T0373794

PRAISE FOR
Josephine's Garden

'Lovers of historical fiction will find *Josephine's Garden* spell-binding, rich and an immensely enjoyable blend of fact and fiction.'
—Blue Wolf Reviews

'*Josephine's Garden* is a rich tale, draped in history, the natural world, passion, motherhood, ambition and status. A perfect vista into the complicated lives of three fascinating female voices from the past, this novel will happily please historical fiction fans.'
—Mrs B's Book Reviews

'[Parkyn] recreates her setting to perfection, warts and all . . . her work is coloured with an authenticity and attention to detail that any lover of historical fiction will appreciate.'   —Theresa Smith Writes

'Parkyn is a master of drawing the reader into a fully realised historical world and bringing women's voices out of the woodwork, and *Josephine's Garden* only confirms her as one of Australia's foremost historical fiction writers. A rich, rewarding historical read that is a joy to be swept up in—highly recommended summer reading.'
—Where the Books Go

'Stephanie Parkyn has written this exquisitely, evoking the gardens and feelings of post-Revolutionary France—as those who were affected by the Terror navigate a new world. Her research has brought these people to life.'   —The Book Muse

'Napoleon's Josephine is a legendary figure, but here Parkyn gives her a voice and a story and creates a richly developed character . . . Parkyn gives insight into a passionate and turbulent time in France's history, but even more, this time in history comes alive through her creation of the feelings and responses of these vibrant, living, feeling and breathing women.'   —NZ Booklovers

'I feel these characters in my bones.'
                                        —Angela Wauchop, *Backstory Journal*

'*Josephine's Garden* invites you to live, breathe and smell the air in post-revolutionary France . . . it's a wonderful place and time for a novelist to uncover.'   —Gill South, *NZ Listener*

'Superb historical detail, engrossing storytelling and a touching rendering of the rollercoaster life of a woman who appeared to "have it all".'   —Jenny Wheeler, *North & South* magazine

'Stephanie Parkyn has woven a luminous, enthralling tale of love, treachery, treason and friendship out of the Empress Josephine's life that is full of unexpected twists and turns.'
                                —Kate Forsyth, author of *Bitter Greens*

'Parkyn's descriptions are a sensory delight, especially where she depicts the process of trying to germinate seeds from the Southern Hemisphere in the damp French environment. Her characters are well-developed and credible, and the story is exciting and gripping. *Josephine's Garden* is an enjoyable read by a gifted storyteller.'
                                                —Historical Novel Society

PRAISE FOR
Into The World

'This enthralling novel is extraordinarily rich in historical detail . . . Stephanie Parkyn vividly brings this world to life. Marie-Louise was possibly the first European woman to visit Van Diemen's Land, but

her amazing story encompasses so much more than this fact. Highly recommended.'
—Good Reading

'*Into the World* is written by an author with a passionate knowledge of the subject matter and genre they're writing in . . . an interesting and enjoyable debut that will have readers anticipating the author's next novel.'
—Books + Publishing

'I was swept away by the suspenseful storytelling as Marie-Louise battles not only the sea, but her self-confidence and self-respect, the attentions of suspicious sailors, and heart-sickness at leaving behind her child. Parkyn deftly builds in themes of loss and discovery, of rebellion and betrayal, of love and duty, delivering a tale that lingers.'
—The Blurb Magazine

'An entertaining debut . . . The details of the expedition and the frictions between the mariners, naturalists and scientists run close to truth, and the narrative is written in an easy style with enough intrigue, adventure and romance to keep you turning the pages.'
—Historical Novel Society

'*Into the World* is a solid example of how fact and fiction can be expertly sewn together to create one vivid historical adventure tale . . . Stephanie Parkyn is one very talented storyteller!'
—Mrs B's Book Reviews

'A well told tale of a fascinating woman and an intriguing and sometimes terrifying journey on the sea. Stephanie Parkyn is to be congratulated on her first novel, one which is sure to find a wide, and satisfied audience.'
—The Mercury

'For those who love historical fiction, this is a must-read.'
—Latitude Magazine

Stephanie Parkyn grew up writing stories from an early age in a book-loving family in Christchurch, New Zealand. She had a rewarding career as an environmental scientist, but is now an historical fiction author with a love of travel, art and nature. She is curious about the human motivations behind the events of history and aims to illuminate women's experiences in her writing. After ten years living in Australia, she has returned to New Zealand and writes from her home overlooking the sea on the Coromandel Peninsula. Stephanie's first novel, *Into the World*, was published to wide acclaim in 2017 and longlisted for the Tasmania Book Prize. *Josephine's Garden*, based on the true story of the woman who became Napoleon Bonaparte's Empress of France, was published in 2019. *The Freedom of Birds* is her third novel.

The Freedom of Birds

STEPHANIE PARKYN

ALLEN&UNWIN
SYDNEY · MELBOURNE · AUCKLAND · LONDON

This is a work of fiction. Names, characters, places and incidents are used fictitiously or are products of the author's imagination.

First published in 2021

Copyright © Stephanie Parkyn 2021

All rights reserved. No part of this book may be reproduced or transmitted in any form or by any means, electronic or mechanical, including photocopying, recording or by any information storage and retrieval system, without prior permission in writing from the publisher. The Australian *Copyright Act 1968* (the Act) allows a maximum of one chapter or 10 per cent of this book, whichever is the greater, to be photocopied by any educational institution for its educational purposes provided that the educational institution (or body that administers it) has given a remuneration notice to the Copyright Agency (Australia) under the Act.

Allen & Unwin
83 Alexander Street
Crows Nest NSW 2065
Australia
Phone: (61 2) 8425 0100
Email: info@allenandunwin.com
Web: www.allenandunwin.com

A catalogue record for this book is available from the National Library of Australia

ISBN 978 1 76087 938 9

Set in 12.6/17.8 pt Garamond Premier Pro by Bookhouse, Sydney
Printed and bound in Australia by Griffin Press, part of Ovato

10 9 8 7 6 5 4 3 2 1

The paper in this book is FSC® certified. FSC® promotes environmentally responsible, socially beneficial and economically viable management of the world's forests.

To my beloved companion, Paul Johnson

PROLOGUE

1807

Rémi

I traced my finger over the letters of my name, printed in glossy black on the playbill. Rémi Victoire. To see it printed so boldly there was astounding. It made me feel real. A family name was important to us children of the Comédie-Italienne. My friend Pascal was simply known as Pascal and it meant he belonged to the theatre with all the other orphans. But to know your family name made you special, it tied you to someone. Everything changed for me from the moment my mother returned. I was no longer just Rémi, I was Rémi Victoire, the orphan whose mother came back.

The playbill announced the opening night of our production and a thrill ran through me to see it. Tonight, I was to play Arlequin in the famous *Arlequin poli par l'amour* by Marivaux. The lead role, no less! I had longed for this chance since I was old enough to watch the actors take their bows before an enraptured audience. I was the first of the orphans of the Comédie-Italienne in Paris ever to take the stage. In a real play, before a real audience. My heart was singing.

Rogerio, our lead actor, had disappeared a week ago. Some said he gambled too much and had had to flee his debtors. Some thought he had been taken by the conscriptors. Others pointed out that he was a carouser who drank to excess and had likely ended his days in the Seine. Whatever the cause, the director was frantic—it was only a week till opening night. I was sad for Rogerio, but I was hopeful too as I begged Gianni for the part.

'You are too young,' he declared.

'I am almost sixteen!' It was true I was small for my age, but I had grown this past summer and I was still growing. 'I could wear heeled shoes.'

'There's not enough time for you to learn the part.' He walked away from me.

Gianni had taught us orphans all the stock characters, reliving the days of his travelling troupes of old, when he was the great Gianni Costantini, famed throughout Italy for his Arlecchino. It was a game for us at first. We orphans would dress up in masks and costumes and play the parts. I always wanted to be the Arlequin in his costume of colourful diamond patches. For weeks, I had watched Rogerio rehearse. I knew I could play the part as well as him.

I jogged after Gianni. 'I can learn all the lines. Pascal will help me.' My friend Pascal knew how I had longed for this chance.

Gianni stopped and turned to me. 'At your age, what do you know of love?'

I couldn't answer that. All I knew of love came from stories.

But out of desperation Gianni had relented, and I was determined to prove to him that I could play the romantic lead. When he saw how I dazzled the audience, he would declare me a prodigy. He would take me under his wing and train me fully in the theatre arts.

Gianni was a master of the commedia dell'arte. I would become a member of the company not as an orphan, but as an actor. A life on the stage was all I had ever dreamed of.

I put the playbill down as Pascal burst into the dressing room. At the sight of me, he doubled over in laughter. I had slathered thick white paint all over my face and eyebrows.

'I am no good with paint,' I complained. 'Can you help me?'

'I'll need a trowel to take this off.' He spat on a cloth and wiped my eyebrows and lips.

Pascal had been with me from the first. My memories began in the theatre and Pascal was always there; playing, chasing, laughing. Pascal had the best laugh, it would make him floppy as a lamb. Once, I made Pascal laugh so hard he rolled off the stage into the orchestra pit. All it took was a well-pulled face.

We orphans of the Comédie-Italienne mobbed together like gulls. We hunted, we fought, we cawed at one another over our possessions. The theatre was our playground, our schoolhouse, our home. In the beginning, we had all been the same, all loved by Gianni, all our parents were dead or vanished. But that changed the day my mother returned and I became different. The golden child. The lucky one.

'Why are you wearing your costume already?' Pascal asked. It was hours before the curtain was to rise.

I shrugged, reluctant to answer. 'I just wanted to.'

I couldn't really explain why I loved to become a character. It felt good to put on those clothes, to become someone else. In the theatre I could be a soldier, a rich merchant, a lover, a spy. I could be anyone. I liked the feel of the smooth velvet as I slid on the tunic with its coloured diamond patches, I liked the weight of the cloak over my shoulders with its bright red lining. None of us had clothes of our own as fine as this, but we had something better: we had costumes.

'I came to tell you your mother wants to see you.'

'Where is she?'

'In the theatre.'

'What does she want?

He shrugged.

I left the dressing room and went to find my mother. Perhaps she wanted to wish me luck. I wondered if she would come to my performance. I knew how she disliked theatre crowds, but perhaps she would make an exception just this once.

Out of habit, I rubbed at the mark on my wrist. When I was little—before she came back—Gianni told me that my mother was a sea sprite who had left this mark on me when she kissed me farewell. It was a promise that she would return for me. I knew it was only a story, but I liked the idea that my mother was a mystical being; that she hadn't wanted to leave me, but the sea had taken her back. Secretly, I'd dreamed of the day we would be reunited.

The day my mother came back I was six years old. She rushed in with her long, blonde hair flying wild like I imagined a sprite's would, and I wondered if Gianni's story was true. She was furious; she screamed at Gianni, accused him of stealing children. She brandished her arm, revealing her burn mark. When she turned my arm and saw the same mark, she gasped like the breath had been kicked from her, and she folded me into her embrace. *You are my son*, she repeated over and over again.

She wanted to take me with her, but I did not want to go. I howled when I realised she meant to take me from Gianni. I held out my hand to him and did not understand why he would not take it, why he was letting her drag me away.

'Stay here,' Gianni pleaded with her. 'What life is there for you out there? Stay with us. We are his family.'

She growled then, deep and menacing. I thought her part animal and part sprite. My mother was a demon. Gianni could not let her take me.

I broke away from her and threw myself at Gianni. She raged at him like thunder and lightning, and I cowered safe in Gianni's arms until the storm passed and silence fell. I twisted my head to see. The pale-haired demon was breathing hard, her nostrils flaring, but as I watched, her shoulders shuddered and she slumped, her skirt billowing out like a dust cloud as she fell. Gianni had defeated her.

I thought she would go, I thought Gianni would drive her out the doors of our theatre, but he whispered in my ear. 'Rémi, this is your mother; we must be kind to her. She will stay with us now.'

My mother's name is Marie-Louise Victoire. She told me I didn't need to be an orphan anymore. I could be Rémi Victoire.

I was afraid of her at first. I hated that we were made to share a room when all the other orphans could sleep together. Sometimes, when she was asleep, I would creep out and run back to Pascal. I shoved him over on his mattress, and he would make room for me, sometimes without even waking. In the morning, I would open my eyes and find myself back in my mother's small room; she had come for me in the night and carried me back to my own cot. When Pascal came to spend his nights on the floor beside me, she let him stay. My mother was kind to Pascal, and it was because of this that I found my love for her.

My mother was sitting in the stalls near the back of the empty theatre. I walked out onto the stage in front of the draped curtains and bowed to her. She laughed and clapped her hands in delight. 'Bravo!' she called, and blew me kisses. I grinned at her. I loved this place. I loved the bright red fabric of the seats, the glittering gold around the boxes rising three tiers above, and the ornate ceiling rose with its painted phoenix in the sky. I loved the smell of oiled boards and smoky candles. Tonight, when the curtains were drawn back, I would stand in a magical forest and gaze out to the expectant faces of the audience, all waiting to be enchanted. I looked out at my mother alone in the stalls and felt pleased to have something none of the orphans at the Comédie-Italienne had: a mother to watch me; a mother to be proud of me. We all had Gianni, but no one else had a mother who was all his own. We two were branded with our special mark, the sign that showed we belonged to one another. I truly felt like I was the chosen one.

I stepped off the stage and walked down the aisle between the rows of seats. When I reached my mother, she had tears in her eyes.

'You look very fine,' she said, with a twist of a smile.

I felt a little foolish then for having dressed so early in my costume. I tried to act nonchalant, like Rogerio would have done, as if taking the stage and performing in front of an audience was no difficult thing.

'Are you nervous?' she asked as I sat beside her.

I shook my curls back over my shoulder. 'No.' But my knee jiggled in the seat and as I stared at those closed stage curtains, I realised that I couldn't remember my first line. It panicked me.

'Have you heard there is to be war in Poland now?'

I shrugged, still trying to remember my first line. I did not pay much attention to Napoleon and his battles. There had been wars all my life; why should this one be any different?

'I am afraid.' She took my hand. 'There's something I need to do. It means we will not see each other for some time.'

I swung around to face her. 'Are you going away?' My first thought was that she would miss seeing me on the stage. 'Will you be here tonight, for the play?'

'Yes, I will be here for the performance.'

I was relieved to have that assurance, but still her words unsettled me. I didn't want her to go away again. What if it was years before she returned? I was gripped by a sudden irrational panic that she would leave me like she had before. That I was not special, I would not have a mother, I would just be one of the orphans again. Like Pascal, who did not know his mother or father. Like little Bonbon, who we found wandering the streets.

'When will I see you again?' I asked.

'It will just be for a few weeks, that's all.' She picked up my hand and kissed it. 'I love you, Rémi—you are everything to me.'

'Then why are you leaving?' My voice cracked like a child's and it embarrassed me.

'I have to do what is best for you.'

I was confused. It was best for her to stay with me. But I was growing into a man and I didn't want to seem like a frightened boy, clinging to his mother's skirts. 'Fine. I don't need you.'

'Don't say that, Rémi. I will return, I promise.'

'Are you going to sea again, like the last time?' Gianni's story of the sea sprite had turned out to be half true; she had gone away to sea after leaving me with Gianni. She hardly ever spoke of that time, though, or of any of her life before coming to the theatre. I feared that if she did go to sea, I might not see her again.

She shook her head. 'No, it's not that.'

'Then where are you going?' I demanded.

'I . . .' She would not meet my eye. 'It's your father, Rémi—he has come back.'

My father! I reeled at this. She had never spoken of my father, and grew angry whenever I questioned her about him. In the end, I had to ask Gianni and he told me my father was a pirate.

'Your father was a good man who found himself trapped by debts and circumstance,' he had said. Debts I understood, circumstance I did not, but from this I gleaned that circumstance could turn you into a pirate. 'He only steals from those who can afford it: the wealthy merchant ships carrying trunks of silver coins and wine.'

'Will he come to find me? Will he make me be a pirate too?' I was half hopeful, half afraid.

Gianni had kissed the top of my head. 'He sails the Mediterranean Sea endlessly, as he has an affliction he cannot soothe. He has wanderlust.'

Wanderlust. I liked the sound of it. A pirate's son. A wanderer.

But now he was here—in Paris. 'I want to meet him!' I said. My heart was pounding. I could have a mother *and* a father.

'If you want to see him, it has to be today. He is in hiding. It has to be now.'

'Now? But the performance is tonight—I can't leave!'

'It is only a few blocks from here. We will not be far away.'

I was excited but my stomach was churning. It didn't feel right to leave the theatre on the day I was meant to take the stage for the first time. And what if we were late? Gianni would be frantic.

The director had been like a father to me, to all of us, I didn't want to worry him—but the chance to meet my own father, to see if he longed for a son as much as I longed for a father . . . I couldn't let this chance slip away.

'Are you going away with him? Is that why you are leaving?'

She swallowed hard. 'No, that's not why we have to part.' She hung her head and I saw a tear slip down her face. 'After you have met your father, I will explain everything,' she said.

I looked around me. The stalls were empty, the orchestra pit deserted. Everything was ready and waiting for tonight. In that moment, I wanted Gianni to come and tell me everything would be all right. Gianni with his singsong voice and reassuring smile. I wanted to hear him give me leave to meet my father for the first time.

'We have to go.' My mother stood and I did too. I noticed how small and slight she seemed beside me.

'Can Pascal come?'

Pascal made everything better. We had always been together, Pascal and I.

'Yes, Pascal, of course—he will be perfect. He will help you.' She was guiding me out of the row, her hands firm on my shoulders.

We found Pascal lingering by the costumerie, all gangly arms and legs, the lute Gianni had given him slung over his back. He loved the last-minute mayhem before a show; the torn seams that needed restitching, the popped buttons, the final touches to each costume. He was learning to tailor costumes from the best in the business, but now I needed him with me.

'My mother says she will take me to my father!' I said urgently, pulling him away.

He gaped at me. 'Your father?'

'We have to go straightaway—will you come with me?'

'On opening night?'

'It has to be now. He is in hiding.' Some part of me was enjoying the drama of this moment. Perhaps my father was a pirate after all. He was wanted for his piracy and he had risked coming ashore just this once for the chance to meet me.

Pascal was still staring at me, mouth open, eyes blinking.

'Come,' my mother said, and opened the side door of the theatre.

'Pascal, where are you going?' a woman's voice called after us. I turned to see Margot, dressed as a fairy for the play. Flighty Margot, needy Margot.

'I'll be back soon,' Pascal called.

Bonbon launched himself at us from one of the dressing rooms, eager to be part of whatever adventure we were setting out on.

'Not today, Bonbon,' my mother said. 'Stay here.'

My mother closed the door behind us.

The house she took us to was on Boulevard Montmartre, a short walk from the theatre. I was jittery. Everything felt unreal to me: the sky too blue, the noise of every horse and cart too loud. My senses were heightened by anticipation. I was glad Pascal was beside me. 'Can you believe this?' I whispered to him, looping my arm through his, holding him close.

At my mother's knock, the door was opened by a man. I studied his face, searching for a resemblance, but I saw no sign of myself in his grey-stubbled visage. When he turned, I noticed one sleeve was tied up where his arm should have been. My mother nodded her thanks to him and we followed as the one-armed man led us through the wood-panelled hall. My heart was hammering. I glanced at Pascal. Neither one of us had been inside a normal home before. Our whole lives had been lived in the theatre.

In the kitchen, the one-armed man dragged the table aside and threw open a hatch in the floor. This must be where my father was hiding.

My mother pointed to a stepladder leading down into the hole. 'Your father is down there,' she said, her voice gruff with emotion.

I gazed into the darkness, never doubting for a moment that what she said was true. Trusting her, Pascal and I climbed down into that hole.

The room beneath the floorboards was so small, we had to bend our heads, not able to stand straight. In the light cast from the open hatch, I saw men's eyes watching me. I smelled the stench of their close-packed bodies, reeking of old sweat. My mouth dry, I peered about in the dim light, wondering which one of the men was my father.

Then the hatch was being lowered and I heard my mother's voice, already distant. 'I will return for you.'

My heart pounded like a thumping fist as I realised she had deceived me. I roared and lunged for the light but was shoved down to the dirt, a man's hand pressed hard over my nose and mouth. 'Shut your worthless gob,' the man hissed. 'Do you want us caught?'

No, no, no. What was happening? I struggled beneath the man's weight. I couldn't breathe. I writhed and struck out. The man only released me when I went slack.

Pascal and I were pushed back to the wall, made to sit beside the stinking privy bucket. We were trapped with these hiding men, imprisoned. I realised I would miss my chance to take the stage and it caused me physical pain; I gasped for breath. Gianni might never give me another chance. I imagined him searching all over the theatre, cursing me. I was letting him down. When my mother said we would be parted, I realised she hadn't meant she was leaving me; she had meant she was abandoning me to this wretched prison. Why would she do this to me, on the very day my dream of taking the stage was about to come true? I burned with hatred. I would never forgive her this betrayal. I bitterly wished she had never found me. I wished I was not the golden child whose mother came back.

Pascal

When Rémi said he was about to meet his father, Pascal was silenced by a white-hot flare of pure, crystalline jealousy. It wasn't fair. Rémi already had a mother, someone special for him alone; why did he need to find his father too? The injustice burned. His friend would have a mother and a father, while he had no one.

Rémi the lucky one. Rémi the golden boy. It had been no surprise when Gianni picked Rémi, out of all of the orphans, for this chance on the stage. He had something special, they could all feel it; something none of the other orphans had. For Rémi was the orphan whose mother had come back. And now it seemed his father had come back too.

But seeing his friend's excitement, Pascal felt ashamed of his envy. He understood Rémi could not miss this chance—and of course Pascal would go if Rémi needed him. It had always been the two of them together, inseparable; he would not abandon his friend now. Rémi and Pascal. Pascal and Rémi. One of his earliest memories was of Rémi climbing a rope above the stage, looking back at Pascal with mischief in his eyes. The unruly curls, the open smile, a face that always lit up the darkness. Pascal could never resist the dare in that sunlight smile. Rémi had dangled high above the stage, stretched out like a monkey, reaching for the next rope. Pascal's chest was tight. He had felt the joy and terror of friendship in that moment; he had felt the exquisite torture of loving someone so much that the thought of their loss was already hurting his heart. 'Come with me, Pascal!' Rémi had called from high above. Pascal had been afraid, but he had climbed the rope after Rémi. And when the one-armed man pointed to the trapdoor in the floor in that house on Boulevard Montmartre, Pascal did not hesitate to follow Rémi down into the dark.

The men startled him. He was slow to understand that it was a trick. Rémi's father was not among these men; it had all been a ruse.

Pascal froze when the man leaped on Rémi, pinning him down. He could not move to help his friend and it shamed him. The boys were silenced, made to sit against a wall. One of the men appeared to be a leader of sorts, threatening anyone who made a sound. He had a fearsome look with a torn and healed lip that exposed his gums and canine tooth. 'I've seen war in Prussia,' he hissed at them, 'and I've no intention of going back.'

So that was why the men were hiding here, Pascal realised: they were avoiding conscription.

Pascal shook with fear, but he tried to console Rémi. 'It will be just a few days,' he whispered when the leader wasn't watching. 'You will see.' Rémi squirmed and fidgeted, gouging the earth with his fingers. He raged against his confinement, knowing that he was missing his chance at a life he craved. Pascal understood. When the two boys were young, they would sit together beneath the creaking boards of the stage and listen to the actors bellow out their lines, hear the crowd roar in laughter or gasp in dismay. Rémi would be jiggling, knee twitching. Not for him the dark spaces beneath the stage—he had always hungered for the light. 'One day I will be the one up there,' he told Pascal. 'I will make them laugh and cry, I will make them love me.' Pascal had never doubted that he would.

'She has taken this away from me.' Rémi stared at him in bewilderment.

Pascal reached across to grip Rémi's hand as he took in their pitiful surroundings. Grey light filtered in from a small grate in the wall to the street.

He counted five men, all of them unshaven, raw-faced. Their bodies were lean, almost skeletal, and they stank. How long had they been here?

The silence was oppressive. He cradled his lute in his lap, longing to pluck its strings, to bring himself some comfort, but he dared not risk the ire of the leader. Hours passed and when he caught the glint of eyes upon him, he ducked his gaze away. All night, Pascal watched the dark shapes of the men and did not sleep.

When the trapdoor was opened suddenly the next morning, Rémi scrambled towards the opening, only to have the men claw him back down and sit on him. 'You will betray us, you little shit. You're here now—be thankful. Wait it out like the rest of us.'

Food was lowered down the hatch and the shit bucket lifted back out. The whole operation took only a few minutes. Pascal blinked, his eyes watering in the sudden light; he had barely adjusted to it before the trapdoor was slammed back down on them.

They ate in darkness; soup and bread and cold omelette. It was good. It distracted him, for a little while.

The day was long and miserable. Rémi fumed about his mother. 'I will never forgive her Pascal—never.' His mutterings earned him a clout from the brute who was their leader.

Pascal was homesick. He felt a twisting around his heart, an anxiousness in his chest. He wondered if they had been missed. Margot and Bonbon had seen them leave. Would Rémi's mother tell them what she had done? He had never spent a night away from the theatre.

The only home he had ever known was with the Comédie-Italienne. All his memories were of the theatre: red velvet drapes rising high above the stage, painted scenes of faraway worlds, dressing rooms lit with smoky candles and faces caked in lead white. Whirling dresses, costumes of bright satin, music, laughter, tears. His whole world was this adopted family of actors and singers. His real parents must be dead, or as good as, and he had no recollection of them. Gianni was enough of a father and mother for all of them. A fierce mothering lion or playful papa bear. All the orphans felt safe with Gianni.

He wondered if Margot would miss him. Margot, the dancer who flitted from love affair to love affair in quick succession. Pascal consoled her whenever another travelling player stole her heart and then moved on. Margot the fluttering bird; iridescent, shining Margot. He would brush her fine, silky hair before each performance. She was like a sister to him.

Little Bonbon would be scouring the theatre looking for him and Rémi. He followed the older boys around everywhere. They had found him as a four-year-old foraging from the scraps outside a patisserie. He was named Bonbon because he liked to pick up sweets that had dropped in the stalls after each performance—the white balls of Anis de Flavigny that had escaped their tins, or sugared violets and candied stems of angélique that had fallen from ladies' laps. Bonbon would fall asleep curled up in the theatre seats, sucking on his sticky thumb, and Pascal would carry him back to a mattress alongside all the other orphans.

Pascal pressed his fingers into his eyelids, willing himself not to sob, not to show weakness before these men. They would soon return home, he tried to reassure himself; this separation from his theatre family was only temporary. Rémi's mother meant to save them from conscription. She had done this to them out of fear. When the threat was over, they would be released.

Pascal remembered her arguing with Gianni. She believed the rumours that Rogerio had been taken in the street by the conscriptors.

'Napoleon fights the Russians in Poland now,' she had said. 'He will seek more men.'

Gianni dismissed her concerns. 'The conscriptors will not target the theatres. People need entertainment to distract them from the horrors. The Emperor knows this. We are safe here.'

Pascal had thought Gianni was right. In the world of the theatre, he had felt safe. Now, out here in the real world, he was terrified.

Through the second night of their imprisonment he meant to keep his eyes open, he meant to let Rémi sleep first and keep watch, but his head lolled, his eyelids drooped and exhaustion overtook him. He woke to the touch of a hand on his thigh. He jerked upright.

A man's face rose above him. 'Lie still, lie still,' a voice soothed. 'I'll take your friend, not you. Just lie still.'

Pascal lay like a bird caught by a cat. His heart banged. The man shifted his weight and touched Rémi.

Pascal swung up his hand and caught the man below his chin. He squeezed. He saw the man's eyes bulge. He said nothing as the man struggled against his grip. Saliva frothed from his lips, but Pascal pressed his fingers up against his windpipe, as tenacious as a dog. He knew then, looking in that man's eyes as his fingers scrabbled against Pascal's grip, smelling the acrid scent of both their fear, that he had the capacity to kill another man. To protect Rémi, he would kill. The man choked, kicking out, and then suddenly he was lifted from Pascal, wrenched back, and the leader with the torn lip had him in a headlock. 'I've warned you before,' the leader said, gripping the man's chin and snapping his neck.

The body fell.

Rémi clutched Pascal's arm and the boys crawled back as far from the man's crumpled form as they could, drawing their feet underneath them, clinging to one another.

Everyone was awake. Everyone was silent.

Pascal heard his own teeth chattering.

'Leave the boys alone,' the leader growled, and took his place beneath the trapdoor.

Pascal trembled all over. A man was dead. The body lay in the middle of the cellar. He had almost killed a man. In the moment, he had only thought of saving Rémi. He bit his lip, determined not to whimper. They must get through this. They *would* get through this, together. They would go home. For the rest of the night, Pascal repeated this over and over to himself.

In the morning, the man's body was heaved out of the hatch with all the other waste.

'I hate her for putting us in this hell,' Rémi whispered to Pascal.

Pascal nodded. Rémi's mother might have thought she was saving them from war, but she had thrown them into a den of wolves.

Days passed and Rémi fell into a torpor. Pascal urged his friend to keep moving, to copy the other men when they exercised their muscles. But Rémi was belligerent, angry. He rolled over and faced the wall.

The name of their leader was Claude.

Claude made Rémi exercise when Pascal failed. He made him eat. As the days turned to weeks, Pascal's fear of the men lessened. He learned their names, communicating in whispers and hand gestures. Some days they played cards and risked speaking when the noise from the street above was busiest. Only one of the men had not already been to war; the others had all been maimed in some way, even if the scars were not visible.

Boredom became his greatest struggle. The anticipation of food was the highlight of each day. Day after monotonous day went by and Pascal despaired of ever leaving this cellar. *You have been forgotten*, his mind whispered to him. *No one cares for you.*

And then, suddenly, they were freed. The trapdoor was opened late one night and they were called up by urgent voices. Pascal was numb, staring at the opening above their heads.

'It's over,' Rémi whispered to him.

They clambered out of the hole, weak and wobbly on their feet. Shaking, they stood in the kitchen of the house on Boulevard Montmartre, holding each other up. Pascal felt Rémi grip his arms and squeeze.

They staggered like old men out into the silent street. The air was fresh and cold—a shock after the stale warmth of the cellar.

Pascal's eyes stung. He breathed deep, gasping with relief. He could go home.

The other men scattered, slinking away along the walls like sewer rats. After two months in that cellar, it was over.

Pascal saw her then. Rémi's mother. She was waiting for them across the street. Rémi's mother—the one who always came back for her son. The one who had tortured them both.

Pascal felt the heat building in his friend beside him, the tremble of suppressed rage. Rémi strode out into the middle of the road and, as his mother reached out her arms to him, Rémi spat upon the cobblestones. Then he spun on his heel, turning his back on her.

'Pascal! Come with me!'

Pascal knew what Rémi was meaning. Rémi was leaving. He would not go back to the theatre and his mother. Pascal could choose to go home to the Comédie-Italienne or he could go away with Rémi. He felt the tingle in his legs. It was time to run. It was time to fly.

He grasped Rémi's hand and they both fled into the night.

Saskia

Saskia stretched one leg up behind her ear. It was a simple move but something that never failed to turn a gentleman's gaze. Saskia limbered up, bending herself backwards, waiting for the audience to arrive. Saskia was proud of her little tent. At almost twelve years of age, she was the youngest performer of the St Petersburg Circus to have her own stage in her own tent. Outside the sun was blazing, sending streaks of white light through the rips in the old canvas. The punters never noticed how tawdry the place really was. Once inside, all eyes were on her. The men were stripped of their coin at the entrance—a silver ducat for a peek—then stripped of their loose change while they stood spellbound, mouths slack, gaping at her contortions.

Her home was a travelling circus. A place of constant movement, of rolling wagon wheels and flapping walls. Castles of tents rose out of flat fields overnight and fell down again whenever it was time to move. The circus had been her home for the last five years, ever since her mother had brought her to it and left her behind. A motherless kitten, a stray. It didn't matter. She was over the shock of it now. She had Svetlana to care for her.

Svetlana would be in the big tent now, charging around the ring, standing on the back of one of her horses. Saskia remembered her first sight of that huge tent with its bright flags and peaked roof. Saskia had been pushed inside by her mother, and the arena was thundering when they entered. A group of six pale horses galloped around the edge of the ring, bare-backed and riderless. Saskia stared at their flashing hooves as they gouged out the sand and sent it flying. A woman in a short, flared skirt of blue satin with matching blue bodice flicked her whip at them from the centre of the arena.

'Svetlana!' the ringmaster called to her. 'Bring us a beast.'

The scent of horse sweat was strong. Saskia knew only one horse in their village, a stout pony always bound to a plough. These creatures were fire-breathing dragons by comparison. She clung to her mother's side as one of the creatures dropped its head before her and snorted warm, wet air into her face.

'Show them,' the ringmaster said.

The woman in the shiny blue skirt vaulted onto the back of the horse, planting her hands on its rump and landing barefooted on the sway of the horse's back. The horse jerked its head up but did not move. The woman, Svetlana, turned about on tiptoe as if she were dancing, like a shimmering butterfly, and then she smiled down at Saskia. 'Would you like to try?'

'Don't be afraid,' Saskia's mother whispered in her ear as she lifted her up to the woman. 'Always be proud.'

Through her leather slippers Saskia could feel the heat of the horse enter the soles of her feet. Svetlana stood behind her, holding out Saskia's arms for balance. Saskia felt so very high, taller now than the ringmaster himself in his tall hat, and the ground looked so far away. When Svetlana clicked her tongue and the horse began to walk, Saskia wobbled, casting a terrified look at her mother.

Lena held her in a defiant stare, chin lifted, cheekbones sharp. Saskia noticed the ringmaster gazing at her mother, sizing her up, like a wild mare he meant to tame.

The horse shied and Saskia found herself in the air suddenly, falling away from Svetlana and the pale horse. Instinctively, she tightened herself into a ball, wrapping her arms around her legs. She landed on her back and rolled, tumbling over and over herself, calves tucked in to her chest until she smacked against a pair of shins. She looked up at a tiny man clapping his hands in glee. 'Can I keep her?'

When her mother disappeared that night, it was Svetlana who comforted her. Who found her running through the campsite, tripping over the ropes, calling out for her mama, alone and terrified. Svetlana took her back to her own bed and kept her warm. She sang to her and told her stories. In the morning, the *skomorokh*, the clown, came to entertain her. He showed her acrobatic tricks. He let her tumble about on the sand. He was a full-grown man with the height of a child and she loved him from the first.

Each night Svetlana told her Russian fairytales, stories Saskia remembered from her own home. Her voice was thick with a strange accent. She scared Saskia with tales of the witch Baba Yaga and monster Koschei the Deathless, who broke his chains and flew like a blizzard out of an open window. She enchanted her with the snow maiden, a child made from snow and conjured by the wishes of her adopted parents. Svetlana wrapped her arms around Saskia and kept her safe.

The circus packed and moved, packed and moved. Saskia lost track of where she had come from. She didn't know if her mother would ever be able to find her again. At first, she was too young to know the places they had travelled, but she learned that people spoke with different languages and wore different clothes. As time passed, the yearning for her mother lessened. She began to forget the life she had lived before the circus.

The circus had set up camp in these fields a few days before and put the word about to all the surrounding towns that the circus had come. They had meant to journey east and return to St Petersburg for the summer, but the wars in Poland had halted all of that. Instead, they would circle about through Prussia, searching for new audiences until the battle was decided. Here, in this countryside of woods and fields and hilltop towns, she was surprised to find she could recognise the words people spoke. The dialect was strange, but she understood it. It reminded her of a place she had not thought about in many years. It reminded her of the place she had lived with her mother: her grandmother's croft on a windswept coast, a place of flocking birds and icy winters.

She remembered skidding on a frozen lake trying to keep up with an old woman, her feet slipping through the frosting of snow and being surprised by ice below. Translucent, crazed and bubbled ice, pale blue like a winter sky. Water frozen in time. She remembered a pair of gnarled women's hands rubbing hers to warm them. Gusts of hot breath. A rough-cut hole in the ice, just big enough to pull a flapping fish from the depths. She remembered her shock on seeing water moving underneath the ice, realising that the thin layer of

26

snow and ice was an illusion of the ground and that there were cold, fishy waters beneath. She must have been young then to have been surprised but not afraid; young enough to trust that something as short-lived as frozen water would hold her up.

Saskia pressed her fingers along the ridge of a metal hook she carried in a pouch around her neck. The fishhook had been a gift from her grandmother. 'Take this,' her grandmother had said, tying the pouch around her neck. 'A hook will always feed you.' She wore the fishhook in a leather pouch beneath her dress along with a feather collected from the cliffs of her home and a shiny black rock her mother had found on the road the day they left. These were the only possessions that had travelled with her from her childhood.

Saskia shook herself. It did no good to remember the past. She was a circus performer now. She climbed up onto her dais and stretched her arms out like a starfish. Ever since the *skomorokh* noticed her talent, she had been training for the stage. She had worked hard to mould her body like this, to be able to stretch and contort beyond most people's capability. It made her feel special to have this ability that no one else had. She was proud to become Saskia the Incredible, Saskia the Twisted Girl. 'See her bend and warp!' the boys were crying outside her tent. Saskia the unbreakable.

The *skomorokh* poked his head inside her tent, his face painted. 'Are you ready?'

She flicked her long, red plait over her shoulder and raised her chin. 'Of course.'

He smiled at her. 'I won't be far away.'

She shooed him off. 'Go, you'll be late!' He should already be in the big tent with the acrobats. 'I am not a child anymore.' *I have my own tent*, she thought with pride. *I am a true performer now.* 'Let them in.'

'Your wish is my command, Majesty,' the *skomorokh* said with a twinkle in his eye and an exaggerated bow.

Saskia wore simple woollen tights and a dress that Svetlana had given her. The short black dress with its whorls of colourful embroidery was the most beautiful thing she owned. She flung a silky cape around her shoulders and turned her back to the door. *Create a sense of mystery*, Svetlana had taught her. *Don't reveal everything of yourself from the first. Keep them wanting more.* She had no curtains to draw around her, no place to hide, so this was her routine, a way to separate herself from the audience's gaze.

She listened as the crowd filed in. The circus boys called out her introduction: 'Behold Saskia the Twisted Girl. She will make your eyes water, she will astound you. Watch her bend and twist into fantastic shapes. She will bend and bend, but she will never break.'

Saskia slipped off her cape and let it flutter to the flattened grass floor. She stretched her foot up behind her head, holding the pose as she spun around on her other toe, taking in the audience as she did so. There was the usual mix of labourers and farmers—few women ever came to her show—but today, in the front row of the crowd, stood a priest. She almost lost her balance. It surprised her to see a holy man in her audience. He stood out from the other men, ramrod straight, face pursed tight, and she felt a strange sense of recognition. The priest was watching her intently.

Svetlana had taught her to hold her face impassive as she twisted her body because her contortions must appear effortless. She covered her shock. She bent backwards until her head touched the floor and she heard a satisfying gasp from the crowd. When she put down her hands beside her head and lifted her feet from the floor, curling her head up between her arms and touching her feet to her mouth in a backwards inverted ball, she was sure she heard a shriek.

She righted herself and moved into another pose, glancing at the priest. He was familiar to her. It must be from a time before the circus. He had to be from her village. Her heart began to thump. Perhaps he would know her mother, or her grandmother.

Saskia pressed her chest down to the stage and flipped her legs back over her head to create a scorpion with her body. The audience broke into spontaneous applause.

What was a priest doing at her show? Should she find him afterwards, should she ask about her home? She had been so young, only seven, when her mother took her away. She couldn't name the place she came from. They'd had no need for names. All they had were the woods, the lagoon, the coast, the spur. There were the fields, the village, the church. It seemed no one had bothered to tell her where precisely she was in the world as no one expected she would go beyond those borders.

And what good would it do her to know the name of it? She didn't want to go back there. She didn't want to know if her mother had ever gone back to that place. Saskia was happy here in the circus. She didn't want to leave.

Saskia pushed herself into a handstand and split her legs apart, bending her knees and stretching them out so that her legs resembled the wings of a bird.

Anger rippled through the crowd. Saskia righted herself. Some of the men had searched their pockets and found them emptied. The boys with swift hands darted from the tent, leaving her alone on her dais, while the men whose pockets had been picked screeched and demanded justice. It all happened too fast for her to react. The priest lunged at her, snatching her from the stage and pushing her out through the back of the tent. The pegs had been removed and the seam of the tent had been cut. He had planned this. Saskia screamed against his hand, barely able to breathe. No one heard.

Outside he had a horse waiting. She writhed against his grip. No, he could not take her away. He pushed her to the ground and leaned his weight on her to pin her down. A gag was shoved into her mouth before she could shout. Her wrists and feet were bound and a sack was pulled over her head.

What was happening? Trussed and loaded across the withers of the horse, a blanket thrown over her, she was being carried away from her circus family. In the big tent, topped with gaily flapping flags, Svetlana would be standing on the back of a galloping horse circling the ring, performing her tricks to the music of drums and horns. How long before they would realise that she was gone? Saskia wriggled against the horse's shoulder, prepared to topple headfirst to the ground if that was what it took to escape. A spitting, roaring anger overtook her. Was she to lose everyone she loved?

The priest held her to that beast as he rode away from the circus. She could see nothing, had no notion of direction. Her head was pounding and her stomach aching from the chopping gait. She felt sick, but knew she must not vomit or she might suffocate. She gathered her courage. When the horse stumbled on the road, she took her chance and flung herself backwards, feeling the brief, terrifying moment of flight. She had done this once before and survived. She tucked herself into a ball. Her head struck the ground with a sickening crack, and blackness consumed her.

When she woke, the pain in her head was splitting her skull. The sack had been removed and her arms and legs were free of binds. It was dark. She breathed in painful gasps. She could smell manure and something else: a rotting vegetable smell.

She was inside a wooden box. Her fingers searched out the confines of the space. She appeared to be in a small casket, like a coffin. She began to shake. She was dizzy, hurting and afraid. Why had the priest taken her? What did he want?

'Don't be scared.'

She flinched from his voice.

'You will be safe here,' he said. 'With me.'

'Who are you?' she cried, her voice croaky.

'You can call me Father,' he said, as he hammered nails into the lid of the box.

PART I

1812

CHAPTER ONE

The smell of hay, manure, piss—I woke with it filling my nose and mouth, face down and chewing on the stable scrapings. I rolled over slowly, not wanting to move my head, feeling the hammers strike anvils behind my eyes. Strike. Spark. I prised an eyelid open.

Ow! Pascal had kicked my ankle. He didn't speak, didn't need to.

Pascal was saddling the mare, buckling the straps with snapping efficiency.

I groaned as I sat up, mouth as dry as feathers. Beside me, a brooding chicken cocked her head with condemnation. I lunged and chased her from my breakfast, cracking the egg and swallowing quickly. The chicken screamed. I shook my head, seeing the barn shift and slide in front of me. The trough. I struggled to my feet, staggering like a penitent to the altar, and scooped handfuls of the water to my mouth, ignoring the horse dung bobbing at the edges. I plunged my head in, felt the baptism of cold water douse the fire in my head.

I drew my head out with a gasp and paused in no small shock at my reflection. I was little cheered by the image in that dark trough. I had twenty-one years but looked twice that in the murky ripples. I wished for a blade to trim those old man's whiskers. As the water dripped and disturbed my visage, a fleeting thought unsettled me. How many more mornings, how many more days could I go on like this?

Pascal gave me no sympathy, the cur, drawing open the barn door and letting the light flood in. The chickens made a break for the yard, clucking with glee.

I pulled a hand down my face, sluicing the water from my skin, my unruly beard. He was waiting for me to apologise, but he should know me better by now.

'Let's go, Rémi,' Pascal urged. He refused to look at me.

With each movement of my head I felt a kicking pain in the back of my neck and I stiffly straightened my back. The grazes on my knuckles throbbed as I held out my hands, opening and closing my fists. No bones broken. I smiled. Took another step. All and all, not a bad night.

Pascal pulled our bay mare from the barn and mounted swiftly. Henriette was a sturdy, round-rumped beast who had been with us these past five years, ever since we loosened her from a cart in a Paris street. Our Henriette was not made for a life of dray work. We named her after a feisty French diva from our childhood who would squeal and kick her dressing room door closed to show her displeasure.

Henriette walked away with a swish of her thick tail and I followed them out of the barn with my eyes trained on the solid spread of her dappled rump. To walk would be good for me. I would walk off my pounding head, and by the time we reached the next village I would be sober. Sober enough to begin again, to weave my magic. Pascal would forgive me then. I looked at his straightened back, the jaunty wave of that feather in his velvet cap, and noted his stubborn refusal to turn and check that I was following.

I stuck my arms out wide and howled to him, like a lone wolf. He still did not turn; the feather in his hat merely bobbed and waved farewell.

That hat. *Pascal, you fiend, I won that hat for you!*

The road headed north. With my first steps, I tottered to the east, righted myself, then stumbled to the west. I steadied myself on a fencepost and came face to face with a sow the size of a pony. She grunted at me and I recoiled from the length of her hairy snout. Her piglets squealed and swarmed for her heavy teats, disgusting me. I shook my head. All I could smell was pungent pig shit. Ahead on the road, Pascal maintained his even pace, a dark shape moving further and further away.

It wasn't always like this between us. When we were first on the road, we were joyous, we were free. A life full of possibility stretched ahead of us. There were hard times, but there were good times too. I hoped Pascal would remember that. It wasn't a bad life we had made for ourselves these past five years. It was a boundless, borderless life. You couldn't get more freedom than the life of a travelling storyteller. We brought our music and our tales to those who needed them. We brought joy.

This was not the life I'd thought I would have, of course; I had dreamed of stardom, my name known in all the famed theatres of the world. But I had made my peace with the loss of that ambition. Now, I had my own stage, one I made out of hay bales or town steps. Imagination was my scenery. My cape was my costume. My vision cleared to show me a brightening sky and I breathed in the scent of meadow flowers, wild thyme and clover.

Pascal had not been himself for some time now. The careless loss of our money angered him, yes. He hated my drinking and brawling, but he should be used to that by now. If I was honest, I knew what troubled him, but I was afraid to let him speak it. I rubbed my finger over the raised welt beneath my wrist, a mark I had borne throughout my life. What he wanted was an impossibility.

I would show Pascal how good this life could be. I squared my shoulders and firmed up my steps. Onwards. There was no going back. No going home. I cleared my throat and rolled out an operatic vibrato to the startled cattle. A showman has to be on form, and if there was one thing that I was champion of in this life, it was the art of showing off.

Before the mile was up, I collapsed face first in the dirt.

I was draped across the pommel of the saddle when Pascal rode under the arched gateway into Gelnhausen. He refused to touch me, not even a steadying hand on my back. Some miles back I had vomited down the shoulder of our mare and valiant Pascal did his best to ignore this ignoble entrance because he was hungry and we needed to make money in this town.

Henriette climbed through the cobbled streets with Pascal singing up to the rooftops of the tall, half-timbered homes, calling to the townsfolk as if he rode a knight's steed and not a carthorse with milky splatter down her leg. As always, he cradled his lute in his arms and played a stirring tune. His voice was strong and commanded attention. *Come and hear the finest tales, the most savage, the most fantastical, as told by the greatest showman of the modern age.* My head flopped and rolled with each step.

When Pascal halted Henriette in the marketplace, I slid bonelessly from her withers and toppled backwards, lying prostrate on my back. Disgusted, Pascal turned his face away. I lay there, head pounding, limbs unwilling, with the walls of the town looming over me—steep-pitched roofs and walls of plaster crossed with exposed wood. Like every other medieval Prussian town, it would have a water well, a town hall, a pillory. I twisted my head to see an abandoned Catholic church with its rose window punched out, like a mouth opened in surprise. I remembered this town. I remembered how years ago we were pelted from those church steps by the devout followers of a strident bishop. They didn't like storytellers here. I almost stirred to warn Pascal, but then remembered that Napoleon had broken the Pope's hold over these lands. These Prussian towns belonged to Napoleon's Confederation of the Rhine now and not the Holy Roman Empire. We would at least be safe from the Catholic bishop.

Pascal sent his music out across the marketplace towards the triumphant spires of the Protestant Marienkirche. He wore striped tights, like a medieval troubadour, and he crossed his leg over the pommel of the saddle, the lute resting on his thigh. He had grown into a strong and handsome man. His skin was good and his smile sweet. I knew it was not only his music that drew the villagers' eyes to him. He promised epic sagas, tales of adventure, tales that would make them weep and swoon. Our mare was already dozing.

I rolled my head towards the crowd as they gathered, looking for the brave, the gullible and the troublemakers. First would come the pigeons from the edge of the square, bobbing their heads. Then the bold geese, the women with their large bosoms and baskets of bread. We loved them for their bravado, knowing it would encourage others, and smiled all the sweeter to reach the girlish hearts beneath their matrons' chests. Each town had this same menagerie of folk. Sometimes, a lone crow would caw and heckle. The skinny dogs would slink around between them all, watching and waiting, sizing up the opportunity for gain. Last of all would come the goats, those self-important men pushing through the crowd, stroking their beards and bleating about public nuisance and keeping the peace and each wanting to take a cut of the storytellers' profits.

We had only moments to capture the townsfolk before the goats would come. Pascal sang and strummed to the end of his song as though his belly was full and his heart content. Confidence sold stories. It made them trust us. It promised them that, if they were patient, something magical would happen.

I roused myself with a roar, springing to my feet with a twirl of my cape. The crowd leaped back, startled, as I swept my arms wide. I burst into life, like a flame in the darkness.

I winked at Pascal and saw the relief wash over him. I had never failed him yet. It was the same in every town, with every crowd: I held them spellbound. When Rémi Victoire told a story, it was impossible to look away.

I hushed my voice to draw them close. 'This is a tale of two lost children . . .'

A gaggle of children pushed forward, keen to be fed on tales of ogres. And their parents too, eager to condemn the wickedness of others and feel all the better for it. At the edge of the crowd, I spotted a clergyman, a raven dressed in black. It surprised me to see a priest at our gathering and I was wary of him. He clutched the hand of a girl, her face partly obscured by the hood of her red cloak.

'They were brother and sister,' I continued.

'Hänsel and Grethel,' a child interrupted, wanting to impress. How it annoyed me when they butted in, destroying the flow of my tale.

'No—they were Jean and Jeanette.'

'Were they abandoned in the forest by their mother and father?' another child asked. *Quiet!* I wanted to shout. I was losing control of the telling, the story slipping from my fingers like a slimy eel.

I strutted about, pointing to the adults in the crowd. 'Their parents were misers, keeping all their money for themselves, and when the children grew older and demanded more and more food, they didn't want to feed them anymore.'

A gruff voice sounded from the back. 'The parents were most likely starving and could not bear to see their children waste away.' The man looked to be a woodcutter from the forest.

Pascal coughed and threw a warning glance at me.

'Well they should have fed their children before themselves!' a woman's voice protested.

I nodded to her, feeding her conviction. 'The mother was wicked. She convinced the father they should lose the children in the forest.'

The crowd clucked and shook their heads in horror. The priest edged around the crowd, towing the child behind him, and I watched from the corner of my eye, uncertain of his intention.

'The first time Jean and Jeanette were taken out and abandoned in the wilderness, they found their way home. But their mother lured them out again, and again. Jean did not trust her and left a trail of crumbs behind them . . .'

'This *is* the story of Hänsel and Grethel!' the belligerent boy insisted.

I snapped, 'There are many versions of the tale, and this is simply a different one. If you will listen, perhaps you will like this one better.'

'We are tired of Frenchmen telling us the way of things.' The man's voice was low, and I felt the threat in the growl of it. His wife gave him a warning glance before looking to the fierce piked roof of the town hall. I followed her gaze. This was not the first time I had encountered resistance to our French tales. Appetites were changing. Only the Prussian version of the tales were popular. After six years of French rule in these towns, the straps were beginning to chafe.

I lost my own appetite for the tale. I gave them the Hänsel and Grethel they knew, with the birds that ate the crumbs, the wicked witch and her house of bread with a roof made of cake and windows of clear sugar to lure the children in. Hänsel in his cage, holding out a bone instead of his finger when the witch wanted to check if he was fattened enough for the pot, and Grethel tricking the witch into climbing inside her own oven, where she was burned to a crisp.

I did not give them the French tale of 'The Lost Children', as I had intended. The bloodthirsty tale of the Devil and his long-suffering, beaten wife. The wife captures the wandering children and imprisons Jean in the barn. Jean escapes and slits the wife's throat, and the Devil chases the children through the forest. It was a thrilling tale the way I told it, but I always changed the ending. In Perrault's version, the lost children forgive their parents for abandoning them. Ha. A likely story. In my version, the children travel the world and live happily ever after.

Pascal, relieved at my restraint, proffered his cap at the end of the story, but we both knew time was short. Already three town goats were blustering out from the *Magistrat der Stadt* and crossing the square in arrow formation. I took the stirrup and swung up behind Pascal. I kicked the mare and she woke with a grunt, leaping forward on the cobblestones, scattering the crowd. For a moment, the priest was in our path. He pushed the child back behind him and I saw her owl eyes upon me. Then the priest jumped aside to let us pass.

We clattered down an alleyway through to the lower marketplace with a string of children following in our wake. I wrapped my arm around Pascal's chest and held him tight against me. My Pascal. I felt his heartbeat, strong and steady. We rode out of this medieval town, passing beneath its witch tower and along the river, seeking a place to light our storytelling fire. I hoped the townsfolk would bring their food and wine to pay us for our tales. Surely then Pascal could forgive me.

The place Pascal chose for our bonfire was under the eye of a church. A spire of dark slate rose like an iron pike from a mud-red nave on the hilltop above us. The sight of it looming on the skyline spiked my neck with shivers. The lonesome church had an abandoned air, like so many other Catholic monasteries and abbeys in these times. A pilgrim's chapel. I didn't think it was a wise choice to camp here given our history with churchmen, yet Pascal had a sense for these places that have a story to tell, and I let him have his way.

I sat beneath the ancient tree with spreading limbs clothed in mosses and creeping ivy that had drawn Pascal to this place. It was a story tree if ever I saw one. An oak from an *Urwald*, a primeval forest, forgotten by the woodcutters. It leaned over the rushing river and its roots had begun to rise out of the earth.

'Are you going to help me with this?' Pascal called, snapping a branch across his thigh.

He had gathered a good-sized pyre of sticks and branches that would soon be spitting and sparking into flame. The town children had followed us here and were likely running home with the word. *By the twisted tree*, they would cry out, the one they had all clambered and crawled through as children, each generation repeating the same old tales beneath its branches.

We needed the good people of this town to be wealthy and bored, for we needed to eat. The villages we had visited of late were rich in eggs and house cows, but little else. Custard. I couldn't look at another bowl of custard, kindly proffered and impossible to refuse. Girls with breasts the colour of custard, hair like summer wheatfields, inviting me home to their crofts and placing yet another bowl of clotted milk in front of me. The whole family gathering to watch, the younger children all bulging eyes and running noses. The mother, earnest, trying to please. The father, lean and wiry, ruddy-cheeked. Narrowing his eyes and weighing up if this wastrel was really the one who would free him from the terror of feeding his whole tribe. I recognised the longing in his eyes, wanting to be released and resisting it all at once.

Was it too much to ask for some salted ham?

Truth be told, I was tired of these pastures. The trees were already turning. No one would come out on cold and snowy nights to hear our tales. We were heading to Marburg, as we did each year to wait out the winter, but something in us both was discontent.

I glanced at Pascal who crouched nearby, blowing on the tender flames, uncertain if he had forgiven me yet. I had been foolish the night before. I had not meant to lose our coin at the gaming table or be caught cheating to regain it, so that Pascal had to intercede with a well-timed blow of his sturdy chair. I would make it up to him, dear, faithful Pascal. He was the only family I had. The only family I cared to have. He did not deserve to starve on my account.

I watched the glowing twigs and dancing sparks as Pascal breathed life into our fire. I smelled the spiced wood smoke as it curled out like aromatic ribbons, travelling on the breeze, along the river, over the hills, up to the lonely church and onwards to the village. Gossamer tentacles reaching out to embrace and cajole and bring out the curious. It smelled of forest sprites and woodland pixies. Of magic.

The girl spooked me, walking out beyond our fire, a pail in her hand. I watched her fill the bucket from the river and turn to face us. The firelight caught her pale skin and shocking hair. She wore it loose and unfettered; long, straight hair of a russet colour I had not often seen here, the colour of autumn leaves, of urns of antiquity, of sun-baked terracotta. She was small and slight, and I judged it would not be long before her parents would be thinking of matches for her—some young man from the next village over. If that was her lot, I pitied her; I did not think much of them, all spotty youths with crowded teeth. Did she want this life? This life of cow udders and custard?

She raised her angled chin, looking sidelong at us over her disdainful cheekbones, her russet hair falling like a waterfall down one shoulder. Bold. Our eyes grazed one another. Hers were large and round and she did not look away. I recognised her as the child in the marketplace, the one who had been with the priest, a servant of sorts perhaps. A strange beauty. What was she doing here? 'Welcome!' I cried. 'Come drink with us.'

The girl with the flaming hair stood her ground.

'We have a little wine.' I gestured to the goat's bladder at my hip.

Pascal snapped a twig across his knee. I could hear the judgement in the violent crack and I refused to look at him.

The girl did not step any closer and held her tongue.

'I know a secret about this tree,' I told the girl.

I rose to my feet, balancing on my toes, shifting my weight from one leg to the other. It is something few understand: that the telling of stories requires the whole body to be engaged. Every muscle, every sinew needs to be ignited.

Pascal fed green leaves to the bonfire and it smoked and smouldered, wrapping us in sweet, perfumed smoke. Above our heads, the branches were contorted like old women's fingers, and I felt the smouldering spark of a story begin to grow.

'Once upon a time, a witch lived here beside this river.'

The girl showed no surprise.

'The witch was very beautiful—so beautiful that many men were afraid to look upon her and even the preening cats sitting in their windows were jealous of her. She lived here because she had been banished from the village.' I turned, setting my cape in motion.

'We have a witch tower in our town,' she said, her voice low and flat.

I had seen the tower as we left the village gate, round-sided, smoothed sandstone with small, barred windows at the top where the women could look out upon their fate.

'I was told that their hands and feet were bound and they were thrown into the river.' The russet-haired girl spoke with such a lack of emotion, such worldly knowledge, that I wondered what had passed in her tender life. She had a Baltic hardness to her voice, deep and solid as rocks dropped into a well.

The fire cracked as it bit on juicy sap.

'The witch's cottage once stood on this very ground.' I circled about, spreading my arms wide. 'On the banks of this stream, high enough to avoid the floods from snow melt, but close enough to save her back when collecting water. She lived alone, except for the goat that trotted in at night to share the croft with her when the winter gales came rushing down the valley.'

Pascal raised an eyebrow at me.

'Why isn't there any trace of this croft?' she asked, jutting out her chin, suspicious, and I caught Pascal's smirk. He knew I hated interruptions. I stared at her with slight annoyance. I noticed the dress she wore was faded black linen embroidered with orange and pink starbursts and whorls of blue and red. Shapes and patterns whirled across her budding breasts like fireworks. The dress was old, worn, almost too small for her. She had been here some time, but she did not belong here.

'The villagers removed all trace of it. They burned it down and took each slab of stone from the hearth and threw them into the river. Pulled out her cabbages and parsnips leaving everything to rot. Over time the wind took everything else and the ash blew far and wide in all directions. They couldn't bear for any trace of her to remain.'

'What did she do that was so bad?'

'Was she very wicked, do you mean? Did she steal small children and lure them into her cooking pot? That I cannot say. Only the goat that visited her shack each night would be able to tell you what she was truly like.'

Pascal snorted.

'A plague came to the town. Some were angry that she could not cure it. Others thought that she had brought it on them. It wasn't wise to live out of town, you see, and not be around to answer what others might say about you.'

'But they banished her here. She had no choice.'

Injustice fired her blood, I realised.

'A wizard came to the town to sell his services. He spoke of towns that had been cured of plague by his methods. Their witch had gone bad, he told them, like a tooth that needed to be pulled.'

I mimed wrenching a tooth from my mouth. The girl did not react.

'Only one little girl thought to warn the witch. She had listened at the window of the town hall, peering through the blown glass. The wizard wore a fine cloak and rode a gleaming horse so she thought he must be very successful indeed. He declared he would take half payment now and half later, once the witch had gone. The grey-bearded men huddled together to discuss his offer. They had to do something. It might work. What did they have to lose?

'So the town masters employed the wizard to rid the village of its curse by casting out the witch from her home. They were not as enlightened folk as we are now. They did not know of disease, only of curses, of wrongs and wrongdoings.

'The young girl heard all this and worried for the witch. She had gone to her for a sore and swollen toe once and the witch had been kind and gentle and wrapped her foot in a poultice that eased the pain a little bit. It didn't seem right to her what they said. She thought to herself, "Well, it could be any one of us accused of bringing death and calamity upon the town without proof," and so she went to warn her.

'The rest of the townsfolk did not think like the little girl. They saw their sons and daughters, mothers and fathers with rings of pustules glowing at their necks and they took fright. They followed the wizard as he thundered down the road towards the witch's croft. He rode a spirited horse and the little girl could do nothing but watch him pass.

'She ran after the wizard. Ahead a great battle had begun. She heard howling and shrieking. She saw sparks of flame shoot up into the sky. By the time the little girl and the villagers reached the spot, a whooshing fire had enflamed the witch's croft.'

I swept back and the majesty of Pascal's burning pyre did not disappoint. The sky was darkening and the flames were roaring up into it, spitting crazed streaks of orange into the lower branches of the twisted tree.

'The witch whirled her arms about her head, howling, snatching at her hair, growing taller and taller, but her legs were rooted to the ground. She screamed because there was no escape. Her waist thickened, her arms grew long and heavy and her wail was silenced in her mouth. She had been transformed into this oak tree!

'The villagers shrieked in fear. What did this mean? She was not dead, but still among them. Would the curse be lifted, would the rest of them be saved from this blackening death? They looked about for the wizard in his velvet cloak and his fine steed. He had vanished.' I lowered my voice. 'But the little girl saw a raven in the branches of the tree, taking flight with his black velvet wings.'

I let my voice fall to silence and turned my face up towards the gnarled branches of the tree.

'She is condemned to stay here for eternity.' As I looked up at the shadowy branches, I almost convinced myself of an angry spirit tearing out her hair each autumn, shivering through the winter and forced to shelter the villagers' children as they climbed among her new leaves in the spring. There was a wrongness in this place; I felt it.

'We don't want your pagan stories of witches here.' A male voice behind me, clipped with anger. The girl leaped, looking younger in her fear. She quickly braided her hair and tucked it out of sight. My hackles rose. I spun to meet him, letting my cape flare out.

Ah. The raven appears. I had forgotten about the clergy. The raven stepped closer to the flames, putting himself between me and the girl. It was the priest from the marketplace. Up close, I saw his face was marred with a vertical scar that ran from one eyebrow to his jaw.

Pascal stirred beside me, doubtless remembering the troubles we'd had with strident priests. He plucked a large branch out of the fire and held it like a brand before him. He had the advantage in height and reach, and a burning limb is a deterrent to wolves of any shape.

Pascal always knew when to loom on my behalf. He stood beside me and balanced on his toes in his fighting stance. I put out my arm to still him. With luck it would not come to blows this time.

'Welcome!' I cried. 'We share our fireside tales with all comers.'

'You should leave.'

'We are quite content here.'

'The town wants you to go.'

'Do the clergy still speak for the townsfolk?' I mimed surprise, knowing full well these towns had been taken from the Pope and given over to aristocratic lords under Napoleon's control.

He studied me. 'The people still listen to their true Lord.'

I had to concede the point. Napoleon's redistribution of power meant little to ordinary folk; they would still pay their tithes, just to another master. And fear of eternal burning hell for their sins did keep the flock obedient.

'In the next day or two, perhaps, we shall journey onwards.'

'You are not welcome here.'

'We shall see. In a few hours we will have an audience of many. Everyone loves a tale of heroic deeds and monsters slain, of fears vanquished and love found.'

'We don't need your kind here.' The priest's face was glowing red by now. The scar on his cheek was a vivid white. He didn't look at all well. 'We don't want you corrupting our children with your lies.'

I rolled my eyes. Not this again. My lies told truths to those who cared to listen. Besides, a story was so much more than truth. A priest of all people should know how powerful a story could be.

I scowled. 'You prefer your own lies, no doubt.'

'If you stay here, you won't be safe,' the priest warned.

I smiled. 'We shall see.' I was glad of the roaring fire at my back.

Throughout this, the girl had been standing as still as a stake in the ground. Now, the priest gripped her beneath the arm, pinching her soft flesh, half lifting her from her feet. She cast a look over her shoulder at me that was part beseeching and part challenge. I almost went after them. Pascal put a hand to my shoulder to restrain me. He shook his head to tell me there was nothing we could do for her. The pail bashed at her legs as the priest dragged the girl up the hill. My eyes flicked up to the church spire, pike-sharp and lethal against the flame-coloured sky.

CHAPTER TWO

Saskia felt Father's hand grip her braid and twist. He thrust her into the kitchen, made her strip before the fire and wash. She dunked the rag in the frigid water, swiping it across her skin, raising goosebumps.

'I told you not to speak with anyone.'

She was shivering.

He pushed her in front of the fire. She felt his fingers crawling through her hair, loosening the braid, revolting her. He took up a hairbrush and tugged it through the strands. He liked to brush and brush her hair until it gleamed like copper. Every night he performed this ritual, and tonight he was rough in his movements, striking at her head with the bristles. His fingers dug into her shoulder, holding her still.

When he was done, he spun her around.

'What did you say to them?'

'Nothing,' she murmured.

'I don't believe you.'

'God's truth,' she said, keeping her face slack. She would give him nothing of her thoughts.

'Put your dress on.'

Saskia obeyed. Svetlana's dress still fitted her after all these years, almost as if her body refused to grow. She was small, lithe and breastless, like a child.

Father took out his Bible and began to read—a monotonous drone, a tale of a sinful woman. She sat cross-legged before him with her head bent as she did on every other night. He thought her cowed. He thought her dull and tamed.

That first time he'd released her from the box she had attacked him. She had raked his face with her grandmother's fishhook and he had howled as he chased her down and caught her. Wild with anger and fear, she bit and scratched. The fishhook fell to the dirt floor and he wrestled her away before she could reach it. He bound her arms behind her and threw her back into the box. She was a harpy, a *vila*, he had screamed at her. She was a demon that needed to be exorcised. She was a dirty whore's daughter who should be grateful she had been saved from a life of sin.

A *vila*. She liked the image. The *vily* of Svetlana's stories were the restless ghosts of unmarried maidens who could shapeshift into falcons or owls. They were powerful and feared. She scratched her fingernails underneath the lid of the box. She would be a *vila*.

The box was his tool of punishment. In those first hours, she had been terrified witless in her solitary confinement. It was no small thing to be alone when you were afraid. She screamed until she was hoarse but no one came to help her. He left her for two days without food and water, long enough for her to wonder if he would ever come back. She imagined she would die there in that

53

coffin. When he opened the box his face was hideous, the wound puckered and stitched, glowing red and puffy. She cringed from him. He offered her water and she gulped it down. 'If you behave you will be freed,' he said to her. 'When I can trust you won't run away.' Then he locked her in again.

When he finally released her to wash the excrement and urine from her body and clothes, she realised she was being held in the earth cellar of a barn. Staggering outside, his hand tight around her wrist, she saw that the barn stood beside a chapel on a hill. Fields of long grass sloped down to a river. Behind her, tangled woods stretched up and over the hills. She blinked at the brightness of the green meadows and sharpness of the blue sky. He took her down to the river and she waded into the water in her clothes, scrubbing at the cloth of her dress, removing her woollen tights. She stood shivering and dripping in the waist-deep water with her back to him, refusing to let him see her tears. That night, he let her sleep on a pallet on the floor beside his boxbed in the windowless room he lived in beside the barn. She watched him bolt the door, saying nothing.

She ached to go home. She wondered if Svetlana or the *skomorokh* were looking for her. She had no idea how far she had travelled away from them. Would they try to rescue her?

In the morning, Father outlined her duties. He would care for her, if she was a good and helpful child. She stared at him, mute with hatred. What choice did she have? She was silent and watchful, yet she did everything he asked of her.

One night, Father forgot to bolt the door. She ran to the river. Should she follow it upstream or down? She had been blindfolded when he brought her here; how could she know which way she had come? How would she find her circus? In panic, she slipped and splashed over the river rocks and it wasn't long before he caught her.

'If you can't be trusted, you can't be free,' Father said, his tone reasonable and his grip tight on her wrist. He tugged her up the hill.

'I can be trusted.' They were the first words she had spoken to him. 'Please don't put me back in there.'

'When I can be sure you'll behave I will let you out again.'

He dragged her back into the earth cellar of the barn and threw her into the box. 'It is for your own good.' This time, he left her alone so long that she was relieved to see him when he opened the lid. For the first time she felt grateful to him for releasing her.

The box was Father's preferred punishment for every misdemeanour. Without warning, he could switch from pleasant to nasty and vindictive, and she could never tell what might rouse his ire. Each time he put her in the box she imagined she would be left there to die, that no one would ever find her. Each time he let her out, he was kind. It became a pattern. He was training her, she soon realised. He thought he was breaking her, like a horse.

She endured the ritual of him washing and brushing her hair each night. The way he touched and stroked her hair was almost reverent. His voice was thick and strange as he cooed over it. She suspected he was touching and rubbing himself in the same way she had seen men in her audience do. She squeezed her eyes closed while he twisted his fingers in her hair. Who was he? Why had he chosen her? She wanted to ask him why he had taken her, but equally she wanted to float away from herself, to pretend that she was not even here.

Afterwards, he lectured her from his Bible. He spoke of women who performed or danced in public as disgusting, vile creatures.

A disgrace to God. 'That circus was an abomination,' he told her. 'I saved you.' Saskia wanted to rip out his tongue.

He had looked familiar to her when she had first seen him in the circus tent. It puzzled her still. If he was from her village, why did he not take her back there?

'Did you know my mother?' she asked him finally one night as he brushed her hair. His hands went still. He stood up stiff and straight and she was too slow to run. He gripped her arm, twisted it behind her back and pushed her out through the barn and back in the box. 'Your mother was a wicked woman.' Saskia learned not to speak of her mother ever again.

The last time he put her in the box it was winter and there was snow in the fields. She feared she would freeze. She shook so much she felt like bones rattling in a cage. When he came for her, he wrapped a blanket around her, carried her into his dwelling and put her down in front of the fire. She stood shaking as he wrapped his arms around her and held her. She didn't resist. She rested her head against him. He patted her back and stroked her hair. It felt nice. She was too tired to fight anymore.

'There is nowhere for you to go,' he murmured. 'You are safe here.'

Perhaps he had broken her in the end. He had convinced her that there was no place for her to escape to, no other place that could be her home, and she never tried to run away again. 'You belong with me,' Father told her, as he brushed her hair each night.

She was made to cook for the few visitors that passed by on pilgrimage. Many were Catholic priests who wandered now without their flock. She trusted none of them with her story. Few townsfolk ventured out this way unless they meant to poach from the forest. A handful came to his services. On Sundays, Father made her kneel in the front row before him while he preached of the need for children to obey their parents. It tightened her throat. She stared at the hem of his embroidered robes. How fine those robes were, she thought; such richness of detail, such expensive fabric, while Father cajoled the parishioners into giving alms to a poor priest.

On market days she played the part of the priest's servant, keeping silent, carrying the eggs and berries and bread and listening. Who among the townsfolk could she trust? She saw they were wary of Father, their laughter false, their warmth extinguished like a candle snuffed as soon as he walked on. The townsfolk thought her sullen and stupid and ignored her. In her veins, ice flowed. She became numb; it was easier that way.

Did they wonder, the townsfolk, how Father had come to possess her? Had they questioned her sudden arrival to that desolate church? No doubt he had spun a convincing story. Perhaps he told them he had rescued her from wickedness and vice and delivered her into the lap of God. The night Father stole her from the circus, no one had questioned him on the road. No one asked him why he carried a stupefied child bound on his horse. A man in a uniform had licence to do almost anything, she realised—especially those in the uniform of God.

'Beware the gentle wolves,' Svetlana had told her once. 'They are the most dangerous of all.'

In town, she listened for word of a travelling circus, still hoping for rescue and dreaming of reuniting with Svetlana and the *skomorokh*. But the circus never came, and as the years passed, she gave up hope of rescue. Deep down, she knew she would have to save herself.

Saskia trusted no one in the village, until she met a herbwoman in the forest. By then, Father allowed her to forage for berries and mushrooms alone. The woman in ragged clothes frightened her at first, flitting through the trees, having no wish to attract Father's attention. The herbwoman had been her only friend. Saskia did not know her name. She was of middle years and mute, since her tongue had been cut out, and they spoke through hand signals. From the herbwoman, she learned which plants were safe to eat and which could poison. She would need this knowledge if she was to run again and survive in the forest. Saskia waited eagerly for the herbwoman with every changing season, looking forward to gathering with her as new flowers blossomed and berries ripened. But when a whole spring and summer passed and the herbwoman did not return, Saskia faced the bleak truth that she was alone again.

From the moment she found the storytellers beside the river, Saskia felt the stirring of possibility. A lone girl on the road invited attention, but three travelling storytellers would scarcely merit a second glance. This was the opportunity she had been preparing for.

Saskia forced herself to calmness, to appear as docile as ever as she sat before Father, listening to him read from the Bible. The sight of her with those men had enraged him and it would make him unpredictable. He might be planning to put her in the box tonight for safekeeping and her heart squeezed in panic at the thought that she might lose this chance of escape.

When Father closed the Bible, she rose and washed the dishes in the pail of water she had fetched from the river. She had to make him think everything was normal. Saskia delivered Father his cup of mead. He took it from her without a word, but she didn't trust him. He was hiding his fury from her.

'Water the animals,' he commanded. 'And don't dally.'

Saskia dipped her head in submission. He was looking for an excuse to punish her. Any moment now, he might call her insolent, or knock something down for her to pick up. He wanted to blame her for something to justify locking her away. As she walked to the door she half expected a blow to the back of her head, a cup thrown at her, or an accusation, but it didn't come.

Outside, the moon was full and the church was bathed in silver light, making sharp angles of black and grey. She hurried to the barn and poured the water into the trough for the house cow and the gelding. The barn was silent. All she heard was the horse chewing on hay from the rack above his head. She took the lantern from the wall and lit it. The crude bunks were empty; no pilgrims were here with them tonight. No one could see her, no one could stop her now.

The door to the earth cellar lay in darkness. Even though it had been years since Father had tried to put her inside it, the threat of the box was always present, waiting for her. And any time Father locked her away could be the time he forgot to come and release her.

Saskia listened hard for sounds of Father stirring, imagining him coming out to look for her. The hinge of the door to the cellar creaked as she slowly pulled it open. The cellar smelled familiar; onions and turnips and damp earth. She approached the box, shivering, catching the old scent of her urine. She tried not to look at it, but the horror came flushing through her. This was the sort of casket that a child's body would be carried in to bury. Quickly, she fell to her knees in the corner, scrabbling at the dirt, digging like a dog, hoping it was still buried here in the cellar where Father wouldn't think to look for it.

She had let him think the fishhook was lost, but months later, when he'd ordered her to lug and stack the harvest of turnips and carrots for the winter, she had searched for it, pushing her fingers through the sludge until she touched the sharp barb. She put it in the pouch with her other treasures: the feather from her home and the stone of black glass. They were her possessions. She would not let Father take another thing from her. She had buried the pouch back in the earth.

Saskia heard a thump from the house and she paused, heart banging. She expected to hear his boots tromping across the yard. She returned to digging, holding her breath, until her hand closed over the leather pouch. It was there. She pulled it out and looped it around her neck. Leaping up, terrified Father would appear behind her, she rushed out of the barn and into the yard. She should saddle the horse and go, but she lingered. She had to be sure he would not follow.

Entering the house, she saw Father had slumped to the floor. If he woke now, he would suspect nothing, perhaps not even realise she had drugged his mead with a sleeping draught. Silently, she ransacked the larder, stole food and money, then she took a knife from the kitchen bench. Each step towards him was slow and cautious. She could slaughter him like a lamb, draw the blade across his neck above his white collar and watch him bleed. She was almost close enough to do it, but her hand was shaking, the candlelight glinting on the steel. She was still afraid of him, afraid that if she drew too close he might reach out and grasp her.

Saskia turned and fled.

CHAPTER THREE

*H*unger gripped Pascal's stomach like a dog that would not relinquish a stick. It gnawed at him. He felt each bite like a sudden cramp. Hunger hurt. He was tired of the ache.

None of the townsfolk had come out to hear their songs and stories and he sat down on the hard earth before a dying fire with his stomach empty.

'They will come,' Rémi said.

'No, they won't!' Pascal snapped. He glanced at the church on the hill. It was in darkness. He rose and kicked dirt over the embers of the fire. 'Come on. I've got a bad feeling. Let's go.'

It helped to keep moving, as if the action fooled his stomach into thinking it would soon be fed. He would not sleep if he had to lie and feel the holes open in his stomach while he waited for the priest to bring damnation down upon them.

Rémi followed with an exaggerated sigh, tugging on Henriette's reins.

Pascal foraged for mushrooms and berries along the verge as they walked, grateful for the silver light of the moon. At least the mushrooms were easy to find. Thick and chewy, they occupied his mouth and filled his stomach. But this late in the season the blackberries were hidden deep behind a tangle of barbed vines and his hands were soon ripped and bleeding. He swore as he pricked his finger again, sucked on his knuckle. He stopped, tasting the iron of his own blood and feeling the heat of a sudden flash of rage burn his chest. He almost whimpered as the frustration flooded through him. He longed for a home, a hearth, one regular meal a day. Was that so much to ask? Ahead, Rémi led Henriette further along the road, oblivious. Pascal slipped his hand among the barbs and plucked a clutch of ripe blackberries from the vine. Ordinarily, he would catch up with Rémi and share the prize. Pascal looked to his fingertips stained with blood and juice, and he took the whole of them into his mouth.

Was this to be his life forever? he wondered. Was this all there would be? Five years had passed since they fled Paris and he was weary of this travelling life. There! He had admitted it. Tired of Rémi risking their lives in tavern brawls, tired of unforgiving earth and poor food. Tired and missing home.

After leaving Paris, their first night out in the open had been terrifying. Pascal remembered they had sheltered in a roadside ditch and he had been spooked by the noises—nameless creatures that scurried through the long grasses and beasts that snorted and bellowed. Rémi had curled up to sleep while Pascal dared not close his eyes. He had drawn his knees up to his chest and kept watch. It seemed he was always watching out for Rémi.

The two men walked side by side in silence on the road that took them north to Marburg, by way of Alsfeld, where they could perform again and hope for better takings. Pascal wasn't optimistic. He could see the taste for Frenchmen and their tales were waning.

'We can't go on like this,' Pascal said.

Rémi slung his arm around Pascal's shoulders. 'Our fortunes will improve. Have faith, my gloom-mongering friend.'

Pascal shrugged him off.

I want to go home. Pascal felt the words forming on his tongue. Five years away from Paris was surely long enough. But what if Rémi should refuse? What then?

'Let's go south this year for the winter,' Rémi said unexpectedly.

Pascal turned to look at his friend. 'South? But we always spend the winter in Marburg.'

'In Marburg, all we will hear is the Brothers Grimm this, the Brothers Grimm that.' Rémi's voice was mocking. 'The Brothers Grimm do not stand up in front of the crowds to test the mettle of their story. They want to hide between sheets of paper, between lines of ink!'

Pascal admitted there was truth to that. 'I hear they mean to publish a book of tales.'

Pascal and Rémi had met the brothers on their first visit to Marburg, when they were boys, new to the art of telling tales. They'd been invited to the brothers' rooms in a half-timbered house to recite their fairytales for a fee. Pascal was pleased they would earn coin so easily. But when Rémi stood before the two law students, who sat with open notebooks on their desktops with pens poised, he had been struck dumb. He had bolted and Pascal had followed, clattering down the narrow staircase after his friend and bursting out onto the street.

Later, they learned the brothers had tried to cajole an old woman's store of folklore tales from her while in a hospital bed and she had refused to speak, content to take her stories with her to the grave. Rémi felt vindicated. 'You see? There is power in these tales. The old woman understood this; she was a keeper of the stories. She could see the Brothers Grimm were unworthy.'

Pascal had been dispirited by the loss of earnings, but did not comment, for he had seen that behind his bluster, Rémi was intimidated by these men of education.

Rémi warmed in his anger, his gestures expanding. 'They do not know the danger of it—to read the emotions of the crowd, to give them more of this and less of that, to know when to add heat or serve a cooling draft. This is something that the artist needs to feel!' Rémi thumped his chest.

If the Grimms published their tales, no one would appreciate the art of the oral storyteller anymore, Pascal thought. Their travelling life was coming to an end, whether Rémi wanted it to or not.

Rémi kicked at a loose stone. 'They have spoiled these towns for us. It is time we journeyed south—to Venice.'

'Venice!' Pascal was shocked; Rémi had never mentioned any desire to see the fabled Italian city before. 'Why there?' Venice was Gianni's home. It hurt Pascal to think of Gianni. It had haunted him how thoughtlessly he had left this man who had been like a father to him.

'Gianni gave us all his stories. We grew up on his tales of Casanova and Carnevale. It would be the perfect place to begin again.'

But Venice was even further away from home than Marburg, Pascal thought.

'Marburg has Katharina,' Pascal reminded Rémi, with a twist in his chest. Silence stretched between them. He glimpsed the look on Rémi's face and knew he was losing his friend to reverie as they walked. Rémi would be thinking of his nights in Katharina's bed and it stirred a sudden jealousy in Pascal. He might win this battle but it would not be without wounds.

It was late morning when they came upon an orchard. *Streuobstwiesen*—wild meadows scattered with fruit trees—surrounded every village in these parts. Pascal's mouth watered. Henriette charged for the trees. She chomped through the fallen fruit, while Pascal and Rémi climbed up into the branches like children, gorging themselves on apples, their fingers and faces becoming sticky with the juice. Pascal grinned at Rémi, giddy with relief at their sudden bounty. He shook the branches, laughing as the apples fell to the ground, and he leaped down after them to gather saddlebags full of fruit. When they were done, they found a stream and splashed into the riffles, overturning rocks, competing to see who could collect the most crayfish to braise for their lunch. Pascal always let Rémi win; he had learned from past experience it meant a more eager companion in their foraging tasks for the next time.

Rémi slapped Pascal's back and beamed at him. 'This is the life, my friend! What more could you want?' His eyes lingered on Pascal's own, making Pascal feel like he mattered to Rémi more than anyone else in the world.

After they had eaten, they washed themselves in the thigh-deep water of a pool. Rémi perched at the stream's edge and tried to shave in the reflection of the calm waters. Pascal took the knife from

Rémi and sat him down on a fallen log. He scraped the sharpened blade slowly down his friend's cheek to his jaw. Rémi closed his eyes, placing all his trust in Pascal's sure hands. His lashes were long and tinged with amber and Pascal felt an overwhelming fondness, despite everything. He tipped Rémi's chin upwards and tenderly shaved the whiskers from his skin. When he was done, Rémi was like a young boy again and Pascal gently wiped the soap suds from his friend's lips.

In the warmth of the midday sun, the men lazed beside the stream. Stomach full, heart full, Pascal enjoyed this moment of stillness. He thought of nothing, no future, no past. He listened to Henriette tugging the lush blades of grass with her teeth, the birds chattering and water burbling. Beside him, Rémi snored softly. Pascal could never stay angry with Rémi for long.

Rémi had his arm thrown back across his eyes and Pascal admired the curve of his bicep beneath his shirt. The drawstring was loose, revealing his smooth chest, and Pascal watched the steady rise and fall of his breathing. Rémi's face lost all bravado when he slept. That loose curling mop of hair and the softness of his mouth gave him a boyish innocence that was never apparent when Rémi was awake. Perhaps that was why every woman Rémi slept with fell in love with him. It came so easily for him, this attractiveness, and Pascal wondered if anyone had ever been able to resist.

Pascal rolled away.

Could he resist Rémi? Rémi wanted to go to Venice and start again, but Pascal longed to go home. Could he go back to Paris and the theatre, on his own? Without Rémi? His breath caught in his throat and he fought the urge to reach his fingers across the space between them, the urge to find Rémi's hand and hold on to it.

I feigned sleep while Pascal gathered our belongings and saddled Henriette, ignoring his sighs and little mutterings about the darkening clouds and our lack of shelter. We would reach the next town soon enough and tell our stories and earn some coin. He worried like an old woman—but hadn't it always worked out for the best? I lay back listening to the bees as they nosed into the petals of the clover.

Above me, a bird wheeled overhead. A *Wespenbussard*. Soon it would journey south for the winter. No one noticed the departure of lone birds, not like the flocks of geese making arrows across the sky on their migration, but one by one these buzzards would leave the north, crossing Italy and journeying as far as tropical Africa, if the stories were to be believed. What a life it would be to fly free of any borders, to have no papers, no new languages to learn. I stretched out my arms on the ground, staring up into the sky, wondering what it would feel like to soar. How did they make their decision to leave? I wondered. When they looked down upon this land, what was the sign that told them it was time to leave everything behind?

'Have you ever thought of going home?' Pascal had asked me some weeks ago. Just spat it out onto the road as we were walking.

'We have no home,' I responded glibly, eager to change the subject. 'We are free.'

He said no more then, but I knew what he was thinking. Sometimes he would spring a memory on me, tales of Gianni, Margot or Bonbon. He peppered our conversations with his reminiscences about our days at the Comédie-Italienne, our youth in Paris. He knew I never liked to look back, only forward, and yet he continued to remind me of the people we had left behind. He made me think of my mother, and I did not like it.

On my outstretched arm, I saw the scar on my wrist where she had branded me. A mark of ownership. Once I had treasured it as a promise that she would return. Now I thought only of her betrayal and I pulled my sleeve down to cover it.

I sat up. Pascal and Henriette turned their dutiful eyes on me and I felt a guilt so sharp it shocked me. Poor Pascal, he did not deserve this life. He had followed me out of loyalty and now he was stuck with this wandering existence. Was it a life for him? Was it enough? I did not know what I would do without him.

I leaped up and embraced him so tightly I lifted him from his feet. His heart beat against mine. Loyal Pascal. I thanked him with my nose pressed into his neck. *I'm sorry*, I wanted to say. *Don't ever leave me.*

Pascal pushed me away gruffly, patted Henriette.

'To Alsfeld,' I said, giving him that.

We broke our little camp just as the first bullets of rain began to strike.

To think I once used to love the sound of rain on the theatre roof. Back then, I thought it sounded like applause, like the wild enthusiasm of a crowd. Now it spattered the dirt road, sluiced down my collar, thrummed on my hat and numbed my fingers, and I hated it.

I sheltered behind Pascal as best I could on Henriette's back, but the rain thwarted our progress, turning the roads to mud. Without a town or tavern in sight, we were forced to take cover in a barn. Poor Henriette looked miserable with her mane dripping, head low, as we let ourselves in. She brightened on spying the towering bales of hay and shook her head like a dog before plunging her nose into the sundried pastures from better days.

Shaking the water from our own hides, I grinned at Pascal, revived. The barn was well built, the hay dry, we had slept in far worse. I spun about, hopeful for chickens, and realised that we were not alone.

Six men looked at Henriette with hunger in their eyes. Battle-hardened men. We stared at one another, not speaking. Their uniforms were peeling from them, faded and threadbare, but still recognisable. They were members of Napoleon's Grand Armée. I felt a cold dread in the depths of my bowel. They were deserters, I hoped, for if these men were reinforcements heading for the war in Russia, we were in danger.

'A story, gentlemen?' I asked in French, stepping forward with a smile and drawing my cloak wide. 'While my good friend lights us a warming fire.'

'How much for the horse?' a thick voice answered in accented French.

'She is not for sale.'

'That's good—we have no money,' a snide voice said in Polish. This met with a snort and several chuckles. I realised they did not know I understood their tongue. I was in the business of words and could speak many languages, for we had travelled far and wide in the Empire. I flicked my eyes to Pascal to see if he understood. We would need our wits to evade these old grey dogs.

The wind rose and rattled the boards of the barn. For Henriette's sake, I judged it wise not to speak of food and our lack thereof. She was noisy in her own appreciation of the fodder.

'May we share this delightful accommodation for the price of a tale?' I was polite yet bold. It does no good to show fear.

The men looked to one another, grey faces hollowed and bitter.

'Tell us *your* war stories,' one of them snarled. He had a long nose and a twitching lip that revealed the glint of a canine. He reminded me of the brute, Claude, and our confinement in the house on Boulevard Montmartre. My hands began to shake. I had a moment to decide. The coin had been tossed—would it fall on the side of truth or lie?

'We escaped,' I blurted out. 'From the clutch of mud and blood and famine. We could not march another day. You see, we are story-tellers, not men made for battlefields. We were with Napoleon when he pushed out the Austrians from Italy, we fought the Spaniards in the mountains and claimed these Prussian towns for Napoleon, but here we have stayed.' Quickly, I added, 'We have not taken arms against Poland.'

'He must've seen fighting as a babe,' one of them sneered in Polish. 'Not a mark on his fresh young skin.'

Unwittingly, I touched the welt burned into my wrist.

Their leader's eyes ranged over every muscle of my body. 'Pretty Frenchman, how many men have you killed?'

I swallowed. 'Too many,' I whispered.

'You weren't in any war, Goldilocks.' The man had me, like a dog biting on my coat sleeve, a nip of my skin caught between its teeth. I needed to turn the tale as deftly as I could, but the dog man would not let go of my flesh so easily.

'Have you killed a man to eat?' he whispered, his mineral eyes direct on mine. 'Do you know what that is like?'

Did he mean to intimidate or to warn of his intentions? Either way, I had decided our stay here should be short.

'Or to slit the belly of your own horse and crawl inside for warmth?' He had a lupine gleam in his eye.

Pascal remained behind me in utter silence. Even Henriette had stopped chewing. Only the rain continued to lash.

The man rose to his feet. 'I bet you were one of those that hid when the conscriptors came calling,' he said, his voice full of loathing.

His words. He could not know what a wound they would inflict. I never let myself remember those months below the floor in putrid darkness.

'Frenchmen that hid in their cellars and beneath their mother's skirts!' another added, 'while we fought their wars for them.' He spat.

We were children again, Pascal and I. We were boys, for all our bravado, and these were men. How could I imagine what they had seen?

Pascal mounted Henriette and spun her about, reaching down for me. I gripped his arm, used his stirrup and was up behind him in a moment and we were riding out into the driving rain, the water coursing down my face, the plates of Henriette's hooves gouging out the mud.

CHAPTER FOUR

Saskia watched the storytellers enter the barn then crept up to peer through a knothole. She recognised the danger at once. Desperate men. Deserters. With the rain hammering her shoulders, she rushed back through the boot-sticking mud to the copse of trees where she had tied Otto and pulled him deeper into the forest.

She had followed the trail of the storytellers since discovering the remains of the smouldering fire in the night. She found them lingering in the orchard and spied on them from a distance, hidden from the road. If Father came after her, he might suspect the story-tellers had taken her with them. She was careful. She waited to see if Father would come for her.

When he discovered her deception, Father would be furious. He despised disloyalty more than anything. That first time she had run away, he had locked her in the box far longer than when she cut his face, as if the physical pain meant less to him. 'You will be loyal to me!' he thundered as he slammed the lid closed on top of her. She could not go back. She would not let him catch her this time.

She jumped. A horse bolted from the barn with both the story-tellers on its back. The solid mare ran with more spirit than Saskia would have imagined possible.

It was time to move. Tying the hood of her red cloak tight about her face, she mounted Otto and followed the mare's hoofprints across the open field until they entered the thick forest. There, she lost sight of the hoofprints among the fallen leaves, and in the gathering darkness, she felt truly alone. The silent spectre of Father loomed in her mind, a black figure on horseback, riding fast along the wet roads. How long had he lain drugged and senseless? She wished she had taken a knife to his throat. She had stood over him with a knife dangling at her side, frozen. She was afraid of him, then and now. Her nostrils flared, disgusted by her cowardice. Saskia urged Otto into a trot, all the while imagining a black crow flapping along the roads behind her.

Otto stumbled on the uneven ground and Saskia slowed him to a walk, willing herself to calm. She led him off the track and he sank into the leaf litter, knees bending beneath him, still saddled. The poor beast was unused to long journeys as Father never left Saskia alone for long. Once he had stolen her from the circus, Father never travelled away like that again. She still had no idea why he had taken possession of her. She had gnawed at that question over and over, always wondering if she could have done anything to prevent him taking her that day. Had she provoked him? Or had she simply been convenient? He gained an obedient servant and she lost a family who cared for her, even if they were not her own blood. They were lost to her now. A travelling circus was always moving. They could whirl away and touch down again any place in the world. How would she ever find them again?

Saskia shivered in her cloak, tucking her legs beneath her as she too sank to the earth. She leaned back against her horse's belly, feeling the comfort of its rise and fall, sheltered under the canopy of the beech forest. Her eyes fluttered closed.

Fragments of memory came unbidden as sleep tried to claim her. She pictured the misshapen trees along the coast bent over by the Baltic wind. *Windflüchter* trees, her grandmother said. Trees that she had thought looked like women with long hair whipped forward over their heads and their toes caught in the earth, fleeing the bullying wind. She remembered walking on a beach, salt spray in her face, the scent of brine in her nose and being startled at the slap and roar of the lunging waves. In the distance, she saw a red-haired woman—her mother—turning away. Saskia tried to run after her. Her mother was laughing into the wind, hair wild with it, whipping across her skin. Falcons were swooping in to hunt along the cliffs. Her mother led her out along the rocky spur, taking her close to the edge of the cliff. Saskia had been buffeted by the blast of wind, her own hair lifting with it as if she too might fly. 'Look!' Her mother's finger pointing, stabbing, as a peregrine falcon hurled itself down to snatch a gull from the sky before her. She had been afraid, looking down at the waves crashing on the rocks far below her. She had panicked and reached out for her mother's hand but felt the looseness of her mother's grip. Did her mother trust her not to fall or simply not care enough to hold her tight?

These were memories from a life before her mother abandoned her to the circus. She had collected a falcon's feather from that place and carried it with her. Should she try to find this place of birds? A place where her grandmother might still live. As she slipped into sleep she dreamed she was being carried by the wind, like a feather caught in an eddy of air, never allowed to touch the earth.

Saskia woke with a start, disorientated. She was damp and cold, and afraid. Through the solid spears of tree trunks, she glimpsed the first shafts of sunlight piercing the mist. She smelled the wet leaf litter. She felt the warmth of her horse at her back and let it soothe her. She was pleased she was not alone.

In the tree above an owl was watching, silent and still. Round eyes, speckled feathers and a solemn stare. Its talons curled around the branch. She had to be a *vila* now; she had to believe she could protect herself. She stood and the bird swooped away on silent wings.

Otto heaved himself to his feet and Saskia brushed the mud and leaves from his legs and belly then ate a little of the hard bread she had taken from Father's larder. The rain had stopped, but the trees dripped pearls of water onto her upturned face, striking her eyelids gently and rolling down her cheeks. She licked her lips.

North. She knew her home was north, even if she couldn't name it. A place of wind and waves and widows. A place of migrating birds. Now all she needed was to find the men that could help her return home.

In the streets of Alsfeld, she walked her horse through the narrow, cobbled lanes, climbing upwards through a town of colourful half-timbered houses with flowers blooming in window boxes despite the lateness of the season. Here the girls wore their hair bound under red Schwalm caps with long black ribbons tied beneath their chins. Saskia pulled her hood forward about her face, feeling out of place. The cloak fell over her shoulders to her waist and covered the foreign embroidery of her dress. Only a black skirt showed out beneath the red cape, and beneath that she wore sturdy woollen tights and boots like all the other girls. Her odd-coloured hair was concealed beneath the hood.

She glimpsed the church tower at the end of the lane, rising square-sided and solemn with a rounded skullcap roof. The windows were arched and long. She had a sensation that it was watching her approach. Worm wit! She cursed her own stupidity. It was the most likely direction for her to run: to the north, towards the place Father knew was her home. For all she knew, he could be waiting and watching her from the steeple tower. He might have passed her on the road while she slept curled up against Otto's belly. He could be slipping through the crowds in search of her at this minute. I must not be recognised, she thought, in rising panic. I must seem like all the others. She threaded her fingers through Otto's coarse mane, steadying herself. He stopped, uncertain, and she leaned against his shoulder, hiding her face. She breathed deep, his scent reassuring. Impatient, he nudged her forward. They were both hungry and thirsty, and she scolded herself. She needed to be a *vila*, with the strength of a lone owl; this childish fear was unbecoming. Saskia quickly slipped out of the gaze of the church windows.

In the bustling town square, a market was held under the open archways beneath the town hall. Here the business of trade was thick and steady. She saw tables laden with bread and eggs and cheese, she saw mounds of onions sliced and served raw with herrings. The smell of bratwurst made her mouth water. She watched the heavy sausages turning over on a hotplate, sizzling and spitting in grease, and caught the eye of the woman who tended them, her arms the size of hams. Would the woman think it strange that she was here alone? She had only ever been to market with Father. She fumbled for her coins, bought a sausage and then bread and stowed the food in her saddlebags.

Otto pulled the reins, tugging her towards a stall of apples. The orchardist winked as he passed her a Goldparmäne, shaking his head when she offered to pay. Grateful for his unexpected kindness, she nodded to him and let Otto nuzzle her fingers and smuggle the apple from her hand.

Saskia heard the men's voices before she saw them. The story-tellers had mounted a small stage on the other side of the square and had already drawn a crowd. People couldn't help themselves, she supposed; they were attracted to anything new, just like beasts of the field gathered about an object to ponder its magical appear-ance. Until they became bored. Or spooked. The crowd clapped and cheered and she saw coins being tossed into the feathered cap of the lute player as he passed it around. He was the one who wore those ridiculous striped hose, like a medieval troubadour. The storyteller was bowing, his cape splayed out. He righted himself snappily with an endearing grin and she felt his gaze sweep over her. She knew he would not recognise her like this, not without her hair on display. All men ever noticed about her was her hair.

She pushed closer to hear their tales. The crowd today was genial and liked the men well enough. She could see the excitement on the storytellers' faces and the troubadour pocketed the coins swiftly, stashing them in some hidden pocket. She wondered if she was the only one among the crowd who was following the route of the money with intent.

The curly-haired bard had worked up a sweat with his tale. Clean-faced and glowing, she saw he had shaved his beard and he was younger than she had thought. He had made a stage out of a board and three crates and now strutted upon it. The people were in the mood for laughter, even she could feel that, and his voice took on a mocking tone. He produced a mask on a stick from behind his back and swept back his cloak to reveal a stitched red heart on his satin waistcoat.

'Kasperl!' The crowd somehow both sighed with pleasure and cheered with excitement. The children worked their way to the front. Saskia moved Otto to a water trough alongside the makeshift stage and settled to watch.

'Yes: Kasperl!' cried the storyteller, covering his face with the long-nosed mask painted with an orange face, lurid blue eyes and red lips. The masked man capered across the stage to a peal of childish laughter.

Then he flicked the mask away and spoke directly to the audience. 'But our hero is in grave peril. It distresses me to tell you good people what has befallen him.' The storyteller lowered his voice, drawing them close. The children shuffled forward, elbowing one another.

'What has happened to him?'

'I cannot say—it is too hurtful, too shameful.'

'You must tell us!'

'I must?'

'You must!'

'He has failed his friend Seppel.'

The mask was replaced with a crying face, the smile turned upside down, the eyes squeezed closed. 'They have taken him,' Kasperl wailed. 'He will surely die!'

The storyteller removed the mask. 'But who has taken Seppel?' he asked the children.

'Was it the witch?' one cried.

'The robber?'

'The wolf?'

'A crocodile?' Every eye turned to look at the tiny child with wide, frightened eyes. They shook their heads and murmured. A crocodile? Where did the child hear such a thing? Where would a crocodile be found in these parts? The child was slapped about the ear.

The storyteller retrieved a hat from behind his stage. Saskia recognised the famous French bicorn and watched as the storyteller settled it on his head and slid a hand into his waistcoat.

Saskia heard some nervous chuckles among the adults. Others shifted their feet and held their tongues. She saw eyes dart to the French municipal guards smoking and sprawling on the cafe chairs at the edge of the square.

'I will take each and every one of you and feed you to the Russian wolves,' the storyteller snarled at the children from beneath Napoleon's hat.

Careful, storyteller, she thought. It's a dangerous game you're playing.

Then Kasperl was back and the hat was gone. 'I must defeat the evil Emperor and bring back my friend Seppel!'

The audience was anxious. The storyteller spoke their Prussian tongue but he could not disguise the French lilt in his words. Was this a trick? she saw them wonder. She had learned enough to understand these lands had been forced to become France's ally once they surrendered to Napoleon. Some people shook their heads, moved away. Mothers called their children to them. She had heard the whispered hatred of the Emperor before, but it was another thing to be found speaking out against him in public.

The tall troubadour stirred as the crowd began to disperse. Even the guards seemed to notice the tension and ambled towards the stage.

Saskia weighed her options. She knew she must not reveal herself. Father could be watching. She needed to hide among these folk and look as plain and simple as any other girl. And yet.

Saskia removed her shoes, tied the laces together and draped them over Otto's withers. Next she unbound her cape and strapped it safely behind the saddle. Her russet hair was pulled up to a knot on top of her head. Then she cartwheeled onto the stage. She flipped and tumbled and curled herself backwards into a ball. Every eye was on her in astonishment. She felt it, their awe, and it awakened in her a remembrance of old. Her muscles were stiff but the routines returned to her body as naturally as speaking an old forgotten language. She walked about on her hands and folded her entire body into the shape of a *Brezel*. She heard them whispering, *Impossible, a freak, the girl must have no bones, she must've been grown in a box!* Ha, Saskia thought. They just about had the measure of it.

From upside down and balanced on one hand, she saw the storyteller was annoyed that she had stolen his stage. Fool. She was saving his life. The troubadour stood stunned. She split her legs apart and reached one foot out. Clasping the feather of his floppy hat between her bare toes, she pulled it from his head, holding out the cap to the crowd.

She shook the hat. She heard the cheers and felt the coins fall into the soft velvet. Even the French militia were applauding. The troubadour picked up his lute and encouraged the children to dance. Finally, the storyteller found the graciousness to bow to the crowd and, in that gesture, claim her.

Now we are three, she thought.

CHAPTER FIVE

'What were you doing?' Pascal hissed at Rémi.

Rémi shrugged. 'I thought it would make them laugh.'

Pascal felt rage rushing through his veins. Behind them a pillory neck chain dangled against the corner of a stone building. He imagined Rémi bound by it and pelted with all manner of refuse. For heaven's sake, this town still used a driller basket for punishment—had he not shown Rémi the poor man driven mad by the children spinning him around and around for their amusement?

The girl brought the horses to them in haste, mounting her own by vaulting onto its back. She stared at them with utter disdain.

Pascal could not meet his friend's eye. Rémi, the fool! Did he mean to get them caught up in these wars after all they had suffered and sacrificed to hide from them?

Pascal climbed into the saddle. 'You cannot mock the Emperor.' He flung the words over his shoulder. 'You will have us conscripted!'

'They despise us oppressors, don't they? I thought they would enjoy it.' Rémi leaped up over Henriette's rump.

The girl spun her chestnut gelding on the spot and cantered out of the *Marktplatz*. Pascal kicked Henriette's flanks and followed the girl as if she had been their leader all along. He was too angry with Rémi to do anything else. Ahead, her red cloak was a beacon.

Passing through the remains of the town walls and out into the countryside, Pascal let Henriette follow on the heels of her horse. He felt Rémi's arms tight around him, squeezing him, and he had the sudden urge to shake his friend away, to let him fall into a ditch by the roadside. Perhaps it was time they parted once and for all. No more Rémi and Pascal. He should return to Paris alone.

The girl suddenly swung the gelding from the road and Henriette followed the chestnut tail without question. Pascal cursed his inattention. He felt Rémi's arms clutch a little tighter around his middle.

The girl dismounted and led her horse behind a thicket of willows. Rémi slid to the ground and walked away from them without a word.

'You have my share?' the girl asked, her small hand held out flat.

Pascal had recognised her at once when she sprang onto their makeshift stage. It was the girl from Gelnhausen. The girl who belonged to the priest. She had saved them from Rémi's stupidity, that was true, and he was grateful; he only hoped the priest was not giving chase. Another reason, he determined, that once he paid her, they should part ways as soon as possible.

He knew the girl had filched some of the coins already, sliding them from his cap into her palm before handing it back to him with a flourish. Her face did not flinch as her hands did their thieving; she stared straight up at him, expressionless. No matter, Pascal thought, she saved us and she is due her share.

'Soon,' Pascal said, loosening Henriette's girth and slipping the saddle from her back. She was sweating from the burst of pace and he took handfuls of long, dry grass to rub the sweat marks from her coat. The girl stood close while he worked and Henriette feasted on the long grass. When he'd finished, Pascal reached into his vest for his purse.

He sat cross-legged to count out the takings. It was a relief to feel the weight of the coins in his hand and he rubbed his thumb across their dull faces. Hard-earned tokens that had passed through hands that threshed wheat, pulled on udders or were scalded by boiling linens. They had been given up joyfully, by people who knew the worth of a little enchantment. He made three even piles of coins on the dirt.

The girl reached for hers.

'Wait.' Pascal gripped her wrist. 'What is your name?'

She narrowed her eyes. 'Saskia.'

He let her hand go. 'With my thanks, Saskia.' He gestured to the coins.

She stashed her share with a speed that raised his eyebrow.

'You cannot stay with us,' he warned her.

She rose to tend to her horse without a word.

Pascal picked up his own share, enough to last a week or more. To Pascal, these coins meant they would buy smoked sausage and fresh bread, perhaps a plate of potato dumplings in a sour cream and bacon sauce. He salivated at the thought. To Marburg, he said to himself, raising an imaginary glass of *Apfelwein* in a toast. To plentiful food and safe beds. After that, he would decide his future.

Saskia returned to sit beside him, bringing out a loaf of bread and warm bratwurst. The smell brought tears to his eyes. She offered it to him.

'You cannot stay,' he repeated, taking out his knife to cut a sliver of the sausage. He held it on his tongue to savour for a few moments, eyes closed, before hunger overtook him.

'You need me,' she said with a shrug.

Pascal felt the truth of it clutched in the palm of his hand and he shifted the coins to his pocket; they would have lost their audience if she had not intervened. But she would only be a hindrance; they could not look after a child.

'You should go back to your family.'

'I have no family.'

'That priest.'

She flinched and Pascal felt ashamed. She went silent then and curled herself into a ball with her arms wrapped around her shins. Like a burr in a dog's coat, Pascal knew they would not remove her easily. She seemed older than he had first thought. Sixteen he would guess. Not so much of a child, but a responsibility nonetheless. He had enough childishness to deal with.

They could take her as far as Marburg, perhaps. Katharina would take the girl. Her house was always filled with actors, singers, musicians. Growing up among a theatre family as he had done was no bad thing. And Saskia had talents, of a sort. She could perform in one of Katharina's cabarets of freakish oddities, her private soirees for the curiosity of the wealthy; it was unnatural the way the girl bent herself like that. Katharina would think she was perfect.

Rémi had walked a little way along the road with his back turned to them and his nose pointing south as if searching for a scent on the breeze. These fights, these confrontations—Pascal couldn't help but wonder if something inside of Rémi meant to put them in danger. What had possessed him to speak of Napoleon? Had meeting those deserters from the army affected him more deeply than he would admit?

Those men's faces haunted Pascal's thoughts; grey and gaunt with death in their eyes. They were a pack of starving dogs. His own hackles rose the instant he'd seen them in that barn, seen the strips of uniforms hanging from them. Pascal knew that when he closed his eyes to sleep they would return for him, those red-rimmed eyes. He had become a boy again in that instant, remembering himself as a frightened fifteen-year-old pressing close to Rémi when they climbed down into a dark hold in the floor with men who looked just as desperate as those.

It was a reminder, meeting the army deserters, like a snort of ammonia, an awakener. They had become complacent travelling in these borderlands already pacified and under French rule. They had seen no warring armies, no blood spilled. They had wandered and recited their fairytales, thinking themselves immune to the events of the world, but they too could be caught by this war. Going home might not be as easy as Pascal hoped. One thing was certain: they could not afford to anger the militia and draw attention to themselves. Entertainers were often overlooked for conscription, but only as long as they remained entertaining. Pascal prayed that in Marburg Rémi would keep to the old tales, the tried and true, the Prussian tales that the Brothers Grimm now peddled to their advantage.

Rémi joined them and swept up his share of profit from the dirt.

'To Marburg then?' Pascal's traitorous voice rose like a question that he did not intend.

Rémi grinned. 'Let's toss a coin. *Zahl* for north. *Kopf* for south.'

And before Pascal could protest, the coin was spinning high in the air.

✎

My coin landed in the mud on its face, *Zahl* side up and I shrugged, ambivalent. Marburg it was to be, for now.

'I am going north,' the girl announced with a shrug. 'You may come with me if you like.'

I barked out a laugh. Oh, how I liked her style.

'We travel together only as far as Marburg,' Pascal grumbled. As if anyone could control the movements of a stray cat! It would be good if the girl travelled with us. We needed a distraction from one another, Pascal and me.

We rode on together and I hummed a tune, in a merry mood. The sun had returned to dry off the roads and set the wet leaves in the trees sparkling. Saskia rode in front on her chestnut gelding, little larger than a pony, and Pascal walked at Henriette's head. Soon we would return to the home of Katharina. I couldn't help but smile. I anticipated a joyous return to her affections, to her ample bed and the soft cushioning of her bosom.

When I first met Katharina, I didn't know her age but I could guess by the subtle lines beneath her throat and the slight creeping of her skin that she was old enough to be my mother. She was still a beauty. A statuesque woman, born for the stage. People whispered that she had once been a celebrated opera singer, that she had even sung for Mozart, but I had never known her to take the stage nor heard her sing. She refused to entertain us at her table, even when tankards and cutlery were banged upon the table in unison, our voices demanding an aria, all of us chanting for Katharina. 'Enough!' she silenced us. 'That was the past. It is your turn now.' Why she had settled in Marburg, sheltering actors and bards and misfits, no one could guess.

It was Katharina who first warned me of the Brothers Grimm.

'Your time is coming to an end, you wandering storytellers,' she had declared. She could be brutal like that, but we all knew it was just her way. I did not believe her then.

Katharina told me the brothers intended to publish a book.

'How many people read?' I scoffed. 'These bound tales are for the rich.' I had waved her concern away. 'The common people will still pay for a tale well told.'

I spoke bravely then, but in truth I became uneasy. Once the tales were set in letterpress, inked and stamped onto the page, would there be only one way to tell the story?

Now, I recalled all the villagers who had demanded their tales be told the Prussian way. Belligerent. Angry. Where once they had been impressed by novelty, now they only wanted their own traditions. They didn't want our French Cendrillon with her pumpkin turned into a carriage by a fairy godmother; all they wanted was their poor ash fool, Aschenputtel, and her stepsisters who cut their toes and heels off to fit into the fallen shoe. They liked their tales with brutal realism and little magic in these parts. Napoleon's wars were rousing a nationalistic spirit and turning them against anything French, and the Brothers Grimm were feasting on it.

Pascal was right. We could not go on this way forever if the brothers published their book.

We made camp beside a river as the light began to fall. Pascal lit our fire while I foraged for mussels in the stream. Saskia caught an eel with a fishhook she produced from a pouch about her neck. The girl was a wonder.

We chewed in thoughtful contemplation, replete. I watched the girl tie the fishhook around her middle finger and turn her hand into a fist exposing the shining barb. She intrigued me. How did she learn to contort her body in such an abominable fashion? A girl with an accent from the Baltic coast, a Slavic dress, a child in the property of the Church. She looked like a tiny gnome under the hood of her red cloak.

Pascal was watching her too.

'We should build a theatre, our own theatre, just as Gianni once did in Paris,' he said.

I turned to him. His eyes were full of light.

'The girl is perfect, can't you see, with her *petit chaperon rouge*? We could perform the tale as Perrault premiered it at the court of the Sun King! I have a bearskin coat to make a costume for a wolf. Imagine a painted forest with butterflies and wildflowers and looming trees. Imagine the grandmother's gloomy bedroom with light through one high window illuminating the girl and leaving the bed in shadow. The wolf in grandmother's clothing. A tale perfect for two players.'

I could see the scenes he described. His enthusiasm was infectious.

Pascal reached for his lute. 'Act One, Scene One: The Innocence.' He played a genial tune. 'Then the arrival of the wolf, agreeable, but sly. The girl is naive, she is trusting.' He trilled his fingers on the strings. 'The audience will know the grave danger she is in.'

I joined in the pantomime. 'Even when the floor is slick with her grandmother's blood she does not suspect a thing. She asks why her grandmother's voice is too deep, her ears and eyes too large, and teeth so sharp.' I leaped to my feet. 'All the better to eat you with.' I snapped my jaw.

Pascal knew I would adore being on the stage, a real stage.

'We could perform in comfort,' he cajoled. 'No more cold market-places. We could sleep in beds with mattresses and linen, instead of cowering in barns or stretched out on the bare earth. It won't matter if the Brothers Grimm publish their book of folktales. We would stay together and be safe.'

I could see how his mind was working. We would start small here in Marburg, but one day he hoped we would take our perfor-mances to Paris.

Oh, Pascal. I looked at his shining face. I know I am going to break your heart.

ꝏ

They talk about me as though I am not here, Saskia thought. The two men so caught up in their imaginings.

The lute player wanted a theatre, he said, he wanted to put on shows. She knew the tale of 'Little Red Riding Hood' as Svetlana had told it to her long ago and they had acted out the parts, taking turns at being the grandmother and the wolf. Svetlana would lie back with a shawl around her and snore like an old woman and Saskia would be the giggling wolf who loved to pounce. Or she would be the innocent child full of questions and Svetlana the wolf

90

with all the answers. She had said it was a warning to gullible girls not to be tricked by charming wolves in disguise, as she tucked her into bed. A lesson for girls not to stray. Even then, Saskia had wondered, where were the tales for young boys, warning them not to become wolves?

Saskia had no intention of appearing on any stage. Imagine it—she would be a ripe plum, low-hanging and easy for Father to pluck. Never again. She would not be a Little Red Riding Hood to anyone's wolf.

Saskia lay down beside the fire, settling behind a fallen log, keeping herself hidden from the road. She had tied Otto deeper in the forest so he could not be seen. Father would look for her, she was certain. Hadn't he told her often enough that she belonged to him? He wouldn't let her go so easily.

She wedged the fishhook between her middle fingers and imagined herself shrieking through the air to attack, like a *vila*. He still terrified her, but she was not going to let him take her back. She clenched her hand above her heart as if she were making a promise. The next man who tried to touch her would lose an eye.

The storyteller, Rémi, took his place by the fire, wrapping his cloak around him and wriggling to get comfortable in the dirt.

'Tell me about the priest.'

Saskia frowned and pressed her lips tight. She couldn't speak of him.

'Will he come after you?'

Hunching down further against the log, she murmured, 'Yes.'

'We will keep you safe,' the storyteller said, full of bravado.

She grunted. A fantasist, that's what the *skomorokh* would have called him. A man foolish enough to believe his own bluster.

Moments ago, Rémi had been duelling with an imaginary foe using an imaginary sword, not caring how ridiculous he looked. He had lunged and feinted, twirled and bounced, flicking his outstretched wrist in an exaggerated fashion while the other hand perched on his hip. She had watched as he strutted victorious before an imaginary crowd. She was not afraid of these travellers, not even from that first moment of meeting. They seemed like boys to her.

The troubadour twitched and whimpered in his sleep like a puppy. She wondered where he stashed his coin purse when he slept and if he would feel the loss of it. He was gentle, but he was still a big man, even lying helpless on the earth. She pictured that long arm swinging up to catch her throat, felt the strength in his grip. An old circus habit to size up a man for risk and reward. She could not help herself.

The sight of his lute tucked beneath his head reminded her of the *skomorokh*, the circus comic who always kept his balalaika close. Memories of her circus family came back to her with force. She had learned to tumble to the music of those strings. She had stretched her young body for hours each day, bending her back a little further every time, while the *skomorokh* told her of the storytelling travellers of old. He boasted that his jests and mockery of powerful men were once so feared that he had been chased out of towns. The St Petersburg Circus had given him shelter too, she had realised then, taking his hand in hers.

She should try to find the circus again, even if Svetlana and the *skomorokh* weren't with them anymore. They had cared for her, protected her, she owed it to them to try even if it seemed hopeless.

Rémi startled her from her thoughts. 'How did you learn to do that with your body?' He traced his finger in the air like a knot.

She hesitated, uncertain how much she wanted to share. 'I grew up in a circus.'

'A circus? Performing tricks on horseback?'

She thought of Svetlana, thundering around the main ring. 'It's more than that,' she said hotly. 'Acrobats, dancers, musicians.'

'And contortionists, like you.'

'Like me.'

'Were you born to it? Did you learn your tricks from the cradle?' He was smirking and it annoyed her.

'You mock me.'

'No, I am interested—forgive me.' He placed his hand over his heart.

Saskia rose up to sitting. 'When I was seven my mother took me to the circus and abandoned me there.'

Rémi looked at the ground and she was pleased she had discomfited him. She was breathing hard, forcing back the hurt of those memories.

'Will you try to find her?' he asked.

'Why would I? She didn't want me; she left me like a kitten mewling at a farmhouse door.' She lay down again and rolled over, turning her back to him.

Rémi spoke again. 'My mother betrayed me once as well.' She heard him poking a stick at the fire. 'I shall not forgive her either.'

She squeezed her eyes shut. It didn't matter that her mother had deserted her. Saskia had no regrets. The circus gave her skills, it gave her strength, and it gave her love. The circus had been her family. They had shown her the world could still be kind, even if your mother no longer wanted you.

CHAPTER SIX

The spectacle of the *Schloss* of Marburg rising out of the mist on a hilltop never failed to take my breath away. Across the valley, the high castle walls and its towers were caught in the warm morning sun and floated on a bed of drifting cloud. Below it the dense jumble of houses clinging to the hillside was entirely shrouded by the fog. Nothing of the town was visible, not the church spires, not the brick walls and slate roofs, only the castle at its peak. It was like a castle floating in the cloud.

We halted our horses on the crest of a hill.

'Half a day's ride,' Pascal said. He stood at Henriette's head and stroked her chin.

I smiled down at him. He had dressed with care. He wore a purple velvet frockcoat that I had once won for him in a game of cards. The dew bedazzled it with jewels.

Below us, the fields were dotted with woods, leaves tinged with gold for the changing season. Blue mist hovered above the ground.

Saskia kicked her horse on as though the majesty of the scene meant nothing to her. We followed our strange new companion.

By midday, we arrived at the entrance to the hillside town, crossing a bridge crowded with traders and their carts, and passing beside an imposing double-spired church. We would stable the horses here and climb the steep streets into the town on foot.

I was in a generous mood and searched my pocket for a precious coin to give a beggar squatting outside an *Apotheke*. When we had extra to give, we always would; it was how we had survived so far, by generosity and charity. Gianni taught us that. If you would not give, how could you expect to receive?

I was pleased to see the shops were freshly painted, with their exposed beams in rich reds, blues and browns against the white-washed plaster. This was still a wealthy town. I smelled the floral scents of a perfumery, and somewhere nearby a baker was pulling fresh loaves from an oven. We passed through a shoe market ringing with cobblers' hammers and I saw Pascal looking at his worn leather shoes. He lingered before a pair of knee-high Hessian boots in polished leather. I knew he was imagining a life of wealth; a life in which he did not feel every stone beneath his soles, where in winter his feet were kept warm and dry. I swallowed the lump in my throat.

Trailing behind us, Saskia looked like a child of the fields and forest in this town. She would need new clothes here, perhaps a new identity altogether. If we stayed too long in this town she would be at risk of the priest finding her, if he was not here already. I glanced around the busy merchant street as if the black-robed priest might accost us.

Pascal had found an abandoned church. He beckoned me over. I leaned through the window and quickly recoiled from the stench. The chapel was now being used as a pigsty. 'The location is perfect,' he said. 'With a little work, perhaps?'

I nodded, noncommittal, then turned away before he could read my face. How could I tell him that I loved our travelling life? That the thought of staying in one place, with the same faces, the same lovers, the same routine day after day after day, filled me with horror? A life on the road was full of novelty. It might be terrifying, uncomfortable, painful even, but it was never boring. Pascal might want to give up this life, but I could not.

The window display of a shop caught my eye and I shrieked.

It was a *Buchhandlung*, a bookshop, and propped up in pride of place in the window was a book entitled *Kinder- und Hausmärchen*.

'*Children's and Household Tales*!' I spat.

So the Brothers Grimm had finally published their collection.

'Pascal!' I called for him, needy, desperate.

He caught my arm, holding me up.

We were doomed, we travelling storytellers, by these word thieves. I saw my future falling away, predicted in the very name of the book, emphatically pressed into the leather bindings. Household tales. No one need leave their homes to listen to storytellers bringing them tales to delight and entertain. Parents could stay beside their own fires, reading the old tales to their children, safe and warm and comfortable.

'These are our stories, Pascal! Not theirs alone to claim!' Next they would be known as Grimms' Tales when it was not the case at all.

'Forget the Brothers Grimm.' Pascal gripped my shoulders, turning me to face him. 'We must create our own theatre. Katharina will support us. We will build a stage for you to command, like you always wanted.'

Pascal didn't understand. No one in Prussia would want his productions of French fairytales—even though it was the French who carried them here in the first place! The stories had been passed on by the Protestant Huguenots escaping religious persecution a century ago and by travelling storytellers like us. I felt my own patriotism rise. It was French *conteuses* like Baroness d'Aulnoy and Madame de Murat, and my favourite storyteller of all, Charles Perrault, who had invented fairytales. Though Gianni had liked to remind us that the first fairytales came to France from Venice through the stories of Straparola. Even the French *conteuses* admitted to drawing inspiration from him. Where had they come from before that? I wondered. Where did those stories begin? Constantinople? The Levant? It did not matter to me. Tales had always changed from one teller to the next, each culture adding a little of their own flavour. When I told a story, it shifted a little with each telling. When you wrote a story down, it became trapped, like a butterfly slammed in the pages of a heavy tome.

Gianni gifted us his tales. 'These stories are meant to pass between the hearts of those who tell them and those who listen.' He told us ancient Roman tales, like 'Diana and the Golden Apples', or medieval tales of witches and demons, and sometimes Bible tales like 'David and Goliath'. He gave us his own Venetian tales. I carried them in my heart and they were the first of my repertoire when Pascal and I needed to make a living on the road. We quickly learned which tales were popular and which would result in dry horse turds thudding against our heads. In those early days, the critics and their missiles were never far away and we both bore scars. Hurling back the insult 'I hear your mother slept with dogs' had only ever ended poorly. But I honed my craft, I improved, and I learned not to retaliate.

I was feeling nauseous, a little dizzy, as I contemplated the book in the window. Was this truly the end? Surely only the rich would read these works; after all, how many people could read? Few. I tried to calm myself. There was still a place for our craft to shine. What vexed me most about the Brothers Grimm was that these learned men, these scholars, had never had to earn their living in the marketplaces; they had never stood up before a crowd and heard their heckles and hisses or felt the sting of the sharp stones they cast. I had earned my right to tell these stories. These men had merely stolen them.

I noticed a flapping piece of paper on a nearby pole. A drawing of two men, their faces turned to the side, prominent noses sharp like blades. Men I recognised from years ago. The Brothers Grimm.

'No, no, no!' I dashed across the street to snatch a flyer from a pole.

'Here! They are coming here, to Marburg, today! They are to give a public reading of their work.'

Pascal shook his head. 'No, Rémi . . .'

I pressed the leaflet into his chest. 'We must go to this public reading. I want to see them perform, these men who mean to steal our living.'

'Bad idea.' Pascal was blunt.

'We cannot let them take our livelihood from us!' To be a keeper of stories was a powerful thing and I would not give it up without a fight.

'Come.' I pulled his arm, dragging him towards the *Obermarkt*.

'Wait! Where is Saskia?'

I looked around. She had been with us only moments before, standing before the shop window. I scanned the street for her bright red cloak.

'She's gone,' Pascal said.

He was right. Saskia had vanished.

❧

Saskia touched her fingertips to the glass. The book had a russet-brown cover with a title embossed in gold. She was captured by the simple beauty of it. A book that was small and easily cradled. She wanted to hold it open in her hands and gently turn its pages. Father's heavy Bible had never inspired the same sense in her. Never had she coveted any object with such intensity. For the first time, she found herself wishing she could read.

Children's and Household Tales, Rémi had said. Inside the pages of this book were stories that grandmothers told their grandchildren and she felt a longing she could not explain—a remembrance of tales told in an earthen-floored cottage with whitewashed walls and thatched roof, on a coast where the wind blew the trees into bent-backed crones. The stories themselves she could barely remember, but the feeling of delight remained. A feeling of wonder. She cast a glance at the bookseller's door then looked back to Rémi and Pascal arguing in the street.

In her heart, Saskia knew there would be many others who felt as she now did, this longing to have the stories for herself, to open them whenever she might please, waiting for no man to tell them to her.

She stepped inside the bookshop.

Saskia opened the book and saw a drawing of a girl resting on the forest floor against a seated fawn, holding its lead in her hand. Saskia almost sobbed. In this drawing she saw herself in the forest with Otto. The girl looked peaceful in her sleep, leaning on the fawn's belly, her head on her arm. Rising above the girl was a guardian angel.

She slowly turned the pages, feeling the soft deckled edges and running her fingers across the text, wishing she could understand the symbols. She longed to learn to read the words for herself. Perhaps worlds existed in these pages that she might remember as her own. Where were her folktales? she wondered. Where were her folk?

She had no name for the place that was beginning to haunt her thoughts. A windswept coast. A wind that made lions' manes of the ocean waves. A wind that blew under the cottage door and into her grandmother's tales—like the one about a magician who cursed a peasant man to be carried by the wind forever more, never to return to his home. She pictured a swirling dust eddy in a yard and remembered her grandmother's horror, her rush to close the doors and windows of the cottage, crying out that the eddy was the dance of an evil spirit. Saskia's mother had taunted the demon wind, lifting her arms and screaming at him to take her from this place. Saskia had been afraid, while her grandmother snapped at her mother, telling her she was a stupid, ungrateful girl to tempt the Devil so. Her mother only laughed and whirled around and around like a leaf carried in a whirlwind.

These fragments of memories of her mother unsettled her. Why did they come to her now? Her mother had plucked her from that home and left her to fend for herself without a second thought. It was her grandmother's home on that wind-beaten coast she now felt pulled towards. Where was this place where people shut all the doors and windows of their huts to ward against evil spirits in the wind?

Stories did more than warn of ogres and wolves, she realised; these shared stories united tribes and villages and countries. Through these lands of shifting borders, of new cultures imposing on the old, she understood why the Brothers Grimm wanted to capture their country's folktales, their heritage, and keep them safe. They wanted to remember where they belonged.

Outside Pascal was calling her name, frantically pacing up and down the sloping street.

Two Frenchmen who could wander freely in these lands, who had no longing for a home. Travelling with them was drawing more attention than she cared for. She needed to keep moving north, to find that windswept coast with the bent-backed trees and her grandmother's cottage.

'Can I help you, little girl?'

A man came forward out of the darkness and she jumped and the book snapped closed. The bookseller twisted his bony hands together and peered at her over a pair of round spectacles that were creeping down his nose.

'Where are your parents?'

She looked back at him, blinking, wondering the same question.

'Are you lost?'

What if she never found the place where she belonged?

In the street, Pascal and Rémi were both calling her name.

လ

Pascal shifted uneasily as he stood across from the town hall, a monstrous building of mottled pink blocks with a steep slate-grey roof and a large clock front at the centre of its tower, Rémi fidgeting at his side. Pascal watched the golden hands of the clock judder towards three o'clock awaiting the arrival of the Brothers Grimm. He knew in his gut this was a mistake.

On his other side, Saskia was silent, her face concealed by her hood. He wondered at the powerful sense of loss he had felt in the street earlier, the shock of her disappearance. When she had suddenly stepped out of the bookshop and into the street, Pascal had fastened her to him, linking his arm through hers. He had been terrified she had been snatched back by that priest. Already he felt responsible for her. Only yesterday he had wanted to leave her behind on the side of the road and today he felt bereft at the thought he had failed her. What had come over him? What did the child matter to them?

He cared too deeply, that was his problem. He had always been a rescuer. He thought of the time they had encountered Bonbon on the street. The dirty child had followed them like a pup, ignoring their attempts to chase him away. Before long, Pascal had picked up the little boy and carried him on his back.

Rémi elbowed Pascal. 'Not much interest.' He nodded to the modest gathering.

This was not their usual crowd. A smattering of well-dressed men in heavy coats and top hats and women in colourful, bell-like dresses with ribbons and bows. The fashions here were like their painted houses: bold. A few children dressed in neat clothes like miniature adults ran around the group, chasing hoops.

Two heralds stepped out of the town hall brandishing long-stemmed golden horns draped with the Marburg ensign. They trumpeted a short announcement, calling for all to gather, leaving Pascal's ears ringing. Curiosity soon pulled more people from their daily business and all of a sudden he felt squashed as the group closed around him.

Rémi bobbed from side to side, tipping up on his toes, trying to catch a glimpse of the men now filing out of the town hall.

A wide-bellied man, who could only be the *Bürgermeister* of Marburg, judging by his outlandish garb, stepped out before the swelling crowd. He was surrounded by other important-looking men in scholars' robes. Finally, Pascal glimpsed the Brothers Grimm, Wilhelm and Jakob, standing close to one another. They looked much the same as they had on that first meeting in their apartments. Both had wavy hair that had been strictly combed and parted, and they wore dark robes.

Rémi punched Pascal's arm and pointed.

The brothers stepped forward, each clutching a copy of their household tales. The mayor welcomed them warmly. He spoke of the need to gather the local stories and celebrate them. A huge cheer greeted his words. Then the chancellor of the university spoke at length on the importance of ensuring that the Prussian folktales and poetry were preserved.

Rémi stretched and yawned loudly.

Jakob, the eldest, stepped forward. The book fell open in his hands and Pascal suddenly saw what Rémi feared most. With a book like this, there was no need for encyclopedic memory; with a book like this, any man could become a storyteller. Pascal caught the look of horror on Rémi's face as Jakob turned the pages, as he realised how easily his special talents, his collected stories, his treasures could be made worthless.

Jakob cleared his throat. When he began to read his voice was weedy.

'Speak up!' Rémi heckled.

Jakob lifted his chin, raised his voice. '*Der Teufel und seine Großmutter.*'

Rémi stirred, nudging Pascal with his elbow. 'That's ours! "The Devil and his Grandmother"—that's our story of the dragon and his grandmother.'

'Don't do anything stupid,' Pascal cautioned. He could not pretend to share Rémi's indignation. The brothers had their stories now and many more to fill their book. But he and Rémi too had traded stories around firesides, learning tales in many tongues, and Pascal knew these stories belonged to no one.

Jakob's voice droned on. 'There was a great war and the King had many soldiers.'

'He has taken the life from it, he has suffocated it,' Rémi hissed in Pascal's ear. 'Look at him. He has no flair.'

Pascal knew Rémi was itching to tell the story of the three soldiers who hid in a cornfield, hoping to desert the army. Tales of deserting soldiers were becoming popular and it was one Rémi had told many times. The soldiers had waited, but the encamped army did not move on, and soon the men were starving. All three knew they would swing from the gallows if they were caught.

Pascal tapped Saskia's arm and raised a warning eyebrow. Rémi was breathing hard, hissing in exasperation, jerking from side to side; he was becoming a dragon that would soon swoop down over that cornfield.

Jakob did not lift his eyes from the page to look at the crowd. He could have no idea what was coming.

'*Eeeeee!*' Rémi clamped his hands over his ears and squealed, writhing about in agony. The crowd turned to look, pulling away from him in shock. As the crowd parted, Rémi seized his chance and burst out into the open space to take his rightful place in front of them.

'Good people of Marburg,' he called, strutting before them, 'I can bear no more of this awful droning, can you? His voice is like a mosquito lodged in my eardrum. It insults my ears. This telling is an abomination and it pains me to see our precious tales so reduced. Would you rather stand here and listen to this insipid rendition, or would you prefer to see a master perform?'

He gave them no time to answer.

The red lining of his cape flashed as he paced before the crowd, appearing as the Devil in dragon form, offering the hiding soldiers a way to escape, offering them seven years of riches and freedom. Rémi always tailored the riches on offer to the desires of his listeners. For this crowd, he described fleet-footed horses and sleek carriages, castles on hilltops and forests in which to hunt. But at the end of seven years the soldiers must become the Devil's servants. It was a terrible choice the soldiers had no option but to accept.

Pascal laid a hand on Saskia's shoulder, guiding her to the edge of the crowd. He watched as the *Bürgermeister* and the officials looked on, stunned by Rémi. He saw Jakob turn to his brother, Wilhelm, uncertain. It would not be long before the town goats took action.

Rémi appealed to the crowd, pointing to the Brothers Grimm. 'Is this the future of storytelling, I ask you? A dry voice slowly clubbing a story to death?'

A snicker greeted his words. Pascal eyed the *Bürgermeister*, who was gesturing to his guards.

'By all means, continue reading,' Rémi urged Jakob. 'You shall have us all sprawled and snoring before you.'

'How dare you!' Wilhelm cried, his hands in fists.

Rémi spun about. 'You have taken stories that do not belong to you and claimed them for your own.'

'This is our culture,' Wilhelm snarled. 'We are protecting it!'

'You are stealing our way of life!' Rémi roared.

He lunged and Wilhelm raised his fists.

'Enough!' Jakob cried, pulling Wilhelm back. 'This is madness.'

The guards were tromping forward from beneath the archways of the *Rathaus*. Sensing it was time for them to flee, Pascal nudged Saskia towards an alleyway that ran along the side of the town hall.

Rémi cried, 'Free our stories! Do not bind and trap them within the pages of a book!' He slapped at Jakob's hands, sending the book flying into the air, its pages fluttering, before it thudded closed on the cobblestones.

There was a moment of shocked stillness before Wilhelm charged at Rémi.

'To me!' Pascal cried, already running. He looked over his shoulder to see Rémi duck away from flailing arms clothed in voluminous sleeves, a scholar's robes not meant for street brawling. Rémi paused to take one cheeky bow before the guards charged at him.

Rémi caught up with Pascal, laughing, giddy with daring. The guards were slow in their ceremonial uniforms, portly men not used to the chase, yet Rémi's recklessness would put the three of them in chains if they were caught.

Rémi dashed ahead, leaping over carts, dodging porters with wicker baskets on their backs, darting between merchants and their buyers. Damn him. Pascal had no choice but to run after Rémi. Saskia fell behind, unable to keep up, and Pascal slowed for her; she did not deserve to be caught up in Rémi's foolishness. It infuriated Pascal that Rémi could be so cavalier, so thoughtless. He should leave him to the guards and protect Saskia. They had done nothing wrong. This was all Rémi's fault.

But then Saskia skidded to a halt beside a barrel. He watched her quick hands twist and pull the stopper, sending oil gurgling over the cobblestones until they were slick and shining and treacherous for the guards.

She had put herself at risk with this act, Pascal thought, by declaring herself one of us.

'Wait for me at the inn,' Rémi called over his shoulder, gleeful, triumphant. 'I will go to Katharina's house!'

'No, Rémi!' It was too late. He had already danced away.

Pascal pulled Saskia down the narrow gap between two houses. He tore her red cape from her shoulders and tossed it through an open window, then he took off his own purple coat and made her put it on, placing her red hair beneath his cap. The frockcoat covered her dress completely. At a glance she could be taken for a boy. They were walking casually as they re-entered the marketplace to merge with the crowds.

Across the square he glimpsed a black-robed figure talking with the *Bürgermeister*. A priest. It made him pause. No, it was foolish to think the priest was the same one from Gelnhausen. This priest could be from a local parish, ingratiating himself and hoping to gain favour by denouncing all travelling storytellers and their pagan tales. Yet he hurried Saskia along, hoping she had not seen him.

'Let's get you new clothes,' he said, pushing her ahead and shielding her from view.

CHAPTER SEVEN

*K*atharina lived among the elite of the city in the first tier of homes below the grounds of the *Marburger Schloss*. I caught glimpses of the castle on top of the hill as I climbed. I wondered if the castle in the clouds was deserted, if anyone still looked down out of its windows. The Hessian landgraves had ruled in this area for centuries before they too had bowed to Napoleon's rule. Now this land was part of the Kingdom of Westphalia, with Napoleon's brother Jerome at its head in Kassel. Katharina believed him to be bankrupting the kingdom and would not hear his name spoken in her home.

Katharina's house was unique; painted in red and green with flowers stencilled on the plaster, it had a roof tower like a witch's hat and all the windows were filled with lead-lined circles of glass. It was a house of several floors and small rooms that were often filled with our colourful brethren. This house was where we came year after year, we dispossessed, we merry travellers. We were a jolly bunch by and large, only fighting over serious matters such as whether Goethe or Voltaire was the better writer. Katharina had liked me from the first, and picked me for her favourite. I never knew if I had ousted one of the other players from her sheets.

Katharina was famous for driving her carriage at a frightening pace around these steep cobbled streets and kept her Hanoverian stabled behind her house. That she could live like this, outside of convention, without a husband, with all manner of men and women in her beds and at her table, spoke of her standing within the town. Her trespasses were always forgiven. Or tolerated, at least.

The street was empty when I approached her door. It was a year since Pascal and I had last crossed Katharina's threshold and it had not been an easy year. She had understood all along that the Brothers Grimm were a threat to us, but I felt radiant. I had vanquished the enemy and their hateful book.

I lifted the wolf's head knocker and let it fall.

An hour later, I lay in Katharina's bed, my arms clasped behind my head in a way I knew she liked. She had been surprised to see me at first, then greeted me with her knowing smile. 'My Casanova,' she whispered and led me up the stairs. I followed the hem of her full skirt and admired the swell of her buttocks. She looked well and I was pleased to see the year had not stolen her beauty. She had changed her hair; the blonde curls were piled luxuriously on her head and coiled down over one shoulder in the Habsburg style favoured by Napoleon's new Austrian wife. She no longer applied love heart beauty spots to the high points of her cheekbones, instead dabbing her skin with rouge in an approximation of the ruddy-cheeked village girls I knew so well. Katharina might not be young, but she had compensations. Now, as I lay back in her pillows watching her dress, I grinned to think of it. She was moving quickly, closing her stays and tying her bows. Stepping back into her striped gown.

'Now, you go,' she said.

'What?'

'Leave.' She flicked her wrist as if to dismiss me.

'Do you joke?'

She turned to look at me as if I should know better. 'You are dangerous for me, my pretty boy.'

I smirked. 'I thought you liked that.'

'You cannot stay.'

'In your bed?'

'Not in my bed or in my house.'

I sat up, annoyed. Her face was still flushed from our passion, and she looked even more desirable as she pinned up her fallen hair. I longed to kiss the back of her neck.

She tossed me my breeches.

'What has changed?' I asked, stunned. Her voice was not teasing, simply direct, imperious. I thought of Pascal and his dream of starting a theatre in this town, here with Katharina. She could not abandon us.

'If you do not know, you are even more of a fool than I thought, *ma petite puce*.' She bent to kiss me then, one quick peck on my forehead as if I were a child.

'Speak plainly.' I was cross.

'A woman who consorts with your kind will be despised when the tables are overturned. Paraded through the streets, head shorn, a target for every cruel and bitter heart.'

'My kind?' I was confused. 'A storyteller?'

She snorted. 'A Frenchman. A coloniser.'

'But I am a traveller.'

'Then you should have opened your eyes. Have you not heard the rumours? They say his Russian campaign has failed. The Grand Armée, which once boasted hundreds of thousands of men, is now reduced to tens of thousands.' She moved to cup my face in her hands. 'Your Emperor can be beaten. Don't you understand what this means?'

In truth, I did not.

'You Frenchmen are not wanted here. Prussia will break away from your Emperor. Our men will not fight in your wars ever again. The next battles on this land will be for our freedom.' She whirled away from me.

I threw the covers from her bed and stood. 'Did you only pretend to care for me then?' I was petulant, childish, but what else could I be? She had made a fool of me. I pulled on my clothes. 'Did I mean nothing to you?' I could not believe that her affection for me had been feigned.

'Once you were the sunlight of my days and the moonlight of my nights, my darling boy,' she said mercifully, 'but now it is time for you to go home.'

Home? I had none. I had walked away from it long ago and I would not go back. Not to Paris. Not to the Comédie-Italienne. And especially not to my mother.

I left Katharina, slamming the door of her room behind me, stomping down the narrow stairs. My footsteps were loud and unapologetic. I realised then that there was no music in Katharina's house, no voices, no laughter. The house had never been this silent. Now there were only closed doors and listening ears. I strode across the landing to the dining room, a place where we had once spent so many joyous nights, with Pascal playing his lute alongside fiddlers or pipers, and threw open the door. I saw them, those men she now sheltered. Those broken men with their grey clothes, grey skin, grey-eyed scowls. She was harbouring deserters now.

I flung myself down the last set of stairs and was almost at the door when she called my name. I turned, a burst of hope in my heart.

'Is Pascal still with you?' she asked.

I nodded, pained that she thought of him and not me.

'You always had too much control over him, Rémi. He wants to go home. Let him go.'

I stared at her, heart working, mouth not. Part with Pascal? Impossible. That I could never do.

'Heed my advice,' she warned. 'This is no place for you now.'

CHAPTER EIGHT

*T*he inn that Pascal took Saskia to was a *Weinstube* with an earthenware jug above the door.

'We came here in the early years, before Katharina took us under her wing,' Pascal explained.

Inside, the floor was gritty beneath her feet, the wood dark and the ceiling low. It stank of spilled wine and stale beer. She thought it empty until a barmaid came out of the shadows, wiping her hands on her apron. 'Look what the cat dragged in. Has it been a year already?' Her eyes were smiling.

'Clara,' Pascal said, opening his arms.

He and the barmaid embraced.

'Who's this?' Clara asked as she drew back, looking at Saskia in Pascal's purple frockcoat and cap.

'A new traveller. Sebastian.'

Just like that he named her. The lie sat smooth and comfortable. Sebastian. She liked the sound of it.

'Where's Rémi?' the woman asked.

'With Katharina.'

'What has she got that I don't?' Clara pouted and thrust out her breasts, then she laughed. 'You want a room?'

'Just a place to rest.'

'Rest or hide?'

'Both.'

She sighed and shook her head. 'You boys. Take the attic—no one will bother you up there.'

Saskia climbed the narrow staircase behind Pascal.

'Come and sing for us tonight,' the barmaid called after them. 'You know I love that voice of yours!'

The attic room was long, with a peaked ceiling and a single window at the far end. Several straw mattresses were cast about on the floorboards. Saskia went to the window and saw a patchwork of slate and terracotta roofs. To her right, the road wound upwards to the castle at the top of the hill.

'Is it always like this?' she asked.

'What do you mean?'

So thrilling, she meant. So exciting. She had enjoyed the chase, the chance to run. The danger didn't seem real to her, not like Father.

'Life on the road,' she answered.

'Rémi can make it unpredictable,' Pascal replied with a wry smile.

'Will you stay here?'

'I hope so.'

She fell quiet. Could she spend the winter here and be safe? Instinct compelled her to keep moving. But she had spent so long on her own. It felt good to have company.

'What do we do now?' she asked.

He grinned. 'We make you into Sebastian.'

Pascal pulled out the clothes they had bought. A man's long shirt, a boy's leather doublet and velvet pantaloons.

Saskia took off his cap and her braid coiled down between her shoulders. She waited until Pascal turned his back before she stripped off her old dress and climbed into her new clothes.

'Are you ready?'

Was she ready to become a boy? Could she hope to fool anyone with this disguise? The new clothes swamped her. 'This is ridiculous!' She looked like a mouse in men's clothes.

'They'll need adjusting,' Pascal said. 'May I?' Pascal gestured to the hems of the pantaloons that sat around her ankles. With her permission he rolled the fabric to mark the place below her knees. She lifted the shirt and let him measure how many fingers he could place on either side of her waist. She glimpsed the starkness of her ribs, saw her skin covered in goosebumps.

He tugged down the shirt to cover her. 'I'll shorten the trousers for you.' He reached for his sewing kit, a fabric envelope filled with needles, buttons and threads. 'I've had to mend our clothes many times on the road.'

Wriggling out of the pantaloons, she passed them to him.

'I used to sew costumes,' he told her, unpicking the cuffs of the pantaloons with practised ease. 'We grew up in a theatre.'

A theatre . . . She tried to imagine it, she had never seen inside a theatre.

'I liked it best behind the scenes,' he continued. 'I was never meant for the stage, not like Rémi. I liked the time between performances best: the artists painting over the screens, the costumiers altering the old dresses to make new ones.'

'What did it look like?'

'It was grand and golden and glorious. The audience sat in gilded stalls rising three storeys high and the stage was hidden behind a rich, red curtain.'

She remembered the boldly striped circus tents that she had once thought were grand and glorious too.

'Rémi told me you were in a circus.'

She nodded. 'I was Saskia the Twisted Girl.'

'A freak?'

'An artiste!'

'What was it like?'

'I was terrified the first time,' Saskia admitted. 'But I learned to close my eyes and block out the audience. I would focus on the routines and perform as though no one was watching.'

He nodded. 'I was the same when we first took to the road and I played my lute in front of others. My hands shook so much I could barely play a tune.'

'How old were you when you left your home?'

'I had just turned sixteen. About your age now, I think?'

She nodded.

'Why did you leave?' she asked Pascal on impulse.

He took up his shears and sliced through the velvet. 'Because of Rémi.'

'Do you miss it?'

He was silent for some time, and when he spoke his voice was thick. 'They were my family,' he said.

Saskia understood. Her circus was a family too. Now, for all she knew, they had scattered with the wind. Perhaps the circus had disbanded years ago, or gone back to Russia or all the way to Spain. Where should she begin? How would she find them again?

She reached for her old dress, tracing her fingers across the raised embroidery. She almost sobbed to think how long this simple dress had been with her, a dress given to her out of kindness when she had nothing else to wear. It had come from some far distant village, a place of snow and frozen ground that Svetlana had sworn she was not sorry to have left. Yet she had kept the dress that reminded her of that home and she had given it to a frightened girl who had grown too big for her own worn clothes.

'Where is home for you?' Pascal broke into her thoughts.

Was it with the circus? That shifting, wandering, makeshift family? Or was it with an old woman in a croft on a windswept coast?

'I don't know,' she answered truthfully.

'What brought you to that priest?' He tugged a needle through the cuff of fabric, unaware of the pain of such an innocent question. She watched the needle stab in and out, the silver flash of it.

'He stole me.'

Pascal put down his needle and tried to meet her eyes but she evaded him. She twisted the loose fabric of the shirt in her fists. *Don't ask me anymore*, she begged silently. *Please don't ask.*

'Why?'

How could she know the workings of Father's mind? 'Perhaps he needed a servant,' she whispered. 'Or a disciple.' She felt Father's hands pressing down on her head as she kneeled before him. She remembered the touch of his fingers stroking her head, the bristles of the brush against her scalp, the tug as he took handfuls of hair, twisting and binding it in a tight braid.

'Will he hurt you, if he finds you?'

She opened her mouth to answer but her voice snagged in her throat. She nodded. She could not go back to the box.

Pascal bent his head to his task, sewing in silence, and she was grateful he did not ask anything else. She watched him stitch, following the deft movements of his hand. Watching him make something new out of the old.

She was going to become Sebastian. She was going to leave behind Father and everything that had gone before. She reached for Pascal's shears and gripped her braid. She found the nape of her neck and sliced at the braid, severing the hair that Father cherished. She felt lightness. She felt unbound. Hair that had been growing with her since childhood. Red hair that marked her out as her mother's child. Why had she never thought to cut herself free from it before?

Gently, Pascal took the shears from her hands, his expression resolute. 'Are you ready, Sebastian? It's time to sing for our supper.'

It was late when Rémi slapped open the door of the *Weinstube* and staggered inside. Rémi tottered forward, drunk and raving. 'She doesn't want us, Pascal!' he wailed.

Pascal leaped to his feet.

Rémi tilted to one side and Pascal caught him before he fell. He slung Rémi's arm over his shoulder and dragged him to the stairs.

Saskia followed, feeling all eyes in the room on them. Her new disguise felt like a flimsy thing; she wasn't used to it yet.

In the attic, Pascal let Rémi fall onto one of the mattresses. Rémi groaned and flung an arm across his eyes. Pascal stared down at him.

'What did she say?'

'She wants nothing to do with us.'

'Why?'

'She doesn't want Frenchmen under her roof.'

'I don't believe you.'

'It's true.'

'Then what are we to do? We cannot perform in this town after your display in front of the town hall. The *Bürgermeister* will chain us to the pillory!'

Saskia squatted down on her mattress with her back to the wall. It upset her to see Pascal so angry.

'Did you ask about the theatre?'

'That means nothing to her, Pascal!'

'You didn't, did you? You didn't even care enough for me to do that.' Pascal took to a corner, radiating fury.

Saskia lay down. The storytellers could not stay here in Marburg, that seemed certain. She listened to them argue with growing trepidation.

'I want to go home to Paris, Rémi. It's time.'

'I cannot, you know that. I cannot see her.'

Saskia put her hands over her ears. In the morning, she would part ways with these men. If Father was following, they would surely draw his attention. She should strike out alone and perform her contortionist tricks from town to town. Her disguise might shield her. It might earn her enough money for food and shelter until she could find her way home. Wherever that might be.

'I am going to Paris,' Pascal said.

'Well, I am not,' Rémi replied.

I am going north, Saskia thought. But it scared her to think of travelling alone. She hugged her knees to her chest.

'Never become attached,' her mother had said on the night she dragged a sleepy Saskia from her grandmother's croft. 'You never know when leaving someone will save your life.'

They were walking on a stony road in darkness with the wind at their backs and Saskia was crying because she had left her twig doll behind. 'Forget it,' her mother snapped. 'We are breaking free from all of that.' They were leaving that windswept coast, leaving her grandmother.

'Take this instead.' Her mother pressed the shiny black rock into her hand. The edges were sharp as Saskia squeezed her fist around the jewel. It was the first present her mother had given her.

Earlier that night, her mother had returned from the fields long after dark, dropping her empty sack to the mud floor like a statement. Saskia lifted her head to see her grandmother scowling, hands on hips. 'Where have you been?'

The sack smelled of onions. All summer the onions had been pulled from the earth and left to dry in the fields. Saskia hated the smell of them.

'Who was he this time? Another man to shame us?' Her grandmother tutted her disgust. 'Always looking for something better, when you should make the best of what you have.'

Her mother dropped down in front of Saskia, holding her daughter's face between her hands. Saskia gazed into her sea-mist eyes. 'Did you know the St Petersburg Circus is in town?' Then she had laughed, a crazed cackle of glee. It had frightened Saskia.

Why did her mother take her that night? Saskia wondered. Why smuggle her away from a home where she was loved and cared for by her grandmother? Saskia now understood her mother hated her life as a peasant in that wind-battered place, but why take her young daughter with her only to abandon her to a circus of strangers? Looking back, she realised her mother had cut herself free of her own daughter with the exact same ruthlessness she had needed to leave her home.

In the attic, Pascal raised his voice again. 'We should go home, Rémi! Forgive your mother. She only meant to save you.'

'She should not have tricked me.'

'At least you have a mother! None of the rest of us had that!'

Pascal rattled down the stairs and slammed the inn door. The sudden silence was complete.

CHAPTER NINE

By morning, Pascal had not returned and I felt bereft. I should not have argued with him, but I was stubborn and hurting and I did not want to go home.

I understood my mother had meant to protect me, but to my boyhood self, the part of me that clung on to hurts, it felt like I had been tossed into a pit of refuse. I was worse than offal, I was worse than stable scrapings, I had no worth. If she could so easily cast me off, if she did could part herself from me yet again, then I must mean nothing to her at all.

I had been the golden boy, the orphan whose mother came back. I believed I was special and that the mark on my wrist made me so. But in that moment, when the trapdoor closed down upon my head, I felt as worthless as a human turd.

She should have wanted to keep me close to her. She should have wanted to put her own body between me and danger. She should not have left me in the ground to rot!

When we had climbed out of that cellar and stumbled into the dark street, I thought of nothing but my own rage. It infuriated me to see her standing there, waiting, like I would rush into her arms and forgive her. I turned my back on her and ran without a thought for anyone but myself. To my shame, I did not think of Pascal or what it would mean for him. He would never have left the theatre if not for me. I knew he would follow me wherever I chose to go.

But no longer.

A terrible thought began to twist and turn in my head. What if he did not return? What if this was how we were to part?

The girl sat up and looked at me with her round eyes. Her hair was short and badly cut. It pained me to see that vibrant hair so hacked and reduced, but I recognised her intent to travel as a boy.

I gave Saskia my hat, a fine, pheasant-feathered cap. 'You'll need this more than me.'

'Thank you.' She settled it down tight on her head.

'You can come south with me to Venice?' I offered.

She shook her head.

A pity. I would have liked her company. And her contortionism was an act we could sell for money.

Together we trudged down the winding stairwell all the way to the gritty floorboards of the inn. It was empty. We lingered, looking at each other. I had no appetite for food. The excess of ale I had consumed after leaving Katharina's still swilled in my gut and made me queasy.

'We should wait for Pascal,' I said. 'He will come.'

She nodded eagerly. Neither one of us wanted to be the first to take our leave.

We waited and at last, the door swung open and Pascal burst in from the street, his cloak billowing. Relief flushed through me.

'I have news,' he said to Saskia.

Perhaps Katharina had had a change of heart. I would forgive her, I supposed, if she was contrite.

'Bremen,' Pascal announced. 'A circus of sorts is camped outside the town. I heard it from two men who had lately travelled there.'

'Was it the St Petersburg Circus?' Saskia cried.

Pascal shrugged, apologetic. 'I cannot say. It was a travelling circus, I believe.'

I read the hope in her face. She imagined it was her circus and she would soon be reunited with her friends.

'A circus would feed us,' Pascal said to me. 'And put a tent above our heads.' It seemed I was forgiven; I felt a rush of gratitude. A circus. It was an idea I had never entertained before, but I could see the appeal of it. A travelling circus!

'Does your circus have storytellers?' I asked Saskia.

'Perhaps it could be so.' She cast her eyes towards Pascal's lute. 'The clowns, the *skomorokh*, were once travelling storytellers.'

'We will go where they have never heard of the Brothers Grimm,' Pascal said, eyeing me meaningfully.

'We could be the Brothers Victoire!' I was excited, already imagining our routines. Pascal's music, my tales and Saskia's unique abilities. I enjoyed the sound of it on my tongue: *Brothers Victoire*. I imagined our names written on flapping banners, on a wagon, on our own tent! Victoire—it was the name my mother gave to me, but it would have to suffice. Pascal had no family name and Saskia had not told us hers.

A circus would carry us away from Katharina's dire warnings that we were despised by these scowling Rhineland serfs who couldn't appreciate that the French had given them equality and freedom.

I caught Pascal's eye and my heart swelled. He had saved us with this plan. I dragged him into an embrace and pressed my lips to the pulse in his neck. He had kept us together. The circus would be a fresh start for us and I hoped he would forget this painful notion of going back to Paris.

The girl was watching me when I drew back and I disguised my tears with laughter. 'We three shall be the Bremen town minstrels! Running away to join the circus.'

Pascal albatrossed his great arms between us.

We strutted from Marburg as though we were celebrated stars of the circus ring. I could not deny I was happy to leave this town and its reminders of those po-faced Brothers Grimm. I would not forget the way they looked at me as if I were a floating shit in their chamber-pot. Our way of life meant nothing to them. Perhaps lone travellers like us could never compete with the likes of the Brothers Grimm and their books, but a circus was a spectacle, a circus could be a stage. A new career beckoned. How quickly fortunes could change when you were free and unencumbered. *See, Pascal?* I wanted to say. *See how much liberty we have?*

At the stables, I was relieved to find Henriette well fed and watered. The chestnut gelding greeted Saskia with a gentle neigh of recognition, while Henriette turned her rump and slashed me with her tail. I reached out to stroke her dapples, cajoling, and scratched the place above her loins that I knew would made her skin shudder.

Begrudgingly, she let me brush across her withers and along the sway of her back to prepare her for the saddle.

An elderly man came out of the stables carrying our tack. He walked bow-legged and weighed down with the saddle and Pascal quickly relieved him of his burden.

'Where are you headed?' the old man asked.

'Bremen,' I answered.

'No fighting there.' He sniffed hard.

'No, not if we can avoid it.'

The man rubbed his grey beard and narrowed his eyes. 'My grandsons were your age or thereabouts when they went to fight in your Emperor's wars.' His disgust was plain. 'What gives you Frenchmen the right to stand here in front of me with your hearts still beating when my sons and grandsons have been taken?'

He had skewered me with his accusation. My heart was beating, and beating hard. I had no answer for him. We had been running from these wars since we were boys.

Pascal saddled Henriette while I stood mute, avoiding the stable-master's gaze.

'The only men left in Prussia are the old and maimed,' he said, scowling. 'Or priests.'

'We have no desire for battle,' I told him.

'And you think my children and their children did?' The old man spat at my chest.

I looked down at the glob of spittle slowly dripping from my vest. What could I say to this grandfather?

I mounted Henriette. The horses trotted out of the stables side by side with Saskia seated behind Pascal on her horse. Above the clatter of their hooves I heard the old man call out, 'I hope they find you! I hope they hunt you down!' His voice was charged and bitter. 'I hope there is no more escape for you.'

༄

Pascal took the road north to Bremen and led them into the valley mists. On either side, tall pine forest closed around them. Fog crept around the rough grey tree trunks and across the road and Pascal shuddered as the cold seeped around his neck. He tried to ignore the sense of foreboding that settled above his heart. He wished the fog would lift so he could see more than a few feet ahead. The words of the old man tolled in Pascal's head. *I hope they find you. I hope they hunt you down.*

He had been shocked to hear rumours of defeats and massive losses in the marketplace that morning. The Russian campaign was a disaster for Napoleon. The Russians had drawn the Grand Armée deeper and deeper into their territory, refusing to fight, retreating and burning the land until the soldiers succumbed to starvation, cold or disease. In the eyes of the old men of this town, he saw a vicious glint of hope. What Katharina had told Rémi was true; he read it in their faces. There was no love for Frenchmen here, and these Rhineland states could smell the scent of change. He began to comprehend the danger they were in.

He had not believed that Katharina would cast them out until he banged upon her door the night before and she would not let him in. The house remained stubbornly in darkness.

Had she pretended affection for them all along? Tolerated them only because she dared not offend the French? It hurt to think that this might be so. Or had she simply seen what was coming for them, the anger and reprisals, and wanted none of it?

For the first time, Pascal wondered what it would feel like to have your home ruled by another. To have your sons taken by a man who cared nothing for their lives, only feeding his selfish desire for a greater empire. He understood the pain of the stablemaster who had lost his grandsons to the Emperor's greed. Napoleon's Empire already stretched from Spain, down into the northern states of Italy and across to Poland. He had tried to take Russia too and failed. Pascal did not tell Rémi and Saskia what he had learned. It was enough that they were leaving. The anger in the stablemaster's voice portended the start of something vicious. These allied states could turn against Napoleon. If the Confederation of the Rhine fell, then French travellers like themselves would not be safe from retribution.

Saskia sat behind the saddle, not touching him, so silent that he turned to check if she was still there. He hoped they would find Saskia's circus or another like it. She would be safer in the circus than on the road with them. He had conceived the plan to take her home, but had not admitted to them that he would not stay with the circus. He cast a guilty look at Rémi, riding alongside him on Henriette. As soon as the girl was safe, Pascal intended to go home to Paris.

Rémi began to whistle. It was meant to be a cheering tune, but in these misty woods the song was eerie, muted. The horses flicked their ears and Pascal saw the droplets glisten on the soft hairs. He felt the clammy moistening of his face and blinked to clear the wetness from his eyelashes. His horse fell back, while Rémi kicked Henriette onwards, trotting forward into the grey mist. Somewhere overhead a kite screamed as it wheeled above the fog.

Then Henriette stopped abruptly and Pascal's horse charged into her rump. He felt Saskia grip his cloak for balance. Pascal could see nothing on the road ahead; the fog was drifting into their faces, hurried by the freshening wind.

Otto's ears flicked forward. Henriette would not budge no matter how much Rémi growled and kicked. Something up ahead had spooked the horses. Saskia clucked her tongue and patted Otto's rump. The horse drew level with Henriette but would go no further.

Pascal exchanged a glance with Rémi and they both listened intently. There: he heard a faint rumble like stone wheels on hard roads, coming towards them. The noise grew louder, becoming rhythmic, like axes chopping in the forest. The horses backed away, snorting.

Pascal didn't like this feeling of exposure. His sense of danger prickled in the nape of his neck. Spooked by a shriek from above, he glimpsed the kite through a gap in the misty cloud. He was staring upwards, looking at the bird, when the first men appeared on the road.

The soldiers marched like wraiths in torn and tattered clothes with eyes cast down to their feet. A company in loose formation, shoulders slumped, heads bare.

The horses shied away into the forest, startled at these apparitions from the mist, and Pascal gathered the reins, bringing Otto to a halt. He felt the same urge to run deeper into the forest, yet he turned the horse, made himself watch, feeling Saskia's arms tighten around his waist. Pascal stared at the men. The skin of their faces was so thin it looked translucent; he saw stark cheekbones and the blood in their veins.

The drummers no longer beat their instruments to spur the marchers on. No voices were heard. Each man moved like an automaton, dragging one foot after the other, boots falling apart or missing altogether.

'Deserters?' Rémi whispered.

Pascal shook his head. There were too many of them. The rumours of defeat in Moscow must be true. These men were the survivors. The road ahead would be scattered with the remnants of the army. They could not go north now—all it would take would be one captain motivated enough to seize them and add three more bodies to his force.

Rémi leaned across and tugged at Otto's rein, swinging the horse around. He kicked Henriette and spurred her forward through the trees, and Pascal let Otto follow, galloping across the fallen needles. They fled south, riding ahead of the tide of wrecked and wounded soldiers.

CHAPTER TEN

Saskia roared out her frustration as they rode. She had no choice but to go with the men, having surrendered the reins of her horse to Pascal—a mistake she would not make again. She clung to Pascal's back, trying not to fall as Otto galloped through the trees and out onto the road. The horses were well rested and ready to run. They were taking her away from the circus and back towards Father. She howled and swore. She wanted to kick and slash and scream her anger to the wind.

From the moment Pascal had spoken of the circus outside Bremen, Saskia had imagined it was her circus, the St Petersburg Circus. She had foolishly let herself believe she would be reunited with her friends, imagining the joy on Svetlana's beautiful face. She had let Pascal raise her hopes and now she cursed her stupid heart. She should never let a man raise her hopes, she thought bitterly, no matter how briefly, for it would only end in heartbreak.

They reached a crossroads and took the route for Frankfurt without pausing.

'Stop!' Saskia cried, tugging at Pascal's arms. 'I'm going back!'

'Don't be a fool,' Pascal cried over his shoulder. 'It's too dangerous.'

'It's my choice! It's my horse.'

But he ignored her. Ahead, Henriette was still charging on, driven by Rémi. They were going south, just as Rémi had wanted all along. Saskia hurled curses at his back.

The horses could not keep up their panicked pace. They slowed to a canter, blowing hard.

'We'll ride on to Giessen,' Rémi called to Pascal. 'Make a plan from there.'

Pascal nodded his agreement without consulting Saskia.

She gripped the cantle of the saddle and pushed herself up to standing, holding out her arms to steady herself on Otto's back. She felt like Svetlana, remembering her boldly spinning like a doll on top of a galloping horse's back.

Saskia climbed over Pascal, knocking off his hat as she pulled herself over him to sit astride the pommel of the saddle. She leaned forward and reached for the reins, pulling Otto to a halt.

She turned to face Pascal. 'Get off my horse.' Her voice was cold.

Pascal flung himself from the saddle and walked back to retrieve his fallen hat. 'You are mad. You will get yourself killed, or captured, or worse.' He dusted off the cap.

Rémi trotted Henriette back to them.

'Ride with us to Giessen,' Rémi urged. 'We will learn more there.'

'It might still be possible to find a way north,' Pascal said to console her. 'Another route to Bremen, away from troops.'

Of course, she knew it was foolish to go blindly into the path of an army. The circus might not even be hers. But if there was still hope, surely she should take it?

'As far as Giessen,' she grudgingly agreed.

*

In Giessen, the retreat was common knowledge. People spoke of shocking losses, devouring reports of Napoleon's defeat like crows in the carrion. She walked among the men in the alehouse, listening to them speak, thankful that strangers paid her scant attention in her boy's clothes. The men of the town had gathered in number here, all clamouring for news, hoping to hear of their sons among the survivors.

A sense of pride and unity was building in these men. They whispered of the Emperor's weakness. The Emperor could be beaten. He was not all-powerful anymore. Saskia saw it plainly. These Rhineland towns were turning against the French. It charged the atmosphere like a gathering storm.

She was hungry. They had not eaten all day and no one had an appetite for Rémi's tales. As soon as Rémi stood up to speak, he was heckled and abused. 'Go home! Go die in your own wars!' They had moved from inn to inn, avoiding violence. Not even Pascal's lute could buy them dinner and she dared not show her contortionism here, so close to Father's reach. Instead, she walked among the men of this alehouse, noting how easy it would be to slip her hand into the men's pockets.

Pascal caught her wrist, shook his head. He pushed her to a booth. 'We do not steal.'

'Not even from these men who would skewer you alive, if they could?'

'We give when we can, we accept charity when we need, but we do not thieve. Every traveller must have a code, a line drawn in the sand—this is ours.'

She twisted her hand from his grasp, still resentful over her loss.

'We need friends in this business,' Pascal said. 'If you steal from them, the world becomes a much smaller, harder place. And it means you can never go back.'

Rémi thumped down into the seat beside them. 'Our only choice is south. Venice.'

Saskia's nostrils flared.

Pascal shook his head vehemently. 'No, we must go home to France. It is too dangerous now to be a Frenchman in these towns!'

'Think, Pascal! The Emperor could be bringing reinforcements across France as we speak. We could be caught between the remains of one army and the beginnings of another! We must go south, while Bavaria and the kingdoms of Italy remain allies of France.'

Saskia could see Rémi's argument working on Pascal. How long could they hope to evade conscription? His brow was furrowed but he remained silent.

'Give me a year, just one,' pleaded Rémi. 'Then we'll go back, when the wars are far away.'

Pascal turned to Saskia. 'What will you do?'

From outside, she heard angry shouts and the chanting of slogans. A window smashed and she saw a brick had been tossed through.

'Come,' Rémi urged. 'We'll be in trouble if they discover we're French.'

In the street, mobs of maimed Prussian men were clashing with the French militia. Shops were being raided and barricades built of chairs and tables. Saskia dodged a bottle lobbed like a missile.

Rémi led them to a cider house. When the barman caught sight of them, he rushed them out the back. 'Boys, it is not safe for you here,' he hissed.

'We'll be gone by morning, Frederic. Thank you for your kindness.' Pascal embraced the smaller man.

'Don't let my wife find you,' the barman said gruffly, but he smuggled them into his storehouse and told them they could hide among the sacks of apples.

'We can't go north,' Rémi whispered. 'It will be like this in any town that has heard the news, where they have seen the survivors, where they have learned their sons are dead. Our only choice is to fly ahead of the reports.'

Saskia understood his reasoning. But grief took hold of her and she gasped and hid her face in her hands. She held back her sobs like a stone in her throat. The pain of it. The pain of a lost chance.

'Travel south with us.' Rémi reached out a hand to her. 'We can be your family now.'

Pascal reached for her other hand, linking the three of them together.

Saskia closed her eyes. She saw the tents collapsing, the carriages being loaded and the flattened grass of an empty field. She saw the wagons rolling away. The circus was a dream, always ahead and impossible to reach.

Rémi kept them moving in search of smaller towns that might have missed the reports from the battlefields. If they saw soldiers in a town, they did not stop. Saskia refused to share her horse, insisting the wide and stout Henriette could carry both the storytellers. She would be the master of her own direction from now on.

Soon they were trading nights of storytelling for board and food, and touting themselves as the celebrated Brothers Victoire. She began to inhabit the role of Sebastian. She copied other boys her age, their mannerisms and ways of moving. As Pascal played his lute, Saskia contorted her body into shapes, a dance of sorts, like the snake charmer and his snake. Afterwards, when the audience had squealed and winced and applauded in astonishment, Rémi would begin his tales, drawing the farmers, traders and travellers close. He told them tales of girls outwitting their wicked stepmothers, princesses saved by handsome princes, of innocents overcoming evil. At the end of his performance, Saskia strutted out on her hands, split her legs to snatch his hat with her toes and proffered it to the crowd, who rewarded them with coin and cheers and laughter. Here in these thick-walled inns, the nights were cold but the firesides were warm. Here the hatred for the French had not reached into people's hearts. People lived as they always had, the push and pull of great armies mattering little to their daily concerns. Each morning the cows still needed to be milked.

Once, she thought she saw Father. A brown-cloaked traveller on a donkey with a scar striking his face. It set her heart hammering. But when she looked again, she saw she had been mistaken. This man was grey-bearded and shrunken; it could not be him. Why would Father travel by donkey like a plain pilgrim? If he could steal a child, he could easily steal a swift horse.

Still, it reminded her to be careful. She wondered if tales of a contortionist might follow in their wake. It was a sight so rare in these parts that people might speak of it after they had passed through. Father could easily follow these crumbs. That the contortionist was a boy would not fool him for a moment.

The Brothers Victoire agreed to alternate their routines. Some nights she did not perform at all, to put greater distance between her appearances, and by day they travelled quickly to reach the alpine passes before the winter snow. If Father had indeed followed her, she hoped he had well and truly lost her trail by now.

From Innsbruck, they rode towards the Swiss Alps, where the weather fouled and caught them on the open road. Pascal took out his bearskin coat to shelter them while the horses turned their rumps to the wind. It frightened her, the quickness of clouds, their darkening overhead. She feared they would be caught out in the blizzard overnight. Rémi's and Pascal's arms were across her back and they kneeled down, clutching one another. For the first time in her life, she felt like praying. The driving sleet turned to hail and she felt the force of nature turning against her. A vengeful God hurled balls of ice from the sky. If it snowed and buried them on the side of this road, no one would ever know where they had died. Nothing would mark the passing of her life. How fragile the human being was without shelter, she thought, and how almighty the elements had proved.

One moment the storm was roaring over her, and the next it had passed almost as quickly as it had come. Pascal stood and shook out the hail from his bearskin coat. Saskia felt weak, humbled. She pressed her fingers to her eyes, willing herself not to cry. She was shaking and shivering so hard her teeth clattered.

Pascal took her hands in his to warm them.

'I thought we were going to die,' she whispered.

'Not us,' he said with a smile. 'Not the Brothers Victoire.'

The Brothers Victoire were rescued by a farmer. A man dressed in furs called out to them from his horse and cart. He waved them over, surprised to see travellers on the road this late in the season. His face was blistered with the cold, crimson cheeks and ice crystals on his eyebrows. He gladly hitched their horses behind his cart and offered them a ride among the pumpkins. Saskia hunkered down beside Rémi and Pascal beneath the coat with the hard globes pushing into her back. She felt a burst of gratitude for the kindness of this stranger. They would not have made it up these steep alpine roads in this uncertain weather without his cheerful aid. The horses snorted and shook their heads as the wheels flicked sleety mud into their faces. The farmer offered to take them as far as Brenner, the only pass open to carts and carriages that wound through the valleys of the Alps.

In the town of Brenner, she found the people of the Alps were friendly. They laughed heartily at Rémi's tales, sang along with Pascal as he played his lute and were generous with their coin when she stood on her hands and proffered the cap with her foot. The signature routine of the Brothers Victoire they had performed in every inn and wayside cafe on the route.

'We don't get much to brighten our days,' a stout woman said, rubbing two pudgy hands together. 'Not many troupes come through here at this time of year.'

'And the last spectacle was not one I wish to see again,' another woman said, her face pinching as if she'd caught a whiff of turned milk.

'Over two hundred thousand men.' The women shook their heads and pulled their shawls tighter around their shoulders. 'Reinforcements from Italy for the Grande Armée. You should have heard the sound of their marching boots.'

Saskia dared not mention the ruined men she had glimpsed coming back from the war in Russia.

'They took our children with them,' one woman whispered to her, grasping her arm.

'They stole your children?'

The woman shook her head. 'The drummers, the uniforms, the horses in shining tack. All marching to adventures, to heroics. How could our boys resist?'

'Even some of the girls,' another said, her gaze falling to Saskia's own loose-fitting clothes. 'Don't let them take you as well.'

One nodded towards Rémi. 'No doubt you have found another way to be free of your village walls.' She chuckled.

Saskia had the distinct impression she had not fooled a single one of these women. But the women said nothing further and drew no more attention to her, as if understanding her need to be one of the brothers while on the road. She left their company feeling undressed.

Through the Brenner Pass, they were blessed with a week of clear weather and their feet now crunched on crisp fresh snow. Jagged peaks rose all around her, sharp against a bright blue sky. Saskia marvelled at the mountain antelope with their curved horns leaping over rocky slopes. In the streams, each fallen log was fringed with sparkling icicles and bridges were topped with pristine snow. She felt this cold like a visceral memory, something deep within her, familiar and comforting despite how it numbed her wrists and made her hands feel lumpen and useless.

The great wall of Alps was now a line of terrible teeth behind them, and Saskia felt her smallness against these towering peaks, and was awed by what she had achieved. Father was behind her now. She may not be going home, but she was going far enough away that he could not find her.

Rémi urged them down grassed slopes like a goatherd, but the horses ignored him and took to the pasture with enthusiasm. Saskia found herself smiling. Here the air was different; it smelled of sweet herbs in the grasses. On impulse, she dropped Otto's reins and threw herself down the slope, wheeling her arms, crying out with delight. Pascal and Rémi followed, chasing and pushing one another. They made her laugh.

She felt exhilaration as she ran, her mouth open, her eyes streaming with tears. It reminded her of tumbling, the wonderful swooping sensation in her stomach, the elation of rolling in the air. Once started, she found she couldn't stop. She laughed all the harder. She was a child again, finding joy in the simplest of things, running down a hillslope through long grasses. She whooped and leaped. She felt free.

PART II

1813

CHAPTER ELEVEN

*V*enice. I swooned to see it at long last. The city of islands shimmered across the water, its towers and domes reflected in the lagoon. The sea was so tranquil that it paled to match the sky above without hint of a line between them, and the city floated on this blurred horizon, glinting in the sun. We had been raised on tales of the mythical Venice and its splendour, its beauty and its darkness. Our Gianni was bound to Venice almost as if it were a mother to him. He had been born of Venice, and we, as Gianni's orphans, must be its grandchildren.

I breathed the sea air into my lungs, hoping to catch a spicy scent of the city. I grinned at Pascal and saw the same excitement in his eyes.

Saskia regarded the city flatly, no appreciation for beauty lighting her eyes, her expression as cool as the pale blue lagoon. I sighed to see it. I hoped she would be happy here, for I had grand plans for our little troupe, our Brothers Victoire. Pascal would play his tunes and Saskia would twist her body in the eye-watering ways that had so far never failed to produce coin from even the most shallow pockets. I imagined performing the stories Gianni had told us as children, stories of blood feuds and vendettas. Venice was the birthplace of the great Casanova: adventurer, seducer, spy and storyteller. His exploits were infamous; the tales of his adventures must surely be beloved here.

Saskia swatted a mosquito from her arm with a loud slap.

All the way down the mountains and through the country-side, I had dreamed that someone here would know of the great Gianni Costantini, once famous for his Arlecchino, a master of the commedia dell'arte. Someone who would give shelter to his students. We needed introductions, connections, a way in to the theatres of this town.

'We must sell the horses,' Pascal announced, breaking into my thoughts.

He must have seen me blanch. I opened my mouth ready to protest. Saskia reared back. 'Not mine,' she stated.

Pascal shrugged as if to say she could do as she wished. He turned to me. 'What choice do we have? In the city we will have no need for them.'

I looked down the coast to where high-prowed boats were launching from the Mestre. I saw the merchant sailing ships at the docks, the small fishing boats. I knew Venice was a city of canals, stepped bridges and gondolas. I had formed pictures in my mind from Gianni's tales. Venice, home of Carnevale, gambling houses, courtesans. A water city, no place for horses. And yet the idea of losing our steeds troubled me. I did not like to think that once we crossed to the island, we would be trapped.

'We can stable them,' Saskia said.

'What with?' Pascal snorted.

'We propose a deal,' she said. 'The stablemaster can sell them after thirty days if we do not return.'

Her idea had merit.

'Thirty days to make our fortune!' I cried.

Henriette pushed her nose into my neck, her soft and hairy lips nuzzling me, as if she knew we were discussing her. Our cantankerous Henriette. I reached up to stroke her chin and we both turned our pleading eyes to Pascal.

'Very well.' He waved his hand as if dismissing us. 'Thirty days.'

The water of the lagoon had turned as dark as the night above by the time we set out to cross it. In the Mestre, we had tried nearly all the stablemasters before we found one who would agree to our scheme. I knew in my heart that we should not trust the fellow, so I whispered farewell to our loyal Henriette and blinked my tears into her mane before anyone could see.

Across the water, the lights of Venice glowed like a host of candles floating on a raft. It was unsettling to feel the boat wobble on the water and leave the solidity of land. I looked to Pascal to see if he felt the same. Neither of us had crossed a body of water before. The boatman had taken our money in his callused hand and now rowed us towards the city. Beside us, the lantern lights of passing boats flecked the dark ripples with orange flames. As we drew closer, I saw the outlines of her domes and towers, this city of myth turned into myriad shades of blue.

The boatman slid us into the heart of the city on water as black and slick as oil. We were silent, wide-eyed. Golden lamplights winked from curlicued windows illuminating the carved facades of the buildings along the canal. Here, the waters were where the light lived, reflecting bright blues and reds from the glass lanterns, while the streets were dull by comparison. Venice. City of dreams. We had arrived.

Winter was the time of Carnevale and I wondered what would greet us on the streets. Gianni had loved this festival, because all the barriers of society came down. Behind a mask, he said, no one was rich, no one was poor; no one could tell who was servant, who was master. Gianni's tales were mischievous. He told us of the pranks the revellers played on one another without fear of being recognised: Casanova once untied all of the gondolas moored alongside private homes and left them adrift on the current. Gianni hinted of the wives and husbands who cruised the crowded streets to find new lovers. He told us of the blood feuds that were settled in the dark streets during Carnevale with stiletto blades. It had chilled us then to think of masked assassins and thrilled our boyish hearts.

I watched the pier grow closer, seeing dark shapes through the mist rising off the water.

'We have no masks,' I whispered to Pascal.

He looked confused.

'The Carnevale.'

I saw understanding dawn. If we had thought to mask ourselves, we could slip more easily into this new town.

The boatman overheard. 'No need for masks,' he grunted as he turned the boat, lining it alongside the pier. 'No Carnevale anymore. Your Napoleon outlawed it.' He spat into the water and the silvery gob of saliva slid over the ripples.

He had recognised our accents. We would need to take more care.

I shared a nervous glance with Pascal and stepped for the first time onto the island of Venice.

The winter mist swirled around us on the wharf. The smell of the fish market lingered pungently even though the benches were bare and waiting for the morning's trade. Now what? Now where? I saw Saskia look to Pascal and then to me.

'To the taverns, Brothers Victoire!' I smiled to embolden myself as much as them.

Pascal slung our saddlebags over his shoulder.

'Follow the music,' I ordered and struck out in a random direction, listening for voices raised in song or argument.

Before long we found our first tavern, a *bacaro*, the door lit by a single lantern. It was tucked in the elbow crook of the riverbank and a footbridge took us directly to the door. I looked to my companions and tried to emulate Gianni's accent. 'All will be well.'

We three entered confidently, Saskia remaining mute in her disguise while Pascal loomed tall in the space. Low-ceilinged, the inn was warmed by fires and the bodies of men pushed close. I smelled the fried sardines in vinegar and my mouth watered, thinking of the *cicheti* that Gianni would make for us. I recognised the balls of cod mousse on slabs of white polenta and smelled liver and onions frying on some hidden stove. I saw bowls of clams in garlic and oil, and men wiping their mouths of juice. They turned and leered at our entry. I strutted as I always did. The publican was a short, black-haired Venetian, not inclined to return my smile.

'We are storytellers,' I proclaimed. 'Will you let us entertain these fellows for coin?'

His eye ranged over the three of us, assessing us as if we were fish strung up in a marketplace. Saskia made herself smaller and plainer than a barstool.

He raised an eyebrow. 'Do as you please. They will pay you if you are worth it; if not, you will likely swim.'

Outside the water slapped at the wharf, and I tried not to think of being tossed into the murky depths to flail with the cuttlefish. I had never learned to swim, never had the need of it. Once I had been thrown into a lake and I sank, lungs burning, my eyes open wide to the green, and I remembered looking up at a sky and wondering how I might find my way back to it when Pascal's hand reached down to pull me out.

I saw the publican call a boy from the kitchen and whisper in his ear. The boy ducked away as though sent on an errand. I didn't like the look of this publican, and it made me nervous as I stepped into the centre of the room.

This was no time to be thrown from my stride. When a story-teller takes the stage, he must breathe confidence. The audience must be entertained, and almost by the force of the storyteller's belief, they will be. I clapped my hands to command attention, as if it were my due.

I flicked my cape back across one shoulder, exposing the bright red satin. 'Let me tell you the tale of the great spy Casanova and his escape from the Doge's prison.'

This was Gianni's favourite story and one we never tired of. Pascal nodded his approval. We loved to hear of Casanova secretly sawing through the floorboards of his chamber with a blade he fashioned himself. The way Gianni told it, we were with the daring Casanova in his cell as he cut a little more each night; we felt his hope as he drew close to finishing and then his crushing disappointment when he was moved from his room just one night before his years of work were complete.

But here a dismissive grumble swept around the small *bacaro*. Faces turned away from me. Of course, they had heard this story many times and all knew how it would end. Quick. Another. I searched my memory. This was a poor start and I felt my tongue begin to trip. I thought of the slick, chill waters of the canal.

I studied the men before me, faces wind- and sunburned from hours out on the lagoon. These were the fishers and the fishmongers. Superstitious, no doubt, as all Venetians were meant to be. What did they hunger for? What would thrill them? Ghost stories of the women who haunted these bridges with their necks slit by jealous husbands?

'There once was a mighty fish that skulked through these canals. A massive fish, eel-like, a long black muscle curling out above the glossy ripples, longer than a gondola. It snacked on sacks of newborn kittens tossed into the canal and leaped up to pluck children from bridges when they leaned out too far. At nights, the beast would take drunken men who slipped into the water and feast on the wives who came down too close to the water to search for them. Any fisherman who set out to catch the creature was never heard from again. A reward was posted, for anyone who could hook the vile fish. Time and time again the fishermen tried, but all failed.'

I paused as the door opened and a cloaked figure stepped inside with the boy the publican had sent. My mouth was dry. I saw a coin change hands, and the boy scurried back behind the bar. The face of the newcomer was shadowed by a hood.

'Who caught it then?' a voice called, demanding my attention.

'Until one day,' I said, resuming the story, 'a boy stood up before the assembled fishermen and declared that he would be the one to slay the beast.' I slashed out with an imaginary sword and stabbed it down between my feet.

'"What will you give me if I rid you of the monster?" the boy asked the crowd. They mocked the boy, they laughed at him; no one thought he could do it. "We'll give you a boat and fill it with gold and riches," they jeered, "with women and wine, with furs to sleep on and fine food to feast on." The boy dismissed their jests. "What will you give me?" he asked again.'

Caught up in my tale, I'd failed to notice that the cloaked figure had sidled around the room to warm himself before the fireplace. His back was now turned to me.

'A fishmonger's daughter called out to the boy. And what do you think she offered him?' I asked, gazing around the room. To my satisfaction, all the faces were turned to me. Even the figure in front of the fire had turned. He spoke.

'Glory,' the man said. 'She offered him glory. She promised they would speak of the boy for centuries to come.'

I frowned, thrown by the accuracy of the stranger's guess. 'You're right.'

The man continued in a deep, melodic voice. 'So the boy fashioned a gigantic hook from a fishmonger's scale and he hung it from the Rialto Bridge.'

All eyes turned to him. Who was this fiend thinking he could thieve my story from me?

I spoke loudly, incensed. 'And what do you think he used for bait?' I asked the room.

I heard his voice reply in concert with me: 'He used his tiny baby sister.'

The gasp around the room told me they were hooked by my tale. I knew that when it was done, we would eat *cicheti* and drink sweet red wine and sit by this fireside in comfort. But all I cared for in that moment was to see the face of this man who knew my story as if it were his own.

As if on cue, the hood fell back. A small man with greying hair stepped forward.

Gianni.

CHAPTER TWELVE

*P*ascal shot to his feet, knocking back his chair. Gianni! Could it truly be? Joy welled up in him, blurring his vision. The man who had once been a father, grandparent, all the family he had ever known, stood before him. Pascal couldn't stop his tears. He swiped his eyes with the back of his hand. Gianni's smile was the same. The kindly tilt of his head, the twinkle of his eyes.

Pascal swallowed the little man in his embrace. Here. After so long apart, Gianni was here.

Rémi joined the huddle. It was as though they were children again, overjoyed to have their father return to them. Now Gianni was the smallest of them all. Pascal felt the narrowness of his shoulders, the thinness of his arms. Pascal pulled back, aware that all eyes were on them now. Gianni was smiling, his face wet, but he placed a finger to his lips and urged them not to speak.

'Come, come!' He ushered them towards the door, with Saskia peeling herself from the wall and following as close as a shadow.

A gruff voice from behind the bar stalled them. It was the publican. 'What about the story? How did it end?' A rumble of agreement rolled about the room.

Rémi swept off his cap. 'Tomorrow night! Return tomorrow night and I shall tell you.' Then Pascal pushed him through the door and slammed it behind them.

Out in the street, Gianni kept them moving. They crossed bridges and splashed through alleys and seemed to turn back upon themselves. How did anyone find their way in this maze? Pascal trusted Gianni completely but wished they would stop soon. He wanted to stand before Gianni, study the lines of his face, ask him how he had fared these past years, see the truth in his eyes. Had he forgiven them?

Gianni stopped before a narrow building. He pushed open a small side door to reveal a stone stairway winding downwards. Pascal glanced at Rémi, saw him hesitate; he hated basements and cellars and rooms with no escape. 'It's Gianni,' Pascal whispered. 'We have nothing to fear.'

Saskia turned to look at them, questioning. Pascal pulled Rémi after him, following the older man.

At the bottom of the stairway, they entered a room with a powerful stench of stagnant water. The flagstones beneath their feet were silted with mud and the walls stained green. Gianni's grin was apologetic, his shoulders lifted in resignation. 'It floods with the high autumn tides.'

He hurried about, lighting brands on brackets around the walls, illuminating the low arched ceiling.

'What is this place?' Pascal asked.

'My boys, my boys!' Gianni held out his hands to them, drawing Pascal and Rémi to him. 'It has been so long with no word. I thought the worst, but I hoped, I always hoped. And now you are here! Sent to me from God.' Overcome, Gianni's small shoulders began to shake. He kissed both their hands then held their faces one by one, studying them closely. Pascal looked into Gianni's eyes for the first time as a man, aware of his height, aware that he was looking down into those grey-green shards of light instead of looking up into them.

Gianni kissed his cheeks, and Pascal felt the scrape of bristle against his own. 'I wondered if this day would ever come. I keep watch for travelling performers arriving to this city. How did you find me? How did you know? Never mind that. You are here! As ever, I cannot stop my tongue, you can see.' He twirled about. 'Welcome to our theatre.'

Pascal took a step back. This basement, a theatre? Oh Gianni, he mourned, what has become of you? Pascal remembered the fine stage of his youth, the troupe of actors, the ardent playwrights, the costumerie, the colour, the fabrics, the movement of it all. So many people jostling, fighting, loving. And what was this? A lonely chamber filled with the stink of rot and decay.

'Napoleon bans our traditions,' Gianni said, his voice bitter. 'The commedia dell'arte is outlawed. Can you believe it? Here, where the art form began, we must hide our performances beneath the city streets!'

That explained these poor surroundings. Pascal shuddered. How like Gianni to put himself in danger to keep his beloved art form alive.

Gianni lowered his voice. 'Napoleon is hated here. He put our enemies, the Austrians, in governance over us to win their allegiance.

You must be careful,' he warned. 'No one likes the French, neither the Venetians nor the Austrians. Speak only our language.'

Pascal nodded.

'And who is this?' Gianni asked, seeming to notice Saskia for the first time.

Saskia turned as if she knew she was being spoken of. Pascal wondered how to introduce her—as Sebastian? He hesitated.

'Saskia.' She said her true name, hard and flat, like an Austrian. She trusted Gianni with the truth. Pascal hoped her accent would keep her safe here.

'Ah! You will be perfect!' Gianni said, an odd smile spreading. 'Come, come join us!' He gestured to her. 'Do not look so glum, Pascal. We have found each other.' He pinched Pascal's cheek as though he was still a child.

Gianni ushered them forward. 'Upstairs,' he urged. 'You must eat, drink. And it is time for you to meet the others.'

'The others? Are they here?' Pascal blurted. 'What has become of the Comédie-Italienne?'

For a moment, Pascal thought he saw anger flash across Gianni's dear face. If they had stayed in Paris, they would know. If they had returned to Gianni and the family, they would know. Instead, they ran away, thinking only of their own hurts. But now Gianni's face held only sadness.

'We lost our theatre. We were swallowed up like little sardines by the whale sharks. Gulped up by Théâtre Feydeau, by Opéra-Comique.' Gianni shrugged. 'After you left, Napoleon squeezed us out. There were to be only four theatres in Paris. No room for the likes of us with our improvisation, our provocation. The only stories that could be told were those he sanctioned.'

'What of Margot, little Bonbon? Are they here?' Pascal felt desperation welling in him. When he imagined returning to Paris, they were always there. When he had pictured his return, there was always a home to go back to.

'We scattered. *Poof.*' Gianni blew on an imaginary daisy head bursting with seed. 'We went all ways. Some took positions with the other theatres. Those who could sing were in demand. All they want in Paris is opera. Opera! They pound their feet and raise their fists, poor fools being fed those saccharine melodramas. Some of the company took to the road to try their luck. Me, I came here, back to my roots.'

'No one is there at the Comédie-Italienne?' Pascal heard his own voice, pigeon-soft.

Gianni turned to the wall, hiding his face. 'The theatre burned to the ground.'

It was too much, this news. Pascal stared at the flaming brands lighting the soot-blackened walls, imagining his theatre as the flames wolfed-up the drapes, feasted on the floorboards, the seats. The theatre, his family. All of it. Gone.

Behind him, Rémi crumpled to the floor. 'My mother?'

Pascal was surprised to hear the ache in his voice.

'Your mother?' Gianni was hesitant. 'I cannot say.' His tone was tender.

Pascal smelled the fetid stench of the lagoon seeping from the walls; it clogged his nose, turned his stomach. He could not look at Rémi, felt no sympathy for his loss—in fact, a worm began to crawl beneath his skin. A slick, black thought: Rémi had made them leave Paris; Rémi had taken them from their family. *Did you think of me?* Pascal wanted to ask. *Did you think of what it would mean for me?* Pascal looked at Rémi, his shocked face, his distant gaze, and felt only a simmering anger. I never could refuse you, he thought, and you knew I would not leave you.

❧

I sank to my knees. There was no Comédie-Italienne, no theatre for Pascal to go home to.

And my mother? What of her? Would anyone have cared for her after the theatre was destroyed?

I gulped air. Gianni had shocked me with his talk of our home turned to ash, our family dissipating like smoke. I recovered myself with a whiff of the putrid lagoon. What did I care for my mother's whereabouts? She had deceived me and I had left her behind. It didn't matter to me where she had gone, for I had no intention of trying to find her.

I let Gianni pull me to my feet. He pointed to an internal door I hadn't noticed before.

A spiral staircase took us out of the damp, sulphurous cellar and up into a cavernous marble hall. I gazed around, marvelling. Gianni's lantern showed a patterned tile floor and the remnants of painted frescoes crumbling from the plaster walls. I saw the Virgin Mary looking beatific, her robe azurite blue and a radiant sphere of gold behind her head.

'This was our *scuola*. Napoleon closed us down, abolished all the *scuole*, our confraternities of arts and crafts, because of their riches and power. Buildings like these lie empty all over Venice.' Gianni's voice echoed against the hard marble, now bare of furnishings. 'I have not always agreed with the guild's power to decide who among us would be favoured and who would not, but there was always charity for those within, there was fellowship, caring. We looked after our own. Now all the *scuole* are disbanded, who will care for the widow of a potter killed in his furnace, or the family of a bookbinder who has fallen on hard times? It is a tragedy for all of us.'

In the centre of the room was a grand marble staircase and Gianni's heels clacked as he climbed it. We followed in silence, taking in the grandeur of the carved balustrade. At the top of the stairs, Gianni stopped before a modest door, little more than a cupboard. 'Come meet my family,' he said to us. His words struck me like a blow. I could not help feeling upset to know that Gianni had another family now. I looked at Pascal, but he would not meet my eye.

Gianni knocked at the chamber door in a coded sequence. Was it truly necessary, this secrecy?

'We are careful,' Gianni explained. 'As I told you, it is illegal for us to perform the commedia dell'arte.'

This made no sense to me; what danger could it pose to Napoleon? When Gianni taught us the roles it was always humorous. Beloved characters, acting out their petty dramas. The commedia dell'arte was harmless.

The door opened a crack to inspect who had knocked, then was flung open. Gianni ushered us inside.

Gianni's players lined up before us, surprise on every face. Among them I recognised Il Dottore in his black scholar's robe, La Signora with her bountiful hair and jewels and a dress that was wide enough to conceal two men crouching on either side of her, and the Arlecchino in his doublet and hose of coloured diamonds.

None of the players spoke. We eyed each other like combatants.

'My friends,' Gianni said to his company, 'allow me to introduce to you some of my dearest children, who I have not seen for many years. Please make them welcome in our family.'

I did not see welcome among the players' faces, only suspicion.

'They too are performers,' Gianni enthused in a way that endeared us even less to the troupe. 'Pascal, I see you still play the lute, as I taught you!'

Pascal touched the strap that crossed his chest and bound his lute to his back.

'And Rémi, my little protégé, your Arlequin was unsurpassed!'

I saw the Arlecchino of the troupe straighten his back. 'Frenchmen,' he said, his voice a mouthful of distaste. 'We don't need your Arlequin in our company.'

We eyed one another. He was a well-built man though a trifle short and those muscles would likely turn to fat with age.

'Of course, here we perform in the Italian tradition, with no scripts. There is no Pierrot, no Arlequin,' Gianni said, deliberately ignoring the challenge in the Arlecchino's words. 'And I now play Pantalone, the greedy tyrant, a character long removed from the French version of commedia dell'arte. Ha! It is no wonder our art form has been outlawed. The French leaders cannot bear to see themselves reflected!'

Laughter broke out, a small reprieve to the tension. But I saw that here, too, we were to be the reviled outsiders. It was a status that all travellers carried like a stink. I was tired of the smell. I had hoped we would escape bigotry here with Gianni.

Gianni swept his arms out to his company. 'We humble players keep the traditions of our people alive even though we risk our own lives to do so. We speak out because if we do not raise our voices against power, what use are we performers? Mere entertainers of the rich? No. I say no. We are the voices of the people; we are their hope. We must use our satires to tell the truth.' Gianni had clenched his fists. He spoke with such passion that the players were lifted by his words. I saw them rise with the noble righteousness of their cause and I saw the genius of Gianni as he reassured the players of their value, so they would be less threatened by the new.

The dark-skinned Il Capitano was first to welcome us. A Spaniard, by his accent—a Moor. Perhaps he understood the burden of being an outsider among these proud Venetians. He had a gentle smile despite his military costume and crossed the floor to clasp hands with me, Pascal and Saskia. One by one, the other players reluctantly followed, the Arlecchino last of all. Overfamiliar, he embraced me, his rough cheek brushing my smooth one, his breath annoying my ear like an insect.

What place would there be for me here with this man in my role?

I planted my lips on his cheeks in an act of aggression.

Gianni clapped his hands. 'Friends, to our rehearsal!'

A series of rapid knocks at the door sent the Arlecchino rushing to open it. 'At last,' he said. A woman stood in the doorway. She was panting from the climb up the stairs, her breasts threatening to burst over her bodice.

'I'm here,' she said instead of an apology. 'He would not let me leave!'

'Our Colombina!' cried Gianni.

This woman astonished me. She captured my whole attention in that moment. I noticed her flashing eyes, flawless skin and the fullness of her rose-red lips. Never had I seen a more beautiful woman. Her dark hair was coiled to one side of an elegant neck, and I was struck with the desire to nibble at the lobe of her ear. Until now, I had not believed in such foolishness as love at first sight. But I suddenly understood that whether there was a place for me here or not, I needed to stay.

≈

As soon as Saskia entered the room her eyes fell on a table laden with food. She saw dried figs, cheeses and nuts. Cured meats. Bread. Her mouth watered. She inched towards the table, stopping only when she noticed the company did not like the newcomers. She could not understand their singsong speech, but she observed their bodies, their faces. She saw suspicion, mistrust, anger, perhaps even fear. What could they fear from us? Saskia wondered.

Costumes hung from wooden racks around the walls and a bare area had been marked out in the middle of the chamber—a circle, like a circus stage. The players paid her no attention, scowling at Rémi and Pascal. She slid a little closer to the table. Then laughter broke out and she was being drawn into the group. Her hands were clasped and her cheeks kissed. She caught the names Il Dottore, Il Capitano, La Signora. The older woman spoke a few words to her in a Prussian dialect, welcoming her, and it was a relief not to feel so much of a foreigner.

'I travelled a lot in my younger years,' La Signora said. 'It helps to know many tongues.'

When the woman, Colombina, burst into the room in an abundance of swirling, mauve silk, Saskia made for the table and grabbed a handful of shaved meat.

Again the voices rose and fell around her. No one noticed her stuff the salty meat between her lips. Her mouth exploded with saliva, and the growling of her stomach grew so loud she thought they must all hear it. Saskia chewed as quickly as she could. At any moment they could be sent back out to the street. She filled her pockets.

'*Ciao?*'

Saskia turned, guilt making her cheeks burn. A boy of about her own age stood before her holding out a plate of figs drizzled in honey and dotted with soft cheese. *For you*, his expression said. He had eyes the colour of the lagoon and hair as pale as milk. She took the plate quickly, embarrassed to have been seen, but not so shamed that she would waste the opportunity. The boy smiled and she regarded him for a moment, confused.

The boy guided her with a gentle touch to her elbow. *Here—you should sit here*, he seemed to be saying as he led her to a pile of cushions against the wall.

She nodded her thanks and the boy sat down beside her. Saskia stole glances at him as she ate.

The figs were sweet and dripping with the honey, and the goat's cheese was sharp. Delicious. She swallowed one after another, and then remembered to slow and let her tongue savour the taste. She might not come across the like of this again if the mood in the room turned against them. When there was only one fig left on the plate, she held it out to the boy.

He shook his head, still smiling at her, urging her on.

She finished the last one and licked the honey from her fingers, wondering at his generosity, uncertain whether to trust this change in their fortunes. This man Gianni was a father figure to Pascal and Rémi, someone from their past. She hoped they would all be allowed to stay because she was exhausted. Travelling on the open road had been hard, harder than she had allowed Rémi or Pascal to see. Many times she was thankful that the driving rain disguised her tears. But here, she was dry and safe and fed.

Gianni clapped and she understood a rehearsal was about to begin. The players were sliding on masks and arranging themselves around the circular arena. Colombina had changed out of her mauve dress and into the patched clothes of a servant. She stood beside the Arlecchino in his bright diamond-patterned hose and doublet. Saskia watched him reach out and place an arm around Colombina's hip in an unmistakable gesture of ownership.

'Cristo!' Gianni called.

The boy beside her leaped to his feet. Cristo. She had the boy's name. It felt good to know it; she would thank him for his kindness. She watched him take his place among the players in their bizarre costumes.

Gianni now looked menacing in a costume that was entirely red, from the woollen skullcap to his breeches and stockings. He wore a golden money purse beside a threatening codpiece. His mask was bushy-browed and hook-nosed. His back was bent. When he walked into the arena, he thrust out each foot, like a heron wading in the marshes, hunch-shouldered, head darting, looking for the flash of a silvery fish. Pantalone—the miser, a greedy old man. She watched as the performance began and was shocked to see him beat his cowering servant with a stick.

This performance did not need language to be understood. Each player took their turn in the arena, acting out their parts with their bodies and their actions. It reminded Saskia of the circus, of the way the clowns would each roll into the field of play and improvise their routines. La Signora swept in with a song on her lips and her skirt wide, pushing it between servant and master. She chastised Gianni as if he were her husband. She walked about in circles, exaggerating each step with a flick of her pretty ankle and holding her arms out stiffly from her sides.

Cristo now took the stage, and Saskia felt a queer flip in her stomach. He wore no mask, no colourful costume, and he had removed his cap. His golden hair flashed in the light. He was dressed in soft velvets, like a Venetian merchant's son. He was pleading with La Signora, but she was resolute, stamping her foot: she would not allow it. She was the mother, and he was her son.

Saskia realised then there was no script, no order to how the story should unfold. Each player took their moment to shine.

Then Cristo turned to look directly at her, beckoning her to him.

She jerked back, instinct telling her to stay where she was. But Cristo held out his hand to her, his face eager. *Come*, his gesture said. *Trust me.*

Saskia rose to her feet. She stepped warily through the other players, conscious of their eyes following her. Pascal frowned. Rémi, gazing calf-eyed at Colombina, barely noticed. Gianni met her with a smile. He coaxed her over the invisible line that marked out the arena.

Cristo stood alone in the middle. Gianni led her over to the boy, and turned her so that she faced directly before him. 'Inamorato,' he said, pointing to Cristo and lingering over the rolling sounds, as if that would make his meaning clearer. Then he pointed to her. 'Inamorata.' He pushed them closer together. She glanced up, saw the fall of Cristo's pale fringe over his brow and the soft smile on his lips. Saskia swallowed, feeling foolish and utterly aware of the boy's body so close to her. Gianni clasped his hands over his heart, squeezing them tight. 'Innamorati.'

The Innamorati. The lovers. She understood.

Cristo was looking at her, holding her gaze, and she felt her own heart squeeze.

CHAPTER THIRTEEN

*I*t was the early hours of the morning by the time the rehearsal finished and Gianni took the three travellers back to his own home. Pascal was amazed by its opulence. Gianni led them to a narrow palazzo alongside one of the canals, then ushered them down a corridor decorated with portraits, tapestries and sculptures. When had Gianni amassed such a collection of art? Pascal felt stunned, wondering if he really knew Gianni at all. In the theatre in Paris, they had seen none of this luxury.

A housekeeper fussed about them, taking Saskia away upstairs to her own separate room. The girl looked dead on her feet. The journey had been long and arduous; he hoped they would be able to rest here with Gianni and his company. It seemed that Saskia had found a role for herself within the troupe, but he was not yet sure if there would be a place for him and Rémi.

Gianni had a servant light a fire in his library while he poured shots of grappa into dazzling crystal glasses.

'How can you afford all this?' Pascal blurted, gesturing to the towering bookshelves, to the sculptures and to an artwork hanging above the fireplace—a vivid painting of Christ in torment, his head covered in thorns, his torso bare.

Gianni smiled. 'This palazzo is not mine. All this belongs to our patron,' he explained. 'He is a generous man. A man who understands that our culture is as vital as a heartbeat. He protects us.'

'He lives here too?' Pascal asked.

Gianni shook his head. 'He has a secret place of residence. Even I do not know where it is.'

Rémi raised an eyebrow. 'This mysterious benefactor sounds too good to be true.'

'Come, sit—tell me all about yourselves. You are storytellers now?'

Pascal didn't know where to start. How to describe five years of life on the road, of nights in barns or wheatfields, of hiding from winter storms? It was a world away from this. 'We were,' Pascal said, with a glance at Rémi, who was sprawled in an armchair.

Gianni took Pascal's hand and kissed his fingers, his eyes moist. 'Thank God you are safe.'

'Have you been here all this time, since . . .' Pascal couldn't bring himself to say, *Since the fire. Since our home was destroyed.*

Again, Gianni shook his head. 'We have been performing for only a few months. It took time to find players willing to risk this way of life. Colombina found us our patron.'

Rémi leaned forward at the mention of Colombina. 'Who is she? A noblewoman?'

Gianni's eyes twinkled in the firelight. 'You had best ask her yourself.'

'She is exquisite.'

Pascal felt a flare of anger. How like Rémi to think of his lust for this woman over all else.

'Why do you risk yourself like this to perform the commedia dell'arte?' Pascal asked Gianni.

'Our artistic traditions have been taken from us. Napoleon dictates which arts he will allow to survive. He placed our old enemies, the Austrians, in control of us and they enjoy belittling our arts. They think us Venetians proud and they enjoy bringing our great nation to its knees. Just as every colonising nation has done to others, they seek to make us ashamed of our unique culture. To replace our culture with theirs.'

Pascal saw his fists were clenched on the arms of his chair.

'What will they do to you if you are found out?' Pascal asked.

'Prison. The dungeons beneath the Doge's Palace perhaps.' He downed the grappa and replaced the glass on a delicate side table. 'This is no light thing that we attempt. Our audiences, too, are taking a risk by coming to see us. They want to show their support for the old ways, want to see Venice restored to its former power. But it would take only one spy among them to expose us all to ruin.' He was leaning forward in his chair. 'If you stay with us, my boys, you must know that this is no game.'

Pascal looked to Rémi, to gauge his intentions. The bitterness he held towards Rémi was making his eyes grow hot. 'I have missed you, Gianni,' Pascal said. 'We should never have left you.'

This was a second chance. Gianni was the closest person he had to a father; he did not want to let him go.

'Of course we will stay,' Rémi said.

'Very well.' Gianni smiled. 'It is late; you must be tired.' Gianni called for his servant. 'Beds for these young gentlemen. Rest well, my boys. Tomorrow night, you will see the company perform for an audience.'

Gianni kissed their cheeks before the servant led them away. Pascal felt tears welling; he was tired and overwhelmed with the news of his childhood home. He noticed how small Gianni looked now, how bent and bow-legged.

As they climbed the stairs, Gianni called, 'Oh and Rémi, do not anger our patron. He comes among us rarely, but when you meet him, please be civil.'

Rémi touched a hand to his chest. 'Me?' he laughed. 'Why would I be anything other than charming?'

'Because I have seen the way you look at Colombina . . . and our patron is Colombina's husband.'

Rémi stopped on the stair and Pascal cursed. Rémi's jealousy could unravel everything. He gripped his friend's shoulder hard and bent his lips close to Rémi's ear. 'If you ruin this for me, I shall never forgive you.'

✎

I leaned back against the slimy wall of the basement, the bench hard beneath my buttocks. No matter what Gianni said, no matter his grand artistic pretensions, this was a poor excuse for a theatre. Wooden bench seats had been arranged in a semicircle and the stage was just the bare flagstones, brushed clean of the inches of lagoon silt. The place stank of rotting seaweed no matter how many saucers of scented oils were burned.

I admit I was irritable. I would be made to watch this farce in which there was no part for me. This improvised art form had long fallen out of favour in France. No one wanted to see these rehashed stories of thwarted love and lecherous buffoons. The French preferred more sophisticated, scripted stories that made use of the stock characters. I was forcefully reminded of the night I was to have taken the stage as Arlequin in a French play, and it rattled me. I didn't want to think of all I had lost when my mother tricked me away from the theatre. I chose a dark corner of the basement to slouch in.

Pascal and Saskia took seats in the front row and we waited for the audience to arrive. I was impatient to see if this benefactor of ours would come. This man who could paw over Colombina whenever he pleased, who could touch her silken skin, press his flaccid, wrinkled body onto hers. This man who owned her.

She could not love him, surely. I remembered the first words she spoke when she came through the door of the *scuola*: *He would not let me leave.* I imagined an arrangement between noble families, wasn't that how these marriages were done? She would have been gifted to him, added to his collection of beautiful objects, and somehow—with her pouting lips, pleading eyes and dark, lustrous curls—she had convinced him to fund this clandestine theatre.

The audience trickled in one or two at a time. When they removed their hoods, I was surprised to see they all wore masks. I saw the long beak of a plague mask, and half masks decorated in the diamond pattern of the Arlecchino and masks with the bulbous nose of Pulcinella. All this must surely be dangerous in a time when the Carnevale was banned. These masks were born of the commedia dell'arte, and I assumed the audience wore them in support of the tradition. I watched them gather, these Venetians in their disguises, and realised that the subversive thrill of it was part of the attraction.

They observed one another from behind their masks and I wondered, which one was Colombina's husband?

Gianni stepped out from the inner door that had led us up into the *scuola*. All the players would enter through this door. There was no curtain, no backstage, no theatre set, no backdrop, just this single door in a wall. He wore his red Pantalone costume and a mask with a long, pointed chin, and he carried a single candle.

'My friends,' Gianni greeted the audience, 'you honour us with your support. We must not let our traditions die!'

I thought his choice of words overly dramatic. I could hear the desperation in his voice. He yearned to keep this tradition alive, to pump new life into it with a bellows. I felt sorry for Gianni. The only reason these people came here was because Napoleon had outlawed it. By banning the commedia dell'arte, the Emperor had made it popular.

And then Colombina entered the arena and stole my breath. She wore a skirt of many frills and, even in her maid's clothing, she shone. How I longed to kiss those lips! The play began and all eyes followed her as she circled about Pantalone, avoiding his amorous advances. Gianni was so convincing as her lecherous employer that I wanted to leap up and slap away his wandering hands myself. He pursued her and Colombina ducked and dived and kept him talking. She reminded him that his wife was not far away, that Il Dottore, the scholar from Bologna, was due to visit. 'Il Dottore,' she cried, cupping her hand to her ear. 'It is him—I hear his droning patter; he bores your wife at the door. Il Dottore!' she cried again, more desperately. The audience tittered.

'Ah, I am mistaken, it is your friend Il Capitano that I hear; he comes to boast of his war stories . . . Il Capitano, is that you?' she called, as Pantalone tumbled her to the ground and climbed on top of her.

Gianni went too far in his performance. I almost intervened, but it was the Arlecchino who bounded through the tiny door to her rescue. He cartwheeled and flipped across the floor and even I was in awe of his acrobatics. The show-off! He seized Pantalone and hauled him from Colombina, booting his behind, pitching him in a rolling ball. The audience laughed at his theatrical overacting. The Arlecchino pretended concern for Pantalone's welfare—surely he must have collapsed on top of Colombina? He threw Pantalone over his shoulder, vowing to take him to a doctor. I had to admit, the Arlecchino was strong; he flounced about the stage with Gianni as if the older man were a sack of downy fluff. He mock stumbled, throwing Gianni into the air and making the audience gasp before catching him again. I scowled. He had the pretty tricks; I would give him that. His physical performance was commanding.

Now La Signora made her entrance, lustfully pursuing her husband. He ran from her, but each time she caught him, pulling his head into her bosom or mauling his oversized codpiece. The audience laughed to hear him call out frantically, first for Il Dottore and then Il Capitano, just as Colombina had done. They laughed to see revenge exacted upon him. And all the while the Arlecchino and Colombina danced, a pretty stepping dance, sweeping arm in arm around the circle of the arena, the lovers reunited. The beautiful Colombina saved by the dashing Arlecchino.

In the middle of the stage, La Signora knocked Pantalone to the ground and vanquished him by swamping him with her voluminous skirts. The audience erupted in applause.

Here, in this putrid little theatre, I saw there was more to commedia dell'arte than tired tropes. The audience relished seeing these beloved characters brought back to life as if they were old friends. The boring Il Dottore, the braggard Il Capitano—I had no doubt they could recite their favourite phrases from memory, they could laugh again and again at Pantalone being spun around on his back like a turtle. There was still love for the commedia dell'arte. Even my jealous heart could see that.

The players linked hands and bowed before the audience. Gianni raised Colombina's hand to his lips. He gestured in thanks to the back of the theatre and I craned my neck to see who was the object of his gratitude. I followed his gaze to a figure standing against the back wall, and I saw the man who could only be our patron. He wore the *bauta*, a political disguise; an intimidating white face mask, square-jawed and frightening, with his head and neck shrouded in a black cape beneath a tricorn hat. I stared at him, radiating animosity towards a man I believed to be my rival.

᳝

Saskia fidgeted on the hard seat, disappointed not to see Cristo take the stage. She was distracted, unused to these feelings of nervous anticipation. She wondered if he was waiting in the rehearsal room, then scolded herself for not paying attention to the performance. One day she would be expected to take her place on the stage if she was to earn her keep among the troupe.

The players returned to the rehearsal room breathless with the excitement. Voices were loud, laughter good-natured and the mood high-spirited. It was clear the performance had gone well. Saskia was carried along with the activity, lost in the whirl of costumes being unbuttoned and thrown onto the floor. She couldn't see Cristo anywhere.

Saskia helped La Signora remove her wide panniers from under her skirts. 'Could you tell me,' Saskia began, hoping La Signora would understand her, 'where is Cristo?'

'Cristo! Ah, my beautiful child, your Inamorato will be with us soon. Do not worry.' She cupped Saskia's face between her soft hands and squeezed. 'You are adorable!'

Saskia blushed. Was her attraction to him so obvious? He was interesting, that was all, and kind. It would be good to have a friend her own age.

The players were lounging on the cushions, drinking wine and grappa. Pascal looked bored and Rémi agitated. Colombina had already left the *scuola* and there was no sign of Gianni. How long should she wait for this boy she barely knew?

Pascal and Rémi got to their feet. 'Come,' Pascal said. 'We are going home to Gianni's.'

Saskia hesitated, torn between wanting to see Cristo and not wanting anyone to see her need for him. 'I am waiting for Cristo,' she admitted, embarrassed.

Rémi overheard. 'You are falling for the milk-faced altar boy.'

'I am not,' Saskia replied hotly.

She was not falling in love with Cristo. Love weakened you. Love made you vulnerable. She remembered the advice of her mother so many years before. *Never become attached.*

'All right,' she said to Pascal, throwing her cloak over her shoulders. 'I'll come with you.'

They left without saying farewell to the others. Cristo's absence had set up a kind of agitation in her chest and stomach that she had never felt before. But she still had her pride. She did not want Cristo to see her waiting around the *scuola* like a love-sick puppy.

When they reached the base of the stairwell, the heavy door of the *scuola* opened and Cristo entered with a lantern and a smile.

Saskia gasped. 'Oh!'

He brushed the sweep of his pale hair from his eyes and beamed at her.

Cristo spoke briefly with Pascal, who then translated. 'He intends to escort you home.' Pascal raised an eyebrow to her in question. 'You are not obliged to accept.'

Rémi sang out in Venetian. '*Bona note*, Inamorata!' and twirled away onto the street.

She couldn't keep the smile from her face. Cristo had come for her. 'I won't be far behind,' she said to Pascal. 'And thank you.'

He nodded and followed Rémi out into the dark night, the door closing behind him.

Cristo turned to her and rolled off a string of words in his beautiful voice, but she could not understand a thing. He stopped, his face falling into a rueful smile when he realised it was hopeless.

'I'm sorry,' she said. 'I wish we could speak with one another.'

His face was as full of confusion as hers must have been a moment before.

He offered her his arm and she took it, feeling his body close alongside hers. They were about to step out into the street when she heard voices raised in argument from outside. A key turned in the door lock. Cristo pushed her back to a corner of the entrance hall and blew out the lantern. The door of the *scuola* opened, letting in the light of the street lamps and Saskia saw Gianni enter shaking his head, angry. He was with a taller man wearing a black cape with a stony white face mask. She had seen him in the audience of the evening's performance, the man Gianni had thanked at the end—the patron. But why was Gianni arguing with him?

Cristo put his finger to his lips in warning to be silent. They waited. Gianni took to the stairs, shaking his head, saying, 'No, no, no,' to the patron. The man stood calmly at the bottom and spoke one final sentence that caused Gianni to pause. Gianni's shoulders slumped in resignation. And then the patron quietly closed the *scuola* door behind him.

Cristo and Saskia remained frozen, bodies pressed together, listening to Gianni's slow footsteps climb the marble stairs. Saskia found her fingertips were resting on Cristo's chest. She felt his arms slide around her waist and pull her tighter to him and she did not resist. He was warm and his neck was soft when she bent forward and touched her lips to it. It was strange to be so close to another, and yet she did not want to pull away. There was comfort in his embrace. There was strength. She was no longer alone. Their lips touched tentatively in the darkness. Soft and warm. She felt like she was home.

CHAPTER FOURTEEN

*M*y face was filling with blood, my traitorous arms beginning to shake. How long had she had me standing on my hands like this, and how in God's good name did she make it look so easy? I had managed to stand and totter on my palms like a toddler, my legs wheeling above me to find balance, but holding myself still took great practice. The world around me looked different upside down. I noticed the battered legs of chairs, the dust-coated carpets, and I found I did not like Pascal and Saskia peering down at me.

My arms loosened, I wobbled, and I turned my fall into a roll, springing back to my feet, returning the world to rights.

Saskia glared at me. 'You'll never be as good as the Arlecchino if you don't practise.'

We were in the room Pascal and I shared in Gianni's home, for I could not bear to have the Arlecchino see my lessons.

'But he has no stage presence!' I tried to convince them.

Pascal snorted.

For three weeks I had been forced to watch the artful Arlecchino and his pursuit of Colombina. The Arlecchino who outwitted the foolish masters. The Arlecchino who contrived to bring the young lovers—the Innamorati—together. He had no grace; he was coarse, lewd, took every chance to rub his genitals over the women. Why could Gianni not see this?

Gianni gave me only minor roles, cursing me with plentiful time for observation and vengeful visions. My imaginings turned to ways the Arlecchino might meet with an unfortunate exit from our company. These were not charitable thoughts, I admit, but my life would be measurably improved if I were to become the next Arlecchino. I watched the rehearsals, criticising the Arlecchino viciously in my head and gorging myself on our patron's fruits and nuts. Oh, yes, we lived a comfortable existence, I should not complain. A wealthy patron provided for us; food was plentiful, and we had beds in Gianni's house. I should've been grateful for it all. Our mysterious patron paid us, protected us, greased the right hands to allow us to perform unseen by the ruling militia. Yet I hated him from the moment I learned our patron was Colombina's husband. When I thought of him forcing his dry old lips on hers, my blood boiled.

I was sick with longing for her. Colombina. I was enduring this to gain her attention. I had to win her. I had to prove to her that I was a worthy match.

'Show me again,' I demanded of Saskia now.

Saskia arched an eyebrow.

'Yes, yes, I will apply myself.' To show her, I tipped myself upside down in the middle of the floor with no wall to steady myself against, and this time I did not waver. My arms, torso and legs were straight and true. I would win Colombina's affections. I held my body rigid as an arrow. I felt invincible.

℀

Pascal shook out the dress Colombina had brought to him, and the skirt of sky blue silk billowed out and settled over his knees. He took a moment to appraise the quality of the fabric, then lifted the hems and tutted in disgust. The skirt was ruined. A tide mark of filth banded the bottom from where Colombina had dragged it through the flooded streets. He shook his head at her. 'This cannot be mended.'

'Remade?'

He grunted, shrugged. Colombina had brought him piles of her old gowns. He could see her expensive dresses meant nothing to her; perhaps they were gifts from her husband and not of her own choosing. Her maid's costume had a frilled skirt made from the coloured fabrics salvaged from her ruined clothes. Colombina climbed into the wire hoop cage that would hold out her skirt around her. She kissed his cheek, and whirled away.

Pascal sat in his makeshift costumerie in a corner of the rehearsal room. Three weeks had passed since they had been invited to join Gianni's troupe and his skills had gradually endeared him to the others. First, he had been asked to mend the rips in Pantalone's red tunic, then Il Capitano wanted more badges of honour on his lapels, then La Signora took him aside and whispered that all her old dresses had tightened with washing and needed to be enlarged. He was kept busy every evening, while the players gathered to rehearse. He learned that the theatre performances were never held at a regular time or day of the week; word of the next performance was sent by messengers. These performances were strictly invitation only.

Pascal ran his hands across the blue skirt, the colour of the Venetian lagoon, knowing the fabric would make the perfect dress for Saskia.

Gianni had come to him a few days before, his face serious. 'We need a dress fit for our Inamorata.'

'Is she to perform on stage?'

Gianni nodded. 'Soon we will have important guests to perform for. If she feels ready, I will ask her to be our virgin of Venice, our child of innocence. Can you make a suitable costume?'

Of course Pascal had agreed. A thrill had shot through him at the thought of putting his costuming skills to use after so long. Pascal had learned to sew in Gianni's theatre, where the costumier took Pascal under his wing, teaching him about the fabrics and their properties, and soon he began to design costumes in his mind. He understood how important the colour and drama of a costume could be to the overall production. An opera singer needed her resplendent dress. A character's clothes told the story of a person. After all, what was Rémi without his cape?

Pascal touched the beaded pearls sewn into the neckline, ran his fingers over the embroidered flowers of the bodice, and wondered if Saskia had ever worn a dress as fine as this. She deserved some happiness.

Making this dress for Saskia gave him purpose. Here, back with Gianni and his new theatre company, Pascal could make a home. Wasn't this what he had wanted? The old life was gone, a hopeless mirage, a fantasy. He should be happy to have a second chance of a theatre family. Yet why didn't he feel content?

He looked across to where Saskia sat cross-legged in front of Cristo, their knees touching, hands wandering towards one another. They had spent long hours together making vowel sounds and rolling their tongues and her grasp of the Venetian language was improving. Today, they shared a pistachio-coloured cake studded with sultanas that was a popular street food here. The boy reached out to touch a crumb on her lip, so intimate, so innocent, utterly unaware of the room around them. Pascal saw her smile, a rare and tender glimpse of happiness. He watched as Saskia, normally so guarded, unfurled for this boy. Her arms were loose, her shoulders soft. Pascal felt an ache of loss, seeing them together. First Rémi and his obsession with Colombina, and now Saskia as well.

Pascal turned away with a tightness in his throat. All the world seemed to be in love, but never him. No one had ever looked at Pascal with the adoration he saw on Cristo's face. He longed for someone to love him as fiercely as he could love them back. Was it too much to hope for?

'She reminds me of myself at that age,' La Signora interrupted his thoughts, speaking from behind her fluttering fan.

Pascal glanced at the size of her and could not imagine it so. He remained silent, pushing down the surge of self-pity that had risen up in him.

'In England, they used to call us the "tumbling whores"—can you believe it? *Madonna mia!* No respect for the art, for our talent. Can you believe they would not let their own women take the stage? Instead, they clothed their men in dresses!'

'Ha! Too afraid of what their women might say when given a chance,' Colombina observed in passing as she made her entrance to the rehearsal stage.

In the centre of the room, Rémi and the Arlecchino circled around Colombina. Pascal sighed. He would be made to watch another display of puff-chested strutting. Their jealous rivalry made fools of them. Rémi lunged into a stretch while the Arlecchino ostentatiously backflipped across the room. These performances had become like wrestling matches, each man intent on besting the other.

Tonight, Rémi played a *zanni*, a nameless servant, and the insults flew between the two men, both relishing the pretence of the play to unleash aggression at one another. As the Arlecchino made to show off his acrobatic skills once again, Rémi stepped on the heel of his Turkish shoe, tripping the man and sending him pitching forward into Colombina, clutching at the frills of her dress as he fell, tearing them from her.

Pascal leaped to his feet with a howl. More work, more repairs—a gaping hole now exposed the wire caging of Colombina's legs. He ushered her over to his costumerie, where she climbed out of the cage while Rémi and the Arlecchino continued to circle one another, barely noticing that the object of their lust had flown.

Pascal fumed. It wasn't fair! He had loved Rémi hopelessly, uselessly, for so many years and that same love had never been returned. How long could he wait and hope for something that could never be? Pascal took out his needle and thread, stitching roughly and quickly. Damn Rémi. It hurt to watch him fall in love with another. It hurt like a physical pain in his chest. Pascal pulled the needle and thread, tacking the torn pieces together and wishing a torn heart could be mended so easily.

In the early hours of every morning, Cristo escorted Saskia home to Gianni's lodgings, stopping beside lampposts, against walls and in doorways to kiss. Her mouth was raw with the kissing, her face stinging, but she could not stop, she could not stop this longing to have her lips touching his.

At first they had no other language than this, the language of smiles, caresses and kisses. When the gondoliers whistled at them, they ran to hide in sheltered archways and Cristo smothered her laughter with his mouth. She pressed her body to his, daring him with her closeness, feeling him respond.

If this was love, she was giddy with it, drunk on it. She had never laughed so much in her life, not even at the circus. This feeling was something entirely new.

This morning they had lingered so long in their walk that the first rays of sunlight were stealing out over the city. When they reached the top of the bridge from where she could see her window in Gianni's house, the light was turning golden, gilding the ripples of the water.

Cristo gathered her in his arms. There was always this sadness to their last moments together, when a whole day would pass without him. She had no idea where his home was, who he spent his days with, or what his family must think of all of this. She dropped her head, eyes welling. What would his Venetian family think of her?

Cristo lifted her chin and kissed her eyelids. The words he murmured meant nothing to her. It was infuriating, not understanding him. She wanted to know everything about him. She wanted to know his favourite food, his earliest memory, his dreams for the future. Who did he go home to when he left her each morning? Cristo was trying to teach her his language but she felt slow and stupid. She pulled away in frustration and sadness. She wasn't used to the surges in her emotions; falling in love was terrifying.

Cristo caught her hand. She let him reel her in for one final kiss. She hated this moment when they had to part. She wished he would stay with her here in Gianni's home and curl up behind her on her bed, but he never asked that of her. Instead, he dropped to one knee with his hands clutched in front of his heart and mimed his anguish. He tried to make her laugh with his antics. He whirled away, arms flailing, in tragic parting, then danced back with a grin. Today she wanted more. She bit his lip on their final kiss. She couldn't smile for him when he left her.

Upstairs, she threw herself at the window, loosening the shutters and pushing them open wide. A cold blast of morning air shocked her face, cooled her blood. The sky was a creamy yellow above the tiled roofs. Somewhere church bells were tolling, calling the faithful to prayer. Saskia shivered and wrapped her arms around herself, wondering whether he was thinking of her. How could she hold his love if she could not speak his language? He would find another girl. He would leave her.

Again, she became anxious. She questioned all his declarations of love. She played their moments together over and over in her mind, reliving the feeling of his arms around her, his hands cupping her buttocks, his desire for her. Was it enough, this physical urge to be with one another?

Did everyone who fell in love feel this way? This uncertainty? It reminded her of learning to stand on another's shoulders, the lurch of her stomach, the fear and exhilaration. She had felt so high above the ground, so vulnerable, balancing with her arms thrust out wide, knowing that at any moment she could fall.

'Cristo, my love,' she whispered.

And then a sweet voice, an angel's voice, sang out. Cristo was there! Cristo stood on the ledge of the bridge, singing her name. Singing of love. She wanted to climb out of the window and join him, but the sheer wall plunged into the milky turquoise of the canal waters. When she stretched out her arm to him, the morning light touched her hand and turned her fingertips to gold.

CHAPTER FIFTEEN

$\mathcal{I}$ followed Colombina, eventually. How could I resist? I had to know which of the palazzi with their balconies jutting over the Grand Canal was her home. I wanted to set my eyes upon the man she went home to at the end of each long night. I stepped out after her as she left the basement of the *scuola*. I spied her burgundy cloak billowing as she walked and trailed her easily through the streets until she paid a gondolier and sprang light-footed into his long, high-prowed boat. The gondolier was quick; no sooner had she sunk into a thick fur than he was poling the black boat between two buildings and I could not follow. She left me staring at the window architraves on the walls of the canal, each one domed like pert breasts with their nipples pointed. Damn her.

I was not used to this chase. Venice was loveless for me. Here I could not be the exotic Frenchman among the village girls who were starved of novelty and attention. Here the French were hated. I had to keep my voice a secret and make myself sound like any other man, to blend in, to be ordinary and unmemorable. Ugh! Worse,

I did not know the rituals of courtship here and my attempts at seduction were met with laughter. Soon, I feared I would be forced to go among the *cortigiana di lume* of the Rialto Bridge and pay for it.

Venice was so much larger than I had expected and each street appeared the same, the walls a mix of mustard yellows, peach and terracotta reds. I walked, fists in pockets, watching my feet climb the endless steps and cobbled lanes, not knowing or caring where I finished. My thoughts were melancholy.

I could not compete with the Arlecchino on the stage. Despite Saskia's lessons, my attempts to tumble like an acrobat had been woeful. Colombina eluded me. How was I to make her notice me? The Arlecchino flaunted his love for her, and somewhere out here in the streets of Venice, her wealthy husband waited.

The buildings pressed around me, the lanes narrower, the canal filled with the stench of tanneries. Here was the ghetto, the Jewish quarter I had heard of, where the poor wretches still lived in these crowded, segregated settlements. Napoleon may have emancipated the Jews in all his territories, but overcoming prejudice was a slow business. Not all the change we French brought about was for the worse, I thought, for surely nothing could be wrong with equality for all men? With the end of serfdom? It surprised me, this feeling of kindred spirit with my fellow Frenchmen. I would never dare utter support for these French sentiments aloud. I examined the thought, with the walls pressing around me, the slitted windows looking down on me. Was being the outsider here in a place where the French were so hated provoking a new fondness for my homeland?

And then, suddenly, I had left the tight squalor of the ghetto behind and was stepping into Piazza San Marco, scattering pigeons, their wings beating at my head. I whirled about. The vast open space was shocking here, where every inch of land was built on. The luxury of emptiness. At the far end of the piazza the first rays of light caught the gilding on the domes of the basilica and I stumbled, almost fell to my knees with the strange mismatched beauty of it. Marble columns in whites, pinks, greens and burgundy rising up to marble archways and a domed facade decorated with Byzantine mosaics of Christ, topped with stone sculptures of golden-winged angels and sphinxes. The four golden horses that should have stood proudly on its balcony were missing—stolen by the thief Napoleon, everyone had told us—but the basilica was still a sight to behold. Figurines were crammed across the top of the facade, a mantelpiece of treasures taken from far and wide throughout the ages and displayed for all to admire the wealth of Venice. It was a hideous jumble. It should not have been beautiful, and yet it was.

The Doge's Palace had brickwork in a woven pattern like a blanket of warm cream and pink, giving this palace with its notorious prison a softness I did not expect. When Gianni told us the story of Casanova's eventual escape from the Doge's Palace, it quickly became my favourite. I had loved how he had used his charm and cunning to escape. Once he broke free of his cell, he disguised himself as a cleric and pretended to have been locked inside overnight. Casanova had walked out of these doors boldly, not creeping and afraid but brave and triumphant. I loved that story almost as much as the stories Gianni invented about my father.

I followed the edge of the palace to the waterfront. The sky was dawning cloudless blue and bringing the lagoon out of darkness. Fishing boats were returning, nets piled high, some with cane baskets for lobster and crab. Tall ships were at the quay and I heard the sailors sing as barrels were rolled up gangplanks and across the decks. Rowers launched small boats in the crisp, breathless morning, ferrying the first customers of the day. I sat down on the edge of the wharf, my feet dangling above the water.

I had never been to sea. My travels with Pascal had never taken me over anything as tremulous and borderless as an ocean. I once saw our theatre painters create scenes of huge translucent waves carrying ships on their crests, and wondered what it would feel like to have the sea fall away beneath you. Or to look out and see no sight of solid land, only heaving ocean all around you. I tried to get my mother to tell me of it, but she resisted.

'It makes you feel small,' she had said at last, staring at the swallowing waves of a painted ocean. 'And it lets you think you can be free.'

Gianni said my mother was not the type for storytelling. 'Not like you,' Gianni teased. 'Words fall out of your mouth like water.'

'My father is a pirate,' I told my mother once.

'Who told you that nonsense?' she had demanded.

I was stunned by her tone. 'Then who is he?' I asked her softly.

She had clamped her lips. Refused even to say his name, no matter how much I begged.

'You have my name. Victoire. It is ours, just ours.'

She never wanted to speak of him. I should have been more suspicious when she came to me with a fanciful story about my father wanting to meet me after all that time. My curiosity was always my curse. I had let her fool me because I wanted to believe that I had a father who cared to have me as his son.

The dawning sun washed the lagoon with pale yellow light, softening the edges of the monasteries on the offshore islands and catching the white sails of all the boats. I could go anywhere from here. All the world was open to me, like Marco Polo leaving the

Adriatic Sea for the first time. Like my father the pirate. A wanderer. I could take my stories to another land, where I would be celebrated.

Below, the ships were readying for sail, cargo loaded, ropes uncoiling from the docks, sails waiting to catch the wind. I could step on board that ship and let it take me wherever it was bound. I stood and lifted my arms, feeling the breeze rise and snatch at my sleeves. I could launch myself with these ships and no one would miss me. Not Colombina, that was certain. Not even Pascal would miss me, not really. He would be better off without me. He and Saskia would make a life for themselves here in Venice. There would never be any lead role for me in Gianni's commedia dell'arte; he gave me only the servants' parts, like the *zanni*, a fool who was often beaten. How long could my pride accept such roles?

I heard a noise behind me, the scrape of a shoe on stone, and turned my head. I glimpsed a burgundy cloak. Colombina.

Colombina put a finger to my lips and stopped me from speaking. I felt myself swoon in the depths of her chocolate eyes. Her pale skin was flushed on the points of her cheeks and the tip of her nose from the cold air. I wanted to speak of her beauty, to let compliments tumble from my mouth, but I felt the pressure of her finger on my lips. When she lifted my hand and tugged lightly, I followed.

We slipped back into the maze of streets, crisscrossing canals over small curved bridges. She stopped me, hands on my chest, to catch a moment when a sudden shaft of light turned the milky waters of the lagoon a brilliant turquoise. The sight captured my breath. I felt her closeness to me and dipped my head, overcome with a crazed urge to push back the cowl of her hood and tilt her lips up to mine. She skipped away and left me clasping for the tail of her burgundy cloak. I followed, endeavouring to take note of her route, but in truth my mind was otherwise engaged, as I imagined removing her cloak, unpinning her hair and loosening her limbs on a bed of furs.

The house we arrived at was not her own, I was sure of that. Our patron would not live in such a slovenly street or in such an insubstantial house. It was guarded by a woman with few teeth and a low-slung bosom. Her sleeves were rolled back and her hands were puffed red and smooth like a blister. Colombina kissed her lightly on each cheek in greeting and ushered me through. The washerwoman bolted the door behind us and returned to her coppers.

Colombina climbed a narrow staircase and I followed with enthusiastic swiftness. Through a window, I saw a courtyard with lines strung across the space, hanging heavy with sheets, pillowslips and white undergarments. I wondered how Colombina came to use this woman's house, but I did not let it trouble me for long. I followed the bounce of Colombina's rounded buttocks up two flights of stairs without question.

That Colombina brought many lovers here I did not doubt, and at that moment I cannot say it concerned me. She halted before a door and I pressed close to her, slipping back her hood and kissing her neck. It pleased me to see goosebumps shiver her skin. She turned and I felt her hips bend towards mine. Her hand was quick with the key and she thrust her hips back to shove the swollen wood, the sudden scrape of the door a scream to my ears.

Immediately, I had to pinch my nose against a gust of fumes. The room was thick with the smell of oil paint and turpentine. I saw rags, pots of brushes, and palettes of oily colours. Easels and canvases were leaning against the walls. There was no bed.

I had expected simple furnishings, I had expected this room to be her escape from the demands of her other life, her opulent life with our patron. I thought this was a place to bring her lovers. No woman as bestowed with beauty as Colombina could be expected to remain faithful to her husband, particularly one who never revealed his own face. I envisaged him old and ravaged by the pox.

I did not expect two strange men to be staring back at me. One was bare-chested with baggy pantaloons made of fur, while the other held an apple in one hand and a flute in the other.

'What is this?' I stumbled over the words, disappointment pricking my voice.

Colombina pushed open the window, letting the paint fumes escape over Venice. 'A tableau,' she answered.

I saw her canvas then, the figures of the centaur and Pan coming out of the woods. She was a painter. I looked from her to her canvas. She pulled the ties of her cloak loose from beneath her chin.

'I need a beautiful boy to be led into temptation.' Her smile was wicked. 'A model,' she said. 'A muse.' She pointed to the men. 'You will be recompensed.' She slipped out of her cloak and tossed it up to catch on a hook.

Anger swirled in me. She meant to buy me, to use me.

'Madame, good day.' I took my hat from my head and bowed low, then turned on my heel and swept out. I clattered down the stairs, not caring if she followed. Taking the wrong door, I found myself rushing through the washerwoman's laundry, fighting my way through the lines of wet linens, snarling in frustration. I punched the sheets before me, found them clinging to my arms, wrapping themselves around me. There was no escape from this yard. I was forced to tear myself free and stomp back through the tubs and coppers, skidding on the soap-slipped stone floor.

Colombina was waiting for me at the base of the stairs.

'Are you finished with your tantrum?'

'You mean to use me as your model?'

'If you wish to. I could not force you.'

'You think that because I am poor and you are rich you can buy me?'

'No different from any male painter who sees a pretty girl in the street and offers to pay her as his model.'

'You embarrassed me.'

'Why? You thought I was bringing you here to bed you? Did you imagine that I, a married woman, would sleep with you? You cannot blame me for the faults in your own imagination.'

My head was spinning. Of course I could blame her for not giving me what she promised.

She continued. 'You care only for the chase and nothing for the quarry. I see you want me and yet you know nothing of me *here*.' She thumped her chest. 'I am giving you the chance to get to know me. To sit with me, to let me paint you. To let me understand you.' She threw the challenge at me.

I was confused, and fearful. What she wanted from me was an intimacy I was not ready to give.

'Please, Rémi,' she said, holding out her hand to me.

The centaur and Pan had gone when we returned to her room. Now I looked about, free of other men's eyes on me, walking the length of the narrow chamber. Her walls were lined with canvases hung up to dry. I was looking for his face, the Arlecchino, wondering if he too had been among her models. The subjects startled me. Leering demons, spirits, nymphs and woodland creatures, half human, half animal. I reached out to touch the vivid red coat of a two-legged wolf and my finger came away smeared blood red.

'Here.' She wiped my hand with a foul-smelling rag. 'This wet winter has been a curse. Nothing dries. It is taking months for these commissions.'

'People want these?' I could not imagine these artworks hanging in the wealth-dripping homes of Venetian merchants, among the portraits of their rich ancestors, of women petting their ferrets and sour-faced men clenching their fists around their possessions.

She stripped my cloak from me and hung it beside hers. When she appraised me, I noticed my poor attire, I saw the patches in my hose, the mended tears in my sleeves. I remembered Pascal drawing needle and thread through my clothes, his rough annoyance when I was stabbed in the arm for cheating at cards in a tavern in Strasbourg, and those first careful stitches mending the holes in our leggings when we were pelted with sharp stones. We were new to the craft then. Just turned sixteen, not long on the road together, and I knew nothing about the nature of crowds and how soon they could turn to mobs. I felt a wave of tenderness for those neat stitches, for Pascal, for his devotion.

'I will pay you for two hours each morning—the light is best here then.' She moved me towards the window. 'Do you agree?'

She was close to me, the light catching all the colours of her eyes. I saw olive, amber, even teal in their facets.

'Agreed,' I said, inclining my head, gathering myself. I did not want her to see how she made me tremble.

She swung away and placed the legs of her easel between us. She peeled back a beeswaxed sheet from her palette, and I watched her dip her brush into the daubs of colour and loosen them with drops of linseed oil.

'How should I stand?' I asked, feeling exposed, awkward, unsure. These were not familiar feelings. I had stood before audiences many times, but this was different. Here my likeness would be captured in paint and committed to the canvas, not held in the memory of my audience. Memories could be argued, lost, misremembered or forgotten. A painting was proof. Proof that I was here, in this moment, in Colombina's eye.

'Like you want to reach up and stroke the jaguar lying on the branch above your head, but you know she will only sink her teeth into your neck.'

She left her easel and stood before me, gently angling my head up so the light from the window shone on my bare neck. She loosened the drawstrings of my shirt and her fingers grazed my clavicles, ran lightly over my shoulders. At her touch, I shivered.

'Like you desire her but you cannot have her,' she whispered.

'That I know,' I said to her, heart open. 'That I can feel.'

CHAPTER SIXTEEN

Saskia woke to a terrible pain low in her belly. It made her groan. She curled up, hoping it would pass. An ache had bothered her for the past day and she had dismissed it as something bad she had eaten.

The pain stabbed at her again, like a knife twisting. She gasped, sitting upright. When she stood, she saw spots of blood on the sheet.

She pulled at her nightshirt and saw the back was stained with circles of blood. Her body trembled with the shock of it. Was she dying? Who could she ask for help?

Saskia knocked at Pascal's door. He looked surprised to see her standing there, with her face ghost white and her hands clutching at her nightgown.

'There is something wrong with me,' she whispered. She didn't want him to see her weakness, but she didn't know what else to do. 'I'm bleeding.'

Pascal's mouth fell open. 'Wait here—I'll get La Signora for you.'

Saskia waited in her room, hungry and sore and scared. It was late afternoon, too early for the players to assemble at the *scuola*. What if it took hours for Pascal to return? What if she kept bleeding and would not stop? Saskia wadded her nightgown underneath her and sat with her hands knitted together in her lap. The pain in her lower stomach had dulled to an ache. Was this Father's doing? Had he cursed her?

When La Signora arrived, she sat beside Saskia on the bed, putting an arm around her shoulders and pulling her close. Saskia felt the woman's softness and smelled the gentle perfume of her face powder.

'There, there,' La Signora soothed. 'There now, it is not so bad.'

'What is happening to me?' Saskia asked.

'Nothing that hasn't happened to us all. There is nothing to be afraid of. One day, all girls have to become women. Did your mother never tell you?'

'I have no mother,' she mumbled. How was she to know this happened to all girls when they became women? In Father's house nothing was ever said. He kept her away from everyone. He kept her only for himself. Svetlana would have held her like this and comforted her, but that life was so long ago.

'Will it stop?' Saskia whispered.

'Of course, my child.' La Signora reached out her fingers to smooth the furrows from Saskia's brow.

La Signora produced some strips of linen she had brought with her. 'Here, we'll tuck these into the gusset of your tights. Climb out of those bloodied clothes.'

Saskia did as instructed, though she burned with shame to be reduced once again to a helpless girl.

'You can have these. Boil them afterwards and dry them well for the next time.'

'The next time?' Saskia echoed. 'This will happen to me again?'

'Every month.'

Saskia felt panicked. Every month? Every month she would bleed?

La Signora shrugged. 'It is the same for all of us.'

'All women? This happens to all women?' How was it possible she hadn't known? Women were plagued by this and kept it secret, wearing bandages, hiding their pain? It seemed incredible.

'Until we are too old to bear children. It is the price we pay for having them.' She sighed. 'You will get used to it.'

'For how long each month?'

'A few days, perhaps a week.'

Tears tipped from Saskia's eyes. It was so unfair. Every month she would have to hide this bleeding. What if she was to take to the road again and pretend to be a boy? These thin rags could so easily betray her.

'Oh my sweet child, do not cry.' La Signora wiped the tears from Saskia's cheeks with her thumb. 'I travelled the world with theatre troupes for many years, and I managed. I would make a pouch and fill it with wool or hay—even dried grass and mosses. It is only blood. It can be cleaned away.'

Saskia sat down again on the edge of the bed. Would others see a difference in her now? Would they see her as a woman and not a child? Would Cristo? Her childhood seemed so far away from her now; she felt like she had lived three whole lives before coming here.

She needed a mother to have told her this. She squeezed her eyes closed to stop the tears.

'You are safe here with us.' La Signora wrapped her arms around Saskia and kissed her temple. 'Other women survive this and you will too.'

℀

Pascal was relieved to see Saskia return to the *scuola* that night. She was pale, but smiling. He remembered what it was like for Margot each month when she would curl up in a corner with a cat pulled onto her lap for comfort. He had no idea what women did to deal with the bleeding and he was thankful they were here with Gianni's theatre when it happened to Saskia and not still travelling on the road as the Brothers Victoire.

Saskia's dress was almost complete and soon she would take the stage here for the first time. He lifted the bodice and drew silver thread through the blue satin, embroidering a tiny owl for her as she had requested, to sit above her heart. He had already stitched the story of the Brothers Victoire into the fabric. Two horses and three small figures lay hidden among the motifs of flowers and curling vines.

It was almost four weeks since their arrival in Venice and a decision would have to be made about their horses if they intended to stay. Pascal was becoming comfortable here and happy in his work, but he could not say the same for Rémi. Gianni had still not promised him a role in front of an audience and Pascal wondered how long it would take for him to tire of this place.

'Will it be ready in time?'

Pascal jumped. He hadn't noticed Gianni was behind him until the older man spoke and rested a hand on his shoulder. Pascal felt the heavy warmth of it.

Pascal nodded. The dress was made and he had only the embroidery to finish. 'When is the performance?'

'A matter of days away. An enclave of powerful men are arriving in the city. Our patron wants us to perform for them.'

'Who are they?'

Gianni looked uncertain, as if he shouldn't speak. His gaze travelled to Rémi and then to Saskia as she rehearsed with Cristo, the two young lovers circling one another in their courtship dance.

'The clergy, a gathering of Roman Catholic priests. They are coming to Venice and meeting in secret.'

'The Church?' Pascal was shocked. 'The Church has never been a friend to commedia dell'arte, you told us that yourself. You told us how you were hounded out of towns all over Europe.'

Gianni held up his hands in defeat. 'I know. I disagreed with our patron, but he insists. The Church resents their monasteries being taken to serve as barracks. Times have changed. We all must lie with strange bedfellows if we want to free ourselves from subjugation.'

Pascal did not fully understand the politics. 'How will the Roman Catholic clergy help us?'

'Our patron wishes to show how the commedia dell'arte does not need to be a foe of the Church. We are on the same side. And our culture, our art, is needed just as much as our religion. We need them to be an ally for us now in our collective fight against Napoleon. Do you understand?'

'I think so.' Pascal felt Gianni's grip tighten on his shoulder.

'A tradition of more than three hundred years cannot be erased by one man.' His voice trembled with emotion. 'Napoleon cannot take our culture from us. If we lose our art, who are we?'

Pascal heard the pain in his voice. Gianni loved theatre more than anything, more than anyone. Pascal bent his head, finishing his stitch and snapping the thread.

'Will there be a part for Rémi?' Pascal asked.

For a moment, Gianni looked stricken. But then he smiled. The smile wiped the pain away. It was the old Gianni, the man who loved them like a father. 'Yes, there is a part especially for Rémi. A part only he can play.'

Pascal was pleased. They could make a home here with these players, he was convinced of it. Once Rémi felt valued here, his restless jealousy would ease. It would be like old times again.

Pascal flapped out the dress, letting the loose threads fall.

'Is it finished?' Gianni asked.

'Let's see.'

Pascal called Saskia over.

'How are you?' he asked.

'Better,' she said with a tiny smile.

He ushered her behind a screen to try on the dress.

Pascal pinned the panniers in place, giving her curves where she had none. Then he eased the fabric of the dress over her head, helping her to manoeuvre her skinny arms through the puffed sleeves. The bodice was stiffened with boning and encased her narrow chest like armour, but the skirt was loose and flowing. She was sky and she was water. She was as hard as ice and soft as new frost. Her hair flamed like a candle. She was beautiful.

Saskia stepped out from behind the screen. Pascal watched as she smoothed down the silk skirt over her widened hips and looked at herself in the long mirror as if seeing herself for the first time. She peeked towards Cristo and her fingertips brushed her neck.

She shone.

Cristo crossed the room to fall to his knees at her feet and take her hands in his. The whole room had stilled to watch the lovers.

Pascal spoke with a lump in his throat. 'Will it do?' he asked Gianni.

Gianni's eyes were wet. He put his arm around Pascal and drew him close. He kissed his own fingers in a gesture Pascal had seen him perform a thousand times before. '*Magnifico*. You have made me proud. It is perfect. *She* is perfect. Our patron will be impressed.' Gianni pressed his lips to Pascal's cheek. Inside, Pascal glowed.

'Now. To rehearsal. Our patron will be here soon to watch you practise.' Gianni clapped his hands, gathering the players to him.

So, the patron was coming here, tonight. Pascal was curious to see Colombina's husband. What type of man would he be? Accommodating and generous, or sinister and controlling? In all the weeks they had spent in this room, the patron had not revealed himself. When a knock at the door announced an arrival, Pascal shot Rémi a warning glance. Gianni went to the door and the room fell silent.

A man wearing a *bauta* mask entered. The city fathers had once worn this disguise when they voted in secret ballots and Pascal wondered if their patron had been one of the rulers of Venice before the Austrians were given authority. A powerful man made insignificant could be a dangerous one. Rémi stood tense, rocking on his toes, as they prepared to meet Colombina's husband at long last. He prayed Rémi's jealousy wouldn't ruin everything for them.

Their patron was tall and did not appear to be corpulent, although beneath the full cloak, who could know? A pair of long, slender hands removed the shroud around his head and the mask over his face. A young man with the features of a Roman god and a dazzling clear complexion now stood before them. Pascal gaped. This surely could not be their patron. He had imagined a much older man to be Colombina's wealthy husband, but this man was hardly much older than Pascal himself.

Colombina greeted him warmly. 'Luigi!' She reached up to hold the sides of his face and kissed his mouth.

Pascal darted a look at Rémi, whose cheeks had enflamed in shock. Luigi was exquisite. Ebony hair, deep blue eyes and red coral lips that made his pearl teeth shine bright. Colombina and her husband matched each other in beauty.

Luigi smiled about the room to greet each of the players and when Luigi's eyes met his, Pascal could not look away.

CHAPTER SEVENTEEN

'Who is this patron of ours?' I asked Colombina the morning after his arrival among us. My nostrils were filling with the vapour of oil paints.

'My husband,' she said from behind her easel.

She pained me. *I know that*, I wanted to snap. She answered me and yet gave me nothing. 'Who is he, what does he do, your *Luigi*?' I sneered his name.

The discovery of her beautiful husband had been torturous. It was bad enough when I imagined her going home to a greying husband, fat and flatulent, with grasping old fingers and flaccid skin, but now I had this young Apollo to abhor.

She leaned out, brow furrowed, as she rendered me in paint. 'He lives in Milan.'

'Milan?' So that was why he had only appeared at that one performance. It brightened my mood to think that he lived far away. 'Why has he come back to Venice now?'

'He is arranging a very special audience for us of influential people.'

I knew of this. Gianni had asked me to perform. He had come to me with his face unusually grave. *There will be risk*, he had said. *I cannot guarantee your safety.* I had thought of nothing but the chance to finally take the stage. I would show Gianni. I would show Colombina and the Arlecchino, even our patron, that I was worthy of this part. *Whatever happens, I want you to know I love you boys, I care for you—please remember that*, Gianni had said, gripping my hands. I had thought his emotion strange. Of course he loved us. I had never questioned that.

Colombina continued, 'This performance will change the course of our conflict.'

'What conflict?'

She looked at me as if I were an idiot. So much derision in those deep eyes. 'Our city has been occupied, our customs outlawed, our churches desecrated, our monasteries closed, our art banned. How can you not see what we are fighting?'

I could see. She was fighting me. A Frenchman.

'I hate to think of you with another man,' I said.

'Keep your chin up,' she instructed, ignoring me. Her brush was harsh on the board, her strokes quick and bold.

'Do you love him?' I didn't know why I asked her; I didn't want to hear her answer.

'Of course.'

I shifted my pose on purpose, petulant, hoping to annoy. I did not wish to be a meek puppy who would debase itself for the slightest scratch of its belly. Yet I was. I ached to know if she could ever love me. What was this arrangement between us? Did she desire me at all?

'We could go away together, perform together,' I urged her. The idea had been brewing for some days now. Colombina and me travelling to all the famous theatres. I was beginning to feel trapped in this city. The damp basement theatre, the windowless rehearsal room, the closeness of the houses, the narrowness of this cramped studio—all of it made me want to run outside and breathe. I wanted us to run away together.

'So I could be yours?'

Yes, I thought, of course. No other man to compete with, no Arlecchino, no Luigi.

'You would have me leave everyone I love so that you may have me all to yourself?' She put down her paintbrush. 'Do you care so little for Gianni? Without his theatre he would be lost. You would have me leave and ruin everything, all for your own selfish desires?'

Why couldn't she see that I suggested this for both of us? I wanted to be with her—wasn't that enough? There was fire between us, I was certain of it.

'I love you,' I admitted to her.

Her laugh was brutal. 'What do you know of love? True, selfless love.' She spoke from behind her canvas so that I could not read her eyes. 'You desire me, that is all. You know nothing of my husband, of what he has done for us, for all of us. There would be no commedia dell'arte without him.'

The commedia dell'arte. Was that all she cared about? Why continue to play at acting in an underground theatre that few came to and no one spoke of? I could not understand it. There was no fame, no glory in this. She performed to minor crowds who came to watch hidden behind their own outlawed masks. The cloak and dagger was alluring, but hardly an illustrious career for someone like Colombina. For someone like me.

'The commedia dell'arte is a dying art form,' I countered. 'Why waste your talents performing these old caricatures in some dank cellar? You are too good for this.'

'Ha, you Frenchmen do not understand. Our art, our culture, it means nothing to you. You would take it all from us.' She was dabbing and slashing with her brush. 'Art is our life. Art lifts us above the fields where the animals feed and fuck. It gives us colour when all else is mud.' I heard the heat rising in her voice. 'Art binds us to one another and reminds us why we live. We must be able to perform our stories or how will we remember who we are?'

She stirred my memories of the Brothers Grimm and their desire to collect their Prussian tales. It was an uncomfortable prickle to feel some sense of understanding for those men. In her presence I felt like a child, concerned only with childish things. She made me feel selfish, banal. When I performed on stage I thought only of the audience and their adulation.

'I perform to keep my traditions alive,' she went on. 'And, most of all, I perform because I wish to.'

I should have known better than to speak again, but I was in a reckless mood. The air was stuffy, the oil paint clinging to my nostrils. My arms were tired of holding her ridiculous pose. How long would we continue with this charade?

'Why would you want to stay in this sodden, stinking city?' I demanded. 'It is filthy. It is unhealthy.'

I knew insulting her beloved Venice would rile her. It satisfied me to see her hurt. I looked out the window over the golden rooftops of another brilliant peach-skied dawn, the cupolas of San Marco round like firm breasts, the phallic tower of the campanile rising above the rooftops. No matter what I said to wound her, Venice was the most beautiful city I had ever seen.

She made a noise that indicated her disgust. 'You know nothing of loyalty, of family. How could I leave them?'

'It is easy,' I said, remembering. 'You turn your back and take a horse.'

'Like you left your own mother,' she snapped.

So Gianni had told her my history. We lapsed into angry silence; even the scratching of her brush was silenced.

'Perhaps you should go back,' she said at last. 'It isn't safe for Frenchmen here.'

Did she mean to Paris, to our ruined theatre? 'Why would I go back?'

'Your mother.'

'I don't need her.' I dropped her pose, reached for my shirt to cover my bare chest. The smell in this room was giving me a headache.

'But what if she needs you?'

Her words probed at my guilt. Who knew what my mother had needed to do to survive after the theatre failed and burned? I had left her in anger. I had left my mother. She could be anywhere and I had no way to find her now.

'I do not want to do this anymore.' I pulled my shirt over my head and reached for my cloak. I didn't like the turn of this conversation. Who was Colombina to accuse me of abandoning my mother? Not even Gianni had chastised me for it.

'Wait!' Colombina plunged her brush in the evil-smelling turpentine, swilled it about, and set it aside to dry.

She only cared about her paintings. Our time together was a simple transaction for services rendered. She was beautiful, she consumed my every waking thought, but I would not be trapped by her.

'I want to show you something. Will you come with me?'

She stepped close. I wanted to storm away to show she meant nothing to me. I was Rémi Victoire. I was the one who left my lovers. I did not like this power she had over me. This power to bind me to her.

She reached up and kissed the corner of my mouth, the tickle as soft as a feather. 'Please?'

I let her entwine her fingers in mine and did not resist.

'What is this place?' I asked her as we climbed through the rusted iron railings of a spear-tipped gate.

'San Zaccaria,' she said. 'A convent.'

We stood in an open plaza overgrown with weeds, the tiles pushed up by sprouting shrubs. The place was deserted. Across the campo, the flat white face of the San Zaccaria church rose several storeys high alongside a sprawling complex of red-brick buildings with a campanile of silent bells. I guessed this to be the remains of a Benedictine convent, where the nuns were once cloistered behind the high wall.

'What is this?' I asked, moving the rusted mechanism of a turnstile in the wall with a reluctant squeal. A portal opened to the outside world.

'A *ruota*, a wheel for the abandoned babies that were left to the Church to care for. A mother can leave her child and spin the wheel. No one need see her face.'

I blanched. It was a squalid place to leave a child. What sort of woman would discard their child like this? I was thankful for Gianni and his theatre, for his promise to keep us orphans safe.

'But there is no one left here to take them,' Colombina said.

What happened to all the unwanted babies now that the convents had been emptied? I wondered. Did they simply slip from their mother's arms into the canal?

Colombina led me into the church. 'I wanted to show you this.'

Inside it was cold and our footsteps rang on the flagstones. She gestured to the altar and the bare marks on the wall behind it. 'San Zaccaria once had the finest Bellini painting in all of Venice, an altar painting of the Madonna and four saints. Your Emperor took it. Looted the art and priceless relics from the Church treasuries.' Her voice was bitter.

'Our art is our soul,' she said coming towards me, pressing her finger above my heart so hard that I felt it bruise. 'We won't let him do this anymore. We must fight back. Do you understand?' She was trying to tell me something with the intensity of her gaze. 'We stood by, helpless, while Napoleon took our painters' art from our walls—Correggio, Bellini, Veronese and Michelangelo. He took our scholars' work from their universities, the words of Leonardo da Vinci. Do you know what it feels like to be helpless, able to do nothing but watch and let it happen? It changes you, Rémi! It is rape. He takes and he takes until you understand that you mean nothing. You are nothing. You are worthless.' Tears were coursing down her cheeks. 'Never again will I lie helpless while a man invades my body at his will.'

I was stunned by her words, by their ferocity, by the truths she had revealed of herself. I reached for her and felt her shudder in my arms.

'This place, this place . . . It is full of memories,' she murmured.

I guessed at what had happened to her here, and it sickened me.

She grasped my hand, pulled me from the church and led me through a wooden gate that had been hewn from its bolts. The remains of an orchard grew on the other side, now a tangle of unpruned trees, and we passed through a shaded cloister. I could feel the presence of the nuns, imagining them gliding through the space, hearing the distant tolling of bells and the chiming of their voices in prayer. The ghosts of this place unnerved me.

A brace of quail burst out of a broken window, wings thrumming like oversized bees, and I yelped and swore. The birds clucked in alarm, fleeing into the branches of the orchard. Through the window I glimpsed a man—a priest. I saw the shape of his long, black cassock. But when I looked again, he had gone.

'Does anyone live here?' I asked Colombina.

'Not anymore. The convents and monasteries were all closed. Most were taken for barracks, but this one remains unused.'

The door for the convent needed no key as it had been hacked open with an axe. I touched the splinters. Such violence enacted on the wood. Not fresh. Whenever this violation occurred it was not recent.

'Some of the nuns refused to leave; it was their only home and they knew nothing of the world beyond these walls. It was cruel to turn them out. They tried to barricade themselves inside.'

'How long has this lain empty?'

'Years.'

'I thought I saw a priest back there.'

'Perhaps you saw a ghost.'

Colombina ducked through the ravaged wood, catching her dress on a jagged edge. I unhooked it for her.

I heard feet shuffling away as we entered a dark hall. I blinked, waiting for my eyes to adjust to the shadowy corridor, listening hard. 'Did you hear that?'

'What?'

'Someone running.'

'This place is haunted with lost souls.'

I shuddered, feeling the chill seep down my back. This awful place. 'Why did you bring me here?'

'Come and see,' she said, as she led me along the row of cells. Most had been ransacked. I saw collections of worthless trinkets scattered across the floor: coloured feathers, pebbles, a book of psalms. Looters had long ago taken anything of value. I saw crude hand-painted drawings of the Madonna and her baby on the walls. I imagined the forcible removal of the women, hearing maddened screams and fingernails tearing at the walls. How frightening the prospect of the outside world must have seemed.

Some rooms were bare of ornamentation, left tidy and undisturbed, showing no trace of who had once lived inside. I frowned.

Colombina explained, 'The highborn nuns took their belongings with them when they were returned to the families that had imprisoned them here.'

'Imprisoned?'

She nodded. 'Not all nuns came here willingly. The Church demanded far less dowry than a marriage match. Some noble families married their unwanted daughters to God instead.'

'So for some, the convent's closure was a good thing. Napoleon opened the doors of the cage and set them free.'

'For some,' she agreed.

She pushed open a cell door. 'This was my cage.'

I turned to her, comprehension dawning. '*You?* You were a nun?'

She stepped back inside the cell, running her hand around its walls, staring up at the single, high window. 'My parents put me here as a child. They thought to marry me to Christ, but I flew out of these walls before they could make me take my vows.'

I stood dumbstruck, my voice failing me for once. It made sense now, this daughter of the nobility living outside of the rules of her society.

'I was one of the lucky ones,' she said, her voice overbright, her eyes glittering. 'When the convents opened my parents were dead.'

I didn't know what to say to her. This awful place. Her shocking confession. She was giving me pieces of herself. Pieces of her life before the theatre.

'My brother, Luigi, inherited the family palazzo. Together we spun a lie of marriage to the outside world to give us both freedom.'

'Your brother? You married your brother? He is our patron?'

'A neat solution, don't you think?' She was smiling at my bewilderment. 'No one recognised me, for I had entered the convent as a girl and was a grown woman when I emerged. I reinvented myself.'

I felt a strange jubilation. Luigi was her brother, not her lover. Hope burst within me.

Colombina pressed me back against the wall and kissed me hard, showing me I had not imagined that passion could exist between us. Her kiss roused me, and I felt her respond, pushing harder against my groin. 'Not here,' she murmured against my cheek.

She took my hand and we both ran from the place, that echoing place, that place of ghosts.

CHAPTER EIGHTEEN

Saskia nervously stroked her hands down the fabric of her new dress. She had never owned a gown. She liked the weight of it, the solidity of its casing. It felt like armour. The silver threads Pascal had stitched into the bodice made her think of etched breastplates. At her request he had embroidered the outline of an owl among the flowers and twining leaves, to remind her of the silent hunter. She twirled in her dress, feeling the majesty of the gown, feeling powerful.

In her short time with the theatre, Saskia had come to love the commedia dell'arte. She loved the simple stage, the improvisation, the way each performance was unique. It reminded her of the circus and how no spoken language was needed to convey the emotions of a story. Stories were shared by gestures, by faces, by the language of the body. In rehearsal, she had thrown herself around the stage, climbed on Il Dottore's back, bounced over Il Capitano when he dropped to a knee to beg for her hand in marriage. And best of all, no matter what course the story took, no matter how many obstacles stood in their way, the Innamorati always found a way to be together.

Tonight, she was to perform for an audience for the first time since their arrival among Gianni's company. She gazed at herself in the mirror. Her red hair had grown and Colombina had brushed and curled it into a twist down her neck. Colombina had placed a velvet band around her forehead as if she were a noblewoman of Venice. The dress Pascal had designed made her feel beautiful, as though she was worthy of Cristo's love.

It was tradition for the Innamorati to be kept apart before the performance, like lovers before a wedding. When she emerged from the makeshift dressing room, Cristo had already gone below to the basement theatre. She felt anxious without him near. A pathetic admission. What had happened to her? She had once prided herself on her cool head, her ability to separate herself from emotion and protect herself. With Father, she had learned to let ice flow in her veins.

Enough. She shook herself. She should be concentrating on her performance. Tonight, she would make them all proud.

Gianni, dressed as Pantalone, made his way towards the stairwell. He smiled at her. She liked Gianni; she trusted him. He spoke slowly to her, in Venetian, and she understood his meaning. 'You are the picture of innocence. You are our beautiful Venice.' She saw then that her dress was the milky blue of the calm lagoon under a clear winter sky. She saw the twinkle of sunlight on the water in the silver threads. Gianni took her hand in his and she noticed the paleness of her skin against his mottled and knobbly hand. 'The audience are important men, but do not be afraid. No matter what happens, the Innamorati will always be reunited.' She wanted to tell him she was a child of the circus; she was trained for this.

Colombina descended the spiral stairs alongside her. Saskia delighted in the need to hold up her precious skirts with one hand, something she had never needed to do before. She no longer felt like a girl. She had entered the secret world of women. Colombina squeezed her hand encouragingly. Had she too felt like this the first time she wore a woman's gown? Together they waited in the stairwell. The audience had already gathered; she could tell from the murmuring and shuffling in the darkness. Pascal would be out there among the crowd and Cristo would be waiting for her onstage.

She thought of Cristo standing on the bridge outside her window, his arms outstretched and singing across to her. Colombina smiled at her. 'Are you ready?' Then she swung open the door and Saskia saw Cristo waiting in the light.

❦

I was the last to descend the stairwell.

Gianni had asked me to play this part and I would not let him down. Years before he had given me the chance to take the stage and my mother had ruined that for me with her lies. I would not fail Gianni now. I understood his commedia dell'arte was more than a tribute to old traditions, more than art and culture. It was a call to arms. I wanted to do this for Gianni. For Colombina.

I had dressed with care, shining all the buttons of my coat, buffing the leather of my boots. Tonight, I was to play the role of Il Capitano and I wore full military dress.

As I waited for Gianni's signal, Saskia pushed past me, running up the stairs in her voluminous gown, her face ghostly white. I almost ran after her. Clearly something had happened out there to spook our tiny ice queen. But then Cristo too left the stage, bounded after her, pushing me aside and chipping plaster from the ageing wall, so I did not interfere. The lovers had their own hearts to mend. Without the Innamorati we had no romance, no lingering taste of hopefulness, but I knew tonight's performance was intended to be far more than a love story.

I wondered if Colombina would be out there on the stage. I wondered what part she would play in this performance.

I heard Pantalone's voice ask in a stage whisper, 'Is that Il Capitano I hear? Friends, we must be silent—he cannot hear of what we speak.'

My cue. I lingered a moment, thinking of Pascal in the audience, feeling sorrow for what he was about to see. Then I stepped into the ring.

↜

Pascal shuffled between the men in their long robes, men in black, burgundy and cardinal's red. He took a seat at the back on one of the hard wooden benches. He felt uneasy. For centuries the commedia dell'arte had crossed swords with the Church. Troupes had been chased out of villages, accused of blatant sexuality and corrupting influence. He sat in the shadows, intimidated by the mass of cloth, the richness of the robes and the austerity of the skullcaps.

When Saskia took the stage, he was proud of how her gown glowed. She was the virgin of Venice Gianni had asked him to create. She dropped her eyes from Cristo and began to step regally about in a large circle on the stage with Cristo mirroring her movements, the two lovers meeting for the first time, watching one another coyly, their circles becoming ever smaller; two young people pulled by an attraction as ancient as life itself. Pascal found himself smiling at their courtship dance and longing for the moment they would accidentally touch. He glimpsed Luigi across the vault, unmasked, his face illuminated by the brands around the walls. When Luigi caught his eye, Pascal's stomach flipped.

Onstage, Saskia had stalled mid-dance, staring out at the audience. Pascal saw the horror on her face. It dawned on him she had not known the audience was men of the Church. He should have warned her. Pascal cursed his stupidity. Fool! Of course she would not know; she barely understood a word of what was spoken in the *scuola*. Pascal willed her to recover herself. She tried to disguise her reaction to these men, but he saw the smile she wore was false. How cruel this must seem. To be reminded of the man who had snatched her from a stage and taken her from her family.

Then, abruptly, Saskia turned and ran, her skirts lifted, opening the stage door with a shove of her arm. Cristo, shocked, raced from the stage after her. For a moment the field of play was empty.

Pascal wanted to follow them, racked with guilt for putting her in this position. He should have thought to tell her. He should have been a better friend to her. He had been distracted by the arrival of Luigi among the players, shaken by the unwelcome nervousness that stole over him whenever Luigi came close.

Their patron was a powerful presence. The tug of attraction Pascal felt confused him. Luigi was Colombina's husband; he needed to remember that.

Colombina was next to take the stage. Pascal saw she had changed out of her usual frilled costume and wore one of her own gowns of red and gold, befitting a daughter of aristocratic Venice, a proud noblewoman. Tonight, she was not Colombina the maid, he realised; she was to play herself.

Pantalone and Il Dottore blustered in, intent on their plans for Colombina's marriage. They must protect her at all costs from the advances of the rapacious Il Capitano.

'Il Capitano, Lord of Knock it Down and Break it All,' Pantalone jeered. 'Here he is!'

And in came Rémi. Pascal gasped along with the audience. Why had Gianni not told him what they intended? His uniform was French, the bicorn hat sideways on his head and the hand placed between the buttons of his waistcoat, the likeness unmistakable. To mock the Emperor—*God's teeth, Rémi, have I not warned you? You will have us killed!*

Rémi's mask was long-nosed and phallic and he sniffed, pushed it forward, prodding at the air. Rémi stalked Colombina and she backed away from him but did not turn her face, it was a dance they performed in tandem without touching, he advancing, she retreating. Il Dottore placed himself between them, and the Emperor showed his annoyance, swiping at him. They ducked and weaved. Il Dottore charged at his shoulder, sent him spinning. There was laughter at Rémi's exaggerated fall. Pascal found his heart beating faster, plagued by a sense of impending danger. He watched Pantalone. Gianni would not put them in harm's way, he had to remind himself of that.

The Arlecchino charged into the stage arena, his movements miming that of swordplay. He waited for Rémi to get to his feet and replace his bicorn, then they circled one another, the harlequin and the General. The Arlecchino was smiling as he lunged with a pointed arm intended as his sword. Rémi slashed it away and turned his back, resuming his pursuit of Colombina. The Arlecchino tapped Rémi's shoulder and bared his buttocks to him, wiggling theatrically from side to side.

If this show had occurred on the street, the crowds would have roared with laughter. The fight was comic, Pascal should be relieved, and yet there was tension in this basement theatre. The priests, the cardinals were perched on the edge of something and no one was laughing. They were waiting.

Perhaps the Arlecchino felt it too, this licence. Rémi chased him and the Arlecchino stopped him with a blow to his chin. Rémi reeled and Pascal felt the punch ricochet into his own chest. He felt the ringing in his own ears, the blood rushing, the desire for revenge. The blow was real.

Rémi shook his head as if to clear it, his mask still in place. Il Capitano was a character known for his false bravado and cowardice. Ordinarily Il Capitano would make his exit now and back away from true conflict. But today, Pascal feared, would be different. Pascal looked to Gianni, wanting to catch his eye, to implore him to stop this performance before it became a brawl.

Rémi raised his clenched fists as if to box his opponent and kicked out with his foot, striking the Arlecchino in his groin. With a howl, the Arlecchino fell to his knees, and the audience cried out foul play. *Oh God*, Pascal thought. *Rémi, you turn them all against you. Is it not enough to pretend to be the Emperor? Must you make them hate you more?*

And, all at once, Pascal realised the intention, the sacrifice, Rémi was making. He *wanted* the audience to hate him. There could be no sympathy for the victim. And Pascal knew what would happen next.

Il Dottore began it, tripping Rémi, sending him sprawling. Then he snatched Pantalone's stick and struck his knees, shins, hands while Rémi curled into a ball. Pascal leaped to his feet. How could he be expected to sit here and watch? Then a *zanni* entered—a servant who was often beaten by his miserly master. The *zanni* squealed with glee and kicked at Rémi's kidneys, stomped on his thighs. Rémi's cries were real. The Spaniard who usually played the part of Il Capitano took his turn to kick the fallen man. Even La Signora entered the fray, putting the points of her shoes into his ribs. The Arlecchino got to his feet, still gasping, and aimed a vengeful kick to Rémi's groin but connected with his bent knees instead. The bicorn hat had spun away from Rémi, leaving his head bare. Those curls. This was Rémi, his friend, his whole life. The man he loved was being beaten to death in front of him. Pascal lunged forward, but his hand was caught and restrained.

Luigi had moved silently around the back of the audience and now wrapped himself around Pascal, pressing him back against the wall with the length of his strong young body. He silenced Pascal with a gesture, his face pleading. He whispered in Pascal's ear, 'Leave it be.'

Onstage, the beating had stopped. He watched Rémi slip in his own blood as he tried to stand; the cast of masked characters surrounded him, shoving him back down. Colombina approached, stood over him as he reached up to her, and she spat on his chest.

And then Pantalone came forward and removed his mask. Gianni was crying. It was Gianni, not Pantalone, who unclasped his codpiece and urinated on the fallen general.

There was triumph in the room, Pascal could feel it. Colombina's voice rose in a nationalistic song, extolling the glory of Venice, all its years of tradition and power. Here in the *scuola*, Pascal felt his Frenchness. How could Gianni do this to Rémi? Had he ever loved them as his children, Pascal wondered, or had he always loved Venice more? When Colombina finished her song there was a loaded silence.

Pascal pushed away from Luigi, suddenly sickened by him. How had he thought this man beautiful? He nearly sobbed, his stomach swilling. We are not welcome here, he realised. This fantasy he had of finding a home in Venice was a lie. There was more than acting in this room tonight; there was hatred, deep hatred, the type that Pascal would never understand. He wanted to be gone from this place. He would collect Rémi and Saskia and take them far away from here.

The clergymen were standing and applauding. The noise seemed thunderous. The patron and Gianni had succeeded in their efforts—the commedia dell'arte and the Church were united against a common foe.

CHAPTER NINETEEN

*P*ascal lifted me and carried me up the stairs and I let him, feeling the pain of every kick and every strike to my body. It hurt to breathe. My ribs were surely broken. My hands were bleeding from the rap of the stick, and my knee was swelling and throbbing. I stank of Gianni's piss. Pascal helped me to strip out of the uniform. Found me my shirt. I winced as I pulled it over my head. I wanted to lie down, to sleep. I could not look at Gianni. Stunned and dazed, I was slow to realise what was happening around us.

Pandemonium. The players were throwing off their costumes, scrubbing off make-up, finding plain clothes. They gathered favourite items and stuffed their possessions into bags. They were packing up and leaving.

Gianni came over to us. 'Go now. It is not safe here.'

'But the performance, was it not a success?' I hoped I had not taken the beating for nothing.

'You were sensational,' Gianni said, kneeling and clasping my hands in his. 'A performance unmatched by any other.'

Despite my pain and humiliation, I still craved his praise.

He stood. 'But now we must part.'

'What?' A cruel stab to my heart. He couldn't mean that, not after what I had endured. 'Why?'

'We will be betrayed. Someone among the clergy will wish to garner favour with the Austrians. It is time for us all to leave.'

'Then why risk this?' Pascal was incensed, jabbing a finger towards the wounds on my body. 'Why side with the Church? They have never been a friend to us!'

'We need the Holy Roman Empire if we are to be free of Napoleon. We had to show them we believe the Emperor could be beaten, to show them our art and religion can unify us against the oppressor. They will help us to fight back.'

'Fight back? What do you mean?' Pascal demanded. 'This is only a theatre.'

Colombina answered him. 'We are part of something much bigger, Pascal. We are gathering powerful groups who can resist the French Empire. We are not just a theatre; we are a Resistance.' She clenched her fist.

'And that is why we must leave,' Luigi said. 'There is more work to do. Not just here in Venice, but Milan too.'

Milan?

Colombina continued, incensed. 'Your French Emperor has tried to silence us, to take our customs from us. We have been victims, but no more. Together we fight for independence.' Colombina pulled Luigi to her, kissing her brother long and hard. When they turned back to me, I saw the same fire lighting their eyes.

She wounded me with that kiss. Did she love me at all? My back ached, my elbows stung, my knee was stiffening. I had taken this beating for her, and it had been used to feed a patriotic bloodlust. I was shaken by their venom. I wiped Colombina's spit from my chest. It had hurt me to have her show such hatred. And now she had struck another blow with this news.

'You are leaving Venice?' I asked, still confused. 'Why?'

'Come with us to Milan,' she whispered in my ear, biting the lobe, grazing her teeth along my chin. She came alive with this danger.

Gianni clapped his hands to chase everyone along. 'La Signora, leave the dresses! We must be gone.'

He came back to us and helped me to my feet. 'Go home, my boys—go home to Paris. It is safest for you there.'

I shook my head. 'We could go to Milan with you,' I heard my own voice begging.

'There is no place for you with us.'

I felt his words like a slap.

Pascal's face loomed before me. 'He's right, Rémi: they hate us here. It's time to go home!' Pascal was angry, roughly packing our things.

'The tide is turning against the French, Rémi, you must see that. You endanger yourselves and you endanger us. Please go home.' Now it was Gianni's turn to plead. 'Find your mother, Rémi. She only ever wanted the best for you. Forgive her.' He was speaking like he wanted to tell me this before it was too late. 'My boys, I love you.' He kissed our cheeks as though this was the last time we would see each other. 'I mean only to keep you safe.'

Pascal was tugging at my sleeve. 'Where is Saskia?'

I looked around, could not see her, but my mind was elsewhere, still trying to fathom Gianni's words to me. I felt like a piece of gristle, chewed up and spat out. I realised Colombina and Luigi had already gone. She had left me as though I meant nothing to her.

Pascal cried out, 'Where is Saskia? Cristo! Saskia!' His voice echoed around the room.

All the players were heading to the door, dressed in travellers' cloaks. Gianni gathered his own belongings and followed them.

'Wait!' Pascal demanded. 'We must find Saskia!'

'We cannot wait—our lives are at risk.'

There were noises on the stair, feet clattering. Had we been betrayed already? I looked up, expecting to see the town militia.

But it was Cristo who burst through the door. 'She has been taken!'

☙

Pascal could get no sense from Cristo. They followed him as he ran back down the central stairwell of the *scuola*. The marble was cold and hard and their footsteps echoed. Out in the street, Cristo pelted down the lane and Pascal raced to catch him by the shoulder and halt him. Rémi was limping behind, holding his ribs, but making no complaint.

'What happened?'

'Gianni's house,' Cristo panted. 'He was waiting for us.'

'Who? Describe him!'

'A clergyman. She called him Father. He had a boat.'

The priest from Gelnhausen! Why would he follow her all the way here? Pascal wished he had prodded Saskia for more detail of her past.

Cristo tried to explain as they hobbled through the dark street. 'In the *scuola*, we argued. I could not understand why she was frightened. The audience had scared her. I tried to tell her of Gianni's plan to leave for Milan. I urged her to go and get her belongings.' He gulped for air between the words. 'Perhaps if I had not, she would be free . . .'

Pascal could not answer him. Cristo might well be right, but this was not the time for recriminations and the despair on his young face was real.

Cristo led them to the bridge over the canal and pointed to a window in Gianni's house.

'When we got to the house, he was in her room. It happened so fast. He pushed her out of the window.' Cristo's voice broke. 'I thought she would drown. Then the priest climbed over the ledge and leaped after her. I saw him drag her into a boat and row away.'

'You should have thrown yourself over after them,' Rémi growled. There was sweat beaded across his brow.

'Which way did they go?' Pascal asked.

Cristo pointed down the canal.

'We must follow. Quick—we need a gondola.' Pascal ushered them towards the canal edge. Rémi could not walk far in his state. 'What did the boat look like?'

'Much like any other . . . Black and high-prowed. I do not know. It was dark.'

They roused a sleeping gondolier by leaping into his boat. 'We need to find a boat with a girl and a priest,' Pascal ordered. How ridiculous those words sounded to his ears, but it was early, there were few boats around—someone must have seen them.

Rémi settled back with a grunt of pain. Cristo rode up in the bow and Pascal sat in the middle. They had failed her. They had all failed her.

The gondolier poled them swiftly past Gianni's house and ducked beneath a bridge. How had the priest known to find her there? She must've been followed, watched, stalked, and they had been blind to it. Pascal should've known that the priest would not give her up—he had acted as though he owned her. Her escape from him must have been an insult to his pride. He had seen this before in men: a possessiveness that turned them into ogres.

He kept his eyes focused on the shimmering water of the canal ahead, scanning each boat they passed. Here the canal was narrow, wide enough for two boats to pass close by one another but not to turn around. Above the night sky was lightening. Soon it would be daytime and these canals would be filled with craft.

'Which way does this lead?' Pascal asked the gondolier.

The gondolier shrugged. 'Where all the canals lead—to the sea.'

The narrow canal emptied them into a wider passage where the boatmen were busying themselves for the coming day, loading supplies and passengers. Cristo looked back at Pascal, distraught. Along the riverbanks, the night merchants—freak-mongers, quacks and even the mask-makers desperate enough to risk breaking the Napoleonic suppressions—were packing away their trade.

Cristo called out to a barge, asking if they had seen a boat with a priest or a girl in a blue dress.

The men laughed. Lewd nudges. 'Try the San Zaccaria. The bishops have been taking girls from there for centuries!'

Pascal felt the hopelessness. Cristo called out to other fishers, but no one had noticed such a boat. They passed alongside palazzi with balconies overlooking the waterfront, thick curtains drawn. They would not find her now. Pascal was meant to be a protector; even as a child he had been trusted to bring the other orphans home when they strayed. He was supposed to look after those weaker than himself and he had failed.

As they passed beneath a bridge and into the Rio dei Greci, Rémi suddenly pushed himself upright, holding his ribs.

'What is it? Did you see something?' Pascal asked.

'Do you smell that?'

Pascal smelled smoke. He thought he heard screams, bells being rung. Here the houses were narrow and butted up to one another like long, yellow teeth, but through a gap he glimpsed a flaming roof, turning the sky to copper.

'She has put flame to it all,' Rémi said.

'Saskia?'

'Colombina.' His voice was strained with emotion, and Pascal did not ask him to explain.

The gondolier poled them down the Rio dei Greci, past the walled convent of San Zaccaria and out to the wide waters of the lagoon. A throng of ships outside the Doge's Palace were loading and unloading cargo, and Pascal realised how easily Saskia could be trussed in a sack and bundled away disguised among the cargo.

Cristo howled his frustration to the falling moon.

She was lost to them.

CHAPTER TWENTY

*D*efeat. I saw defeat in their faces. Cristo falling into despair and Pascal resigned. We needed a place to think; we could not circle about these canals like a dog seeking a scent. As we bobbed beside the Doge's Palace, the sea stretched out before us, disturbed only by the distant islands and their monasteries. Day was breaking over the lagoon.

Cristo knew somewhere he could take us, he said. Pascal paid the gondolier as we stepped onto a platform outside a severe-faced building. We followed the boy without question as he unlocked a door and led us inside.

By now I had stiffened with the pain of the beating and my teeth were chattering. Pascal put his coat over me.

'Where are we?' he asked Cristo.

'The Pietà,' the boy said, as if we should have known.

We were in a passageway lit by a single lantern. He took us to a door and jangled his chain of keys to find the right one while I shivered. I hoped wherever he was taking us was warm. I did not want to think of Saskia and what cold floor she might be lying on. It seemed to take an age for the boy to find the key and turn it in the lock.

It was not warm, but it was light.

The dawning sun streamed through the long arched windows and bounced around the white walls. The smile of God himself seemed to enter me through these windows.

'What is this place?' I asked in awe. I shielded my eyes from the brilliance.

'The Santa Maria della Pietà, church of the Ospedale della Pietà,' he said. 'There is no performance today; you will be safe here.'

He took us up a spiral staircase and I was reduced to a crawl. Pascal lifted me up as easily as if I were a toddler and slung me over his shoulder. I submitted to this ignoble treatment with only the barest whimper.

We entered a curtained chamber and Pascal laid me down on a wooden pew. I felt every beaten part of me throb. It was a pain I had felt before, yet somehow the pain of a beating was more palatable when you knew you had deserved it.

'You will be safe here,' Cristo repeated, his hands moving uselessly at his sides, his mind distracted. He worried for Saskia, I realised, and it made me think more kindly of him. I shuddered to think what she might be facing. Had that priest taken her by boat back to the mainland? Were they already on the road towards the Alps? How had he found her? He must have followed us from tavern to tavern on our journey south.

Pascal crossed the chamber to a balcony which looked down through an ornate, gilded grille into the nave of the church. 'What is this room?'

'The women sing from up here, their faces screened from the viewers below. Surely you have heard of the all-female choirs of the Ospedale della Pietà?'

Pascal shook his head.

'Well, they are very famous.' Cristo seemed annoyed. 'Vivaldi composed here for them.'

When we made no comment he continued, 'The hospital has been taking foundling children here for hundreds of years. They raise us, give us a home, teach us skills. For the girls it is singing and they perform here, behind these grilles. Like music from the heavens.'

There was a curious longing in his voice. I pushed myself up.

'You were one of these foundlings?'

'*Genitoribus incogniti*,' he said. 'Parents unknown.'

It struck me then that I knew nothing of this boy other than his moon-eyed love for Saskia.

'They called me Cristo d'Angelo, because the angels must have left me here. The abbess here was very kind to name me so. Foundlings from other places are sometimes slurred with names like Proietto, Abbandonata, Esposito.'

Castaway. Abandoned. Exposed.

'How?' I asked, thinking of the turnstile in the convent wall. 'How were you deposited here?'

'Through our *scaffetta*. I was lucky to be left as a newborn. The hole is only big enough for a tiny baby. Sometimes older babies have been smeared in oil and had their bones broken when they were stuffed inside.'

I winced. Pushed through a slit in the church wall! He spoke dispassionately, as though this meant nothing to him.

'You are not angry? You are not hurt by what your mother did?'

He shrugged. 'The mothers are desperate. We have such a fine reputation for care of infants. And many are hopeful that when they give their daughters to our choir, they are offering them a better life.'

He was proud of this institution, proud to be a foundling. His revelation shocked me.

Cristo dug deep within the pocket of his sleeve and carefully extracted a cut card. He held it out to me, cupped in his hands. The image was of the Virgin Mary, dressed in her blue robes and with the face of a child depicted on her chest, but the holy card had been sliced cleanly in two. He held only the top piece of the card. I stared at him, confused.

'Sometimes a baby is left with a token, a mark, or one of these: a holy card sliced in two. It means my mother meant to return for me. She kept the lower portion so that one day, she could prove I was hers.' Cristo smiled down at the card in his hands with a devotion that amazed me.

I thought of the mark on my arm, the scar I shared with my mother. She had fulfilled her promise to me while Cristo's mother had not. Had it helped him to know that she wanted to return or hurt him to think she never did?

'What would you say to her, if she were to come looking for you now?'

He tossed his golden head back. 'I think it is too late for that.'

'Yet you keep her card?'

'Of course.' He stowed the halved card back into his sleeve.

He confused me, this boy. I did not understand him. How could he care for a mother who never came back?

'And you?' Pascal asked Cristo. 'What do you do here?'

'The boys are taught a trade and the girls who have no aptitude for song are taught to be domestics. At sixteen we are sent out to make our way in the world.'

'But you are still here,' I prompted.

'I never learned a proper trade. I failed at woodwork, had no strength for labouring, refused to work in the tanneries. I wanted to sing, only to sing. But boys have no place in this choir. The abbess took pity on me, so now I help to run things. I organise deliveries, meet the traders at the gates. I have the keys to many places here and I can come and go as I please. I have more freedom than these women who sing. They are married to the Pietà; they cannot leave.'

'But you sought out Gianni. You still want to sing, to perform?' I understood this desire. Now he reminded me of myself.

'Gianni found me. I was singing the "Gloria" in this chapel, when he heard my voice. The voice of an angel, he said. He said God must have brought him to me.'

'And now he has left us all,' Pascal said sourly.

'No.'

I looked at him. Pascal turned from the grille. 'What?'

'Tonight we are meant to meet in the Mestre, on the mainland shore. We were to disappear after the performance at the *scuola* and each make our own way across the water. Then we would ride together to Milan.'

'Gianni planned this?' Pascal asked. 'Did Saskia know too?'

Cristo shook his head. 'I only told her tonight. Gianni was afraid she would tell you.'

I felt those words like another blow. Gianni did not trust us. A cavern opened inside of me; we meant less to him than he did to us. Our father Gianni did not want us.

'We left him too once,' Pascal said with fatalism in his voice. 'Perhaps he has not forgiven us.'

'Saskia,' I said, to turn his thoughts from blaming me. 'We have little time.'

'Who is this man who has taken her? Is he truly a man of God?' Cristo asked.

Pascal shrugged. 'He pretends to be is all we can say. He wears a costume of virtue, but what he wants with Saskia, we do not know.'

'He must have had help. Where would a man of the Church take a child?' I asked.

Cristo pricked up. 'To an abandoned abbey, perhaps? A convent?'

I looked at him, eyes widening. San Zaccaria. We had passed the convent walls on the Rio dei Greci. I remembered the figure of a priest I had seen when I went there with Colombina. Was it possible he had been hiding there all this time? That would explain how he and Saskia had disappeared so quickly; there must have been an entrance from the canal. 'I think I know where he has taken her!'

∽

In pitch darkness, Saskia felt her way around the walls of the pit. Her knees were wet from the sodden floor and the walls damp with mould beneath her fingers. She made herself feel her way with her hands, searching every flagstone, prising her nails into loose mortar, pushing and pulling. The space was not tall enough for her to stand. She crawled blind except for her hands reaching out before her, fingers feeling where the slime of the algae changed to spongy moulds above the tideline. She imagined green walls turning to black. She smelled the salt water. Somewhere along the bottom of these walls the tide entered and retreated. She would not let herself think of anything else. There must be a grate to let the water in.

Now she was calm, purposeful. She moved systematically, searching every inch of the walls with her fingers, storing the information that her hands found, mapping out her cage. Earlier she had woken in this cell not knowing how long had passed—perhaps hours. She was hungry, thirsty and frantic. She had thrown herself at each of the four walls, scrabbling and clawing like an animal. *'Aiuto! Aiuto!'* she screamed, knowing enough Venetian now to call for help. No one answered. She had scratched her throat raw from screaming at these walls. She had stripped off her gown, the wet weight and the tangle of its skirts enraging her. She shivered in her cotton underclothes. Was this her punishment for running away? Was she to be kept here in this hole and drowned with the tide? She had lain down on the dress and when she thought of Cristo, she had wept.

Cristo had told her the company meant to leave for Milan that night. Saskia had not understood why he was speaking of Milan. Why would Gianni leave for Milan? It made no sense to her. Why had no one mentioned this before? 'We were sworn to secrecy,' Cristo had implied with his gestures. 'Gianni did not want the Frenchmen to know.'

In Gianni's house, everything happened so fast. As she reached for her belongings beneath the bed someone had gripped her around the waist. She twisted as she struggled and recognised her assailant. Father. She screamed and he pressed a pomander of foul-smelling nostrums into her nose and mouth, gagging her with it as he tipped her out of the window. She remembered falling but not how or where she landed.

She thumped her fists against the wall. She should never have fallen in love. It had dulled her mind and weakened her. For that matter, she should never have come south. She should have left Rémi and Pascal and continued on alone, forced herself to be brave. For a moment, she dropped her head in despair. But this was no time for regrets. With a shuddering breath she willed herself to continue her search, to place one hand after the other around the slimy walls.

A grate! Barred, but wide enough for her to slide her arms between the bars up to her elbow. Her hand plunged out into dark air. Swivelling her wrist, she stretched her fingers out, hoping to touch something, anything that might help her escape. She pressed her ear to the grate, listening. There were echoes, the slap of water against walls, but nothing more. No voices, no gondoliers, no markets. Only bells, distant bells.

She lay down and peered out through the grate. The grate was something at least, some hope. The bars might be rusted; they might be worked loose. In the distance, she saw light dancing on the water and casting reflections onto the curved roof of a tunnel. Daylight. She made out the shape of a colonnaded crypt. Down here were the bodies of noblemen, cardinals, perhaps even doges, buried in stone tombs. Father had hidden her with the dead. What if Father never came back? What if he left her to die like this, among all the other corpses?

He was forcing her to remember his control over her. The damp cold, the smell of rot and decay, the fear of never being found. Those memories she had locked away, but now they rushed back. How she had kicked and scratched and beat upon that coffin to no avail.

How he had taken pieces of her spirit each time he put her there. How he had made her grateful to him.

What could Father want with her? Why follow her all this way? She thought of his hands stroking her hair. He was obsessed with her and for some reason he couldn't let her go. She had been foolish to believe herself free of him. 'But why me?' Saskia railed aloud.

Saskia smelled smoke. Perhaps Venice would burn while Father left her here to drown with the rising tide. The tide would come like a salty brine to wash the city streets and she was down in the catacombs beneath them. The smell of smoke was nauseating. Now that it had found its way through the grate it seemed to be trapped here with her. She coughed, and felt panic welling in her. If not the tide, then this smoke would steal her air.

She began to tremble. Would Rémi and Pascal look for her? Would Cristo?

Milan. Cristo would be gone to Milan while she was here, back in her box, waiting to see what Father intended to do to her.

But there must be an entrance to this pit. She kept hold of that thought as she continued her exploration, reaching up to touch the ceiling above her head. It was wood, not stone. In fact, it was planks of wood, like a floor. This too was a good thing. Wood could rot, wood had borer and knots that sometimes became holes. Her fingers tapped across the floorboards until they reached an edge and traced it. A trapdoor. Now she understood how she had been lowered into the cell.

She crouched beneath the trapdoor and felt for her dress, running her fingers along the seams of the bodice. Finding the fishhook in its hidden pouch, she ripped open the seams and gripped it tight.

She felt the strength in her thighs, imagined the moment the latch would be drawn back and she would rise out of this cell like a *vila*. A *vila* in owl form, with claws she was not afraid to use.

Saskia woke to movement above her. Footsteps on the boards. Then silence. She sat up. If she screamed, a pitying ear might hear her. If it were Father who listened, she knew he would ignore her until he was good and ready.

She heard a chair scrape across the boards and the creak and groan as a man sat down.

'Can you hear me, child?'

Father's voice. She would know it anywhere. Her heart hammered.

'I am disappointed. You should never have run from me. I thought I had lost you forever until I saw you in the window of that house as the boy sang to you from the bridge. How beautiful you looked. How like your mother at the same age.'

Saskia's stomach lurched. He'd admitted that he knew her mother. Why was he telling her this now? He never wanted to speak of her before.

'Did you know your mother never wanted you? She was going to drown you in the ocean as a baby. I was her priest. Her confessor. She trusted me to keep her secrets.'

He said this to goad her into speaking, but she would not respond; she would not give him the satisfaction of hearing her voice trapped beneath his feet. Yet, she wanted to hear him speak about her mother. Even if what he said was lies, she longed to know more.

'She was a spiteful, ungrateful child. She didn't know how fortunate she was with me. She forced me into hurting her.'

Saskia's breath came quick, nostrils flaring.

'I wanted her to come away with me. It was time to leave that godforsaken windy coast. I had tired of it. And your mother hated that peasant existence. She should have come with me.'

Saskia conjured up a vision of the trees, the *Windflüchter* trees. She had always seen them as bent-backed old women chased by a bullying wind. But now, she imagined them as lines of women facing the ocean, women who endured no matter what was thrown at them by the gods of the sea. They stood up to the wind, bending backwards with their hair streaming out behind them, refusing to be shifted.

'When she spirited you away to that circus, it angered me. You are my child. She had no right to take you away.'

What was he saying? What did he mean by this?

The hairs of her neck prickled. He was her father. That was it. Why had he never told her this before? The thought of his fingers tangled in her hair each night made her want to vomit.

'She ran away from me! She deserved to be punished, she deserved what happened to her. We could've had a life together. She should not have run; she had no right to take you away!'

Saskia understood now that her mother was dead. She would never have abandoned her on purpose.

'I put my hands around her throat and squeezed,' Father said. 'It was satisfying to watch her die.'

Saskia closed her eyes. She had long known that monsters existed outside of tales. All these years, she had blamed her mother too much and her father too little.

'I couldn't take you then, but I returned for you, didn't I?' His voice was wheedling.

Ha. I was no use to you as a child, Saskia thought. He returned only when she was old enough to be his slave. He must've heard the St Petersburg Circus was close and taken his chance to steal her away. Saskia gripped the fishhook in her fingers. This gift from her grandmother, from a home far away.

She understood he was telling her all this to terrify her into submission. She refused to be afraid. Silently, she shifted into a crouch.

Saskia heard the topple of his chair as Father stood. Her heart pounded out a powerful rhythm and her mind was steady. This man, her father, a man who was supposed to care for her, would tyrannise her no longer. She tilted her face up to the hatch.

'I am willing to forgive your disobedience, my child. We are going to leave this place, but remember what happened to your mother. No one runs away from me. If you run, I will snap your neck.'

The hinges of the latch shrieked and the noise propelled her upwards, joining her voice to its cry. She was upon him before he could leap back, she wrapped her legs around his torso and pinned his arms to his side. She plunged the hook straight into his eyeball, feeling the barb pierce the jelly of his eye, and she wrenched her arm back. The eyeball hung from its socket.

She ran from him, light-footed and sure, while his screams of torment chased through the corridors behind her.

CHAPTER TWENTY-ONE

*P*ascal and Cristo followed as Rémi led them through the abandoned convent of San Zaccaria searching each cell, even the abbess's rooms. Pascal moved quickly, feeling his dread mount as they pushed open every door to find it empty. Rémi was certain that he had seen a priest here, but Pascal was losing hope. Rémi explained that Colombina had been confined here in this convent and it shocked Pascal. Colombina a nun? He could not imagine it. He was glad that she had found a way to flee this sorrowful place.

'Can you hear that?' Rémi whispered.

Pascal listened. He thought he heard feet pattering on the flagstones below, followed by a thud.

They took the stairs down to the frigid basement, and Pascal smelled the rankness of the lagoon. Cristo led them into a kitchen with large open fireplaces at one end. In the corner, a table had been pulled back, a chair overturned and a cellar trapdoor raised. The three men looked to one another.

'She's here!' Pascal cried and rushed to the trapdoor.

Cristo leaped down into the cellar. Pascal glimpsed her dress, the sky-blue skirt, and a jolt passed through him. But as Cristo cried out in anguish, he saw the truth. The dress was empty; the panniers had given it false life. He climbed down and picked up the dress he had made for Saskia, clutching the shimmering silk.

'She was here,' Pascal said, voice thick with loss. 'We are too late.'

'The canal!' Cristo shouldered past Pascal, climbing back up into the kitchen.

Rémi and Pascal ran after the boy, ducking down a passageway lined with mildew and mould and skidding to a halt at the waters of the canal.

Pascal saw old storage boxes and barrels stacked along the walls. Here was a passageway into and out of the convent—a secret internal waterway that allowed boats and their passengers to arrive unseen. 'The deliveries were received here,' Cristo explained. This must have been how Saskia had been brought here too.

At the end of the waterway, curved wooden doors were spread wide open to the Rio dei Greci. The bright opening glared back at him.

A boat had carried her out of here and they had missed it.

Pascal sank down to his haunches. For a moment, he had thought they had found her. Elation had welled up and flowed away. They had been so close. He clenched the fabric of Saskia's dress in his fists.

'Quick!' Cristo pulled him up. 'The campanile.'

Pascal nodded in understanding; from the bell tower they might see the boat that had taken her. Hurrying back the way they had come, with Rémi limping along behind, he dared to feel hope. They were close to finding her. She had been here. Pascal and Cristo swiftly climbed the narrow steps of the tower, leaving Rémi to drag himself up behind.

From the belfry, Pascal had a view of the streets and canals snaking out from the convent and all the way across to the islands of the lagoon. He ran from window to window. He saw the domes of the Basilica di San Marco and the rectangle of the Doge's Palace. Below, in the canals, black gondolas were moving slowly like ants following each other's trails. He scanned the waterways, looking for any boat moving swifter than the others.

Rémi wheezed as he hobbled to the belfry wall and planted his hands out wide to steady himself against the stone.

Pascal traced the Rio dei Greci, still hopeful there would be some sign. To his right, the canal spilled into the sea between all the trading ships; to his left, the slick green of the canal was crossed by bridges, jammed with boats both tethered and moving. From this height it was impossible to see who was carried in these boats. She could be bound and stashed beneath covers in any one of them. And even if he caught sight of her, what could he do? From here, he was too far away to help her. Pascal cried out in frustration. Saskia was gone.

Cristo slumped down against the belfry, defeated. 'I have lost her forever,' Cristo moaned, dashing the tears from his eyes with the backs of his wrists.

'We have to keep looking,' Pascal declared.

Cristo shook his head in despair. 'She could be anywhere. He could be taking her on a ship to any place in the world.'

'Then we will try the ports. We will ask every ship.'

'I'm sorry, but I must go. I have to leave with the others.' Cristo pushed himself to his feet.

Rémi twisted his head to look at the boy. 'You are going to Milan?'

Cristo wrung his hands. 'Gianni promised I could sing. He has plans for a new theatre. I cannot miss this chance to go with them.'

'Saskia loved you and you are going to leave her?' Pascal replied, incredulous. He couldn't keep the venom from his voice. The boy disgusted him.

'If she breaks free of him, she will come to Milan to find me. It is my only hope of seeing her again.' Cristo sounded tortured. 'I have to believe she will come to Milan.'

Pascal was still clinging to Saskia's dress. He had failed her. What use was he if he could not keep those he loved safe? He hurled the dress from the bell tower with a roar. The dress plummeted and the skirts spread out like a tail fan, like a falling bird. When it hit the canal, the dress floated, rocking gently in the wake of boats, forming the shape of a woman. An empty illusion, mocking him. He watched as the shape of her was pulled down beneath the murky waters.

※

For hours we searched the boats along the riverfront, calling out to each one to ask if a girl had been seen. Cristo left us. When the afternoon shadows grew long, we returned to search Gianni's house and found it cold and lifeless. Gianni, his housekeeper and all the servants had packed and fled. We crept back into the *scuola* to collect our things, finding the rehearsal room in the same state of disarray as we had left it. Pascal embraced his lute and returned it to its rightful place across his back. We exited through the basement, where my blood still marked the floor. Pascal half carried me from that place and we found a church where I could stretch out on the rigid pews and rest my beaten body.

I threw an arm across my eyes. My mind swirled with confusion and loss. Our Saskia had been taken from us.

Our time here with Gianni confused me. Gianni had welcomed us, he had shown us love, and now he had turned his back. None of them was deserving of our loyalty. Not Cristo, not Colombina. Not even Gianni. Oh, how it burned to think he had not told us of his plans! He used me, then cast me aside. Colombina too. I swallowed a lump lodged in my throat. I had been made a fool of by her and her brother. I would not think of Colombina. But as I closed my eyes to sleep, she slid back into my thoughts.

After Colombina had showed me the convent, she took me to a room above her studio. A simple room furnished only with a sumptuous bed, layered with white covers and pillows smelling of lavender oils. When she kissed me, I felt her desire, her need for me. We made love with the winter sun streaming through an open window. Her passion was startling; she was unlike anyone I had been with before. She made me feel like I was the most important person in the world to her. I had never felt so necessary. Afterwards, she lay with her head on my chest and I traced my thumb over the curve of her shoulder, realising then that I was lost. I had given her the whole of my heart.

I awoke with the light beginning to rise through the stained glass, feeling bereft. Gianni had left us behind and Colombina did not truly care if I followed her or not. All she cared about was her politics. I understood their cause—Napoleon's intrusion, his theft of art, closing institutions that were centuries old, establishing new rules and codes of living, forcing them to live under the Austrians' rule—all of this was an insult, a violation. Gianni could not live like this. To lose their own governance was to become impotent.

Gianni I forgave. It was not easy for a man to bend to the will of another. But Colombina I could not forgive. She had tricked me. She had betrayed me with her false love.

When I had stood on the campanile of San Zaccaria with all of Venice laid out below us and saw Colombina's house smouldering and blackening the sky, I realised she had wanted to disappear completely. But in doing so she had wiped away all evidence that we had ever been together in that studio, that she had ever tried to catch the likeness of me in her paint. The bed where we had made love was turned to ash.

With heavy hearts, Pascal and I arranged passage on a boat leaving for the mainland. I would not miss Venice and its winter fogs. I had tired of the stench of oily fish, the cawing gulls, the maze of streets that seemed intent to make you lose your way. I had tired of entrapment.

'You sold the gelding!' Pascal had the stablemaster by his throat, and I did nothing to restrain him. Pascal backed the fellow against a wall of leather straps, yokes and bridles.

Pascal had paid the man good money to keep our horses, taking a boat across to Mestre after a month to pay the fee. I had been lost in my lust for Colombina, while Pascal had protected our horses. I had almost wept with gratitude when he told me. Now, the man's treachery enraged us both.

'I did not,' the stablemaster stammered, attempting to push Pascal away. 'A boy came for it.'

'A boy?' My mind leaped ahead.

'Cristo?' It took Pascal a moment longer to comprehend, but then I saw his eyes go wide. 'Could it be?'

'The boy said he was your brother, Sebastian. He paid for extra hay for this one.' He jerked his elbow to Henriette, who regarded them all with close attention. 'I should charge you for the damage. She's been kicking the walls and gnawing the stall door since the other one left.'

'Could it be her?' Pascal whispered to me.

'It must be her!' I gripped Pascal's forearms, suddenly filled with an overwhelming joy. Tears came gushing to my eyes in a ridiculous display of relief. Saskia had escaped the priest. I could barely believe it.

Pascal turned back to the stablemaster. 'The boy, which way did he ride?'

'How should I know?' The stablemaster pointedly rubbed his neck where Pascal's hands had gripped.

I fished out a gold ducat.

The stablemaster inspected it and sniffed, wrapped his fingers over it. 'Seen galloping on the road to Padua, I heard.'

I grinned at Pascal. 'She rides for Milan.' Cristo was right. Of course she would chase the boy! There was still hope.

When I mounted Henriette, I threw myself forward in the saddle to wrap my arms around her solid neck. It caused me pain to do so, but I did not care. I was joyous. I had missed her. I had missed this travelling life. She flicked back her head in surprise at my exuberance. I lay my cheek against her mane and stroked the smooth hair beneath her neck. Pascal walked beside us, lost in his own thoughts. Gratitude surged through me and I thrust out my hand to him. I didn't want to travel alone. I needed Pascal by my side. I waited with my hand outstretched, hoping he would return the gesture. Finally, he slapped my open palm and we hooked our fingers together. We had each other. The Brothers Victoire, still victorious. We need only find Saskia to be complete.

Ahead the road curved through bucolic countryside. I noticed spring flowers were blooming and the bees were merry, supping on sweet nectar. The swallows chased one another in their courtship flights. The air was crisp and clean, the sun warm on our faces. Breathing deeply stabbed my ribcage, but it was worth it, for the air was spiced with wild thyme. It felt good to be on the road again, to take up our old life, like a warming, well-worn coat.

Overhead a pair of storks slow-flapped across the sky, returning to roost from their winter sojourn. Perhaps they would make it all the way to Paris to build those precarious nests on church spires in the city. I wanted to point them out to Pascal, thinking the sight might cheer him, but I swallowed the thought. Selfishly, I was unwilling to remind him of his desire to return home.

We took the road for Milan. We would travel through the Lombardy states still loyal to France and take our tales to the firesides of inns along our route and beg for a place to rest our heads and food to fill our bellies. It would be like old times.

How I would laugh to encounter Gianni and Colombina on these roads! Would she travel in a caravan like the troupes of old with a covered stage dragged on a cart? It amused me to think of Colombina sleeping in barns, her once perfect hair now mussed and tangled. I pictured her standing in her finery, with the farmer's wife pointing out the slop bucket in the corner, the Arlecchino dusting chicken feathers from his shoulders, Il Capitano and Il Dottore knocking the mud off their shoes and Cristo climbing into the loft, ashamed of his selfishness. And Gianni, he would be laughing, rubbing his hands, invigorated to be on the road again.

I saw drawings once, a sketchbook he kept from his early years on the road showing gatherings of players, some part-clothed in costumes of elephants or bears, singing around firesides. People of all colours and sizes, all the variety of humanity. Gianni had said that troupes were often havens for the outcasts. He had once confided to me his shock at encountering a woman who hid a part penis beneath her skirts. This image had tormented my boyish mind in fascination and repulsion. What if I were to be tricked by a woman like that? I thought nothing then of the woman and how she might feel to reveal such a thing to her lover.

In Gianni's pictures, there were always children. Children running after the rabbits and chickens that travelled with them. In the drawings, I saw mothers suckling babies to their breasts as the players sat among their wagons. In our theatre, there had been no babies, only orphans, only children already formed. My brothers and sisters were found, not made. I had seen pregnant women in the streets, I had seen babies in slings around their mother's chests, but I hadn't understood how a child was created. Back then, I never questioned why there were children in Gianni's troupe, why the women were pregnant. Until now, I had not concerned myself with the consequences of leaving lovers behind me in every village.

I shook my head to dispel these uncomfortable thoughts. Colombina had got beneath my skin. She had a way of making me question myself that I did not enjoy. I swatted at a bee buzzing in my ear. It flew off to bother Henriette and then swooped back at me. I swung my arms in irritation.

No, I could not imagine those pampered Venetian players on the road, putting up with the dust in their noses, blinking the grit from their eyes, eating only eggs and rabbit meat. I did not expect to see them plying their craft in the streets of Padua or Verona as we would be, or spinning tales in taverns for a night on a mattress stained by decades of bodily exudations. I had no doubt that Colombina and her patron would provide amply and comfortably for them all. It would take us some weeks before we would reach Milan, and they would have flown far ahead of us.

In Milan, we would seek out Gianni's troupe, but only to find Saskia. We would not stay. We were not wanted by Gianni and I would not debase myself by begging for his affections. I need not see Colombina; I would not even try to seek her out.

CHAPTER TWENTY-TWO

Saskia left Venice convinced that fate would reunite her with Cristo. Why else had he appeared in her life when she least expected to fall in love? The strength of that conviction powered her heels into Otto's flanks and drove her to Padua and each of the towns en route to Milan.

Saskia spent her saved coins on nights in cheerful inns in Verona and Brescia that reminded her of Rémi and Pascal and the Brothers Victoire. She remembered how Rémi would bounce up onto a table, letting his cape flare as he began each tale and how Pascal would stroll between the tables, strumming his lute. She wondered if they had searched for her, and if anyone had told them of Gianni's plans to take his troupe to Milan. She hoped so.

When she arrived in Milan, Saskia was shocked by its sheer size. She had believed that simply arriving in the city would be enough to find Cristo. But the streets were choked with people coming to witness the imminent unveiling of the new *duomo*. She followed the crowds, swept along into the centre to see the monolith standing at the far end of a rectangular piazza and hidden behind great sails of canvas draped over scaffolding. In every pale-haired boy, she looked for Cristo.

That night she toured the theatres, watching their doors, waiting to see the nobles arriving in their finery at the Teatro alla Scala and following the masses flocking to the ballet at the Teatro della Canobbiana. This was wrong, all wrong; these theatres were too large, too popular. Anything Gianni created would be small and intimate.

How would she hear of a new theatre? A feeling of desperate loss clouded her view of the city. She walked the avenues and watched the groups of Milanese as they ate steaming bowls of saffron risotto. She expected to find the Arlecchino drinking and carousing on the street. She looked for Colombina behind every fan and veil.

After paying for lodgings, bread and cheese, and a stable for Otto, her purse was fast losing weight. A room of her own in the boarding house had cost nearly all of her savings. The proprietor had a stale, mousy smell and a suspicious eye; what boy needed a room of his own when twenty could share one basement for a fraction of the price? But he made no comment and took her money. She needed to find work. She went to the stage doors of theatres, tipping herself up onto her hands, folding herself into knots. Noses were lifted in contempt, backs stiffly turned, and she was made to feel as worthless as a beggar. They laughed at her. *Find yourself a freakshow*, they seemed to say. *Our performers are artistes!*

She watched the boys of the city, followed them, saw errand boys, altar boys, hawkers, and boys selling roasted chestnuts. Boys were handing out leaflets and pasting them on pillars, notices of the latest plays and performances. Boldly, she tapped the shoulder of one boy holding a pot of glue and brush, made him turn, but her stilted attempt to ask him where he came upon such work earned her nothing. The words she had learned in Venice were little help to her here among the Milanese.

She traipsed through the cobbled streets day after day. How long could she wait for Gianni, for Cristo? In her darkest moments of terror, a suspicion crept into her mind that they might not be coming to Milan at all.

Saskia ventured into narrower streets, heading away from the grand avenues and into the dim laneways. She asked for any work that would pay. A shadow world spawned around the theatres, an industry fed from the spill of theatregoers. Here, the voices were a loud clatter of unfamiliar tongues. Tall drums were beaten by quick hands. Bottles were passed around groups with eager smiles. A small boy sifted through broken pipes and picked out tobacco with nimble fingers. Migrants gathered in these narrow alleys. Wasn't this where she belonged? She shifted between pickpockets, whores, touts and mountebanks. She had nothing to fear from thieves, at least; her money, by now, was spent.

The *lucciole*, the fireflies, wore yellow scarves and tiny bells on their gloves. They hummed and called to her sweetly and raised their skirts above their ankles to reveal their towering chopines and torn stockings. Like mosquitoes in Venice, the air here was thick with them. Saskia shrunk away from their caresses.

A man shoved her shoulder, spun her about and slammed her face into the masonry. His body covered hers. His hardness prodded her buttock. He hissed an amount in her ear. The shock froze her for a moment, as if her mind was slow to understand her liberty had been taken from her. He offered money again, and began to tug at the drawstring of her pantaloons. So this was how a fair-faced boy might make his way in this city. Saskia twisted and slashed at the man's face, catching his jaw with her fishhook, and when he howled, she ran. She heard hoots and cheers from the *lucciole*, but the tinkling of their whores' bells seemed like mockery. She dashed back through the theatre district and did not stop running until she reached the open piazza before the new cathedral, feeling the need for light. She shook, revolted, understanding how brittle life was for any child on the street.

Saskia was jostled and knocked as the crowds gathered before the *duomo* for the unveiling. It seemed the day had finally come to reveal the face of it to Milan. A good crowd like this was ripe for quick hands to plunder their pockets, she thought. Could she become a thief? A little misdirection, an innocent blunder, her small hands seeking out the weight of a purse. At the circus, it had been expected. But she had never been a master of the art and she imagined herself stabbed by a stiletto blade in retaliation. Thieving or whoring—were these the only options left to her if she were to survive in this city?

She wheeled out of the crowd, escaping the press of people, until she found a solid wall. She sank down cross-legged on the cobbles, knowing there was one last option left to her. Hunger gnawed at her belly. Her head bent with the shame of it as she turned the palms of her hands into a cup.

'We are not beggars!' Her mother's voice snapped in her head. She remembered their arrival at the circus, her mother brushing her down, tilting up her chin. 'We have something that they want— never forget that.'

The memory of her mother was sharp and vivid. Her bright red hair. Her angled jaw like carved marble. For the first time Saskia felt grief for her mother's death. Memories of her were no longer tinged with anger. That night, she hadn't meant to leave Saskia with the circus; she had loved her daughter enough to take her away, to run from Father, to want to protect her from him. Saskia's throat grew tight and sore. She felt an overwhelming sadness for her mother's lost life, for the life they could have had together.

Her mother had hated that peasant croft and the endless seasons of sowing and digging onions from the fields. Saskia remembered her whirling around and around in the wind, hoping it would carry her away. It was no wonder she fell prey to a man offering salvation. How long before she learned he was a monster? Saskia's memories couldn't tell her. She had little recollection of going to church, but she must've been presented to him, her mother must have taken her to him. He would have made her stay silent and keep his secret, while she bore the shame of giving birth to an illegitimate child. Father would have believed himself invincible.

Father. Her father. The monster who had stolen her was her own father. From the beginning, he had revelled in the fact that she was his creature and that his possession of her was absolute. She had a sickening understanding of him now. When he had stroked and admired the rich sheen of her hair, she realised it must have reminded him of her mother, Lena. He would have touched her in the same way. He would have flattered her. Slowly, cunningly, he would have convinced her mother to become his.

But her mother had resisted him in the end. She had run from him. Saskia felt a shiver of pride and love for her mother. He had murdered her mother because he could not bear that she had defied him.

What kind of man could take the life of someone he had loved? He was evil. She could find no other explanation for it.

He would not stop pursuing her, she understood that now; he was driven by something primal, something that could not be easily put into words. He had to believe he had total control of her. His domination of her made him feel strong. All powerful. Each time she escaped from him, it made him feel weak. He was convinced she belonged to him and he had to take her back. He would never let her be free.

Saskia closed her eyes and felt her mother's arms wrap around her. It was the last moment they had together. Her mother had been so proud, so pleased Saskia had won them a place in the circus. She had picked her up from the floor of the circus tent and had squeezed all her limbs, kissed her cheeks. 'We will be safe now,' her mother whispered. 'We will be safe here.' Saskia's final memory of her mother was the warmth of her lips touching her forehead as she was carried off to bed.

In the piazza, Saskia lifted her head. Her mother's final gift to her was the knowledge that she could survive. She was resilient and she could save herself. Saskia parted her hands and the begging cup broke in half. She would not beg. She had worth. Even her mother had seen it once.

Moving through the crowd before the cathedral were Romany women telling fortunes from open palms and migrant boys touting white pebbles from the construction site as holy mementoes. She heard the peddlers of holy relics hawking their wares. This was where she needed to be: among the gawping tourists and the gullible. When the shrouds were dropped and the scaffolding dismantled, more and more people would come into the city to see the *duomo*.

They would keep her fed. The theatres might not want her, but here among the people of the streets, the performers and the charlatans, she could find her place. Emboldened, she stood and cartwheeled twice and her hat fell flat upon the cobblestones, open to the sky.

༄

Pascal had seen many churches and cathedrals in his travels, but never before had he been to an unveiling of a cathedral that had taken centuries to complete. He had a tingling sense of the momentous as the clanging of all the city's bells could be heard on the outskirts of town, calling them in. The construction of the *duomo* had begun five hundred years before and had only been finished because Napoleon ordered it to be so, and now they were riding into Milan on the day that its magnificence was to be revealed. It made the roads a nightmare.

Henriette struck out with her hind leg and squealed to demand space from a blinkered carthorse that was pushing its muzzle into her tail. The driver cursed and snapped his whip and sent the horse trotting past Pascal and Rémi with a narrow glare. They rode into Milan on Henriette's back, keeping high above the masses swarming through the city gates.

'How are we supposed to find Saskia in all of this?' Pascal asked Rémi, not expecting to hear an answer.

When the congestion of carts and carriages became too great, they stabled Henriette and continued on foot. Despite the throng of people, Pascal discovered the streets of Milan were surprisingly clean, the cobbles swept and shiny, the minerals in the pink granite sparkling. This was a city made for show, he thought, with its glittering facade.

Pascal glimpsed the cathedral by accident. He turned his head to look down a lane and saw the fierce white of its spires blazing against a vivid blue sky. The sight of it was pure radiance. He had never seen such beauty, such shining light, emanate from stone. He tugged Rémi down the street and into a grand piazza. He gazed in awe. The *duomo* rose before them with multitudes of spires, each one rising ever higher towards God.

For the first time in his life, he felt like falling to his knees and praying. There was something in those carved white spires and pinnacles that thrilled his heart, that made him want to sing. The cathedral was music made with stone.

Rémi roused him, urging him away from the touts. The piazza was crammed with people. A flower seller pushed a bloom into his face promising the gift of love and threatening the curse of impotence. A man looped coloured braids around Pascal's arm, gripping his hand and refused to release him without payment, until Rémi kicked the man away.

Rémi pulled at him. 'Come on, we are here to find Gianni.'

'Saskia,' Pascal said. 'We are here to find Saskia.'

Rémi nodded. 'Of course.'

'Don't you think they might be here now, to witness this moment?' He wanted to stay and gaze a little longer at the pure beauty and brilliance.

'We will never find them in this crowd.'

'Saskia could be here.' This spectacle was drawing all the street performers into its embrace. Stilt walkers loomed above their heads. Fire swallowers tossed flaming brands into the air. Purveyors of religious artefacts spread out locks of hair and fragments of bone, and mountebanks cried out their cures for pox and ailments of the gut. Where else would a contortionist ply her trade?

Rémi shrugged away a boy who had his fingers in the folds of his cloak. 'Pascal! We cannot linger here, we will be robbed blind.'

At last Pascal conceded, following his friend towards the edge of the piazza. As he went, he cast a glance back over the heads of the crowd to see the majestic spires once more, wishing he had space and time to gaze upon them in peace.

And there she was. Saskia. Upside down on the cobblestones, standing on her hands.

Pascal elbowed Rémi in the ribs then barrelled towards her, halting just in time to let her flip into a backbend and right herself before him.

Her owl eyes went round before he swallowed her in his embrace. He squeezed and squeezed until she beat upon his chest with the flat of her palm. She was laughing when he finally pulled away.

They spoke in unison.

'How did you find me?'

'How did you escape?'

Rémi flung his arms around them both, squeezing them all together again.

Pascal's eyes were wet. Against all the odds, they had found her. It was a miracle, a true miracle. She looked unharmed; she looked well.

'You came,' she whispered.

'Of course,' Pascal answered.

Rémi gripped each of their hands and made them dance about in a circle. 'We must drink to our good fortune! We must feast and be merry!'

'Wait,' Saskia said. 'Cristo. Have you found him? Do you know where Gianni's troupe is?'

Pascal ached to see the hope in her face, the yearning for that unworthy boy. Wordlessly, he shook his head.

Saskia turned her face away, hiding her sorrow.

'We will find them,' Pascal assured her, reaching out to touch her arm. Feeling the thinness of her, the skin and bone.

'We will.' She tilted her chin up to him. Her smile was brave.

He studied her in silence. He wanted to know what that priest had done to her, why he had taken her, but he was afraid to ask her for more than she was willing to share.

'Have you eaten?' Pascal asked.

'A little.'

'Well, we shall dine and you can tell us everything,' Rémi said. 'Then we will make a plan to find Gianni. It is impossible to think without full stomachs. With three minds and three hearts, we shall not fail.'

Rémi danced ahead, skipping through the crowd, twirling about for the sheer fun of it. 'We are reunited!' he called back to them, spreading his arms wide and forcing the crowd to veer around him.

Pascal shared a wry grin with Saskia. 'Rémi is still an idiot.'

'Some things won't ever change.'

'Let's find a quiet place to talk,' Pascal urged. 'We thought you were lost to us.'

Saskia led them away from the crowds, towards the theatre district. Pascal saw banners announcing world famous operas and he halted before the Teatro alla Scala. La Scala, that mythic place of world premieres. He could hardly believe he was here, in Milan, home to one of the principal opera houses in the world. Coloured banners on each side of the entrance advertised the season of *La Pietra del Paragone* by Rossini. Pascal heard music, an orchestra tuning, the instruments being warmed. His heart was beating faster. He missed this world. He missed the madness and the joy.

Pascal hungered for a glimpse inside those solid doors. He pictured a lobby with chandeliers. He closed his eyes and saw himself walking up carpeted stairs, the walls hung with framed posters. The door of a private box was swung open for him and he marvelled at the view from its balcony, the gilded boxes across the void reaching six storeys high. He saw the semicircular amphitheatre with the crowds jostling in front of the red-curtained stage. He could imagine it all. He could hear the hum of voices. He could smell the perfume of powdered wigs. But when he opened his eyes, he saw the doors still firmly closed.

'Come on,' Rémi said, 'Gianni won't come to a theatre like this, Pascal.'

Saskia nodded in agreement. 'They turned me away.' Pascal took one last look at the Scala, wondering if he would ever cross the threshold. Dressed as he was in rough travellers' clothes, he would never be allowed inside. He promised himself he would return one day, dressed in finery, and take his place among the elite of Milan.

As he let himself be led away, a plain, hand-drawn banner tacked on a pillar flapped in the breeze and drew his eye. An advertisement for a new theatre.

OPENING SOON. CAST WANTED FOR OPERA BUFFA
AT THE TEATRO VENEZIA.

'Rémi!' Pascal snatched the playbill.

Opera buffa was the lighter, comic style of opera that Gianni loved. The Comédie-Italienne was once famous for it.

Today, on this day of wonders.

Teatro Venezia.

'It has to be.'

CHAPTER TWENTY-THREE

I should have guessed that Gianni would choose an abandoned monastery for the site of his new theatre. Beside the modest chapel—a squat church, plain-walled in brown brick with a single round window above the door—was a fanciful gothic cloister with pointed archways and decorative spires that I couldn't help but admire. It put me in mind of the flying buttresses of the Notre-Dame de Paris. The Monastero di San Benedetto surprised me with its beauty.

The three of us watched the comings and goings through the monastery gate. Workmen entered carrying planks of wood and we heard the ringing of hammers. I was certain we had found them. A stirring of excitement fluttered in my chest. This feeling lasted only a few breaths, though, to be replaced with stinging hatred as I remembered the Arlecchino, Il Dottore, Il Capitano and the others brutally attacking me. Out tumbled the memory of Gianni urinating on me and Colombina's spit.

Saskia surged ahead, but I pulled her back. It had been two weeks since Gianni and his players parted from us without conscience. I could not be sure what reception we would find.

'So do we simply walk inside?' Pascal asked.

Saskia made the decision for us. She shrugged off my hand and slipped through the iron gates.

I stalked across the cobbled street, chin lifted high, cloak pushed back over my shoulders. It amused me to imagine Gianni's face when he saw us, or Colombina's. They did not expect us to follow them to Milan.

The courtyard was overgrown with tufted grasses and an ancient olive tree straggled upwards. Pascal went to it, placing his hand on the gnarled old trunk as if to find a heartbeat. I knew he felt his senses stirring, that he felt this derelict place could have the magic.

Inside the darkened nave of the chapel it took a few moments for my eyes to adjust. The brick walls were blackened by candle smoke. The chapel opened out into a much larger space, with stonework arms that held a brick ceiling above us, and there, in the middle of the aisle, Saskia had leaped upon Cristo and wrapped her legs around the boy. They were cinched tight in an embrace, lips joined, spinning around and around and around.

I watched as the boy kissed every inch of her face, heard him beg for her forgiveness. I wondered if she understood his words. Would he admit that he had abandoned the search for her and thought only of his own future? This pretty child-man, caught in time between adult and boy, not quite one or the other.

Cristo spied us and called out, running to us, begging us to translate his words.

'I should never have left, I have been in torment—please tell her.'

Pascal admonished him. 'If you loved her you would not have abandoned her.'

'Please tell her I am sorry.' His young face was full of anguish.

'He admits he behaved like a faithless shit,' I said to Saskia.

'We searched for you,' Pascal growled. 'He should have stayed with us.'

She shook her head, tears in her eyes. 'It doesn't matter.'

She faced Cristo. 'I found *you*,' Saskia said in faltering Venetian. 'I love you. I forgive you.' Her hard voice. Those soft words. Their kiss.

I ducked my eyes away from their love. Had I been any less selfish at Cristo's age?

Pascal coughed, the sound ringing out. It broke the lovers apart. They grinned, sheepish and giddy. Did all lovers look so foolish? It made me think of Colombina. Where was she?

'Come see the others,' Cristo urged.

'Wait.' I touched Saskia's arm. 'Do you mean to stay?' I searched her face. Those round owl eyes looked back at me, solemn and haunted. We were about to lose her to this place, to Cristo, to Gianni and his troupe.

'I will be safe here,' she whispered.

I steeled myself for seeing Gianni once again and my heart flipped traitorously as I wondered if Colombina would be among the players. If she was, I need not speak with her, I would ignore her.

Saskia took Cristo's hand in hers and we followed them out of the church and across the courtyard. Ahead, two voices rose in argument. A man and a woman.

'I cannot have him do these things to you! I cannot let you say these words of subjugation. Choose another play, not this one.'

We turned a corner of the cloister and there they were. Gianni in the centre of the players. Our Gianni with his new family. It hurt to look at him.

'You misunderstand,' Colombina argued. 'These methods Petruchio uses to tame his wife can be a mirror to us. They show how some men treat their wives, to cow them, to break them.'

My heart floundered. Her beauty was captivating. Despite my best intentions, I could not take my eyes from her face. I watched them without a word. Intent on their argument, no one had noticed us.

Gianni spoke. 'People will think we mean to instruct them!'

'The audience are meant to feel discomfort, to wonder if this is a comedy they are laughing at. They should feel a prickle of truth nagging at their conscience.'

'You give the audience too much capacity for abstract thinking. You think they will understand if we say one thing and mean another? You forget I have been in this business for many years.'

'Some will wonder why not just beat the shrew and be done with it,' interjected Il Dottore. 'I would.'

Gone were the Renaissance velvets and Venetian masks; the players were dressed like the Milanese. Colombina and La Signora wore stiff, shining gowns buttoned to their necks. I could not see Colombina's husband, Luigi, among the group.

Colombina paced along the covered cloister, colour rising in her cheeks. 'We are to be a theatre for social change, are we not? Isn't that why we are here? We must expose cruelty and injustice when it exists.'

How could anyone resist those eyes, that face?

'Very well,' Gianni relented. 'For our premiere we perform *The Taming of the Shrew*.' Gianni clapped his hands. 'Bertoni's version in opera buffa.'

La Signora shrieked with all her considerable might. She had seen Saskia. Beside us, the lovers were once again tangled in one another's arms. La Signora rushed forward and swallowed both Cristo and Saskia in her voluminous embrace. The other players looked at us in silent shock. I could not meet Colombina's eye. Gianni regarded us evenly, no surprise on his face, no welcome. Worse than that, I saw, for a fleeting moment, disappointment.

Now was our moment to leave: we had found Saskia, we had returned her to her lost love. There was nothing keeping me here. But when I stepped forward and opened my mouth, I surprised even myself.

'I will play Petruchio.'

'You will not!' cried the Arlecchino, stepping forward, a multi-coloured cape pinned across his shoulder. He swung to Colombina. 'I was to be the lead in this play!'

'Shush—I promised you the lead and you shall have it,' Colombina said to him, her eyes bright as cut crystal. 'You will play Kate, the shrew.'

The Arlecchino was stunned to silence.

I fell back at this. 'You duped me!'

'What?' she mimed shock. 'You thought to play Petruchio so it could be *you* who tortures *me*? Is that what you presumed?' She walked towards me with exaggerated slowness, swinging her hips from side to side. 'You who would pretend to be my soulmate, declare love for me, marry me'—she had clasped her hands above her heart—'then, as soon as you take me into your house, twist my mind? You who would give me food and then take it from me, give me clothes then strip them from me, make me believe that the moon is the sun, make me agree with everything you say just to keep the peace?'

Colombina always could tie me into knots. I had imagined she would play the part of Kate, but not for the reasons she threw at me.

Il Dottore laughed. 'The witty shrew has you there!'

'There are to be no female actors in this play,' she continued. 'Cristo will play Kate's sister, Bianca, so that when the older men gather to bid for her among themselves'—she gestured to Il Dottore, Il Capitano and Gianni—'they will be bidding for a fellow man.' She was breathing hard. 'Do you see? I want to put a man in our shoes.'

Gianni threw up his arms. He thought it nonsense, but had no more will to fight her. Instead, he turned to me. 'One performance, I will give you that. You should go home.'

Again, Gianni took his knife to my heart.

As director of the Teatro Venezia, Colombina had taken the largest room in the monastery, the friar's office, for her bedroom. It was furnished with sumptuous rugs and tapestries, paintings from Venice and statuesque urns. This room would never have seen such luxury. It was late that night, long after we had been shown to beds of our own, before I gathered the courage to rap my knuckles on her door. I longed to know if we would resume our former intimacies. Colombina had my whole heart, my every waking thought, but I did not want her to know it.

'Who arranged all this?' I asked as I stalked about her room.

The friar's desk had been pushed against the wall and her bed now took centre stage. She leaned back among her ample pillows, watching me.

'Luigi prepared everything for us in advance.'

'Where is he, your husband?'

'My brother,' she replied.

I waved my hand, dismissed her words. 'Luigi, your brother. Why isn't he with us? I thought you had to come to Milan to be closer to him.'

'What does it matter? What is he to you?'

Evasive, my Colombina. Answering questions with questions.

I stood before one of her paintings and shivered. It was cold despite the warming of the season. I suspected this monastery was always cold, even in the height of summer. The painting towered gilt-framed above me and I felt buffeted by the power of it.

Colombina saw my regard of the picture. 'It is a copy of the original,' she said.

'You did this?'

She shrugged self-deprecatingly, but I could see she was proud of it.

'There is so much . . .' I struggled for the word. 'Rage.'

She nodded. 'Artemisia Gentileschi. Her paintings were her revenge. She was raped.'

I couldn't meet Colombina's eye. I studied the painting. Two women with fleshy arms held a man down on a bed. One gripped his hair and pushed his head back; she held a long sword against his neck. Blood trickled down the mattress. His eyes were wide and knowing. It terrified me.

'And this one?' I pointed to a portrait of a Venetian woman in fine clothes, jewels, a loose blue scarf around her neck and one nipple enticingly exposed.

'Veronica Franco, a courtesan and published poet. She lived and penned her works at the same time as Shakespeare.' Colombina's voice was quickening. 'Listen to this.' She pushed herself up to her knees, twisting the sheet up in one hand before her breasts, the other arm wide and gesturing like an orator. '*Although we may be delicate and soft, some men who are delicate are also strong; and others, coarse and harsh, are cowards. Women have not yet realised this, for if they should decide to do so, they would be able to fight you until death.*' She punctuated her quotation by thrusting an imagined knife into the mattress. Her performance was mesmerising. 'Veronica wrote that in 1580! To think that a woman from hundreds of years ago had the same conviction as I do today.'

Her dark eyes glinted, but as I watched, her shining face grew sad. She sank back against her pillows, deflated. 'It is both inspiring and disheartening.'

In this friar's room, she had surrounded herself with her heroes. And I realised this was not Gianni's theatre; it never had been. It was Colombina who was our puppetmaster, who pulled on our strings to make us dance.

An easel straddled one corner of the room. She was painting again here in Milan. I glanced about, wondering if she had saved my portrait from the flames. I flipped through a stack of boards and saw men in rich clothes and uniforms depicting their rank, but their faces were grotesque. She had painted their features in exaggeration, a mouth filled with horse's teeth or the nose of a pig. I saw a general with ears of a donkey. They would have made me laugh if I did not sense the danger in them. These were parodies. She was mocking the statesmen of Italy. And no man of power liked to see himself made ridiculous.

'Is this why you set your studio alight? To leave no trace of your activities?'

She sighed, sorrowful. 'Luigi thought it was quickest to erase our presence there. And I agreed. Yet I could not let my work burn away to nothing.'

'But the washerwoman living beneath? Such risk to her.'

Colombina looked horrified. 'We moved Sister Louisa first! She is the housekeeper now at our palazzo, taking care of it while we are gone.'

'A sister? From the convent?'

'She was kind to me when so few others were. When the convent was closed, I took her in. San Zaccaria was a prison to me, but it was her only home.'

'And you returned to Luigi.' I drew out his name with the usual distaste.

'Yes.' She challenged me with her arched brow. 'I became my brother's wife.'

I circled the room, trailing my hand through a rack of her gowns. 'What is your name, your true name?' I was tired of pretence; I wanted to know something real.

She laughed. 'Which one? There is the name I was given by my parents, the name the Church bestowed on me, the name I took to play my brother's wife and now this, the name I choose for myself: Colombina.'

I chewed on that. It still felt like she held something back, that she hid herself from me.

'Why are we here?' I pushed.

'Philosophy at this hour?' She smiled and patted the bedclothes. 'Because you wish to be my lover?'

'Not here in this room.' I drew my arm in a wide arc. 'Here in this monastery, this city. Why not stay in Venice, the city you profess to love? You have abandoned her!'

As I'd hoped, I riled her into speaking rashly.

'Not true! We have saved her. The Austrians who rule there will turn against Napoleon in a heartbeat; they need only to believe the other allies will turn with them. The Roman Catholic Church is now with us. Prussia will be next . . .'

She stopped her rush of speech and bit her lip, watching me, wary. Ah. So it was out between us. She did not trust me. A Frenchman.

'I have no love for our despotic Emperor. I have been running from his press-gangs half my life.'

She regarded me, struggling with her distrust. Finally, she made up her mind.

'We are here in Milan because Luigi works here to weaken Napoleon's Kingdom of Italy. Our theatre has a part to play in reminding the people of Lombardy that they don't need the Austrians or the French; they belong to much older traditions. We can be unified through our paintings, our food, our music, through the stories of who we are. We can be Italian.'

'Ha! You would abandon your hopes for the Republic of Venice, your dreams of restoring her to glory and autonomy?' I did not believe her. Venetians were arrogant; they thought themselves above all others.

'How would you know what we want?'

'I have travelled far and wide and visited many towns. Each one thinks it is better than its neighbour. I see no difference with nations. Each one wants to impose its way of life on the others.'

'The Kingdom of Naples, Rome, the Republic of Venice—all of us will one day be united. I am convinced of that. Napoleon's Empire will fall. We will make it happen. And when it does, we will not be ruled by the Austrians or the French. We want to govern ourselves, Rémi!'

She spoke with such certainty, yet I could not believe it would come to pass as she described. Napoleon was still Napoleon. He had lost battles before. This loss to Russia was crippling, but he would triumph in the end. The Empire would hold. Colombina risked her life for nothing.

But with her words I felt a curious fear begin to twist. The idea of a shift of power unsettled me. I did not like the thought that the Empire would fall. It was not a good feeling to know that about myself, that I might prefer Napoleon's domination because it gave me and my kind safety. Could I live beneath the will of another, subjugated? I would enjoy playing Petruchio to the Arlecchino, my every whim obeyed, to have him leap when I said to leap. Could I play the part of Kate? All my life I had lived in a world where Frenchmen were hated and feared, but never powerless.

It was then I caught sight of her painting of me, humiliated as a satyr, a man with horns and a goat's ears and legs, propped carelessly against the wall, unframed. I cannot say I took to the likeness. Was that how she saw me—as a bestial woodland spirit intent on seducing nymphs?

'What are you doing here, Rémi? Why come back to us?'

I was hurt she did not know that I had come because of her. I looked away. The women in Gentileschi's painting seemed to lunge out of the frame.

'I see I am not wanted.' I made to leave.

Colombina sat up in bed, letting the sheets fall from her breasts. They swayed as she moved and cleared my mind of all notions of departing. She took a tendril of her unbound hair and stroked her own nipple.

For a girl raised in a convent, she knew how to enflame.

Like a terrier, I went to her.

CHAPTER TWENTY-FOUR

*P*ascal looked about with an expression of bewilderment, assessing the poor state of the theatre in the monastery chapel. The pews had been pulled back into a semicircle, but there was no curtain, no sets, no orchestra pit. For that matter, no orchestra. How did Gianni imagine they could perform an opera buffa like the old days in Paris?

'Good, you brought your lute!' Il Capitano beamed at him, taking Pascal's hand in his to pull him up to the stage, the dark skin striking against Pascal's winter pallor.

'This is no Teatro alla Scala,' Pascal murmured.

Il Capitano laughed. 'Indeed not. But it could be. A deconsecrated church with some imagination . . .'

'And hard work,' said Il Dottore.

'And money,' La Signora added.

'And we conquer the world!' the Spaniard finished.

Pascal cast his gaze over them all, the Venetian players. He barely knew who they really were behind the caricatures. He was wary of them now, remembering how gleefully they had attacked Rémi and how easily they had abandoned the Frenchmen in Venice. Could he forgive them? He had hated them all while watching their viciousness on stage that night.

The players had welcomed Rémi and Pascal the night before and given them beds in the monks' quarters. They had eaten together at a long table in a dining hall. He had looked for Luigi but found no sign of him. He felt conflicted. It still shamed and disgusted him to think he had let himself be restrained by Luigi when he should have stopped what was happening to Rémi on the stage. Pascal had trembled at Luigi's touch—the long length of his thighs pressing against him, his hands circling Pascal's wrists. He had submitted to him with barely a pretence of fight and it mortified him. Luigi was tall, but not nearly as strong as Pascal; he should easily have overpowered the other man. Starved of physical affection, the shock of Luigi's body so close had paralysed him. He did not ever want to feel that helpless again.

Yet a part of him had hoped to find Luigi here, had expected to, and when he hadn't it left him hollow.

Gianni remained distant, standing at the back of the church as if to repel them with his coldness. He had made it clear he did not want them in his theatre, so what were they doing here, among these players? What was Rémi thinking, to want to play the lead in one of Gianni's productions when all he ever spoke about was the freedom of a life on the road?

Colombina climbed up on the stage beside Pascal and rested her head against his shoulder as if nothing had changed between them, as if she had not fled the *scuola* in Venice without a word of farewell to him. 'I'm sorry,' she whispered. Then, like a butterfly, she whirled away, clapping her hands the way Gianni did to draw the players around her. She was as bright and colourful and mesmerising as ever.

Pascal watched Rémi gravitate to her, his eyes never leaving her face. The two circled one another as though they were not even aware of the other players. He ached to see the tenderness between them, but he finally accepted that he had lost Rémi to another.

As the days passed, Pascal graciously accepted this new turn of their fates. He was weary of an exile's life and grateful for a safe place to sleep and food to fill his belly. He set to work without complaint, adapting the costumes of the commedia dell'arte to this new production and claiming part of the monks' dining hall for his workshop. For Gianni, Pascal took inspiration from Pantalone's red merchant costume and made a fine red waistcoat. He tailored neat satin pockets and stitched gold buttons into place. He invited Gianni to try it on for size, and he hovered nearby, hoping for approval. Gianni donned the waistcoat in silence. Pascal found his coldness heartbreaking. He rationalised that Gianni showed antipathy towards them to force them to go home thinking they would be safer in Paris. But what was there for Pascal in Paris now? The theatre was gone. His home had been with Gianni and it hurt to think that Gianni did not feel the same. Pascal stole glances in the mirror, studying the older man's familiar face. In his expression, Pascal found no answers. Finally, without meeting his eye, Gianni nodded to Pascal that it was good.

The Teatro Venezia slowly took shape over the weeks leading up to opening night. Money was found and workers came, erecting scaffolding and building theatre sets. The play was set in Padua and

Verona, both towns Pascal and Rémi had lately travelled through. Pascal helped Colombina to paint the village streets on great sheets of canvas, old sails that he had stitched together.

'What do you think?' she asked, standing back and chewing on the end of her paintbrush. She had sketched out the street to give the illusion of depth, expertly extending the small stage. It looked convincing enough to walk along.

'It will pass,' he said.

Pascal doubted Colombina's choice of play would be understood as she intended, but grudgingly he admitted it felt good to be building something from nothing. They were giving new life to this monastery that had been home to Benedictine monks for centuries. Little by little, they were creating their own home.

In rehearsal, Colombina was fearless.

'You must believe you are worthless now,' Colombina directed the Arlecchino.

His face revealed his struggle. He glowered at Rémi. Hatred simmered between the two men, and Pascal feared it would soon erupt. She was asking the Arlecchino to submit to Rémi's will.

'Here . . .' Colombina pointed to the line on her script. 'When Kate tells the other wives to be the hand beneath their husband's foot, we see she has been brought so low as to believe it herself. She has been squashed beneath her husband's boot!'

'Can we not have her speak with irony? Can she not retain her spirit?'

'No! We must see the cruelty of it. We must see her broken and believing her inferiority.'

She wanted the audience to think of themselves in Kate's place. To see a man in Kate's clothes. Pascal understood. There would be no make-up, no softening of the Arlecchino's jaw; he would retain his clipped beard. Pascal watched that jaw clench. To admit inferiority to another man, to Rémi of all men, was tearing at the Arlecchino's pride, at his very self.

'I cannot do it.' He ripped at the dress, bursting the seams, until it fell away in pieces.

'Hey!' Pascal cried out in frustration.

'You must act!' Colombina caught the Arlecchino's arm, pulled him back to face her. 'You must act as though your survival depends on it.' She shook him. 'Act the part until you forget who you were before.'

The Arlecchino hung his head, breathing hard.

'You wanted the lead. Now play it.' She spun away from him, stamped her staff on the stage. 'Again!'

Pascal saw the workers on the scaffolding had paused to watch. They stared at her. Colombina did not speak like a woman. She spoke like a man accustomed to being obeyed. Pascal saw knowing looks pass between the men. They would not allow themselves to be ordered about like that, their faces said. By a shrew.

Pascal began to worry for Colombina. He did not think the Milanese public would understand her intent; and if they did, he worried even more that they would not take kindly to it.

As the opening drew closer, tensions in the Teatro Venezia grew greater. Shouts were exchanged, curses spat, tools dropped from heights. When the workmen finished, everyone was relieved. A circular stage had been built before the altar with a ring of scaffolding all around to hang the scenery canvases behind the stage and drape curtains across the front. Tiers of seating had been constructed on wooden frames. The boards were bare of ornamentation. This was no Teatro alla Scala. Pascal feared that no one would come to the premiere performance of the Teatro Venezia.

It was not only this fear that disturbed him. Weeks had passed since their arrival with the players and there had been no sign of Colombina's brother. It had set up a terrible agitation in his heart, this wondering when Luigi might appear. If he lived here in Milan, then why had he not visited the theatre? His dreams were tormented by the tall, black spectre of Luigi in his cape and *bauta* disguise. The hard white mask loomed above him as he lay on his pallet mattress; he felt smothered by the man's body, unable to push him away. He had woken tangled in his sheets and with a full erection that demanded attention.

Pascal wondered if he imagined the frisson between them. What experience did Pascal truly have of love, or lust? One foolish, drunken night with a farmer up against his barn, where the man took Pascal's cock in his mouth. Pascal burned red at the memory. He had gasped at the wet heat of it, amazed at how delicious the motion felt, drawn up to the points of his toes as the pleasure climbed and the release came fast and powerful.

The farmer quickly dropped his own trousers and pulled Pascal to his knees, prodding his fingers into the back of his head. Pascal opened his mouth, felt the man's cock press against the back of his throat and almost gagged. His face was pushed repeatedly into a scratching curl of hairs. The man groaned and pushed his hips out from the wall. The hot, spurting fluid came as a shock, filling his mouth with the taste of soap. Pascal spat.

The man struck Pascal hard across the face.

Trembling on his knees, hose stripped down to his ankles, Pascal looked up at the farmer and saw shame and anger. He saw that he was to be blamed for this man's urge to be with men.

The farmer turned away in disgust, buttoning his trousers. 'Get away from here.'

An eighteen-year-old boy with no experience of sex and reeling from the transaction—both the pleasure and the price taken for it . . . Pascal cowered, ashamed and guilty. He felt as though he had betrayed Rémi. It was ridiculous—Rémi was even now being seduced by the farmer's wife inside the house—but he felt unfaithful. He had cheapened the nature of his love for Rémi by giving in to this lustful act.

Rémi would not agree with such an idea, he knew. Rémi would tell him to seek his pleasures when and where he could. Pascal never spoke of that night. His face burned even now with the confusion of that moment. He felt as though his own body had betrayed him.

When he thought of Luigi, he felt the same dangerous confusion.

He needed to see Luigi again to know what these feelings meant. Pascal had spent so much of his life agonised by unrequited love, perhaps it had become habit and he had simply transferred his lust to another unattainable object of desire. Surely, Luigi would come to their premiere? He would seek him out, Pascal decided, he had to know if there was ever hope of love for him.

On opening night, Pascal watched the audience arrive and find their seats. He was anxious for Colombina, hoping the crowd would appreciate her retelling of *The Taming of the Shrew*. An audience made to feel foolish could soon turn upon the players. But that was not the only reason for his nerves. He stood at the back of the theatre searching the faces of the crowd for Luigi. The middle-class merchants, clerks and craftsmen had all trotted out in their best clothes, folk intent on looking wealthy, but none of the elites of the city. The Teatro Venezia had not proved itself yet. To his dismay, he couldn't see Luigi among the theatregoers.

The audience settled and the lanterns around the church were extinguished one by one. Pascal had been certain Luigi would come and now he felt heavy with disappointment. He gradually lost his view of the audience to the darkness until just the stage was lit for the first performance of the Teatro Venezia . . .

The performance concluded with a smattering of polite applause.

Pascal listened to the confusion among the departing crowd.

'Where were the actresses?'

'Could've at least given him a shave!'

Laughter from those nearby who overheard.

From a woman: 'What was the point of it when we have so many pretty actresses? This is Milan in 1813, not England in the Middle Ages!'

And her husband: 'Should've just beaten her and be done with it!'

More laughter. The audience left bemused, but not angered.

Pascal watched each person pass him by until the chapel was empty and the sounds of their footsteps had faded away, and he knew with absolute certainty that Luigi had not come.

Gianni brought the company together on the stage. Every face looked glum and no one met Colombina's eye.

'I made a mistake,' Colombina admitted hotly. 'I should have had the male parts played by women. To show men how it would feel to have women decide their fates and control their tongues.'

Gianni shook his head. 'You ask too much.'

Colombina raged. 'Must we wait five hundred years for men to see their actions and be appalled by them? *My tongue will tell the anger of my heart, or else my heart concealing it will break,*' she spat, quoting Kate from the play.

Gianni put out his hand to pacify her. Pascal wondered if Colombina would slap it away. 'You remind me of someone I knew years ago, in Paris. A playwright, and a very brave woman. Olympe de Gouges. No one wanted to put on her plays. I was the only one.' Gianni's face was saddened by his memories. 'She died for her convictions.'

'Some convictions are worth dying for.'

Gianni frowned at her. 'You are young. You don't know of what you speak. War and revolution are not games.'

Colombina reddened. She turned back to Pascal and the other players, taking command. 'Then let us perform a tragedy. *Giulietta e Romeo*. The original Italian version, Luigi da Porto's story—no more Shakespeare.' She looked straight at Saskia. 'For our lovers.'

CHAPTER TWENTY-FIVE

Saskia worried that her voice would not be good enough. She worried that she would not be able to learn the lines. When Gianni brought her the script she had nearly burst into tears. How could she admit she could not read?

Cristo saw her distress. 'What's wrong?'

She shook her head, too proud to admit her weakness. She waved away his concern. She would find someone to teach her.

'You cannot read,' he said, understanding. He did not laugh or mock and she was grateful. 'I will help you. We will learn these lines together.'

She kissed his mouth. 'Thank you.'

Saskia agreed to perform because Cristo asked it of her.

'We are the Innamorati,' he said, as though that made them invincible.

Cristo spent each day teaching her. He pointed to a line of script and spoke slowly. *'Sei piu bello di un angelo.' You are more beautiful than an angel.* She kissed him again, her lips lingering on his. As she repeated these words of love she was memorising, she could understand more and more of the language. She followed his finger on the text. It was a thrill to see each word formed on the page and know that she could unlock the key to decipher it. These lines she could memorise. Cristo and his smile made her believe that anything was possible.

When Gianni spoke of the woman playwright in Paris, it had come as a revelation to her that new tales could be written; that they were not just told and repeated or collected like the Brothers Grimm had done. That someone might invent a story and commit it to paper was something she had not considered, even though it stood to reason that a tale must be born somewhere. That a woman might create a story worthy of repeating seemed shocking. And what if that someone might one day be her?

Il Capitano helped her learn to write. He taught her the alphabet, the coded symbols she would need to build her own worlds out of words. He had been a scholar once, he explained, back in Spain. His father had wanted him to go to university in Seville, but he had run away with a theatre troupe instead. 'We travelled to London, Paris, Venice. I learned pieces of many languages.' But the theatre troupe had folded and left him destitute.

'You don't want to go home?' Saskia asked him, as she formed a row of letters with full bellies and sloping backs.

'I owe Gianni my loyalty. He took me in. I will follow wherever he decides.'

She nodded, understanding how the gift of shelter and safety in this dangerous world could make you both grateful and beholden.

*

On a rare day of freedom, Saskia and Cristo explored the city together. She showed him the marvellous edifice of the grand cathedral, and he showed her the stray kittens around the walls of the Castello Sforzesco. When it rained, they dashed inside the Pinacoteca di Brera among a gaggle of scholars, finding refuge in the library stacks. The books were lined up on shelves so high that ladders were needed to reach those at the top. Saskia tilted her head back. For hundreds of years this knowledge had been gathered, generation after generation. She remembered the bookshop in Marburg, how she had been awed by the towers of books, awed by how much there was to learn. She remembered how she had turned the pages of that book by the Brothers Grimm and been struck by the desire to read.

An ornate winding staircase in the far corner of the room took them to the upper levels. She noticed the gaping holes where books had been pulled from the shelves, like gold teeth extracted from an unwilling mouth. 'Napoleon claimed these volumes for France,' Cristo explained. 'Original codices by Leonardo da Vinci and works by all our great thinkers.' In the galleries, she saw the shadow marks on the walls where large paintings had kept the distemper from fading for centuries. The Milanese did not try to hide the loss; they left evidence of the theft visible for all to comprehend.

They were discovered by a strident librarian and chased out from the galleries for not being scholars. Hand in hand they ran, laughing, into the streets. Outside, Saskia flung herself at Cristo, twining her arms around him and holding tight. She loved that she had Cristo with her constantly. She loved that when he crept out from his own monk's cell each night and into hers, that she had him all to herself where they giggled together beneath the scratchy wool covers. From the first, theirs had been a language of touch. She adored the feel of his naked skin against hers. In the mornings, Gianni frowned at them, but said nothing.

La Signora had taken her aside, pressing a sheath of pig intestine into her hand. 'For Cristo,' she said demonstrating its use. Saskia felt her face flame red. La Signora wagged her finger and pointed to Saskia's stomach. *No baby.*

Saskia felt a clutch of fear in her gut to think of it. What would she do with a child?

La Signora had smiled and kissed her fondly, pulling her to her ample bosom. 'Inamorata,' she murmured into the crown of Saskia's head.

The lovers meandered through the streets of Milan, holding hands, pretending to be betrothed. It was nice to imagine that they were destined to be joined together. Saskia wore one of Colombina's old dresses that Pascal had adjusted to fit her. She felt like a young woman who could soon be married. Whose parents might have made a match for her.

'Where are your family?' Saskia asked Cristo.

'I have none.'

'You must,' Saskia said, laughing, before realising he was serious.

'My mother left me,' he tried to explain, miming a baby handed away in his outstretched arms.

'Mine too,' she said, struggling to find the words. 'My father killed her.'

It shocked her to say it aloud.

Cristo stopped walking. He turned her to face him. 'That priest?' His brow was creased with concern. 'He killed your mother?' When she nodded he gripped her arms hard. 'Will he come for you again?'

She shrugged. 'I do not know.'

Saskia didn't want to think about Father. About how he had tracked her down once before and might easily do so again.

'And your father?' she asked him.

He swiped his hands together as though dusting flour from them.

She looped her arm through his. 'We have each other now.'

CHAPTER TWENTY-SIX

I held Colombina to my chest while we lay in her bed. She was soft and warm and the tendrils of her hair tickled my armpit, but it was a rare thing to have her relaxed in my arms and I did not want the moment to end.

'What was it like, to be the orphan whose mother came back?' she asked.

I sighed. She was going to ruin this time together with her questions about my mother. With the arrangements for *Giulietta e Romeo* taking her attention we had precious little time alone. I was surplus to everyone's requirements, needed only for practising swordplay as some nameless thug. Through boredom, I was forced to watch the young lovers in their rehearsals. Some days it hurt my eyes to look upon their happiness. Today had been one of those.

Now, Colombina forced me to remember my mother. How I'd learned to run to her when I needed consoling. How I had been pleased to have a mother to watch out for me, something none of the other children of Gianni's theatre had. The truth was I had always felt special because she came back. It had made me superior and perhaps a little too cocksure, I could admit that.

'It made me who I am, I suppose.'

'What was she like?' Colombina asked.

I cast my mind back to those times and recalled that she was different from the thespians. 'Quiet. Contained. Never one to join the group.' I remembered she had liked it best when it was just her and me, the two of us watching rehearsals, or when we went to bed each night and I nestled in the crook of her arm and she sang to me. It occurred to me now that she had never truly felt at home in the theatre; she was an outsider and she had only stayed because of me.

'Why did she leave you at the theatre with Gianni?'

'I don't know.'

'You never asked her?'

Colombina flung her arm across my chest and entwined her legs with mine. I suddenly felt invaded by her closeness, by her questions.

'I don't want to talk about my mother.' I had been a self-centred boy with little interest in my mother's life, but then my mother was someone who could deceive her own child. I was determined not to feel guilt. 'She betrayed me.'

'My mother betrayed me too. She gave me to the nuns and she never came back for me. I was only eleven. I never saw my mother again.

'For years I cursed my parents with calamity and disease. I was expected to pray for them, to ease their passage in the afterlife, but I refused. I prayed for my parents to die in vats of burning oil or to drown in the canal. They perished because I wished them dead and that is the great guilt that I must bear.'

I was a little shocked by her confession. 'What happened to them?'

'A contagion. It took the entire household. Luigi had been sent away to school in Bologna and when he returned to claim his inheritance, every servant had died or fled. Then Luigi conceived a plan to rescue me. He pretended he had married and that his wife would soon join him. In our home, there was no one left who might recognise me. I was fortunate that Luigi came for me and gave me back my own home, as his wife.'

Luigi the saviour. It still troubled me that Luigi meant so much to her and yet we had rarely seen him. In Milan, our patron remained as mysterious as ever.

'Now, I wish I could ask my mother why she did this, why she put me in a prison when I was just a child. My parents could visit me and speak to me through a grille from the parlour, but my mother never came. My father brought me sugared almonds, as if the sweets would assuage his conscience, until eventually he too ceased to visit. She never came. I hated my mother for that. She would've left me there forever to pray for her soul and never laid eyes on me again. I was fifteen when I was freed from their tyranny and my nun's hell.'

She sat upright. Until then, she had related her history with little emotion, but her eyes were shining now. 'I want to confront my mother, to ask her how she could have forsaken me. If my mother was alive, I would find her and demand to know.' She pushed her finger into my chest. 'Your mother lives, you could find her—don't you want to ask her why she left you?'

'I am not interested in her reasons.'

'That's a lie,' she said accusingly. 'Why else have you followed Gianni here?'

For you. I came here for you, I wanted to say. But she was right, it wasn't only that. Gianni had my story and it was time I took it from him.

I found Gianni alone in the chapel extinguishing the candle flames, his back turned to me. I hovered, uncertain, among the pews. Gianni dropped his head almost as if he were praying.

Colombina had prodded me towards this confrontation. She had made me wonder about my mother and why she had left me at the theatre. Where had she gone? Why, years later, did she return for me? I had never asked. Colombina had been angry that I could demand of my mother something she could never receive from her own. Answers.

Emboldened, I went to Gianni.

'I am too old for fairytales,' I said, baring the mark on my arm that he had once told me was from the kiss of a sea sprite. 'I want to know the truth.'

He stared at me for a long time, then he sighed. 'What do you want to know?'

I wanted to know why my mother left me with Gianni at the Comédie-Italienne. Why she couldn't stay. I held up the mark on my wrist. 'What does this mean?'

'Don't judge your mother harshly, Rémi. She did what all pregnant, unwed women do. She meant to leave you with the Church, and she marked you so that she would find you again.'

I reeled. 'What do you mean she left me at a church? You told me she gave me to you.'

Even as I said it, I knew it couldn't be true. I remembered. My mother had not known Gianni when she arrived that day, a wild woman on the storm. She had accused him of stealing her child.

Gianni's face went pale. 'Forgive me, Rémi, I thought it for the best. To give you a gentler story.'

I wasn't the chosen one. I wasn't the beloved child left in Gianni's care until my loving mother returned. I was no better than a whore's brat, unwanted and discarded on the steps of a church. I pictured the *ruota* in the convent wall in Venice. I was a child conveniently disposed of. Everything I believed about myself had been a lie. I wasn't the golden child; I was never destined for great things.

'She abandoned me.' I rubbed at the mark on my wrist as if I could erase it. Few babies survived being left as foundlings. In Paris, the *enfants trouvés* were tainted from birth with the slur of their mother's debauchery. No one cared what happened to them, hidden away in the Maison de la Couche, where they were suckled on rags soaked with goat's milk or wine and slept five or more to a bed. Plenty of wet nurses kept taking payments from the Church for babies already dead. She had condemned me to a miserable life and, most likely, an early death.

I didn't know whether to hate her more for burying me away in that cellar or for the knowledge that she had never wanted me at all.

'Many women had no choice. Have you not seen enough of the world to know that? What else was she to do? Sell you to a beggar or a juggler? Sell you to a fiend who needed an innocent child's blood for witchcraft? You were lucky that you came to us.'

I flinched from him. If I was a baby dumped at a church door among thousands of others, how did I come to be in Gianni's theatre?

'What happened to me?' My voice was hoarse.

He gestured for me to sit and he took my hand in his. I felt like a child again, with all the rage and hurt of a boy, needing to be soothed.

'Do you remember me speaking of a woman playwright who staged her plays with us when no one else would do so?'

I shrugged, impatient.

'Colombina reminds me of her. Olympe de Gouges was memorable the moment she walked into a room. She glowed. All eyes were drawn to her, but she could be frightening with all that intensity, all that passion. She wanted to put on plays that would change the world. The establishment thought her mad, or dangerous. Time and time again the Comédie-Française rejected her plays. They ignored her and it infuriated her.'

I could imagine that a woman like Colombina would be fearsome if she had no outlet to express herself. But I wondered what this woman had to do with me. I tapped my foot.

'She wrote so many plays she formed her own company. Her lover, Jacques Biétrix de Rozières, financed her. He provided her with a home, allowed her freedom to write. A patron of sorts. But then one day she sold us everything—her sets, costumes, even some of her players—and she never wrote a single play again.'

'Why?'

'From then on, all was politics.'

'What does this woman have to do with me?'

'She cared for you as a baby.'

I closed my eyes. All my life I had had this recurring memory. I was being lifted from the floor, held tightly to a warm soft chest. Fear was making me gulp back sobs and a woman was rocking me, soothing me. I had thought she was my mother.

'She raised you until the night she was arrested.'

'Arrested? What happened to her?'

'War and revolution. Neither are kind to women who dare to speak. Only the mice survive.' His eyes grew distant, fixed on the floor. 'They accosted her in the street while she campaigned against all that was unjust in this world, then imprisoned her. She was executed. Beheaded.'

I winced at his words.

'I think I remember her,' I murmured.

Gianni nodded. 'The man, Biétrix de Rozières, brought you to the theatre. You were two years old. The household staff had deserted and the home was requisitioned by Robespierre's men. He didn't know what else to do with you.'

'Why did this woman have me if my mother meant to leave me with the Church?' My mother had meant to leave me in a box. I thought of the oiled children of the Pietà shoved through slots to lie alone and crying in the dark. My mother had run away, but this Olympe de Gouges had kept me. 'Why did she go away to sea? Why did it take her so long to come back for me?'

He shrugged. 'Those are questions for your mother. Why not go to Paris and ask her?'

Not this again. I was happy here. I was in love with Colombina. Why would I leave?

We both fell silent, retreating to our respective corners.

'Find your mother, Rémi. Let her explain it to you. It is dangerous for you here.'

'Why are you so eager to be rid of us?' I couldn't disguise the hurt in my voice.

'You must see what is happening. When the French Empire falls, there will be anger, hatred—the innocent will suffer! I have seen this all before, Rémi, please believe me.' Gianni gripped the sides of my face. 'I had to leave Paris during the Revolution. I know what it is like to be a hated foreigner. They will hunt you out like ferrets after rabbits. It is safest for you to be in France!'

I wanted to believe that he meant to send me away for my own good. To believe he still cared for Pascal and me. Gianni was the only father we had. But his words were like hands pushed against my chest, shoving me away.

CHAPTER TWENTY-SEVEN

*T*he spring turned quickly into the heatwaves of summer and the sun bleached the colours from the city with its glare. Pascal hid inside the cool dining hall that had become his costumerie. *Giulietta e Romeo* was to be a much grander affair than *The Taming of the Shrew*, which meant weeks of preparation. More players joined the troupe. The families of Montecchi and Cappelletti all needed to be dressed in matching tribal colours and Pascal found girls and boys with an aptitude for the needle to assist him. An orchestra joined the company to perform the score composed by Zingarelli. Colombina adapted the libretto. This opera had first been performed in Milan at the Teatro alla Scala and Gianni was nervous.

'We want them to love us. We want them to be proud of our Italian theatre.'

Pascal understood that Gianni did not need to keep his theatre secret here. This form of theatre was acceptable, the subjects safe, the story predictable. It had none of the danger of the improvised satires of the commedia dell'arte. They did not have to fear the authorities of this city. But if the Teatro Venezia were to survive, their performance had to be sensational. They had to win hearts.

Gianni remained distant, but he voiced no objection to their continued presence in his company, and Pascal was pleased he had not forced them out. Where else would he go? He had companionship here, he had industry. His yearning for Paris was lessening with each passing day.

Pascal unrolled the bolt of pale blue silk across the tabletop. For Saskia—their Giulietta—he needed to conjure another dress. He tried not to dwell on what had happened the last time he made a dress for her. He chose the same colours, needing to make this for himself as much as her to overcome this superstitious fear that he would lose her again.

'*Ciao*, Pascal.'

When he heard his name spoken in that musical voice, Pascal swung about, knocking a roll of fabric against a line of jars and sending pearl buttons and silver pins dashing across the stone floor.

Luigi stood there, a smile on his lips.

Pascal dropped to his knees, sweeping at the beads and pins, swearing as they pricked his flesh. Fumbling fool, he cursed himself.

Luigi deftly reached for a broom, corralling the errant buttons.

Pascal picked himself up from the floor sucking the blood from his thumb. His feelings were tangled. Desire or disgust. He took the broom from Luigi to still his shaking hands.

'It has been some time since we last met. I hope you remember me.'

'Of course—you are Colombina's husband. How could I forget.'

'I am her brother.'

'I had thought we might see you here before now.'

'My apologies. You are right, I should have come. I should have welcomed you.'

'No need.' Pascal turned to hide his flushed face and put the broom safely aside.

'I hope we will be friends.'

They were innocent words but they set Pascal's heart flailing. He risked a glimpse at Luigi. What did he mean?

'I am concerned we did not part on the best of terms.' Luigi stepped closer to him and Pascal could smell the exotic spice of his scent. He backed away.

'As you can see, I have many tasks I must attend to,' Pascal said crisply.

'Of course, I will not detain you from them. Perhaps this evening we might share a glass of wine at dinner? I bring important news.'

'Perhaps,' Pascal murmured.

Luigi bent and scooped up the pearl buttons from the floor. He held them out to Pascal, pressing them into his cupped hands. Pascal felt the warmth of his hand, the soft pads of his fingers touching his skin. It caught his breath. Luigi smiled his dazzling smile and Pascal's stomach somersaulted. Then Luigi bowed and took his leave.

Pascal sank into the nearest chair, thinking of Rémi. Could the heart transfer its love to another so easily?

Luigi was coming for dinner. That thought spurred Pascal to action. He draped a long table in the dining hall in a cloth of shining pewter fabric. Raiding Colombina's packing crates, he found amethyst-hued glass goblets and napkins of golden damask to set at each place. He found silver candlesticks of different sizes and styles. The plates he placed before each chair were varied: Chinese porcelain, Dutch delft, English blue willow or Spanish majolica. Colombina must have collected them from travellers, Pascal presumed, just like she had collected this mottled company of friends.

'To us all!' Gianni made the toast as the troupe sat down to eat. Glasses were clinked, eyes met and laughter shared. 'And greetings to our patron.' Gianni stood at one end, smiling delightedly, while Luigi was seated beside Colombina at the other end of the table. Pascal found the sight of him magnetic.

Luigi got to his feet, raised his glass. 'To the Teatro Venezia—to your success!'

The assembly drummed their feet on the floor, hammered fists against the table, and the plates jumped and clattered as the crescendo rose. 'Huzzah!'

Dishes of minestrone, veal cutlets and hearty ossobuco were brought out by the cooks that now ran the kitchen, set down and admired. Beside Pascal, Rémi arm-wrestled with the children whom Gianni had adopted into their number. The Teatro Venezia was becoming like the Comédie-Italienne in Paris, he realised: a sanctuary.

Pascal's hand trembled as he lifted his glass to his lips and stole a glance at Luigi. All through dinner Pascal wondered if Luigi would approach him. The fluttering in his stomach almost put him off his food. Once, Luigi looked up and met Pascal's gaze directly, catching him staring. The shock of it was like a collision. Pascal's eyes leaped away.

La Signora got up from her seat and insinuated herself close to Luigi, commandeering his attention. Pascal was torn. Perhaps he had interpreted Luigi's intentions wrongly; Luigi did not mean to single Pascal out from all the others, he meant he was wanting to share food and wine with them all. Pascal felt stupid. He was about to make an excuse to leave, when he heard Luigi's chair scrape back on the flagstones.

Luigi rose to his feet once more. 'My friends, I bring news. Prussia has turned against Napoleon. The alliance is broken!'

Around the table, everyone cheered. Pascal exchanged an uneasy glance with Rémi, who took a deep slug of crimson nebbiolo from a discarded goblet.

Luigi explained that Prussian armies now fought with the Russians against Napoleon.

How should he feel about this news? For the past five years they had travelled freely through the Prussian provinces that were allied to France. The people had been willing to hear their stories and their songs, hadn't they? They had parted with hard-earned coin, had laughed and shared their bread. Or had they merely played along to keep the peace? He did not know what to think. Would Napoleon fight to regain his territory? Would the peaceful villages they had visited become battlegrounds, blown apart by cannon fire because a battle for governance was played out in blood and smoke and splintered homes?

Rémi looked equally troubled by the news.

Pascal saw faces shining with hope that the Emperor would fall, that the Kingdom of Italy would one day be ruled by their own people. Pascal wondered how much blood was yet to spill. Once again, he felt his otherness keenly. The company ate and drank with gusto, picking and sucking at the remains of bone shanks, voices loud. Only Gianni looked grave. Pascal stood up from the table, resisting a final glance at Luigi, and left the company to their celebration.

*

Late that night, Pascal woke to the sound of his door creaking open. He lay on his pallet of straw and listened, heart thudding. He had no need to ask who had entered his spartan monk's cell. Pascal pushed himself up against the brick wall and waited for Luigi to speak.

'I was sorry to see you leave tonight.'

Pascal said nothing. What did Luigi mean by coming to him like this? He saw movement and heard the groan of a chair as Luigi sat.

'Have you seen what one hundred thousand pairs of shoes looks like?'

Pascal frowned into the darkness, confused.

'No,' Luigi continued. 'I imagine not. But I have seen warehouses full of shoes. As you know, when the French first came to Lombardy with their conquering army in 1796, they pushed the Austrians out and made us pay for our liberation. They took money—many millions of livres—and our priceless works of art, the words of our most famous thinkers. I am sure you have heard about this. But they also took our food, our clothes, our horses and our oxen. They took the barley and oats from our fields, and the shirts from our bodies.

'Not only here. It was the same in all the conquered dominions. From the provinces of Prussia, the duchy of Parma or the Republic of Venice. One hundred thousand pairs of shoes from Bavaria. From the Netherlands, one hundred and fifty thousand pairs of shoes and the same amount of coarse linen trousers. They took fine stocking breeches, spatterdashes and bales of silk as well as farmers' coats and hats. It was deliberate. They left us shivering, naked and exposed. When we were poor and broken, when we had nothing left, we had no choice but to accept protection. It was how each alliance was forged—by taking so much from us we had no other choice.'

Pascal listened to Luigi's words, shocked that he had not fully understood the consequences of invasion. He thought of the shrew in Colombina's play and the methods Petruchio used to tame her, taking her food, her clothes, to make her doubt who she was and what she believed. These methods of domination were not dissimilar.

'I know these things because it is my job to draw up the lists of requisitions. Crops to feed Napoleon's troops, an abbey for a hospital, money, clothes, shoes. I record it all.'

Pascal listened in silence.

'And it is also my job to keep taking, to keep making little slices into flesh, like a physician with his bloodletting knife, to bleed a little here and there. When Napoleon needs more for his Empire—more men, more food, more horses—it is my job to bleed the limbs.'

Luigi paused and Pascal could hear his breathing.

'Twenty-seven thousand Italian men went to war in Russia for Napoleon. I helped to send them.' His voice broke. 'Less than two thousand survive. We tell no one this. How can we tell their mothers? We keep this secret, but there will be a time of reckoning, Pascal. For sixteen years we have carried this leech upon our backs. I want you to understand, there must be a day of retribution.'

'Why are you telling me this?' Pascal's voice was hoarse.

'I don't want you to be hurt, Pascal.'

Why should Luigi care for him? He detested the French. It was clear he was a spy, a man well placed in the Milanese government—an aide of the Viceroy of Italy, Eugène de Beauharnais, perhaps; someone who heard news of the Emperor's defeats when few others were privy to them. Luigi worked against the French Empire to bring Napoleon down.

Pascal heard Luigi stand and cross the room towards him. He felt the weight of a figure settle down on his bed. He turned his head, breath quickening.

Luigi bent close to him and brushed his lips against Pascal's ear setting the nerves of his neck alight. He whispered three words that made his heart thrum.

'I missed you.'

CHAPTER TWENTY-EIGHT

Saskia and Cristo lingered in bed together on the morning of the premiere of *Giulietta e Romeo* long after the others would be at the breakfast table. She wanted to hold him like this forever, her head resting on his chest. It was one of her greatest pleasures to have his naked skin touching hers.

'Let's stay here,' she said, rolling on top of him and kissing his neck, his ear, his jaw.

'All day?' he asked, laughing.

'For evermore!'

'You forget our adoring public. How can we disappoint them? The season is about to begin.'

She ducked her eyes from his. A sliding, sickening sensation disturbed her stomach, like the rocking of a boat, whenever she thought of having to perform.

'Do you really think I can do this?' she whispered.

Saskia rubbed her throat. It hurt to speak let alone to sing.

In rehearsals, La Signora had practised with her over and over. 'Try again,' La Signora had called up to her, her face alight with hope that this time Saskia would find all the right words and all the right notes. Already Colombina had amended the play for her; she only had one song to make perfect. Saskia stood on her balcony. Her shoulders were tight, her chest stiff. She made herself relax. She breathed deep as Cristo had taught her when they had practised for hours standing facing one another, breathing in unison, chests rising towards each other. She relaxed her throat, tilted her head from side to side and front to back. The sooner she mastered this song, the sooner she could climb down from this scaffold and be with him. The music of Pascal's lute floated up to her. She smiled and smoothed her hands down the dress he had made for her. The pale blue silk was light and supple with no heavy panniers to drag her down. The bodice was shot through with more seams of silver braid, stiffened with quilting, yet flexible. It let her sing. It let her move.

Far below her, La Signora sang the note again, eyebrows raised, chin lifted, her shoulders bobbing ever higher, as if by demonstration alone she could force the wind into Saskia's diaphragm and push it out through her vocal cords.

Saskia tilted her head to look up into the plain brick cupola of the monastery chapel. Here there were no paintings of angels floating into the clouds, none of the gilded ornamentation of the churches Cristo had showed her in this city. There was only the plain simplicity of bricks knitted closely to one another. Impulsively, she climbed up on the rail of the scaffold. She heard the panicked cries from below and did not look down. She was a circus performer; she had balanced on heights far greater than this. She closed her eyes and spread out her arms.

She remembered standing on the edge of a cliff, with the wind buffeting her clothes and lifting her hair. She heard the cry of the falcons on their migrations, remembering how she had stood with her mother on that windswept coast, frightened and exhilarated. She wanted to do this for her mother who had meant to fly far away from that place and give her daughter a new life. She wanted to do this for Cristo. For Pascal. For all of them. She wanted to make everyone proud. Saskia had opened her eyes and sang.

'I think you will be magnificent,' Cristo said now, his voice full of confidence. 'We will be triumphant. This is only the beginning.'

Saskia nestled even closer to him. He believed she could sing.

Cristo spoke excitedly. 'One day we will perform in all the great theatres of the world. Teatro alla Scala, the Palais-Royale, the Globe!' He imagined their future together and it made her love him more.

'They would take you, but not me,' Saskia said. 'I was not born to sing as you were.'

'There will be parts for us both,' he assured her. 'You are so beautiful you will light up the stage!'

But Saskia wasn't sure she wanted a life on the stage. Already her eyes had been opened to new possibilities. She thought again of the woman in Paris whom Gianni had mentioned; the one who wrote her own plays, who invented new stories rather than performing the old. Now that she had begun to read and write, Saskia hungered for new words, collecting them and their meanings like children collect coloured stones or shining beetles. One day she would write her own plays. She clasped Cristo's hand, knowing that they imagined different futures, but hoping that together they could make both their dreams come true. She was happier than she ever expected to be as she lay with her ear on his chest, listening to the solid beat of his heart.

He stroked her hair and whispered, 'Be with me for the rest of our lives.'

She lifted her head, her eyes questioning, unsure if she had understood his words.

'Will you marry me?' he asked softly.

She sat up abruptly, suddenly aware of the danger of her feelings for Cristo. If she were to lose him, it would tear her heart from her chest, it would finish her, and she understood why Giulietta had taken her own life when she thought Romeo had died. Without Cristo, she could never hope to feel this kind of happiness again. She looked into his eyes, meeting them fully. Everyone she ever loved had been taken from her. Could she commit herself to him? Could she open herself to the risk of loving someone once again?

Cristo drew himself up against the headboard, embarrassed by her silence.

Saskia reached out and touched his lips with her thumb. She stared at him with wonder. It was too late; she had already given him her heart. In one word, she tethered herself to him.

'Yes.'

౸

When the chapel doors were flung open that night, the audience poured into the theatre. The house was filled to capacity. Pascal climbed high to watch the audience filing in, a buzz of excitement building in the crowd, everyone curious to see Luigi da Porto's love story of Verona returned to the stage.

At the back of the theatre, Pascal waited for his cue. He spotted Luigi among the military men on their raised seats overlooking the stage and his heart jittered a little, even though he knew to expect him, for Luigi had promised he would come. The men Luigi sat with were dressed formally in military uniform. Were these the French statesmen he had placed himself among? Was the moustachioed young man beside him Eugène de Beauharnais?

A cacophony erupted in the theatre as the orchestra banged their drums and sounded trumpets. Pascal had no more time to ponder Luigi's companions. He leaped to his feet, shucking off his cloak and revealing his colours. A wooden sword, painted silver, hung at his side. All around the theatre, actors were leaping up from their seats then climbing over the audience and dashing for the stage as the orchestra played.

The audience squealed with delight as the Montecchi and the Cappelletti kin clashed in the aisles. Pascal fought the Arlecchino, false blade flashing. Il Capitano led the charge for the stage, vaulting over the drummers and into battle. Pascal took a theatrical sword to his chest and tumbled into the orchestra. He rolled away quickly out of sight, retrieving his lute and taking a place to the side from where he could view the stage and the audience. With this vicious fight between the rival houses, the play had begun.

Rémi was among the combatants from the house of Romeo Montecchi, his movements bold and eye-catching, relishing his moment on the stage. The Arlecchino played Tebaldo Cappelletti, whom Romeo would later slay. The aggression moved from the street to the private houses, to a ball where Romeo would see Giulietta for the first time. She, the daughter of a Cappelletti? And he, the son of a Montecchi? Their love was doomed from the start. Pascal watched the reactions of the audience when Saskia and Cristo stepped onto the stage. He saw the tension of this impossible match; he saw the hope catch in their hearts.

Pascal had designed the set himself, an ingenious system of circling curtains that could be drawn around to change the backdrops from the street scene, to a ballroom, to a garden, or fall away entirely to reveal the bare brick of the chapel wall behind. Saskia climbed the scaffolding of her rickety tower to wait for Romeo, hidden from the audience's view. She faced the curtain, her fists clenched at her side.

The scene was coming to an end. Gianni sent children running around the circular face of the stage, hidden from the crowd by a false wall, pulling a curtain along with them. The drapes disguised the scene behind until the painted ballroom was replaced with a garden scene. By the time the front curtain had been fully collected on the opposite side, Romeo was waiting in the shrubbery and Giulietta was revealed on her balcony above.

Pascal heard the gasp of appreciation from the crowd. His stage engineering had worked seamlessly. In triumph, he searched for Luigi, who met his eye and smiled.

Pascal fumbled for his lute, heart trilling. Only his lone, clear notes would accompany Saskia's voice. She had nowhere to hide.

He struggled to master his own nerves, knowing that Luigi was watching him. He could imagine how Saskia felt to be standing on that balcony, all eyes upon her. She must be weak at the knees, sweating under her make-up, terrified her voice would come out wrong.

Pascal began to play, the lute comfortable in his embrace. When Saskia opened her mouth to sing, her voice was sweet and clear, each word filled with longing. Pascal was overjoyed for her. As she reached the end of her song, Pascal wanted to leap to his feet and applaud with the crowd. Her performance was perfect. The lovers spoke their passions and declared their love for one another and Romeo climbed the trellis wall to touch his lips to Giulietta's in a forbidden kiss that made the audience swoon and sigh.

The expression of their love reminded him that Cristo and Saskia were to be married. Their announcement had come as a shock that morning, stunning the company to silence. Cristo had bounded into the chapel, wrapping his arms around Saskia, crying out for a priest to marry them. It should not have been a surprise, but Pascal had been speechless nonetheless. She was still a child to him. The lovers barely knew one another. Yet hadn't Romeo and Giulietta fallen in love and given their lives to one another on far less—one brief meeting and the strength of love at first sight? Pascal had gone to her and embraced them both.

Saskia had begged for a simple, quick affair which had mortally wounded La Signora and was soon overruled by all the company. 'It should be lavish,' La Signora enthused and she took on the role of choreographer. The wedding was to be in a month, after the season of *Giulietta e Romeo* ended, here in this chapel.

Pascal had already turned his mind to her dress. He envisaged her walking down the aisle of the chapel in a gown shimmering like crystal. Saskia had no traditions of her own to draw upon, for when he asked her where she came from, she couldn't name it. She seemed to be a child of northern conquests, Celtic and Hun. He pictured her flaming hair coiling down over an ice-white gown. None of these traditional thick Italian fabrics in colours of red wine for this bride. They would make her look like an overdressed doll.

From across the theatre, Pascal felt Luigi's gaze on him. Pascal hardly noticed the passage of the play now. He had seen it rehearsed so many times—the secret marriage, the families' violent feud, the death of Tebaldo at Romeo's sword, Romeo's banishment and the lovers' separation. 'What shall I do without you?' Giulietta cried. 'My heart forbids to live any longer.' Saskia delivered her line with a throbbing ache. When she promised to cut off her hair and disguise herself as Romeo's valet, Pascal's thoughts wandered to his moments with Luigi, the accidental brush of his hand across Pascal's own when no one was looking, a touch to his thigh, an arm looped around his waist pulling him in and then letting him go. The work of a moment to be wondered at later; had it happened at all? What kind of relationship could he hope for? Was it simply desire and lust, secret trysts in the night?

Publicly, Luigi remained Colombina's husband, but he did not sleep here at the monastery with her. Luigi must have an apartment in town, rooms he rented—a palazzo of his own, perhaps. Pascal liked to imagine Luigi gliding through fine rooms with warm Turkish carpets and furs draped over leather armchairs. He saw tall windows opening out to rooftop views of the spires and pinnacles of the *duomo*.

He did not like to imagine Luigi with companions. But a man as young and beautiful as Luigi must have many. Rich, intelligent Italian men, stylish and sleek draping themselves about his rooms like decorations. Jealousy roiled his stomach. He imagined witty conversations filled with wry remarks and much laughter. Pascal could not compete with men like that. In such a room, he would be the oversized cupboard in the corner, where all the dashing young men threw their cloaks.

In the audience, Luigi murmured to his companions and pointed to his wife. Colombina commanded the stage every time she stood upon it, even when she played the dowdy aunt who finds Giulietta's lifeless body, drugged insensible with a fake poison, a trick to avoid being married to another man against her will.

On stage, Romeo was told of Giulietta's death. Pascal watched the audience as they realised Romeo would miss the crucial message that her death was a ruse to reunite the lovers. He saw mouths open in despair.

Soon the backdrop curtains would fall and the stage would be bare. The scene in the crypt where Giulietta comes to life would be enacted here in this very chapel; the austere brick walls and arched windows would serve as the stage scenery itself. As intimate as if the audience were with the lovers inside the crypt.

Romeo, in grief at the sight of Giulietta's unconscious body, took his own life. Giulietta woke to see her lover dead, his spirit departed. She took his face and dug her thumbs into his cheeks, drew his cold lips to hers. She shook his shoulders, pummelled his chest; she would not let him leave her without a fight. She screamed at him, called vile insults, pulled his hair. The audience had tears on their cheeks to see her anguish. And then, when all hope was lost, she took his dagger and slid it into her heart.

Silence.

Pascal heard no sound. No scuffle of feet, no cough, no shifting creaks of the tiered seats.

Pascal stood in his Cappelletti colours, Giulietta's kin. The actors of the feuding families came forward from their places in the audience as they had at the very start of the play. Solemnly they walked onto the stage and circled their fallen children. Montecchi

317

and Cappelletti joined in vigil, each man promising to end this blood feud. This was how Colombina chose to adapt the original, removing Luigi da Porto's chastisement of women who did not love as selflessly as Giulietta, to end instead with an admonishment of powerful men and the senseless loss of their children.

How many innocents must die to bring the warring parties to peace? Pascal wondered, looking down at the entangled bodies of Saskia and Cristo.

As the audience rose to their feet and cheered, Pascal gazed out into the crowd, searching for Luigi. From the well-lit stage all the faces of the audience were lost. It unsettled him. He felt adrift on this floating island of light while all around them feet stomped, hands clapped and voices roared their appreciation. He longed to know if, in these times, an Italian could truly love a Frenchman. If love could ever overcome blood.

CHAPTER TWENTY-NINE

'Will you go home to Paris after Saskia and Cristo are married?' Colombina asked me as baldly as that, between the dab of her brush in a pot of vermilion and the slash of it on her canvas. The wedding was to be held in just a few days' time.

I covered my disgruntlement somewhat poorly. 'Grown tired of me?'

She frowned as I shifted my pose on purpose. She had me standing bare-chested in a pair of striped tights with one foot up on a stool. I wished she would paint faster. I felt a fool. I needed only a jester's cap and three coloured balls and the transformation would be complete.

'I thought you might take this opportunity to leave us.'

She said it so lightly, it pained me.

'Why would I go?'

'Gianni said you asked him about your mother and that he told you to seek your answers in Paris.'

'Did he put you up to this? Did he ask you to release me?' I would not put it past Gianni to meddle. He knew I had fallen in love with Colombina. He knew I would only leave if she rejected me.

'He means to protect you,' she said. 'If you want answers, you should leave before it becomes too dangerous to do so.'

There was war through Prussia now, just as Katharina once predicted. Prussian men now fought against Napoleon, when they had once been allies. If the Emperor was defeated, we French storytellers would never be welcome back in those lands where we had spent so many years. The Austrians, too, had turned against Napoleon. They controlled Venice, so we could not go back there. The same would be true of Milan, if Colombina and Luigi achieved their goal of turning the Lombardy states against their ally. The borders of my world were shrinking.

'What is Paris like?' she asked.

Paris. Paris did not feel like home. I barely remembered much of it beyond the theatre. Muck-filled streets that ran like sewers in the rain. A city of urchins on street corners scrapping for dropped coins.

Except, one time I remembered my mother taking me to see a great parade of wagons and carriages. We had followed them through the heart of Paris, along the Seine and around the Tuileries Palace. She held my hand and, unused to such restraints (I had been my own protector for so long), I strained against her grip. At the Place de la Révolution I saw a hot-air balloon for the first time, a swell of peach-and-gold-striped canvas and a swaying basket rising above me, and felt my mother squeezing my hand so hard I thought she had broken it.

These were the spoils Napoleon had taken from the churches, the libraries, the art galleries of Milan and Venice. I had been there in Paris when these treasures were paraded through the streets. The price of losing a war, an accepted part of the game for those with the power to play it. But for the common people? I now understood their culture had been taken from them without consent.

'Paris means nothing to me,' I answered.

'If you stay with me, you could be my *cicisbeo*.'

'Your what?'

'My lover, my companion. In Venice, everyone knows marriage is a commercial transaction. For love, we noblewomen have our *cicisbeo*.'

'You mean me to be like a *mistress*?' I was a toy for her and nothing more. She would stay married to her brother and would not even admit that she loved me. Was I supposed to follow her around like a devoted lapdog?

I knew that I loved her. As proof, I had wasted hours standing half dressed in all manner of demeaning poses for her to paint. But did she love me in return? She confused me, pushing me away and at the same time asking me to stay.

'I will stay, if you say you love me.' I jutted my chin high, determined to claw back some dignity.

I could not see her face behind the canvas, only heard her hog's-hair brush scratching.

Colombina peeked around the side of her easel and appraised me. Without a word, she gestured for me to return the flute to my lips and pretend to play the instrument. Was there no humiliation I would not submit to?

Of course I wanted to stay with her. I loved this theatre life. In Milan or Venice, I would live in luxury with Colombina. I would want for nothing. Pascal was happy here in her theatre and I knew she would look after the both of us. But my pride . . . it hurt me. The man should be the one to dictate whether he stayed or left.

'What do you think?' Colombina spun the canvas about.

I sighed. Once again she had painted me as half human, half goat. A horned freak of nature with the chest and head of a man and the hairy hind limbs of a beast. My cloven feet danced in a meadow as I played my music and the merry maidens cackled around me.

Luigi chose this moment of my great humiliation to burst into the room. He stared first at me and then the painting. I crossed my arms over my hairless chest, wishing for a cloak to pull across me.

'Where is Pascal?' he cried.

I was shocked by the panic in his voice.

'I came as soon as I could. They are coming. A raid. I'm sorry— we had no warning.' Luigi was breathless. I had never seen him so discomposed.

Colombina leaped to her feet, knocking a jar of turpentine to the floor.

'The war in Prussia?' she asked.

He nodded. 'Napoleon has lost the Battle of Leipzig. He retreats while Russia, Sweden, Austria and all of Prussia are now joined in coalition against him.'

Colombina clapped her hands. 'But this is good news!'

'You don't understand. This is no time for celebration. Napoleon needs more men. Almost forty thousand have been killed, wounded or are missing in the battle. The conscriptors are coming—they will take all able-bodied men with no exception.' He turned to where I stood, gaping at his news. 'Help me,' he implored. 'I cannot find Pascal.'

I began to run.

℃⊃

Pascal liked this time of the morning when the streets were quiet. Only the house-proud matrons were out scratching the cobblestones with their brooms and the shopkeepers preparing for the day's trading by rinsing the night's urine from their doorsteps. The cats watched him as he passed, stretching and lolling on thresholds.

Pascal had left the monastery that morning intending to ride out in the countryside. It was an extravagance to keep a horse stabled in a city when he had so little need of her, but he returned to the stablemaster each week to pay her fee. Henriette had been through all manner of storms with them. She was family; he could not let her end her life yoked to a cart. He had paid to stable Saskia's horse too, just in case she ever had need of him again. The spectre of that priest was still present in his mind.

This would be an autumn wedding, and Pascal had been tasked with gathering decorations for the wedding banquet. For Saskia, he pictured a table heavy with rambling roses and threaded through with canes of blackberry, the prickly leaves of holly and their shocking red fruit. For Cristo, he imagined white flowers, with petals soft like wings. White wings for the boy with a voice of an angel.

Pascal had already bought Saskia a wedding gift. It was a book. A beautiful book with green leather binding and gold embossing, the page edges marbled with green and blue inks. A different sort of book. Inside were no fairytales, no sonnets, no stories taken from ears and given to eyes. It was not a book of Bible stories drawn by monks and illuminated with gold leaf. This book had no stories at all. In fact, the pages were blank.

'Write the story of your life together,' Pascal would say as she opened it. 'Write a great love story.'

He smiled to think of it. He knew she loved to collect words, and now she could collect them and shape them into her own story.

The first thing he noticed when he reached the stables were the gates hanging from their hinges. Then he was struck by the deathly silence. He passed through the thick stone walls, and gasped to see all the stalls open, the courtyard empty, the horses gone. The place was deserted. He called out for the stablemaster, heard only his own heart pounding in his ears. He searched the hay barns and saw a trapdoor hastily closed. He wrenched it open and pulled the man from the pit.

'What is the meaning of this?' Pascal roared, his temper fired by panic. 'What has happened here?'

'Do you not have eyes in your head, boy? The conscriptors, of course. They took the horses and would've taken us if we hadn't hidden.'

The stableboys peeped up from the hole.

The stablemaster looked Pascal up and down, taking in the youth and strength of him. 'I'd run if I were you.'

'They took the horses,' Pascal repeated, realising how sheltered his life had become in the sanctuary of the Teatro Venezia. This war and its voracious hunger had barely touched him. Now, Henriette would end her life on some distant battlefield.

'He took my livelihood,' the man said, 'but I will not give him my life. No one is safe. You'd do well to hide yourself.'

The man jumped back into the pit and pulled the trapdoor shut.

Rémi, Pascal thought instantly. This was what Rémi's mother had been afraid of all those years ago. This was why she had lied to Rémi and hidden them both away. They had been together through so much; he could not abandon him now. He had to return to the monastery before it was too late.

He ran towards the theatre in the wake of the conscriptors. In the streets, women wailed and beat their hands against their chests. They screamed at him as if it were his fault. Husbands and sons had been dragged from their homes; no one was safe. Not the theatre, he prayed. The season was not finished, *Giulietta e Romeo* had two more nights to run. Then Pascal realised the stupidity of his thoughts. No one would care about a play when war had come to take their children.

When he reached the monastery, all he could hear was someone screaming.

℃⊃

Saskia was falling into an abyss.

Her screams could tear the bricks from the walls.

℃⊃

When Pascal threw open the door, my heart leaped. I was convinced he had been taken, that he was lost to me forever. Luigi ran to him and wrapped himself fiercely about my friend. I pushed Luigi away. Pascal was *my* friend, *my* brother. But Pascal pushed us both aside and took Saskia in his arms.

'Cristo?'

Saskia moaned, unable to speak.

'What happened?' Pascal looked to me.

'I could not find you,' I said. We had searched the monastery for Pascal, while Gianni rounded up the other players, taking them to hide beneath the stage. I had thought Saskia and Cristo safe with Gianni.

'Did the conscriptors come?'

I shook my head. We had waited, watching the bolted doors, but the conscriptors never came. Only Saskia returned, shouting and slamming her hands against our doors with murder in her voice. 'We didn't know they had gone to buy rings for each other,' I explained. 'Cristo was taken in the street.'

I could picture the armed militia appearing in ranks spread across the street so that no one might pass. I heard the sound of their boots and the clatter of their swords. Cristo would've had nowhere to run.

Saskia struggled in Pascal's arms and twisted away from him. She was running now, running for her cell, and I knew what she intended. I cried after her, 'No, don't do this!' She slammed and locked the door behind her.

When she came out, dressed for the road in her boy's clothes, Pascal and I were waiting.

'You will waste your life. Cristo would not want that,' I told her. She walked on.

I stepped in front of her, blocking the way.

'Let me go,' she growled.

'I cannot do that.'

'Then you are no better than any man who means to confine me.'

Her words stopped me like a slap.

'It is my choice to do this,' she insisted.

I stared at her, this child we had come to think of as a sister. But she was not a child. She was older now than Pascal and I had been when we left our home, and she was already far less naive.

With great effort, I stepped aside. 'We are your family too—I hope you know that.'

She went to Pascal, thanked him in silence with her arms circling his body, her head bent into his ribs. It choked my chest to see it. She seemed impossibly small, and I felt a surge of love as if she was my child to protect. Pascal bent down and whispered something in her ear. 'In case you ever have need of sanctuary,' he said, straightening. Then he rubbed her skinny arms and let her go.

She turned to me next, and I held her tight. 'Find Cristo,' I said. 'Bring him home.' Empty words, meant to cheer, for we both knew we would not see one another again.

She wiped the tears from her face. 'I will.'

Luigi waited in the shadows looking like a kicked dog. 'I couldn't do anything to stop this.'

'Take me to them,' she demanded of him. Her tone was hard and cold. She had become a sharp-edged diamond again, the way she was when we first met, a small stone able to scratch the strongest metals. Good, I thought. This will protect her.

Luigi nodded and Saskia followed him. She did not look back at us.

'We had thought that priest would take her from us,' Pascal said. 'We should have known there was a much greater villain to fear.' Pascal and I watched her walk along the unlit hall until she was swallowed up by the darkness.

Our company sat around the dining table, morose and ashamed, while the candles burned down to stubs. We had all been spared.

Il Capitano, Il Dottore, the Arlecchino, myself and Pascal. All fit men. Fighting fit. Pascal hung his head and I couldn't meet his eyes. We should have gone in her place. How could we stay behind and let her go to war? I had no wish to fight, but I suffered from the shame of knowing that we grown men had escaped while our children had been sacrificed.

It was late, but none of the company wanted to be alone. La Signora was weeping quietly. Gianni had gone to pray in the chapel. I could not bear to think of Saskia alone among the soldiers.

Luigi's heels snapped rapidly on the flagstones, interrupting the vigil. I felt an unconquerable hatred for this man.

'The Teatro Venezia was not targeted in this raid because they wish your performances to continue. For civic morale.'

I snorted, rolled my eyes. The city was in mourning. Few would care for our opera now. Besides, our Innamorati had been taken.

'Has she enlisted?' Pascal asked.

Luigi nodded.

It was done. Saskia would fight for France on some Prussian plains in a battle against her own people. She would die, while we lived.

Pascal scraped back his chair. Stood. 'Where have they sent her?'

'They march to Paris.'

To Paris? I swung my head to look at him.

'The Russians and their allies mean to take it.'

They mean to take Paris? I shared a look of confusion with Pascal. The armies would invade France? I reeled, trying to make sense of it. France could fall. France could be occupied. Never had I imagined this was possible. Soldiers marching on towns, artillery fire, explosions, children running in the streets. Their revenge for our Emperor's greed could be brutal.

Colombina, sitting alone at the end of the table, had risen to her feet. 'Prussia has thrown out the Emperor, the Confederation of the Rhine has fallen, Austria has broken their alliance and the Kingdom of Italy will soon follow. We can return to Venice!' Her shining face was radiant, charged once again with fervour, but I could not believe she thought only of her precious cause and so little for Saskia and Cristo. Her yearning to throw out the oppressors clearly mattered more to her than anything—or anyone—else. At a time like this, when we had lost our children, I could not look at her.

Luigi took a step towards Pascal and I saw their fingers entwine. Now I was losing Pascal to this fiend.

'My place is here, with the government,' Luigi said to Colombina. 'I cannot leave.'

Russian armies were marching on our home. Paris could be invaded. I looked into Pascal's face—my Pascal—and saw the youth with the sandy hair and soft doe eyes who had followed me every-where. Pascal, who had been my comfort, my protector and my only friend for so long. His face was stricken with the same indecision I felt. Where did we belong?

I began to understand his longing for home, for the safety of a place that would protect its own.

Luigi moved closer to Pascal. *Stay with me*, his presence said.

Colombina kneeled beside me. 'Come with me to Venice.' She picked up my hands and kissed them.

Friendship or love?

Gianni had been right all along: there was no place for us here. I looked to Pascal and whispered a word in a language I had not spoken for so long. 'Maman.'

PART III

1814

CHAPTER THIRTY

*P*ascal kept his eyes closed, listening to the soft rainfall dampen the streets below. Outside his window, the drains trickled with falling water. He kept his eyes closed knowing that to open them would bring in the hard edges of reality. He had made his choice to leave Luigi; there was no going back.

Rémi stirred and kicked out in his sleep. Pascal rolled towards him, opening his eyes. The furs had slipped and Pascal pulled the cover up over Rémi's shoulder. What were they to one another now? Brothers? Friends? Or simply travellers returning home?

It was winter now. The travelling had been difficult as there were few coaches to be had and most were filled with émigrés fleeing for their homelands.

Luigi had passed a heavy purse into Pascal's hand before they left Milan and the funds had paid to silence the suspicious. Men of wealth need not fear the conscriptors they hoped. Luigi had dressed them like Italian ambassadors and Pascal and Rémi played the part knowing their lives depended on it.

It ached, this loss, even so long after they had parted. The memory of that last moment pained him. Luigi gruff and silent, dressing him in heavy robes while Pascal stole guilty glances at him. Luigi tightened the cord of the velvet cloak around his neck with rough, quick tugs. They faced one another, both men equal in height.

'I will come back,' Pascal promised.

'You won't.'

'I will.'

Luigi knotted the ribbon at Pascal's throat. 'It will not be safe for you to return. Soon all Frenchmen will be driven out of Italy.'

'Then you will come to me.'

'Why would I? You have made your choice.'

Pascal blazed. 'Rémi needs me. He is a brother to me!'

'Ha! You may deceive yourself of that but never me.' Luigi turned away to pick up his gloves and shove his fingers into the leather. Fingers that had been the first to trace along Pascal's clavicle and over his bare chest, to follow the line of hair down his stomach.

He gripped the silk of Luigi's shirt to pull him against his body. Pascal felt the fire of his loins and twisted his hand in the fabric of Luigi's shirt, holding him tight. How could he willingly let his lover go?

They stared at one another. Luigi hooked his fingers over the band of Pascal's breeches. Pascal groaned. He could let Luigi strip him naked, let his mouth give him such exquisite bliss, but he found he could not release him. They moved against one another, rubbing quick and hard, groins pressed tight and bodies arching away, until Pascal felt his chest expand and his loins explode.

Pascal rolled away from Rémi, his erection hot and hard from the memory of Luigi. He stood and pulled the furs from the bed to cover himself and went to the window. Sleet streaked the windowpanes and he traced the rivulets with his bare finger. On the streets below, two beech martens screamed and fought and scampered along a stonework fence. Somewhere, a woman's voice was raised in argument. It was strange for him to hear the French language spoken, familiar as an old coat, yet one that did not fit so well as it once had.

Pascal had followed Rémi again without question, despite his love for Luigi. All through the difficult packhorse climb from Turin through the Col du Mont-Cenis he had pondered this strange hold Rémi had over him. He left Milan not knowing whether he would ever see Luigi again, just as he had once left everyone behind in Paris, all his family, all those he loved. But it was more than just Rémi. He had felt the call of his childhood home, his place in the world. Rémi must have felt it too. When the word *maman* slipped from his lips, he must've felt that same sensation. How could they stay away and leave those who loved them to face an invasion alone? He belonged in Paris and he had to take this chance to get home.

In the last weeks, the bitter frosts had kept the ground frozen, but soon the roads would thaw and turn to slush and bog down the wheels of carriages and carts. Their final leg to Paris would be slow. Already, they had been on the road for three months. Even with their fine clothes and bulging purse of money, they had to travel on the lesser roads and take circuitous routes to avoid the movements of the army. Napoleon had lost Spain earlier that summer and troops were retreating across France by forced march, heading for Mainz on the Rhine border. Pascal and Rémi listened for any rumours of regiments that might cross their path. They spent weeks in Lyon, cooped up in a hotel room, while the French army camped outside the city en route to the eastern border. Enemies were gathering to the east. Russia, Austria, Prussia—all had sniffed the Emperor's weakness and now they were intent on punishment. Luigi's time of reckoning had come.

The thought of Saskia out there in some freezing field, camped out while waiting for battle, gave him a physical pain in his chest. He thumped at his breastbone, kneading his knuckles against the bone. Another horror had come for her and she had walked into it willingly to find her love. Would he have done the same? She was braver than either he or Rémi. For years they had avoided these wars, running from place to place and blaming Rémi's mother for their exile, yet she had only tried to protect them from this fate. Wouldn't he have done the same for Saskia, if he could?

Pascal turned back to Rémi on the bed and saw he was awake and sitting up against the solid, carved headboard, watching him. They stared at one another without speaking—Pascal standing at the window with a bearskin pulled around him, Rémi leaning back, chest bare.

Rémi spoke. 'They say Napoleon gathers his armies to the east of Paris, near Brienne. We could try to find her?'

Could they find her among the thousands of men? Could they steal her away? Pascal pictured any number of possible deaths—they would be shot as deserters, they could be captured and made to fight anyway then blown to pieces on a battlefield. On the other hand, there was bravery, honour and duty to a friend. Their eyes shied away from one another's.

We are cowards, Pascal thought. We do not want to go to war.

CHAPTER THIRTY-ONE

Saskia swung her drumstick and beat the tambour in time with her steps. Her feet were swollen and sore and her fingers numb with the icy cold, but still she walked and struck the calfskin snare drum as rhythmically as breathing. It had been this way for months.

Luigi had assigned her a place among the drummer boys. She wore a black uniform buttoned high up to her throat and a tall black hat, and carried a round drum slung by a sash across her chest. There were mostly children in her regiment, and she marched alongside them in their oversized uniforms, firearms fixed with bayonets pointing to the sky. A long train of boys taken from the streets of Italy and swallowed up from the towns in their path. The recruits were nicknamed 'Marie-Louises' by the older soldiers who marched with them, a reference to the Emperor's new bride, because they were all so young. Among the soldiers she had heard a mix of languages spoken; some she recognised, others not. She felt no kin with any of them. Her nationality meant nothing to her—she thought only of finding Cristo.

Those first few hours as the conscripts were corralled into their regiments had been agony. She had scanned every face with growing panic. Cristo wasn't in her regiment or any other around her. As they set off from Milan, it was impossible to see who was ahead and who was behind. She had imagined that by joining the draft she would find him easily, but from that first night on the road she recognised the impossibility of the task. The camp stretched miles and miles along the roadside, row after row of tents filled with thousands of men and boys, and she had only the hours after dark to look for him. The first few nights she had crept from her tent, evading the officers on watch, and despaired to see the dotted fires stretching away far into the distance. The northerly breeze brought her the scent of smoke and stung her eyes to watering. If she tried to move between the camps, she would be shot as a deserter.

Saskia had returned to her tent, curling up on a thin mat on the hard ground, feeling like being sick. She missed Cristo. It was excruciating to know that he was with her on this march, either ahead or behind, and yet she could not reach him. She would stay alive, she promised herself then; she would survive this gruelling march and find him.

The young recruits were taught how to beat their drums by veterans of the Old Guard, the *grognards*, as they walked. The snare drum was slung low and fell to the side of her hip, its weight bulky and awkward. She learned how to hold her batons and strike with alternating hands and sing to help the rhythm, *ta-ga-da* for a simple stroke roll, right-left-right. Practising the paradiddle repetitions took her mind off the enormity of what she had done by joining this army. Left-right-left. Right-left-right. The repetitions required all her focus, as she trained her left and right hands to strike with the same skill, so that neither side was dominant. The webbing of her thumbs blistered. For days on end, they marched and beat their drums. She learned the rudiments required to announce the reveille—a wake-up call—and the rudiments for a call to arms or a retreat, and she sang along with the other Marie-Louises as they practised their double beats in unison: *papa-maman, papa-maman.* Children singing for their parents.

Saskia found two other girls marching among the troops with bayoneted muskets over their shoulders. She watched them closely. The girls did little to disguise themselves, their short hair, caps and a uniform lending them an anonymity of a kind. They had questioned her with a simple bald stare and she had returned their gaze with a nod. They spoke little but watched out for one another, these girls who had been found in the wrong place, or had followed their brothers and boyfriends, or had simply wanted to escape. The hardest thing, Saskia found, was the lack of privacy. On the march, she drank little and learned to hold her bladder. One of the girls had a silver tube that let her piss standing up with the other men. Latrines were dug each night, but these were always shared, three or more men along a wooden plank. The girls coordinated, always visiting the latrines together, never leaving anyone alone. Perhaps the young boys in her regiment were too shocked by their own predicament to notice there were girls among them, or perhaps they simply did not care. Saskia was far more wary of the older soldiers and she kept her fishhook close.

On rest days, the drummers and the new soldiers were taught the basics of fighting: how to stick a bayonet into a straw man; how to fire a gun; how to kneel and hold a musket and bayonet so that advancing forces would impale themselves. She could see that not even their training sergeants expected them to be proficient in these skills. Most of all they were taught to hold. To hold formation. To hold the line. Heroes held, cowards ran. They were there to make up numbers, to be the first squads to take the cannon fire. After the carnage, the Imperial Guard and the dragoons would ride through and complete the attack. Saskia intended to be far away when the day of battle came.

As they marched northwards, the weeks turned to months and the weather grew brutal. Her hopes of finding Cristo dwindled with each passing day. It was all she could do to put one foot in front of the other.

In the evenings, she collapsed, exhausted, by a fire and waited for her turn to eat. A simple bowl of stew or soup with rice and beans, yet she looked forward to the meal as if it were a banquet. Tonight, as every other night, the company gathered to eat and recall past battles and heroic deeds. The same tired stories were passed around the Old Guard, each soldier taking his turn to embellish.

'I was at Austerlitz when we split the Russian forces in half!' boasted one of the Italian soldiers.

Saskia saw some boys were excited by these tales, their eyes glistening, each hoping for his own chance to be a hero. How easily they could be manipulated and cajoled by promises of glory and importance. It angered her. All of it, the codes of honour, tales of camaraderie, the flash of uniforms, badges, ranks and medals—all tricks to persuade these boys to stand in a muddy field and face the cannons.

Someone passed a lute around the circle to one of the boys.

'A ballad to stir the troops,' one soldier said. 'Make me into a song.'

The boy put down his pewter bowl and reluctantly took the instrument. The musicians all had their part to play in this masquerade, and it sickened her to watch it.

She hated that she was part of this mechanism of control, that music and story and song would be used to drive children to their deaths. Every one of these soldiers must know it was false, that their lives meant nothing more than a number. Whichever side had the most numbers would win. Why go along with it, why believe this nonsense? But she knew, of course she knew, that there was no other choice for these men, and they had to believe in the glory and the solidarity or else what was the point of their sacrifice?

The boy strummed a few hesitant notes and then looked up to the heavens, lost in creation, and in that moment he reminded her so much of Cristo when he was about to sing that she almost sobbed. What was she doing in this war? How had she ever thought she could find Cristo in this madness?

She pushed herself back from the ring of boys around the fire, dropping her bowl and clutching her stomach while laughter followed her. Saskia ran towards the latrines then ducked away, vomiting on the frozen earth. She retched until there was nothing left of her rations, until she could taste the bile, the taste of fear.

The Young Guard, the Marie-Louises trudged towards Paris, on roads made thick with thawed mud and the boot prints of thousands of marching troops. Saskia slogged along in the train of men, concentrating on pulling each foot from the sucking mud. Artillery wagons became bogged in the sludge and had to be pulled free by gangs of soldiers. The going was slow.

As they crossed the Haute-Marne, the rolling landscape seemed confusing to her, each small village looked the same as the last, nestled in frozen fields between patches of woods that looked bleak and cheerless without their leaves. Occasionally they passed a grand chateau with its gatehouse and sweeping drive leading up to a shuttered mansion on a hill, and she tried to fix it in her mind—a landmark she might need to remember.

Saskia twisted her head to glimpse the train of camp followers snaking across the slopes. Behind the troops came the wagons of cooks, laundresses, whores, musicians and sutlers selling victuals and liquor from the back of their wagons. The camp followers made a sprawling, nomadic village composed not only of travellers desperate for the trade, but also soldiers' wives and children. Even when chased away on the General's orders, the followers eventually regrouped and rejoined the baggage train—the army was like a dog that could not be parted from its fleas. Through this swarming, uncontrollable mass of humanity, Saskia was certain she would make her escape.

At nightfall, the troops reached Brienne-le-Château, where a military school had been taken as a headquarters by the Cossack and Prussian forces. As they set up camp, the soldiers were quick to anger and officers harsh in their reprimands. Latrines were dug and the queues were long. For the first time on this long march of months, they were about to face the enemy.

Saskia waited in her tent, listening for the sounds of children breathing deeply and murmuring in their sleep. Most of the boys in her tent were younger than her; twelve or thirteen, she would guess, perhaps some as young as ten.

She crawled out under the flap of her tent dragging a small bag of supplies she had managed to steal. She had to risk going to each encampment of men and asking for Cristo. If she found him, they would sneak out to the sutlers' wagons and find a way to disguise themselves among the free camp followers. It was not much of a plan, but it was all she had. This was her last chance to find him. This was not her war. She wanted no part of the killing come the dawn.

The soldiers were retiring to their tents. She picked her way between the glowing embers of their fires, edging close, asking everyone she encountered if they knew her brother, Cristo.

'He can sing,' she said to one.

'He has beautiful golden curls,' she said to another.

The men sucked on their clay pipes and shook their heads, faces full of sorrow, missing their own brothers and sisters.

Between the tents, she moved softly, avoiding guy ropes and pegs in a way that reminded her of her years in the circus. She remembered the night her mother left her, when she woke to find her gone. She had run blindly into the ropes, falling, cutting her shin, getting up and tripping again. She had been running between the tents, crying in panic and calling her mother's name, slow to realise that she had been left behind. And all along, her mother had been dead.

She was creeping around the blackest corners of the camp when a hand gripped her collar.

'Where do you think you're going?' the soldier growled at her.

She struggled free of his hold. 'Latrines,' she said.

'I'll take you.'

He pushed her on and she clutched her stomach, hunching over as she walked. It took no effort to feign illness; she felt nauseous and her heart hammered at her throat. Her hopes of escape were slipping away. She contemplated running. Would he have time to load and fire before she could vanish into the night? She heard him cough, a rattling pipe smoker's cough. Had she enough tobacco to buy her freedom, perhaps?

When they reached the latrines at the edge of the camp, she reared back at the stink. Her eyes watered. She blinked and saw that guards were posted as close as fence railings around the entire perimeter of the camp. Even if she found Cristo, they would never get through. Any thought of escape was useless.

She gagged against her hand, then spun around and vomited on the soldier's boots.

On the morning of battle, the sun hung low and red against a blue-smoke sky. Mist hovered over the earth, shrouding farmhouses and making the fields, strewn with abandoned ploughs and overturned carts, appear ghostly and treacherous. Saskia's breath puffed out in front of her and she shivered, her whole being trembled as she lifted the sash of her drum and slung it over her shoulder.

The recruits were called into formation and marched alongside the troops as they moved forward. They halted and waited. Her knuckles were stiff as she gripped her drumsticks. She could hear the men near her breathing. So many had never faced battle before.

Ahead, the barren fields were dusted with light snow and the chateau sat stark and solid, high on a hill. Saskia was stationed so close to the front of the assembled troops that she could see an avenue of bare linden trees along the road and make out the gilded tips of the iron gates. Behind it, the Russian army waited. There was no escaping the battle to come. Her stomach surged and she spat her breakfast onto the snow.

She jerked at the signal of the bugle horn. Saskia struck her drum with all the others. Right—left, left, right. Left—right, right, left. She was calling the regiments to arms, striking fear into the enemy as her boots tramped the frozen earth. The drummers were sent marching along the front lines of troops. Young boys whose uniforms were too loose, pimpled faces that showed the brutal shock of what they were about to endure. The older soldiers lifted their chins, staring up at the chateau behind her. Saskia kept her eyes trained on the Young Guard, her hopes rising and falling with each passing face. The soldiers stood in square formation, so many rows deep that she had little hope of seeing every one of them. Each regiment was nearly a thousand strong.

This was war. At any moment these men would march forward and enter the lottery of life or death. She felt sick again, her stomach churning. The sounds of their drums grew louder, stronger. Booming tympans were called forward. The soldiers straightened and gripped their weapons.

Her gaze travelled up to the four generals sitting on horseback on a slight rise to the rear of the company. Some had cheered to know that Napoleon himself had ridden from Paris to direct the course of the battle, while others had sneered and called him the Corsican ogre. She stared at him, hunched down on his ghostly horse, and felt nothing. She recognised this absence of feeling, this cool separation of her emotions. Her time with Father had given her that.

Over the hill, the enemy soldiers rolled out the cannons. The orders changed and she beat the calfskin of her drum with all the other drummer boys, the call to charge. Ta la. Ta la. The rhythm thudding like her heart. Ta la. Ta la. The drummers moved back and the Young Guard marched forward. She searched for Cristo as the recruits stomped past her. He must be among them; fate had put them together once, how could it not help her now?

Boys and men streamed past. She wanted to call out and halt this madness. They would be cut down as soon as they came in range. She hoped against hope that Cristo wasn't here—that after this sacrifice she had made to find him, it was somehow a mistake, that he had run away before they even left Italy. Perhaps he was with Colombina and Gianni; perhaps he had returned to the Teatro Venezia after all.

She heard the call to halt and hold. For a moment all was silent. Then she saw a distant puff of smoke and heard a crack. She cried out at the shock of it, to see the middle of the square of men crumple. The first shots boomed and smoked and shattered people, and she screamed with all the others.

She closed her eyes and beat her drum. This must be what hell is like, she thought. She smelled blood and gunpowder, heard shrieks and felt the thump of the cannon fire reverberating beneath her feet. She prayed that Cristo had escaped long before now.

Dirt and stones sprayed her, stinging her face, but still she squeezed her eyes closed. She heard horses' hooves like the rumble of thunder and felt them coming from behind. She heard the officers scream their war cries, rousing themselves and the troops for the coming battle. The dragoons rode through and she felt the air suck at her, pulling her forward, almost toppling her from her feet with the force and speed of their beasts. She imagined she would be knocked down and trampled into the mud. She stood her ground, beat her drum in relentless monotony as bullets pierced through the lines of men and horses around her. She heard a child's scream and, alongside her, a snare drum fell silent. Her body shook violently, but still her wrists maintained the rhythm on her drum.

A general shouted orders in her ear. A new message needed to be sent back to the commanders on the hill. Automatically she obeyed, changing the pattern of her beats.

Ta rum, ta rum, ta-ta-ta rum.

She heard others pick up the beat and join her. The drummer boys were stationed around each regiment and she strained to hear how many were still able to beat their drums. She understood now why the army needed so many young drummers—not all of them would survive, and there needed to be enough left for the message to be heard.

A bugler sounded his horn, three blasts. Saskia stilled her hands. For a moment there was a complete, shocked silence. No booming cannons, no rifle shot, no drums. She opened her eyes.

Nothing could have prepared her for the sight of people torn apart, split open, guts spilling, limbs far flung. Of people butchered into pieces. Nothing. She retched. Her throat burned, her eyes stung. The air was as rank as the latrines. She looked down at her hands, her drum, the front of her uniform, all splattered with blood and dirt. Her hands were shaking uncontrollably now, her fingers were sticky with others' blood. Was it over? She looked out over the battlefield as the smoke began to lift and revealed the heaped mounds of bodies and the cratered fields. Had Cristo lived?

On the earth beside her a drummer boy lay as if asleep, his perfect face untouched but for a single bullet shot through his forehead.

CHAPTER THIRTY-TWO

For almost a month Pascal and I had been caught in a noose. The French had fought battle after battle against three separate forces from Silesia, Austria and Russia. First in the east at Champaubert and Montmirail, then north at Château-Thierry, then backtracking to Vauchamps, before marching south-east to Mormant and Montereau, and finally returning west to Méry-sur-Seine. By the end of February, Napoleon's army had almost completed a full circle back to Brienne, and we had been trapped in the middle of it all.

This morning Pascal had woken in one of his moods and had loomed about our room in his furs like a growling bear. We had made it as far as Troyes, a medieval town of half-timbered houses that reminded me of our travels in the Rhinelands. Our lives together as travelling storytellers now seemed a distant memory.

'There are battles all over the countryside.' Pascal spoke as if it were my fault.

He was angry because he felt guilty. He believed he had failed Saskia, but the girl had chosen her course of her own free will—we were not responsible for that.

'We have a chance to break through this circle of war,' I countered. 'We are going home to Paris—isn't that what you always wanted?'

He growled something about wishing he'd never left Milan.

Pascal loved Luigi, I knew that, but it was his choice to come with me to Paris; I did not make him.

'Why not return to Milan, if you are going to blame me for your heartsickness?' They were words said snappishly, as I was sick of his moods. I did not mean them. Of course I didn't want him to leave me.

Over these past weeks, as the battles surrounded us, he had become ever more agitated. Nothing pleased him. Each night we shared a room out of long habits of thrift, and my every noise and movement annoyed him. A vigorous scratching, a long piss in the corner of the room, even a yawn could irritate him into sighing and complaining. We fought like an old married couple and I wondered if this constant pecking and sniping was what led one partner to finally push the other out of the nest.

'Today we will reach Paris,' Pascal said ominously. 'We should begin our search at the theatre.' He was reviving an old argument. We could not agree on where to go when we arrived in the city.

'The Comédie-Italienne has burned to the ground! Why torture yourself by picking over the remains of our old life?'

Pascal thought we would find a trace of them there—Margot, little Bonbon, some of the actors and actresses who made up the company. I thought it foolish and had told him so. We could never go back.

'Far better to try the Comédie-Française, who surely would have taken the best and brightest among them. Margot, certainly, would have found a home there.'

'But your mother,' he said, 'she was not one for the stage. Don't you want to know if she left anything that would lead you to her? How can you not want to see? This is why we left Milan. We came to find those we left behind!'

'If you want to search the theatre, then go. You don't need me to hold your hand.'

'Fine!' he shouted. 'We will go our separate ways.'

'No, Pascal.'

He was pacing the floor. 'You should go back to that house on Boulevard Montmartre. Your mother took us there. She must know the man who hid us. If you want to find her, he will know.'

'I can't go back there.' The remembrance of that place filled me with a sickening dread. It made me feel trapped just to think of it. The walls of this room were pressing in on me.

'We left everyone because of your selfishness. It's your fault. You don't even care enough for your mother to find her. Do you care for anyone other than yourself, Rémi?'

He riled me into speaking rashly. 'Your trouble, Pascal,' I informed him, 'is that you are too weak to know what you want for yourself. You are too weak to fight for it. You would rather blame me for taking you away from the people you love than blame yourself for lacking courage!'

Pascal threw a shoe against the door. 'I should never have left Luigi for you!'

'You should thank me for releasing you from the clutches of that lizard.'

That, it seemed, was the final straw as Pascal had packed his belongings without another word to me.

At the coach-house in Troyes, Pascal paid for two fares to Paris, loaded our cases and played his usual part of an Italian nobleman on government business. We spoke in Italian-accented French when we greeted our fellow passengers. We took seats apart from one another and gazed out of our respective windows at the wintry countryside. Freezing mist blanketed everything.

Pascal and I sat in wretched silence, avoiding each other's gaze while the carriage jolted and lurched along the pitted roads. The last stretch of our journey together, our arrival in Paris, our return home, would be spent in this torture. I touched the cold window-pane and let my fingertips burn.

I was alone with my thoughts as the carriage rocked us closer to Paris. I thought of Saskia and Cristo, snatched up by this war, and it filled me with melancholy. I did not like to think of Colombina, as it caused a tightness in my chest and a pain in the pit of my throat. The memory of our parting was still raw. 'I will come back,' I had said to her. 'I love you.' Even then she was too proud to admit she loved me in return. Her one true love was her homeland. But the kiss she pressed on my lips in the last moments of our farewell gave me hope. 'Be safe,' she had whispered. 'Return to me.'

Pascal was wrong to think I did not want to find my mother. I simply did not want to go back to the charred remains of our old life. I did not want to see it as it was now; I wanted to remember our majestic theatre as it appeared to me as a small boy, when it was my entire world, when it held all my hopes and dreams and I could think of no other heights of success than to be on that stage and adored. Our home had been glorious.

In the theatre, my mother and I had climbed up into the boxes together, pretending we were rich and glamorous members of the audience. At age thirteen, I knew how to act like one of them, for I had watched them all my life. I held out my arm for her like a gentleman. She was famously sparing with her smiles, but she smiled each time I did this.

We loved the dress rehearsals best, when all the costumes and scenery were in place. Sometimes I saw Pascal below, running off on some errand for Gianni, little Bonbon tagging along behind. I could've called out to them, could've invited them up, but instead I kept silent, sitting close beside my mother.

We critiqued the performance. Margot overacted in her death scene as she always did, but she looked exquisite when held in the arms of our leading man, Rogerio. I wanted to be Rogerio, holding his dead lover in his arms. One day, I promised myself, Rogerio's parts would be mine.

At the end of each performance we bounded to our feet to applaud and cheer. Margot winked and blew me a kiss as the performers took their bows. I couldn't wait to be grown. I couldn't wait to take the stage for myself and have my mother watch from the audience.

Our imminent arrival in Paris was dredging up memories that had been long buried. I was coming back to find my mother and I was confused by this unusual wash of protective feelings for her. For so long I had nursed my sense of betrayal. Every time an audience took offence at my tales and cast a stone, I blamed the hurt on her. Every hunger pang, every needling wind through threadbare clothes, I blamed on her. But as the years of our self-imposed exile passed, as I began to enjoy our wandering life, I thought of her less and less. I didn't need her or want her in my life, so I simply did not think about her.

Since that tragic day when Cristo was conscripted, I better understood the flavour of my mother's fear. I could forgive her for luring me to that cellar in Boulevard Montmartre now, knowing what she meant to save us from. But the fact that she hadn't wanted me at all, had meant to dispose of me at some squalid church infirmary rife with sickness and malnourished foundlings, still caused me pain. She must have known it was a death sentence for a child. But she had come back, Colombina had reminded me, when many other parents did not. She marked me because she meant to return for me. I turned over my wrist to see the burn. It was small comfort. What if she had been too late?

Colombina had wanted answers from her mother, answers she would never be able to get. I still had hope that my mother would give me her story. I had a place to start. As well as the name of the man Olympe de Gouges had lived with, Monsieur de Rozières, Gianni had furnished me with a description of his house on the Rue du Buis, near the Bois de Boulogne. I intended to begin my search for my mother there. She had gone to them once before for aid—perhaps she had gone there again. Let Pascal search the ash and rubble of our youth; I wanted none of it.

There were still some hours left of this interminable ride. I recognised nothing familiar in the landscape, having never travelled far in my own country until that night we fled. Growing up in the theatre district, I had no desire to go elsewhere. My whole life in Paris had been lived in the streets around the Comédie-Italienne. Even that hateful house on Boulevard Montmartre where we were entombed beneath the floorboards had only been a short walk away.

We hit a rut in the road with such force that a man beside me squealed in shock. I tried to catch Pascal's eye. I hoped he had forgiven me a little, but his face was stone. I sighed aloud, knowing he would hear me.

The carriage was halted at the city wall so the authorities could examine papers and collect taxes from the merchants. We jolted forward again in frigid silence, passing beneath an arched triumphal *barrière*. We had returned to Paris. If I had expected to feel a surge of emotion at this moment, I did not. It disappointed me, vaguely, how little I felt for the city. Pascal too looked down at his hands and not out into the streets. The horses pulled the wagon as far as the Marais and stopped to disgorge the passengers. Whatever Pascal decided to do now was up to him.

I got out of the coach without looking at Pascal. Paper boys flocked to us, shouting the headlines about the advance of the enemy troops towards Paris. I felt a small shudder of concern, despite my efforts to persuade myself that Paris could not fall; no foreign army had taken her in four hundred years. Pascal paid the boy and took a paper from him.

I tightened my cape around my neck. I could say one thing for Colombina's brother: he had dressed us well. Warm capes and rich velvets—I had never known such luxury.

Pascal took our cases from the driver and set them on the ground. I reached for his hand and kissed his gloved fist. I felt like I was falling from a cliff and scrabbling for purchase. Did he truly mean to leave me? There were tears in my eyes, a welling of emotion I was struggling to control. We were parting after everything good and terrifying and exhilarating that had gone before, all our lives spent together. Was this how it was going to end?

We'd had a life of words, and now we had nothing to say to one another.

He nodded once then turned from me.

'Pascal! Don't leave, not like this. Forgive me!'

He walked away.

Tears streamed from my eyes. It was undignified, my sobbing, but I did not care. He couldn't leave me—not like this.

'Pascal!'

I had challenged him to leave, and now he was actually doing it. I never thought he would. But perhaps it had to be this way; perhaps it had to be in anger. Our time together had been wonderful, but it was over.

Pascal turned a corner and vanished from my view.

CHAPTER THIRTY-THREE

*P*ascal shifted through the remains of the theatre. From the outside it had looked like any other derelict building lost to fire; part of the roof had caved in, exposing the scorched beams, like ribs of a carcass. The stone facade of the building remained unharmed, but inside, the furnishings were turned to ash, and the debris infested with the nests of rats and mice escaping the winter cold. Anything left of value had been scavenged long ago.

The costumerie was gone, reduced to blackened waste. He could see right through to the stage where once there would've been the mighty sheets of canvas, the painted set screens and the magnificent velvet curtains. All was burned. It was unrecognisable as his home. He tried to find the voices of his fellow orphans—Rémi's laughing call to some new game, the giggling Bonbon following along behind. He heard silence. Only the charcoal scent of smoke still lingered.

Pascal wondered if Rémi was even searching for his mother. In his dark mood, he doubted Rémi cared at all for his mother's safety. He might not hate her as he once did, but he did not care for her.

All he wanted to know was his own story. What had happened to *him*. Selfishness. As ever. Rémi had never appreciated how privileged he was to have a mother. Never noticed how jealous it made the other orphans, how jealous it made Pascal.

What did it matter now? Pascal could not summon the energy to wonder who his parents were or what had happened to him in those early years that he had no recollection of. His memories began here and it was the love in this theatre that mattered. This was what stung him the most when Rémi refused to come here and see for himself what remained of their home. Did nothing matter to him? Was he truly heartless? It was clear Rémi did not care as much for his theatre family as they had for him.

Those words that Rémi hurled at him, accusing him of lacking the courage to follow his own path and blaming Rémi for that weakness, were false. Pascal did blame himself for the defect of character that kept him loving Rémi. He did not blame Rémi for pushing and taking and never giving. Instead, he hated him. He had come to hate Rémi for knowing that he had this power over his oldest friend and exploiting it. Pascal had sat in that carriage on their final leg into Paris and boiled with rage. For so long, he knew that I wanted to come home, Pascal thought, but he would never bend an inch for me. We only came when it suited *him* to return. Everything on his terms, never mine. Enough. Rémi's power over him ended on this day.

Pascal stood in the wings of the theatre, from where he had liked to watch the performers rush out to greet the crowds. He had loved the energy behind the curtains, that moment of transformation when an actress turned from one person into another. He thought of those moments now as if he were an actor about to step onto the stage and become someone new. Would he be able to change himself as easily as a performer slipping on a mask?

He scanned the burned rows of theatre seats that had once been filled with excited people chattering like birds and preening their feathers and were now just blackened lumps like gravestones. His gaze travelled up to the seats in the gods and the private boxes where he had once seen the Emperor and his wife. He remembered the red and gold paint, the gilded carvings, the scalloped curtains. All gone. The boxes were falling to the floor below, their colours peeled and replaced with ash grey and charcoal black. There was no one here to watch his transformation, the moment he stepped out on this stage and became his own man.

Then Pascal heard a noise, a thud, like a log of wood dropped onto a hearth. It came from the pit where the orchestra once played. Perhaps an animal had made its home here for the winter. He thought of the beech martens that found their ways into cellars and larders at this time of year. Or perhaps a fox. He moved softly, freeing a shank of wood from a fallen wall.

He crossed the stone floor, stirring flakes of grey soot that had gathered like snow flurries. He saw no animal prints in the ash. Above his head, parts of the roof had crashed down, letting in shafts of grey light. Pigeons had flocked in, staining the black walls with streaks of white. Was it safe, he wondered, to be creeping around inside the ruined theatre?

Then he caught sight of a figure huddled beneath the stage. She had long, bedraggled hair and was dressed in strange garb: a rich man's culottes, a sailor's jacket. She was bent forward, coaxing a small fire to life on the flagstones. Rémi's mother—it had to be.

She looked up. A pale, young face marked with blue smudges beneath her eyes that made her older than her years. He dropped the charred wood in his hand.

'Margot?'

She straightened, gasped in shock.

'Margot, it's me—Pascal!'

This was a reunion he had not expected. Margot, the pretty star of Gianni's theatre; singer, dancer, actress, she could turn her hand to whatever the play demanded. She had always been like a sister to him, snaking her thin arms around his neck and kissing his cheek, making him blush. What was she doing here? She could've found work in any number of theatres. Margot was a flower that thrived on the adoration of others; she shouldn't be hiding away in the dark.

'What has happened to you?' Pascal asked, shocked.

'You are so tall, so big,' she said, crying openly.

Pascal rushed to her. 'Why are you alone here?'

She held him, sobbing into his chest. 'I knew you would come back. I knew it. I told them all that you would come back.'

'Don't tell me you waited here for us. Why would you do that?' The thought that she might have wasted her life waiting for them to return terrified him; he could not live with that on his conscience. Margot had always needed lovers, dancing from one man to another—he never imagined that she would be living here in the ruins of the theatre wearing remnants of the costumes, without anyone to care for her.

He stroked her hair while the memories assailed him. Margot hated being alone. Many times she had made him sit and practise playing the lute while she brushed her hair and sang. Sometimes they painted one another's faces and grimaced at each other in the mirror. Then she would tire of him and push him out of her room, send him off to find Lucien or Pierre or whoever was her favourite beau at the time. He didn't mind. It was nice to be needed by her.

'I have missed you so much,' she sniffed, pushing him back so she could look at him. 'The others thought the worst, that you had been captured and taken into one of these hideous wars. They told me to leave. But I wouldn't leave—I knew you would come back.' She hugged him again and he felt how thin she was beneath the coat.

'Why did you stay?' he asked, bewildered.

'I should've told you the truth,' she sobbed. 'Then you never would've left. I should've told you that you were my son.'

He heard her words and was slow to react. Margot was his mother? What trick was this? He drew back, staring at her. Should he feel a rush of love for her? Well, he did not. There was nothing in his heart.

Margot looked up at him, eyes doe-coloured, and he saw their resemblance to his own. He felt an unexpected burst of fury. All those years together, her teasing him like a sister, and she never said a word. All that time he had believed he was no different from all the other orphans, when he could've had a mother.

'Why didn't you tell me?' he demanded.

She shook her head, shivering. 'I couldn't. It wasn't done. There were rules we all had to live by. Besides, I would've been a bad mother—you know what I was like. I couldn't be trusted with the care of a child. It was better that you didn't know.'

'Better that I was an orphan?' His voice was bitter. He could've been the golden boy, like Rémi. He could've been special. Instead she kept him ignorant. He felt like a fool. 'Who is my father?'

She chewed her lip, creased her brow, said nothing.

'Tell me.'

She shook her head, just once. 'It doesn't matter.'

'It does to me.'

'Why?' She showed a flare of anger. 'Why does a father matter to you more than me?'

Pascal ignored her anger. 'Did Gianni know him?'

She looked up to the gaps in the roof. 'Please don't ask me anything more.'

An idea came to him, one that filled him with confusion. 'Was Gianni my father?' Gianni had always loved him as a father would, but if it was true, why didn't Gianni ever tell him?

But Margot shook her head sadly. 'Oh my boy, my beloved boy. Even I don't know.' She dipped her face and he saw the tears spill. 'It could have been any one of them,' she whispered.

He twisted away, remembering Margot as she was then, a waif in sheer silks, flighty as a swallow, alighting on any male arm that was held out to her.

'You were too young to understand the ways of the theatre.' Her voice was hollow, emotionless, resigned. 'He could've been any one of the men Gianni arranged for us.'

Pascal jolted, turned back to her. 'What do you mean?'

'How do you think a theatre survives? Its patrons, of course. And patrons must receive their due.'

'All of us? All of the orphans? We were bastards?' He thought of the dancers, the singers, the opera divas. Why had he never wondered why the Comédie-Italienne sheltered so many orphans?

'Not all of you, but some. The girls would go away for a time. The patrons paid. It was part of the deal—none of them wanted bastards coming back to make a claim on them. Sometimes foundlings were left with us. Or Gianni took pity on the urchins he found in the street. Most men grew hardened to the sight of begging children, but Gianni never did.' She wiped the tears from her eyes. 'We were a family, weren't we? You were happy?'

He could ease her suffering, but he didn't want to.

'So Gianni made you his whore.'

He expected her to flinch, to show her shame, but she stared straight at him. 'Yes.'

She shamed him then with that stare. How could he blame her? She must've been a girl not much older than Saskia when she was pregnant with him—perhaps younger than Saskia.

He had idolised Gianni, but he was just a man, with flaws like any other. This was the reality of the theatre Pascal had loved, and he had been blind to it.

He struggled to master his emotions. Here was Margot, his friend Margot whom he had thought of as a sister. He could not feel for her as his mother. Now that he knew the truth it did not change how he felt for her. He could not conjure up feelings that were not there. She could never be his mother. How was a son supposed to feel?

His legs felt weak, he sank to the floor.

Margot knelt in front of him. 'I wish I had told you from the start that I was your mother. I never thought that you would leave. When you didn't come back, I was distraught—I hated her for taking you away from me.'

Rémi's mother. It always came back to her.

'Did you know of her plan that night?' he asked. 'Did you know she meant to hide us?'

'Ha! She told no one until it was too late. You know what she was like: wilful, independent, a loner who thought she knew better than the rest of us. She admitted it when Rémi did not take the stage that night. She did not trust that Gianni would keep him safe.'

Pascal sat silently, staring at the fine drifts of ash stirred up by his presence here.

'Where is she now? What happened when she came back?'

Margot screwed up her face in that way she had when she didn't want to tell the truth. As if it pained her.

'We fought. I didn't mean to do it. I just hated her so much for taking you away.'

Pascal narrowed his eyes. 'What did you do to her?'

'It was an accident.'

Oh God, had Margot killed Rémi's mother? After all this time, was Rémi searching for a dead woman?

'What did you do, Margot?' He stood and she clung to his arm.

'I didn't mean to,' she repeated. 'But when she came back without you after you had been gone for months, after she promised you would return, I was so furious that I pounced on her. I wanted to claw her face, to hurt her any way I could. They pulled her away. Then Gianni told us we were finished—the other theatres had bought us out and he was leaving us. I picked up the lantern and threw it. I was pleased when the hot oil splashed her skirts, when the fire seized the curtains and threatened her. I wanted her to burn, to suffer like I was suffering. Gianni too. He sold us out!'

'*You* did this?' Pascal looked about at the ruins. 'You burned our home?' He almost couldn't bear to ask. 'Was she killed?'

'Gianni saved the old hag. He cared more for her than he did for me—for any of his girls!'

Pascal could imagine it: Gianni beating at the flames licking at her skirts, the curtains already burning. The paper and wood of the stage sets, the oil paints, the lights all around the stage . . . This was how theatres burned down all the time. The upholstered seats of the theatre would soon catch, row upon row of candlewicks. Backstage there would be panic. All the costumes, the feathers and lace, would burn where they were thrown. The stagehands would rush through with buckets of water and sodden blankets, but it would be too late. The heat now would be insufferable, the smoke filling lungs and choking everyone.

'Did they all escape? Tell me—did they all live?'

Margot wailed and began to rock, her hair falling loose around her face. She looked like a madwoman. His heart plummeted.

'Tell me who?' he croaked. He wanted to shake her. This woman who was his mother; this woman who had ruined everything.

'I didn't know he was hiding there,' she wailed. Her mouth was open, tears streaking her face. Pascal squeezed his eyes shut. No, no, no. But he knew. He knew little Bonbon would have been crawling between the rows of theatre seats, looking for coins and sweets and fallen treats.

'Don't leave me!'

He was running back along the aisle of the ruined theatre, away from this mausoleum she had made her home. Rémi was right, there was nothing left for him here. You could never go back.

'I waited for you!' she pleaded. 'I love you!'

He did not stop.

CHAPTER THIRTY-FOUR

For days, Saskia and the Young Guard had been engaged in minor battles and skirmishes with divisions of the Prussian army to stop them reaching Laon. The fighting that day had been light. She was becoming numb to the massacres. How strange, Saskia thought, to have become so accustomed to the sounds and sights of mass slaughter that a few hundred deaths seemed trivial. She could detach herself from the horror. She seemed to have a special knack for it.

After every battle the drummers were sent to help ferry the wounded on stretchers to the medical tents. That first time, when Bonaparte's forces finally took the chateau after the Russians slipped quietly away in the early hours of the morning, had horrified her. All around, the dead were being dumped into the holes made from artillery fire and buried. Her gaze swept across the full swathe of the battlefield, appalled by the decimation. How would she know if Cristo were among those consigned to the mass graves?

The living cried out in torment. She helped lift a broken body onto a stretcher and, then gripping the handles, heaved it up with a grunt, feeling the weight of the wounded soldier in her shoulders. She walked with her head down, focusing on her boots as she navigated the pitted earth. Over and over again she trudged between the battlefield and the triage tents, until the sight and smell of bloodied body parts became almost commonplace. She thanked God she was not among the soldiers tasked with burying the dead. With the living, she had hope.

Walking through the ward, she searched the faces of the men in their low-slung hammocks. The facial injuries scared her the most: the men with jaws blown off, eyes gouged out, cheeks opened up to expose the rows of teeth. How little it took to change a human visage into that of a monster. Men sweated and moaned and occasionally cried out in terror. She made herself look in every face for Cristo. He was not among the wounded that day, she was sure of it.

A pile of bloodied bandages discarded on the floor made her stop and stare. Her monthly bleeds still hadn't come, she realised. At first she had blamed the poor food and long days of marching; she hadn't wanted to consider the fact that the nausea, the exhaustion, the missed bleeds were all signs of pregnancy. But after three months since she left Milan, she could no longer delude herself. The condom of pig intestine had failed. Soon there would be no hiding her condition. Soon she would have to make her escape with or without Cristo.

That night, the survivors in her tent moved closer together on the floor, shifting their mats to disguise the gaps where friends once lay. Saskia listened to the chattering of their teeth, the gentle whimpers and snuffles as the boys finally slipped into sleep. It terrified her, the thought of a baby. How was she to raise a child? Her pulse pounded in fear whenever she let herself think of the future.

Now weeks later, as she surveyed the remains of the battle, she folded her hands across her growing belly. Even amid the brutal shock of each battle, she held on to hope. There was something miraculous within her: new life. She was carrying part of her and Cristo's love. She had kept herself and her child alive and it gave her a flicker of faith in her strength.

'Live for me, Cristo,' she whispered. *We will be a family together*, she promised them both.

When the orders came to pack up camp and march again, she pulled her drum across her stomach like a shield.

In early March, Saskia was at Craonne, less than a hundred miles from Paris. The Russian forces had taken the plateau around the Chemin des Dames road and occupied the farm of Heurtebise. Saskia was stationed with Marshal Ney's Young Guard in the hills on the right flank, watching the Russian army arrange itself into lines across the marshy valley flats. Those flats were treacherous; the day before she had seen horses sink to their hocks. A weak sun rose over the woods beyond, while the air was breathless and still. She pulled her hat down to her collar against the cold. Any fool could see the Young Guard were grossly outnumbered.

In all these weeks, Cristo had not been among the wounded she had ferried from the battlefield, nor among those that filled the hospital tents. He was either lucky or already dead. She had grown weary of the continual searching, the cycle of hope and crushing disappointment. She felt outside of her own body, as if she were watching herself go through the motions of this war but it no longer had the capacity to shock or wound her. A fatalistic hopelessness swamped them all.

By eight o'clock that morning, it was obvious the Russian forces meant to fight. They now stood in gleaming straight-backed rows. Saskia scanned the slouching men beside her. Grizzled veterans smoking clay pipes with firearms slung across their shoulders and thin boys with stunned, hollow faces. A mismatched assortment of clothes made a poor excuse for uniforms; some men had great-coats but most made do with farmers' clothing. Some wore scarves wrapped around their heads beneath their caps to ward off the cold. When she looked at their feet it almost made her cry: boots too large, taken from fallen comrades, and leather slippers that would give no relief from the frozen mud. This had the capacity to move her. Was Cristo standing out there in his own shredded shoes? She was grateful her boots were sound and she had guarded them fiercely, using them for a pillow when she slept with the laces tied around her neck, knowing that if she was going to run, her life would depend on them.

Bread and brandy were shared about. If Cristo were here, he could not avoid a battle of this size; all their forces would be called upon, even those with less than twenty days' service, even those who were injured. From her position on the ridge, she could watch it all play out. She could see the Russian soldiers lined up on the plateau facing the windmill at the head of the valley from where Napoleon would direct the battle. Soon she would see men cut down like stalks of corn by a scythe, men and horses mangled, their bodies melting into snow.

She stood waiting for her orders, her hands frozen around the drumsticks.

Marshal Ney galloped over on his horse to rally his troops. He wore a fine coat with a high collar embroidered in thick gold braid. She was used to the sound of his voice now, becoming familiar with the French words for honour and duty. Marshal Ney halted his horse beside her. She was close enough to look up into the man's face and notice his bushy sideburns and cheeks that were ruddy with the cold. There was sweat on his brow and wisps of hair escaped from his bicorn. He ordered a round of artillery fire that burst out and broke the peace. Smoke billowed. Jeers from the waiting Russian soldiers rang out as the volley fell short. They sounded so near. Saskia shivered, waiting for the return of fire. When the Russian cannons cracked and bit the earth, she flinched, but the French soldiers on the plateau stood unharmed, out of range of the Russian guns.

Suddenly orders were shouted and she beat her drum with all the others. Marshal Ney sent the Young Guard forward to attack the Russian flank. Men stomped past her. Broken men who could do nothing but follow orders and put one foot in front of the other. Some limped past her, the wounded patched and sent back out. All they needed to do was stand. Stand in formation as the cannon shot rained down. The side with the most men standing always won.

She beat her drum with the same automatic motions. She was as broken as any of them. A slave to the routine of camp life, numbed by battle and becoming increasingly convinced that she could never break away and be free. Each night, deserters were found and shot.

She promised herself this would be her last battle. This would be the last time she sent men forward to their deaths. If she found Cristo, she would run, take his hand and run. Even if she did not, she would take any chance she could to desert. This search for him was futile, she had to admit that. She should never have come to this war, it had nothing to do with her, and she had a child to care for now.

Cristo.

An apparition. Had she conjured him from longing? She saw his sweet face, as he marched past her. She noticed the chin strap of his hat cut into his soft cheek. His eyes were trained on the shoulder of the man in front. She found her voice and cried his name, but the boom of a cannon stole it away. He passed her without glancing her way, and she let him go, helpless in the moment, immobilised, even after all her imaginings of a heroic rescue.

He was here. She watched the top of his hat among the mass of soldiers marching headlong into a wall of smoke. He was walking into carnage. Saskia felt panic welling in her. She had to stop him. She realised in horror that it was her beating drum sending him forward. Ta la. Ta la. Ta la.

Out of the corner of her eye she spotted movement. A horse rode hard and fast across the face of the hillside—a messenger. It drew her eye from the impending battle. The horse stumbled, then righted itself. As it reached the ridge line, Russian shot thudded into the earth. She swung her head to look for Cristo, but he had disappeared in the smoke.

She heard the messenger cry out as the horse skidded to a halt. It was one of Napoleon's aides. She saw him grip the reins of Marshal Ney's horse. The aide was pointing to the east. He was angry. They were meant to wait. She understood the words he spoke, *renforts militaires.* Reinforcements. She guessed there were not enough artillery on this side to protect the Young Guard from attack. In dismay, she realised that Marshal Ney would never admit his mistake and call a retreat.

Saskia dropped her drumsticks. She threw off her drum and pelted forward into the smoke, no longer caring if she was shot in the back for leaving her position. Find Cristo, she thought. Take him home.

She ran alongside the marching troops, coughing in the smoke, her eyes smarting. Soon they would be in range of the Russian guns. 'Cristo!' she screamed. The old soldiers glared at her while the young looked terrified, too terrified to break out of formation. They simply walked on behind the man in front. 'Cristo!' she called again, voice hoarse. She wanted to pull them away. 'Go back,' she cried. 'It was a mistake!' She had to make them understand, she had to save Cristo before it was too late. She couldn't come this close and lose him. A cannon blast tore through the company up ahead, and she was thrown to the ground as metal shot sprayed into the men's bodies. Her ears were ringing, and all other sound was muffled; she couldn't hear the shouts and the drums or the men screaming. The survivors got to their knees. All around her, guns were being loaded in the expectation that Russian soldiers would come storming through the smoke. She stood, looking for Cristo.

Then, through the thick gun smoke, she saw him turn, and his beautiful eyes met hers. Her heart sang out to him. His hat had been knocked away and she saw the white gold of his hair. He looked like her angel. She saw him recognise her, she saw his mouth fall open, as if he were singing. Hope surged through her. There was still a chance they could be together. The shouts and wails of men around her were dulled by the roar of her own blood. Cristo moved. He was coming for her. Then something punched her chest and her world turned upside down and stole Cristo from her view. She was tumbling through the air, mind wheeling, slow to understand why she was flying.

She woke, eyes and mouth full of dirt, with the weight of men across her back. Had she been unconscious? She couldn't be sure. She spat and coughed. She crawled forward, digging her elbows into the earth. Cristo, she remembered, as she pulled herself out from beneath men's bodies. She felt no pain as she pushed herself to her feet.

In the chaos of the battlefield, she saw the crater where Cristo had been standing. She roared in anguish. She cried out for him, stumbling forward over broken bodies, pushing and pulling at dead soldiers, looking into each of their faces. She crumpled to her knees.

He was there. How could he be gone? Why couldn't she find him? They had almost been together again. She covered her face with her hands, bending forward, screaming into her palms. She thumped the earth with her fists. He had to be here.

She crawled through the mangled bodies. There was so much death. The wounded cried out to her but she couldn't help them. She thought only of finding Cristo and taking him from this place of horror. She tugged at the piles of bodies until fatigue overcame her and she couldn't lift herself from the ground.

Hatred burned inside her. Hatred for this place, for these men who sent boys into impossible battles, knowing it was a lottery of death. She screamed at the futility and the waste. Her hands, her clothes, her face, all were covered in the blood of others. She had lost Cristo. She slumped, sobbing. She had to confront the truth; she would never see Cristo again. He had been torn from this world.

The battle continued around her. More recruits tromped forward. Horses pounded over the fallen. Soon the enemy would be upon them and she would be sliced through by a bayonet as the soldiers ran them down. They were coming. She could hear their war cries, feel the power of their horses' hooves vibrate the earth. She waited to welcome a blade through her chest. She understood that she would die here, in this place where Cristo had fallen. She crossed her arms over her child, the only gesture that made sense to her in this senseless place.

A riderless horse trotted out of the smoke, spooked and lame. The horse slowed and she saw the bullet wound to its rump. It stopped, nostrils and sides bellowing, head high as it sniffed the air. Which way to run? It seemed uncertain. Saskia stood and soothed it with her voice. She approached the trembling beast. Blood streamed down its hind leg. She gently stroked its neck and felt the heat of it. The warhorse snorted and stamped its plate-like hoof. She reached for the stirrup. This was her chance. Cristo was gone. She couldn't stay here any longer.

She flung herself across its back like another fallen soldier and let the warhorse pick its way through the battlefield. A lone horse limping towards a copse of trees, moving slowly with a dead rider on its back, drew no attention to itself. In the last throes of the battle, as the drummers beat out the signal to retreat, Saskia and the horse slipped away into the woods.

CHAPTER THIRTY-FIVE

I found the Rue du Buis on the outskirts of the city between the Bois de Boulogne and the River Seine. Gianni had described the house of Olympe de Gouges as sandstone, shuttered, and three storeys high. On close inspection, the paint was peeling from the shutters and grass was struggling out from cracks in the steps. The place had an abandoned air. I feared there would be no one home after all, that Monsieur de Rozières had left Paris now the true numbers of battle losses were becoming known, that I was too late.

After several loud knocks and a despairing wait, the door was opened a crack. I glimpsed a shining dressing gown, a head of grey hair neatly combed across a balding head. De Rozières himself, I presumed, with no staff to tend him.

'Monsieur de Rozières?'

'Who are you?'

I decided at once to be honest. 'You knew me as a babe. I once lived in this house with you.'

He drew back in shock, and I thought I had lost him. Quickly, I continued, 'My name is Rémi Victoire.' I licked my lips. 'I am looking for my mother.'

His eyes ranged over me then. Clouded blue eyes, with the whites yellowed with age. He opened the door wider. He was an odd figure. Apart from the neatly combed hair, he seemed dishevelled; his face was stubbled with grey, his neck thin and skin loose. The robe was woven with fine golden threads in paisley swirls, knotted at his waist, but his slippers had holes in the toes with tufts of wool escaping the leather. He was older than I had imagined.

I followed him into a music room of sorts, a salon with a pianoforte in one corner and sheets of music strewn on the floor beneath. The walls were lined with books and I saw an escritoire with drawers of paper, and a gaming table set for backgammon. On the pianoforte I noticed a portrait in an oval frame. A beautiful woman, like Gianni had said, wearing a towering wig of silky white hair. Olympe de Gouges had serious, large, dark eyes that were shining. Her face was soft, and not what I expected of a female playwright who harangued men for their hypocrisy. I wanted to go closer to the portrait, to lift it and see if I could conjure this woman to life. It was due to the kindness of this unknown woman that I was still alive.

De Rozières offered me a seat, brought me a brandy and poured another for himself. I saw his hand was shaking. 'You have surprised me,' he murmured. 'I had not thought to see you ever again.'

'So it is true?'

He collapsed into an armchair of rich, red velvet. 'There was a child, a foundling baby, that we cared for, that is true. If the boy is indeed you, I could not say.'

I lifted my sleeve to show him the burn. He stared at it, unmoving.

'Your lover, Madame de Gouges—I believe she knew Gianni Costantini at the Comédie-Italienne?'

'Oh my dear Olympe,' he said, closing his eyes for a moment, remembering. 'Gianni indulged her. She wrote plays that the Comédie-Française would never stage. They were too risky, too aggressive, too offensive to the conscience of the comfortable bourgeois. But Gianni couldn't say no to her. Then again, he didn't have much choice. The fashion was for French plays in those days, and I was happy to finance her passions. You see, I too could not say no to her.' He smiled ruefully.

I knew all this already, and I tried to keep the impatience from my voice as I asked, 'And she knew my mother?'

'They were once friends, I believe,' he replied. 'Marie-Louise and Olympe.'

He fell silent. His arm was limp across the armchair and I could see the raised blue veins down his long hand. I was about to get to my feet and shake him, when he spoke.

'Don't blame your mother,' he said with a sigh. 'It was Olympe's idea to leave you with the church and for your mother to take flight. She couldn't bear for anyone to be caught and held against their will. Freedom mattered so much to my poor Olympe, she thought it should matter to everyone as much. She couldn't abide the thought of being trapped. I asked her to marry me, you understand, many times. I loved her, and I was no scoundrel, but she would not have me. She liked what we had together; she loved me, but she would not be bound to me.'

All this was very well, but it had nothing to do with me. 'Why did my mother have to run away?'

'Marie-Louise's father was an important man and the scandal of an illegitimate child can ruin an entire family. To some, it is the greatest sin. Your mother wasn't safe from them and neither were you. They might have tossed you from a moving carriage to protect themselves from shame.'

I recoiled at his brutal imagery. Her own family deserted her. I tried to imagine what that would be like. I had difficulty comprehending that a father would not care for his daughter, that her life—and that of his grandchild, too—was of so little significance. I knew the stories, of course, of mothers cast out with no means of survival, bastard children dropped into the Seine like unwanted kittens, but to know that it was oneself who mattered so little is another feeling altogether. My upbringing had not prepared me for this. The theatre may have been an unconventional family, but a family it was. We were loved. I felt a surge of gratefulness for Gianni and the family I had been raised with.

'Olympe was meant to leave you at the church, but she could not. She told me she took you to the *tour d'abandon*, the baby hatch, and wrenched open the door. But when she saw the cold, dark slab, she couldn't leave you behind.' He looked into the fire, lost in his own reverie. 'We had lost our own baby some years before, our Julie.'

I wanted him to tell me what my life was like. Was I a burden, was I cared for, was I loved? I asked none of this. 'And what happened to my mother?'

'Years later, your mother came here looking for you. She had been to the Hôpital des Enfants-Trouvés, where they keep a register of all abandoned babies and their markings. There was no record of you. She showed me the mark on her arm, the one that matches your own.'

I pictured her arriving at his house as she had looked that day in the theatre, her hair long and wild, her clothes coarse and plain. A madwoman. I couldn't imagine de Rozières opening the door for her; she must have forced her way in.

'Where had she been all that time?'

'Your mother told me this fantastical story of a voyage around the world—I could hardly believe it. Olympe had sent her to a friend in the port of Brest and from there, she told me, disguised as a man, she had joined an expedition searching for a lost explorer in the South Seas!

'I told her what we had done, that we'd had to pretend you were a foundling left on our doorstep, as Olympe did not want your father to find you. I had to tell her that the revolution Olympe fought for had turned on her; Robespierre took her freedom and then her life.' Tears were moistening the creases of his eyes.

I plucked a handkerchief from my sleeve and proffered it to him. I didn't want to feel sympathy for this man. 'You took me to the theatre and you washed your hands of me.' It occurred to me that by his actions I had been abandoned yet again.

He blew his nose. 'If Olympe had lived, I would've kept you—I would've been a father to you, please believe that. But alone I didn't know what to do. I was grieving, lost, hopeless, not fit to care for a child.'

'Where is my mother now?'

'I have not seen her in many years. How could I know?'

'Are you sure? She didn't come to you when the theatre burned?'

He shook his head.

'What of her family—would she have gone to them?'

'She had risked everything to be free of them. She would never go back.'

'Tell me who they are.'

'She had changed her name to Victoire when she returned. I did not know her before.'

So it was true. Victoire was an invented name. I am not real, I thought. I am a fiction.

I fell silent. There was nothing more I could learn from badgering this tired, sad, old man.

'I failed you,' he said eventually. 'I should have cared for you myself.'

I looked about this room, tried to imagine myself here, brought up as the son of a clerk. I could not.

'It was for the best that you took me to Gianni,' I conceded. At least I had that memory, of being placed in Gianni's loving arms.

But de Rozières shook his head. 'I took you to the theatre but the Italian troupe had already escaped. It wasn't safe for them to stay during the terror of the Revolution; only the French players remained. Gianni had gone. Didn't he tell you this?'

Gianni had lied to me again. He wasn't even at the theatre; he had run from the threat of violence like a mouse. Could I trust anything he had ever told me? 'If not Gianni, then who did you leave me with?'

'I gave you to a woman who promised to care for you. She said the theatre would be your home. She had a little boy about your age.'

A boy my age.

It had to be Pascal. I pictured a serious-faced boy with sandy brown hair and soulful eyes. A boy who had been there from the first.

I found my heart was beating with some force.

Pascal belonged to the theatre more than me. He was truly a child of the theatre. I should never have let him go back to the Comédie-Italienne alone; it was cruel. I should have gone with him.

I pushed myself up to my feet, thanking de Rozières who seemed stunned at my departure. I had learned all I could from him and moved quickly through his house.

Dear Pascal. I felt a jolt of panic to think I might never see him again.

When I returned to our theatre looking for Pascal it was ash, all ash.

'Pascal!' I stood on the ruined stage and cried out, spooking the pigeons into flight.

It was deserted, abandoned by all but the rats. Pascal wasn't here. I felt destitute yet again to see it empty. This place hadn't been our home. It was never the place. It was always the people. And they had scattered. *Poof.* I sneezed violently from the ash.

Pascal had left me. I felt the ache of it anew. I had imagined I would find him here, rebuilding and setting everything to rights, and I would ask him to forgive me. Now, I felt as low as a thief, a faithless cur who did not deserve a friend like Pascal. I was too late.

I left the piteous remains and walked, aimless as a flâneur. I crossed the bridges of the Seine, back and forth, watching the water glide beneath me. Had my mother stood here long ago? Had she thought about ending it for both of us in those days when she learned her family would not support her?

My mother. I had come here to Paris to find her after all and yet I lingered, beset with indecision. Where would she go, if not to her own family? What profession would she choose? My mother was skilled: she could mend and cook and turn her hand to many trades. She could be anywhere in this city—if she was still here at all. She might have disguised herself in men's clothes again and returned to sea. She was resourceful, she was a survivor; there was some comfort in that.

The promenade along the Seine had many denizens plying their trade beneath the shadow of the bridges. I took a seat to watch the furtive clerks scurry past, intent on a little pleasure in their noon repast. Across the way from me, an old whore rested on a park bench. Too tired to stand and flaunt and chase the custom, she simply eyed me boldly across the path. Slowly she raised her skirts. To my shame I felt my loins stirring, uncontrolled. I saw her baggy stockings, the hairs of her shins, the bones of her knees and the dark patch of shadow between her thighs. She sagged back on the bench with a lewd grin and a question in the quirk of her eyebrow. I stared at that pit of darkness and wondered how many children had come from it.

Was this how ageing, destitute women made their way in the world?

I rose and foraged in my pockets for the last remaining sous. I paid her to pull her skirts down.

'Do you know a woman called Marie-Louise Victoire?' I asked of her.

She smiled and I took fright at the state of her teeth.

'Every one of them is a Marie-Louise now,' she scoffed, tossing her head towards the whores in their tatty blonde wigs. 'Before that they were all Josephines, or Marie-Antoinettes. I don't know a whore alive who will give you her true name. We trade in fantasy, my love.'

'She'd be about your age.'

She whistled. 'Not many who can stomach the trade as long as me. Likely dead. You'd best find a new companion.' She patted the seat beside her.

I spluttered. 'I'm not looking for . . .'

'You'd be surprised how many men pay for a little mothering.'

This was futile. Did I hope to interview every whore in the city? She called after me as I left her. 'I like her name—Victoire. I might take it for myself!'

I had now spent the last of Luigi's money.

I was hungry as I walked the streets, feeling sorry for myself. I needed Pascal to chide me into better humour. I hammered at the door of the Comédie-Française until I roused someone to answer my enquiries. The brute who answered had no knowledge of Marie-Louise Victoire, or Margot, or any of the actors from our theatre. 'A man named Pascal, then?' I asked with hope in my voice. 'Has he been here?' The door was slammed in my face. The gaudy banners in the streets proclaimed the coming operas. Gianni was right: all was opera now. It made me think Cristo would do well here if he made it out of the war alive, and the thought of Cristo and Saskia on the battlefields sank my spirits still further.

On street corners, Parisians exchanged morsels of information, still shocked, still disbelieving that there were battles being waged less than a day's ride away. How could such a great empire crumble in so short a time? How could enemies be marching towards Paris?

My stomach growled and my thoughts turned to my predicament. I needed food and board. For several nights, I entertained at a gentlemen's club, telling bawdy stories of my exploits with foreign women. All invented, all Casanova-esque. I was accosted by a bespectacled man who wanted me to rank the sexual willingness of women from a list of nationalities that he pushed into my hands. He wanted to publish a guidebook. He licked his parched, red lips so often that even I was disgusted by him. 'Is your Prussian lass more willing than your Alsatian?' he called after me. I did not return to the club.

I wasn't good at being alone. Too much time in my own head made me wonder if I truly was the selfish shit that Pascal accused me of being. I missed Colombina. I wondered if she had returned to her beloved Venice and if I would ever see her again. The unaccustomed pangs of loss caused me great suffering, but was I capable of selfless love, like Saskia, facing battle and almost certain death to find her boy?

Or capable of faithful love, like Pascal?

Or dutiful love, like a son for his mother?

A hard stone seemed to be wedged in my throat and I could not swallow it down. I felt guilt, I felt loss, but was it grief, was it love? Or was I simply feeling sorry for myself?

Pascal was right—I did not deserve to be loved.

There was only one place left I could think of to trace my mother and I had been avoiding it. It was the house on Boulevard Montmartre. My mother knew the man who hid us under his kitchen floor. She must have known him from her life before the theatre. It was irrational this swill of disgust I felt for that house. Pascal recognised it as a safe haven, yet I could not. But this man who had kept us from conscription might be sheltering her now. Pascal had known it all along. I had to go back to that house.

CHAPTER THIRTY-SIX

Saskia led the warhorse through the trees to the edge of the forest. She peered out across a field to a farmer's barn and lodgings where a single candle flickered in the window. Both the horse and her were quivering all over. She had not stopped since leaving the battlefield, but now she paused, weighing up the risk of leaving the cover of the woods. The horse favoured its hind leg, resting it on the tip of its hoof. It hung its head, mane clumped with drying blood, a creature as brutalised by this war as she was and she tenderly combed the forelock from its eyes. They had wandered for hours through the trees, following the woodcutter's trails, always keeping the sound of battle at their back. Mercifully, no one followed them, but soon the army would send out patrols to round up the fleeing deserters. And even if she wasn't caught, she would face a freezing night with no food or shelter. Her teeth were chattering with the cold. Steam rose from the horse and she nestled close to its side, watching for movement in the house across the field.

She could not think further than this one night. She did not let herself think of Cristo, because each time she did the feeling of loss was so overwhelming, she had to stop and weep, and the crying left her exhausted and weak. This was a time to be strong, a time to remember all the trials of her life that she had overcome. Each time she had faced adversity on her own, she had survived, and that knowledge gave her confidence. She had triumphed before and she would again. For now, she had to find shelter.

The barn alongside the house was in darkness. It might be possible to hide inside for the night, if the barn door was unlocked. Yet she held back. What if she was caught and the farmer turned her in rather than risk punishment for harbouring a deserter?

The daylight was fading and she would have to make a decision. She would die if she stayed out in the freezing woods, and her child would die with her. That thought motivated her to coax the horse forward towards the farmhouse.

A small herd of cream-coloured cattle watched her cross the field, sliding their jaws in slow, rhythmic motion. She pulled the horse to the farmer's door and knocked. She would not try to hide unseen in the barn; she would have to be bold, because she needed help.

She knocked again and a startled flurry of French words were called through the wooden door. When she didn't answer, a woman opened the door a crack. The woman took one look at her—a drummer boy spattered with gunpowder and blood, and slammed the door. It was as Saskia feared: they would not help a deserter. She waited, hoping that the woman's shock would pass. She felt faint. She prayed that these people would take pity on her, that they would not turn her away or, worse, send her back to the army.

The horse tugged on the end of its reins, backing away as if it too felt uneasy. Neither one of them would go back to war, she vowed.

Eventually the woman spoke from behind the closed door. 'What do you want?'

It took a moment for Saskia to understand her words. After months with the French army she had picked up some of their language, but her understanding was simple.

'*Une robe*,' she replied. A dress. Saskia said nothing else, but of course she wanted far more. She wanted food, she wanted a place to hide.

The answer had provoked the woman's curiosity, as Saskia hoped, and the door was cracked open again. The woman's red-rimmed eye studied her. She was not old or young, but past child-bearing, Saskia would guess.

'*Pourquoi?*'

'To wear,' Saskia replied.

The woman slipped out into the yard and grabbed the horse's reins, pointing to the military-issue saddle and chiding Saskia in words she did not understand. The woman dragged the horse into the barn and Saskia quickly followed. A pair of goats bleated in surprise.

The woman was still talking as she closed the barn door behind them. Saskia caught the word *fille*. She could guess what the woman was asking: 'You want to travel as a girl? Is that it? Think you will escape the draft?'

'I am a girl,' Saskia said with a tiny shrug.

The woman gripped her chin, twisted her head from side to side, squinting in the poor light of the barn. The woman took Saskia's arm and towed her back outside and into the house. She brought a candle close to Saskia's face.

Saskia took off her cap.

When the woman released her grip, Saskia felt bruised by her fingers.

The woman muttered something but the only word Saskia recognised was death.

Mourir, la décès, la fin, le trépas—the French had so many words for death and dying. For killing. She had learned them all in her time at war.

She scanned the room, blinking, grounding herself. Inside the cottage she saw a table with a single bowl set for a meal. Rough wooden furniture. No one else. No man's boots at the door. No thick jacket hanging from a hook. This woman's husband and maybe even her sons would've been taken by these wars. Saskia smelled the soup bubbling and the smoke of the fire. Her stomach growled. The woman set about finding another bowl, ladling the soup, gesturing for Saskia to sit.

'*S'appelle?*'

'Saskia.'

So long since she had told that simple truth. 'And you?' she asked.

The woman breathed heavily before she answered. 'Natalie.' Then she sat and picked up her spoon. Saskia slurped down the soup, burning her tongue, unable to stop herself. She ate the food without tasting it, and Natalie pushed her own untouched bowl across to her.

When she'd finished the second serving she wiped her mouth with the back of her hand, suddenly embarrassed by her desperation. She felt naked before this woman with her solemn gaze. Saskia wasn't used to trusting a stranger. They regarded one another across the table until Natalie seemed to make a decision and rose to her feet.

Natalie set to work boiling water above the fire and filling a copper basin for Saskia to wash. She promised to alter one of her dresses for Saskia by the morning. Saskia went to her and clasped her hands over her heart in gratitude.

Please make it loose, she begged Natalie, with her gestures. It had to last her, this dress, through whatever the coming months would bring.

Natalie gave her privacy while she went outside to burn the uniform Saskia had worn; there could be no trace of a deserter in the house. Saskia lowered herself into the water. The roundness of her stomach was obvious to her for the first time and she stared at it, disbelieving. She hadn't washed like this, fully naked, for months. Now there was no denying the trouble she was in. Saskia covered her face with her hands and began to sob.

Afterwards, Saskia—wearing a nightgown for the first time in a long while—climbed up a ladder to a loft bed where children might once have slept. Down in the kitchen, she heard Natalie drag out a large chest and fossick through the contents. She heard the heavy weight of shears against the tabletop, and the soft humming as the woman began to stitch.

Saskia lay down on the straw mattress and nestled her hands on her belly. She closed her eyes and immediately saw Cristo in that final moment, his face turning to her, the curls of his hair loose without his cap. He saw her, she was sure of it; their eyes had met across the mud and blood and fallen bodies, she had held him with her gaze. She felt the grief welling inside her, pushing upwards against her sternum, her heart, her throat, choking her. It hurt, this feeling in her chest, this tightness. She wanted to weep, she wanted to cover her face and scream, but she did not.

She opened her eyes wide, not letting herself remember, not letting herself feel. She could make herself go numb. It wasn't real. After all, she hadn't found his body on that field. She hadn't seen his beautiful face glazed and still. There was still hope. Perhaps he had been thrown by the blast and merely injured. If he lived, she would find him. The Innamorati were always reunited in the end.

In the morning, she woke to the sound of cocks crowing. She was confused at first, not understanding where she was. She looked up to the rafters close above, and heard the thunk of an axe slicing through wood somewhere outside. She lay on the bed feeling the aches in her body. Then she remembered Cristo, the loss of him flooding her with fresh agony. She rolled over so her cries were muffled by the down pillow. Saskia wanted to curl up into a ball and stay hidden in this loft. She wanted to weep bitter tears and rant at the injustice of the world. Why had fate brought them together only to tear them apart?

When Saskia had gathered herself, she climbed down the ladder into the kitchen. There, Natalie produced a dress for her to wear. She held it out with kindness and Saskia accepted it gratefully.

Natalie turned her about and placed her hand on Saskia's belly, a knowing look in her eye.

Saskia nodded, tears welling.

She removed her nightgown and stood in the middle of the kitchen with her arms above her head as Natalie pulled the plain cotton dress over her. It was gathered beneath her breasts and loose around her stomach as she had asked. The full skirt touched the floor and disguised her boots—military boots she was determined to keep even if they marked her out; she would need their solid leather soles beneath her.

'*Merci*,' she whispered. They smiled at one another.

Saskia looked into the woman's weathered face. Natalie was strong, but she was ageing, and she was here alone. What if she stayed with this woman in the French countryside? Here there were no reminders of Cristo, of the life they dreamed of together on famous stages in famous cities. Natalie was kind and generous, she had given a stranger food and clothes and a safe place to sleep. It felt good to be protected. Natalie had sheltered her at great risk to herself. Saskia could repay her by working the land for her. It would be a safe place to raise her child.

But here she also saw a life of mud and pig troughs and pitchforks and piles of manure. It was a physical life, a good life, but a life like the one her own mother had run away from. Year after year, watching the same fields turn from frozen white to luminous green, changing with the seasons, yet always the same. This was not a place to learn to read and write. It was not a place of books and plays. What would become of her dreams if she chose to stay here?

She had to think of what was best for her child. Who would help her when the baby came? She watched Natalie move about the kitchen, preparing a breakfast of bread soaked in eggs and milk and fried in butter, humming as she worked. In her crocheted shawl, Natalie reminded Saskia of her grandmother. Was it time to find her own kin? Along the coast where she grew up, the seabirds would be returning, flocking to the offshore islands to breed. The terns and gulls, sharp-winged in shades of white and grey against the wave-rounded rocks. If she found her way to that thatch-roofed cottage on the edge of the sea, would her grandmother take her in? This wild child, another shameful red-haired slut with a bastard in her belly. Her chest ached. If she flew home, would they let her land?

Natalie asked her to fetch a pail of water and Saskia hastily slipped out of the warm kitchen and into the yard. Outside the air was brisk and she took several deep breaths. It was pointless to think of a home in a place she could never hope to find. The pump squealed as she worked the handle, drawing water spurting into the bucket. She needed a home, so why not stay here? She could help this woman; it would be a good life.

The boom of cannon fire made Saskia yelp and drop the bucket, spilling water across the yard.

The day's battle had begun again. She saw smoke rising beyond the woods. It panicked her. The battlefields were moving closer. Soon these fields would be churned to mud by thousands of boots and hooves, and gouged out by cannon blasts. She had seen houses set alight by gunfire. Homes would be ransacked, livestock taken for food, women raped.

The crackle of gunshot pattered the sky and she flinched, covering her ears with her hands.

It wasn't safe here. Saskia could not stay and wait for the soldiers to swarm over these farms. She had to think of herself and her child now. She ran to the barn. Natalie had already stripped the army saddle from the horse and hidden it away. The heavy warhorse moved stiffly, reluctant to walk, but thankfully the blood from its wound had dried. Saskia clicked her tongue and led the horse out.

Natalie stood on her threshold watching her, face full of sorrow.

'Come with me,' Saskia urged, pointing away from the booming guns.

Natalie shook her head and raised her hands in hopeless sub-mission, as if to say, *And go where?*

Saskia mounted the horse bareback as Svetlana would have done. She had an address in Paris where Pascal had told her to go if she was ever in need of sanctuary, a house on Boulevard Montmartre. She would go there.

CHAPTER THIRTY-SEVEN

*P*ascal picked his way through sandbagged streets. An argument spilled out of a shop in front of him as two men wrestled over loaves of bread. Nerves were frayed in anticipation of a siege on Paris and accusations of stockpiling caused rows and violent scuffles. He dodged the men and walked on towards the city gate.

War was coming to Paris. No one could deny it now. The last battle at Arcis-sur-Aube had been a catastrophe. Pascal could hardly imagine being one of Napoleon's twenty thousand men and seeing reinforcements of eighty thousand Austrians arrive upon the plains. If Saskia was still among the soldiers, he hoped she had run for her life.

Grim-faced, people muttered together on street corners. Napoleon had turned his troops east to cut supply lines for the enemy rather than bring his army back to defend Paris. The air sparked with tension—how could the Emperor abandon Paris in this final hour? The Parisians felt betrayed. He had taken so much from them during these long wars to build his Empire; why was he deserting them?

Those who spoke in his defence clashed with his detractors and there were frequent brawls in the streets. Regardless of his intentions—the Austrians, the Russians, the Prussians—they were all coming, and Napoleon's troops were too far away to help.

That afternoon, the streets of Paris were strangely subdued as Pascal made his way to the northwest of the city. There were no rallying cries, no shows of nationalistic fervour to threaten the approaching enemy.

He expected disbelief, panic, but not this quiet acceptance, this hopelessness. Many had boarded up their homes and left the city. He wondered whether Rémi had found his mother, if the two of them were safe. He thought of Margot and how he had treated her with such disdain. She had waited for him all that time. He was ashamed of his reaction. He understood the reality of the theatre now; they had lived in a fantasy world, blind to what Gianni asked of his actresses. The director had tried to shield them from the truth with his tales. He had once told Pascal he was delivered to the theatre by a guardian angel, a white-winged creature that had descended from the skies carrying a baby in his arms. Pascal had never repeated that story. Of course he knew it to be nonsense, although a tiny part of him had wanted to believe it. It was a beautiful story to give to a child, far better than the truth: that Gianni had whored his mother to a wealthy patron.

At the city wall, a brief volley of artillery fire startled him. Pascal made for the nearest church and climbed its bell tower. A meagre army had stationed itself on the hill of Montmartre. Pascal heard the officers call out their practice drills and the drummers strike their drums. The Imperial Guard arrived on horseback and Pascal watched as the cavalry charged in one direction then turned and charged back the other way, as if oblivious to the enemy making camp behind them. Lines of men stretched out across the fields, wagons rolling, tents rising. He expected the Imperial Guard to repulse them, but the enemy soldiers were simply allowed to set up camp. They waited for the morning's battle like labourers waiting for a day's work in the wheatfields. He heard singing. He heard laughter. The enemy was making itself at home.

Pascal walked around the bell tower, catching glimpses through the open portals of the whole city. He could see Notre-Dame, the Tuileries Palace and all the hovels at the foot of this church. The stone city walls were crumbling in places and he wondered if too many stonemasons had been lost in these wars. He was seized with the strangeness of the moment, watching history unfold. How many of them would remain, come tomorrow evening? Would the city fall? Would there be massacres in the streets? He felt giddy and gripped the lintel. He had hungered to come home, but he had never imagined he would return to a city under siege. Did he want to face what was coming alone?

As the sun slid west, painting the sky with red, the enemy soldiers continued arriving from the east. Pascal stayed to bear witness as the defence troops gathered on Montmartre hill, hopelessly outnumbered, and yet they still beat their pathetic drums, and the cavalry still thundered across the field on their horses in small bright bursts.

წა

I had little time left now to find my mother before our city was invaded. The enemy had arrived at our gates. Soon there would be chaos; fighting in the streets, roads clogged with those seizing their last chance to flee. I waited outside the house on Boulevard Montmartre. This house had ended one life for me and forged another. I wondered if there were deserters beneath the floor of the kitchen even now, sitting silent and fetid in the dark.

Moments earlier, the man I presumed to be the master of the house had passed me on the street and dashed up the steps to enter through the front door. I saw a stern face beneath a tall, black hat. He had a serious demeanour, walking quickly and with purpose. I had almost called out to stall him, but my courage failed me.

I rapped on the door several times before the man I had seen on the street pulled it open. He was not the one-armed man I remembered from years before.

I stared at him, inexplicably tongue-tied. He looked at me with annoyance. At his feet were two large trunks.

At last I found my voice. 'I believe you knew my mother—Marie-Louise Victoire.'

'No,' he said, pushing the door closed on me.

I risked my foot, stuck out my arm. 'Wait. She brought me here. She knew you. Seven years ago, my friend and I spent months below your floor.'

He glanced about and silenced me with his frown. 'Are you an imbecile? Hush!' He dragged me inside and slammed the door shut.

In the hallway, the light was dim, but I saw the grand staircase winding up through the middle of the house and I remembered coming here. I remembered the smell of the oiled wood and my shock at seeing framed paintings on the walls and rugs on the floor. I had never been in a proper house before. I'd had no idea how other people lived.

The master seemed to live alone in this great house; there was no sign of servants or companions. An ageing man, his face softening and folding with the years, like a bulldog, his dark hair greying at the temples. He was dressed for travel with sturdy boots and a heavy coat.

'You mean Louis Girardin.' He said it like a statement.

Just like that I had her name, my name. Girardin. Rémi Girardin.

'Is she here? I am trying to find her. Do you know where she is?'

'You'd better come with me.'

When I was here before as a boy, my heart was in my mouth—I was about to meet my father for the first time. I felt a similar trepidation now. Did he mean my mother was here?

He pushed open the door to the kitchen and I saw two figures seated at the table. Emotion flooded through me. Pascal! Here. He had come back. Sitting across from him was a woman wearing a mob cap and a simple, peasant's dress. She scraped her chair back and stood. My God. Saskia.

I gasped and ran to her, folding her in an embrace. Our Saskia lived. I squeezed my eyes closed as I held her. 'How . . .' I murmured. 'How did you find us?'

'Pascal,' she said. 'He gave me this address before I left Milan. Monsieur Labillardière was kind enough to let me in.'

Of course, Pascal. Dependable Pascal. He had thought of this as a place of refuge, while I thought of it as a place of torture.

Saskia stepped back from me and ran her hands down the front of her loose dress. Her stomach was small but unmistakably round. My mouth fell open. I drew out a chair and sat heavily.

'Cristo's child,' I said.

She nodded.

'Does he live?' I whispered.

She turned her head and would not look at me, hating to show her vulnerability, even now. Our brave Saskia.

'Where will you go?'

She shrugged. 'I have no home.'

My mother had been in this same predicament once. Perhaps Pascal's too. Had anyone been there to help them?

'You have a home with us, wherever we are.' I looked to Pascal and he nodded. 'What will we do?' I reached out to hold her hand, offering my other to Pascal. He didn't take it.

Monsieur Labillardière coughed, reminding us of his presence. 'If you mean to stay here, I must disabuse you of this notion. The house is sold. I am leaving for the countryside before this madness descends on us. Might I suggest you do the same?' He gestured towards his hallway.

'My mother,' I said, remembering why I had come. 'Do you know where she is?'

'How would I? We have had no reason to correspond.'

'You were her friend. She came to you for help.'

'We sailed together once. We were companions, not friends.'

'You helped her once; surely you care for her still?' I glanced at Pascal. 'To survive a journey together, to share suffering together, it binds companions to one another.' Was it too late? Were we still friends after everything that had gone before?

'Or breaks them apart,' Pascal muttered.

'It makes them family,' I hissed to him.

'Families don't desert one another,' Pascal rejoined.

'Enough!' Labillardière interrupted. 'Félix Lahaie. The gardener. If anyone knows where your mother is, it will be the gardener. Go to Versailles. He has a nursery there. I believe your mother's family came from that town.'

He silenced us with this news. *Go to Versailles.* As the night was closing in, with an army gathering at the city gates, with Saskia pregnant, with the roads choked with refugees. *Go to Versailles.*

We would be safer in Versailles than here in Paris. I turned to Pascal. Would he come with me? Would he forgive me for taking too much from him and never giving as much in return? I had to know.

'I am sorry, Pascal. I am sorry for my ill-considered words, for my selfishness, for my self-centred arrogance, for being a shitty friend.' My apology was genuine. I understood who I was.

Pascal was looking at his hands folded in his lap. Slowly, he rose from his chair and put his arms around me. He felt warm and strong and my heart was bursting. He whispered in return, 'I am sorry I wanted too much from you.'

When we separated, both of us were grinning. Rémi and Pascal. Pascal and Rémi.

'Will you come with me to Versailles?' I asked.

He shrugged. 'I have made no other plans.'

I laughed and squeezed his hands in mine.

'Saskia, will you come?'

Saskia had laid her head down upon her arms on the tabletop.

'You can stay and rest if you wish,' Labillardière said, 'but I am leaving. The city's defences are abominably weak—a few half-dug trenches and feeble barricades, and an army of young conscripts stationed at Romainville.'

'The Young Guard?' Saskia lifted her head. 'The Young Guard are to defend Paris?' She spoke in French.

'For all the good it will do,' Labillardière scoffed.

Saskia struggled to her feet. She looked exhausted. Pascal lifted her into his arms.

Labillardière steered me towards a dusty, disused salon with ample couches and a rocking chair beside the window.

'Pass on my respects to Lahaie, if you see him. And your mother.' He spoke stiffly.

I owed him my life. This man had hidden me in this house at great risk to himself. I understood that now, with the benefit of my years away. If I had encountered him that night when we fled from the hole in his kitchen floor, I might have kicked his shins. When I was hurt and wanting to hurt.

I bowed to him. Not flamboyantly, as I once would have, with a great flourish of my cape and grand sweep of my hand as I dipped low. Not as a storyteller with a wicked smirk. Simply, sincerely, and I hope with grace. 'You saved my life,' I said truthfully. 'I shall not forget your kindness.'

He turned and promptly abandoned his house.

✧

Pascal did not sleep through the night.

He squirmed in his chair, unable to get comfortable. This house was haunting him. It would be easy to run from this place again, to follow Rémi, to let him make all the decisions. They could flee Paris and start a new life, all three of them. They would help Saskia with her child. They would be safe. Yet he wrestled with his guilt. He remembered how he had left Margot alone in the shell of their theatre and he was ashamed. He had visions of a ransacked city, of foreign soldiers breaking down doors and women cowering from the coming assault. How could he leave Margot in that wrecked theatre with no more defences than sticks and stones cemented with ash?

He remembered her as she had been, young and careless. A waif. A firefly. She was simply Margot—no more, no less. He could not think of her as his mother. She'd had her chance to tell him the truth when he was a child, to give him a mother when he had none, and she had held her tongue. He could not forgive her that. But then he had always been the one to look after her, even as a small boy. Why should that change now?

He still mourned the loss of Bonbon, the little boy who'd followed them about, saddened that they had lived and grown into men and he had not. Pascal grimaced. If only he had gone back; Margot would never have fought with Rémi's mother, there would never have been a fire. Guilt churned in his stomach. But he had not cared enough for them. He had chosen Rémi; he had followed him without a second thought for anyone else.

There was nothing left for him in Paris. But could he leave? Could he leave without knowing what had become of Margot?

⁂

Saskia was exhausted to her core, her limbs were lead weights, she could barely lift her eyelids to find the chaise and stretch out beneath the window. Yet she could not sleep.

She relived the moment of Cristo's death on the battlefield. Was she sure he had been hit? There was so much smoke. She had looked for him, turning over men's bodies to see their faces. Again she wondered, what if he had been thrown from the blast like she had? What if he had only been injured? What if he had lain unconscious, buried in dirt, while she had taken her chance and fled?

She had left him there. She should have made sure. After everything she had gone through to find him, why had she not waited?
Why hadn't she returned to gather the fallen as she had done after
every other battle?

She placed her hand on her belly. The safety of her child had to
come first, she knew that. But her heart ached.

Saskia had ridden away from Natalie's farmhouse driven by panic
and fear. The sound of those guns had terrified her. The horse
was valiant, and she rode it until it foundered from the wound to
its rump and she couldn't force it to run any further. Gently, she
slipped the bridle from its head, stroked its velvet muzzle in thanks,
and let the horse wander loose in a field.

She reached the city walls on foot. The road was empty, the
gates barricaded with broken furniture and wagons. Old men and
young boys were digging trenches around the base of the walls.
They gawped at her as she clambered through the barricades, but
said nothing.

The gates were closed and bolted, but a sweaty guard climbed
down to heave them open a crack. He waved her through, like he
was swatting a fly. He growled a barrage of fast French at her and
she did not answer him. No doubt he wondered why she was out
alone on this road with the city about to be under siege.

'Boulevard Montmartre,' she called, then followed the direction of his pointing finger. With these two words to anyone she
encountered, she made her way through the cobbled streets.

Pascal was already in the house when she arrived at the door.
When the scowling man led her into the kitchen, Pascal cried out

in shock. As he embraced her, she felt all the tension leave her body, her muscles relax, her jaw unclench. She didn't have to be alone anymore. She pressed her face into his shoulder and choked back a sob. He would help her with the child she carried. Pascal would not desert her. She felt his arms around her and she loved him for his loyalty.

'I am waiting for Rémi,' Pascal had told her, convinced that he would soon come. And he had.

She couldn't tell them about Cristo. She couldn't tell either of them that she had found him on the battlefield and lost him. Those moments were all muddled in her mind. She didn't want to believe he was gone. She refused to believe it.

If the Young Guard were returning to the city, she had to wait for them. She had to know for sure.

⁀ᗉ

I woke when Pascal shook my shoulder. I was annoyed with myself for falling asleep in the armchair when I had promised to keep watch.

'Listen,' Pascal hissed.

I heard the crack and boom of cannon fire from the east. We looked at one another. Saskia's large round eyes were haunted. It would not be long before the enemy was swarming through our streets. I was filled with the urgency of impending loss, plagued with the feeling I would lose my chance to find my mother.

All three of us rushed out into the crisp dawn. The street was deserted. For a moment, all was eerily silent. Then cannons boomed again and I felt the earth shudder beneath my feet.

'Quick!' I urged.

But Pascal caught my arm and tugged me back.

'I can't.' He shook his head. I knew he was thinking of the time seven years before when he had made his choice to run with me.

'You must. It's not safe here—the city is under attack.' My voice was hoarse, desperate.

'I have to stay.'

I stared at him, feeling bereft. Hours before I had experienced the euphoria of his return to me and now I was losing him all over again. He had dug his toes in like our dear Henriette and I could not pull him with me. Damn you, Pascal. I blinked away my tears. 'Saskia, we have to go.'

The girl shook her head. 'I'm staying.' Her gaze was fixed on the flashes of artillery fire. I saw the glow of orange smoke against the eastern sky. We were close enough to hear the war cries and the beating drums.

'I have to know if Cristo lives.'

I opened my mouth to protest: the boy was surely dead, so many had been lost. But how could I extinguish her hope?

'I will protect her,' Pascal said, taking Saskia's hand in his.

I know you will, Pascal. I know you will, better than I ever could.

I reached up to cup my hand behind Pascal's neck and pulled his forehead to mine.

'Farewell,' I whispered.

This was the last. I swallowed hard, and then I let them go.

CHAPTER THIRTY-EIGHT

I worried for Saskia and Pascal as I walked from Paris amid the scattered refugees, listening to the distant artillery fire, imagining scenes of battle in the Paris streets. Riders overtook me carrying the news and it was soon cried out from every town. Paris had fallen. The Russians had walked through the Arc de Triomphe; the city had surrendered to Tsar Alexander. Napoleon was beaten.

The Emperor would not be forgiven easily by his people. I learned he had made it to the Château de Fontainebleau with the remnants of his army. Some were sure he would bring his forces on to take back the city. Some thought he should be slaughtered in his bed for his neglect. He was to abdicate, they said. He was to be exiled. I scowled. A gentleman's agreement would be made; the leaders of these nations would protect one another in the end, but not the millions of men they had killed and left nameless on a battlefield.

As the day was ending, I walked the long avenue up to the Palace of Versailles, seeing for the first time the ironwork fence bent and broken by angry mobs during the Revolution years before, its gold leaf scraped away. Chains held the battered gates together. Through the bars I saw the wings of the chateau spread wide across the empty courtyard. Even in the failing light, the gold ornamentation around the slate roof sparkled and glimmered. The chateau was empty now, former home of kings, forsaken by this Emperor and waiting for the next.

The end of an empire. It was over in less than a day. The French people were tired, too tired and heartsore to fight anymore. They had nothing left to give.

I slumped down in the gutter and found sleep leaning against a stranger, our backs holding one another up.

I woke. The stranger who had loaned me his back was gone and I was sprawled out on the cobbles.

In Versailles, the refugees of Paris were not welcome. Doors and windows were boarded up, shops had closed their shutters and hotels had posted signs—*complet*. Anger rose in me as I strode through the streets of the town, and I began to hate these people of Versailles with their closed doors and closed hearts. I imagined my mother returning here to her family seeking sanctuary and being turned away. I saw a child's shoe left on the road. I tried to calm myself. I would need the help of the locals if I was to find this Félix Lahaie. He was my last chance to find my mother.

I asked at the Jardin du Roi, the kitchen gardens for the palace near the edge of town, for the gardener, Félix Lahaie. They knew of him. It set my heart beating faster. A sallow-skinned youth told me he had once been the chief gardener for Empress Josephine and had established a specialist nursery for the growing of exotic plants on the outskirts of town. I didn't know what to expect of the man as I entered through the stone gateposts and walked down a long driveway, passing furrows of turned earth and regiments of cultivated plants.

A modest stone residence stood among a cluster of glasshouses and barns at the end of the drive. The place appeared deserted. I listened hard. Flies buzzed. Had he fled with the news of the Emperor's defeat? Did he fear retribution as one of Napoleon's regime? I knocked at the door. If this man had run, then I had no hope of tracing my mother. I knew of nowhere else to try.

I knocked again, mouth dry.

The door was opened by an ape. An ape lightly covered in orange hair and wearing a frilled dress.

I blinked and did not move.

The ape pointed down the hall and I shuffled past. Even now, after all I had seen, there was still capacity for shock.

A small girl, perhaps five years of age, with bright white hair ran out to meet me.

'Have you come for lunch? You're late,' she said, then flounced back up the hall in her white dress with a bright blue ribbon around her waist.

I followed cautiously through the small dim rooms; the child seemed as fleeting as a ghost. The ape padded softly after me. Ahead I heard voices and laughter and the clink of cutlery against plates. Stepping out into a walled courtyard, festooned with hanging flower-pots, I saw a large table had been set and the family were gathered around. Dishes of food filled the centre of the table and I salivated at the smell of the roast meat. How long had it been since I enjoyed such a feast? The voices fell silent as they saw me. The orange ape silently took her seat beside the blonde-haired girl and picked up her knife and fork.

The man I presumed to be Félix Lahaie pushed back his chair and stood. 'How can we help you?' He had a soft face creased with the lines that came from smiles and laughter.

I was strangely affected by this simple scene. The little girl bright-eyed me over the rim of her soup bowl. Men and women dressed in plain and hardy clothes, whom I took to be workers from the nursery, stared at me. A woman with flushed cheeks and golden hair rose from her seat at the table. I saw her cast a nervous glance at her husband.

I whipped my hat from my head and crushed it in my hands in front of me. 'I was lately with a man you know, a Monsieur Labillardière. He sends his regards to you, hopes you are well.'

'Jacques! What does he want with us now? We haven't heard from him in years.'

'No, you misunderstand me—he doesn't want anything from you. I asked him to help me find my mother. Perhaps if I can speak with you alone, Monsieur Lahaie?'

'Your mother?' he replied, ignoring the request for privacy. 'Who is she?'

'Marie-Louise Girardin.'

The man's mouth dropped open. 'That is a name I have not heard for many years.' He shook his head in disbelief and I felt my hopes plummet. She was lost to me. In that moment, I realised how much I had let myself believe Lahaie would know where she could be found and I was surprised at how destitute this made me feel.

'Come with me, son.'

I let Félix Lahaie lead me away from the table, tears prickling my eyes. I was embarrassed by my weakness. I had let myself be vulnerable when I should not. I was Rémi Victoire—the storyteller, the bard, spinner of tales and wearer of magic cloaks. I was not used to being Rémi Girardin, the motherless son.

Félix walked with me through his yard. 'I knew your mother when we sailed to New Holland. She helped me once to make a garden on the other side of the world.' He smiled over his shoulder at me and his eyes were kind. I didn't know this story and it made me feel better to hear him speak of her. I wanted him to tell me more.

Félix moved a little stiffly and I noticed the grey hairs streaked through his brown locks; I put his age at fifty years even though his face appeared younger.

'I collected most of these seeds on that voyage. Your mother helped us then with our collections, Monsieur Labillardière and myself.' He gestured to the rows of plants. He paused for a moment to touch the dusty round leaves of a scraggly grey sapling as though still surprised at the miracle of it all. He looked around him proudly. 'We began this nursery when the Empress left Malmaison, to safeguard all her work after the divorce.'

We continued on towards a milky glasshouse.

'A woman came to us a few years ago needing work. A woman by the name of Marie-Louise Victoire.'

I stopped walking.

'It was the woman I had known all those years ago as Louis Girardin. She passed herself off as a young man about your age when she was on the ship with us. And lo! There she was standing in front of me. She had taken her grandmother's name—Victoire.' He smiled. 'We thought her dead, but despite everything, she had survived.'

CHAPTER THIRTY-NINE

*I*nside the glasshouse the air was thicker. Hot and heavy and hard to breathe. My mother hadn't seen me. She kneeled on the floor tending a row of potted plants, staking each one upright. She was dressed in coarse linen trousers and a shirt, cinched at the waist by a length of twine, like a peasant in a field. Here, she wore men's clothes for practicality, not disguise. I watched her work, a stone in my throat. I shuffled forward and she looked up. I saw her eyes widen with the shock, then the slow realisation. She climbed to her feet. When her eyes met mine, I wanted more than anything to know what she was thinking.

She wiped her hands on her clothes. She had aged. I saw grey strands in her pale hair. She looked uncertain as she came forward. I let her look at me. She reached up to touch my face.

'I dreamed of this day, but I never truly believed it would come. I thought you were lost to me forever.'

I pulled back from her touch. She dropped her hand.

'I pictured how you might look as each anniversary of your birth passed. I worried how I would recognise you. Now look at you. I missed the moments when my boy turned into a man.' Tears were streaming down her face. 'How foolish I was—of course I would recognise you. You are the one true love of my life.'

I had come to find my mother, but now I was reluctant to speak, reluctant to show my wounds. My eyes moved from the straggling plants in their terracotta pots to the dusty panes of glass above our heads and back down to the scarred benchtops of the nursery. I could not meet her gaze.

'Why did you leave?' Her voice was aching.

'You know why. You tricked me. You left me in a pit to rot for months!' I couldn't keep the hotness from my voice.

'I did it to protect you!'

'You made me think I would meet my father.' My words swelled with all the self-righteous indignation of a wounded boy.

'Why did a father matter so much to you?' She sounded bitter.

I raised my eyes to her face and, to my surprise, she looked hostile. In all these years away, I had fixated on my pain, how I could not forgive her. I had not, until this moment, thought that she might not forgive me.

'Every boy wants to know who his father is.'

This time, she was the one to look away. 'I meant to keep you safe.'

'I know that. But you stole my future. My career on the stage meant everything to me and you took it from me without asking. I hated you.'

She reeled back from my honesty. 'Then why have you returned, after all this time?'

'To save you.' Those words sounded melodramatic even to my ears and I knew they were not the whole truth. 'I thought you might be facing this war alone.'

'I have managed well enough without you.' She busied herself arranging seed trays on the bench beside her.

I had hurt her. But her hurt wasn't fair and it angered me. I would not apologise for leaving her when she had meant to abandon me from the first.

'You never wanted me,' I accused. 'I know you meant to leave me with the Church. Didn't you care that I might have died there!'

She stared at me, alarmed. I saw her struggle with what she should say.

'No more stories,' I said to her. There was a time for stories and a time for truth. Truth was what I had come for. I wanted to look into her face as she told me how she could leave me for dead and sail around the world. I wanted an apology, I wanted to see her remorse. If there was no remorse, then I wanted to see that too. It was selfish of me, but it was truly why I had come. I wanted to see shame and guilt on her face. Did she care enough to show me that?

'I know you didn't give me to Gianni to care for. I know that was a lie. How could you leave me?'

She hung her head. 'I had no one.'

'That's not true. You had that woman, Olympe de Gouges, and her benefactor.'

'I didn't know what else to do,' she whispered. 'I never meant to be away so long. I had to leave, and when Olympe came up with a plan, I had to take the chance. It was only by accident that I went on a voyage of many years. I grieved for you. Please believe me. I did not leave you lightly.'

She tried to reach for me again, but I moved away once more. I was a child again, not willing to be consoled. Her face showed her pain and I was glad of it.

'I always meant to return for you. When I arrived back in Paris, after all those years away, I learned Olympe de Gouges had fallen victim to the Terror. I couldn't find you at the church or foundling hospital, and I was frantic. I paid the amount they asked for raising you and then they asked for thirty francs more to check the records. I could not believe it, those fiends! To earn that money took me some time is all I will say of it. I went back with hopes raised, but when there was no record of a baby with a burn on his wrist in the register, I felt despair like never before. I was at my lowest when I sought out de Rozières. The only light of hope was that Olympe had not given you to the Church after all, that she had kept you safe, loved you, and that you had been healthy and unharmed.

'It was stormy on the night I came to the Comédie-Italienne. I went immediately, the moment that de Rozières told me what he had done. I hammered on the theatre doors, rousing a guard, almost mad with the desperation of coming so close to finding you and fearing that I would be too late. I pushed my way in and demanded to see the director. I showed him my burn. When he brought you to me, the sight of you was like a kick in my chest. You were a grown child, six years had passed; I was nothing to you, but you were everything to me.'

She stopped to press the tears from her eyes with the back of her hand. All of this had come out of her without pause, in a frothing torrent of admission.

'I remember,' I told her. 'I remember you frightened me when you first came to the theatre.'

She nodded, leaning on the bench for support. 'I am sorry for that.'

'And my father?'

I saw the tightening around her eyes; it irritated her that I cared about him. 'He had no wish to know you. He abandoned me when I was pregnant, denied all connection to me and married another woman who could advance his station. I will give you his name if you wish me to, but he is dead, parted from his head in the Terror.'

How was I to feel when learning all of this? My mother wanted me and my father did not. Why did I still feel her betrayal and nothing at all for him?

I still did not understand why she'd had to leave Paris. 'Why did you leave me?'

She stared at me, knowing exactly what I meant: not the mechanics of why she could not support me in a world that had no place for unwed mothers, but how a mother could leave her own child, not knowing if it would live or die. I wanted her to admit she should have stayed with me, no matter what. She had abandoned me twice, and I could not forget that.

'If I tell you, you will only hate me more.'

'I have come for answers.'

She sighed. She pushed her hands into a pot of dirt, and her shoulders sagged. She looked defeated. 'My father was once a gardener at Versailles.'

'I was told your father was an important man, one who would be shamed by his unmarried daughter and her bastard son.' My voice was strained.

'He became that. He married a wealthy widow after he let my mother die in childbirth.' She spoke plainly, without emotion. Was I to believe my grandfather was a monster?

'He was a controlling man. He needed absolute power. I had shamed him and I had disobeyed him. It infuriated him.'

'He wanted us both dead?' I asked.

She shook her head. 'My father did not turn me away when I was pregnant and unwed. He offered to care for us both.' Her words were slow and reluctantly given. 'But I could not let him control me, I could not be bound by his rules for my life and yours. I was to be married off to some malleable friend and live a life of servitude to my father. So I risked your life. I risked my own. I could not be trapped by him again.'

I backed away, taking in her words. The truth was out between us. She did not need to flee her family; she had chosen to. She had left me to save herself from a life of confinement. The pain in my throat was high like the pressure of a thumb, stopping me from saying more. Did I hate her, now that I knew the truth?

We both were wounded beasts. We regarded one another, seeing the faults in ourselves. I was a wanderer, not meant to be bound to any one place or person. I had wanderlust, Gianni had once said. I had believed it to be from my father, but now I knew it was my mother all along who could not abide to be tied down.

She had kicked and scratched like a cat put in a sack. She had clawed a way out for herself. We were more alike than I had credited.

Without saying a word, I stepped forward and swept my mother into my embrace. My cloak folded around her, and I felt how small she was under those loose clothes. I felt her stiffen, then claw at my shirt, felt her shoulders shake and tremble. I held her until her convulsive sobs subsided. I did not know if we could ever forgive one another for our hurts. We were both too proud for that. But we understood one another's pain and perhaps that would be enough.

'Where are you going to go?' my mother asked, sensing I would not stay.

I could not answer her.

I would likely not see my mother again. When I left Versailles, I would not come back here. The world would change, new borders would be drawn, France might face occupation, but my mother was safe here with these people.

I would not go back to Paris. Pascal would find a new family at the Comédie-Française or some other theatre, I was sure of it. The colour, the drama, the petty rivalries: he would love it all. Or perhaps he would follow his passion and return to Luigi; that was for him to decide. I would carry him in my heart always, but it was past time for us to part.

The question for me has never been: Where do I belong? It has always been: Where will I go next?

I walked from that nursery in Versailles with the wind pushing me south—to a distant, floating city and a woman named Colombina. I had to know how that story would end.

The fate of Saskia and Cristo, I would never know. But I could picture them in the chaos of the Paris streets; the heavy artillery rolling in, the gun smoke, the horses, the sound of gunfire and the Young Guard falling back under the onslaught. I saw Cristo, splattered in blood and blackened by smoke. I saw him turn and recognise Saskia, I saw her run to him, pull him to safety within the shattered walls of a house. I saw her take his hand and drag him down to a kitchen with a secret cellar beneath the floor. I saw them shivering in the dark with the firestorm raging outside, foreheads touching, each cupping their hands over the other's ears so they would not be afraid.

Our Innamorati would be reunited. That is the story I chose to believe. For what is the point of stories if they do not give you hope?

As I left the nursery gate, I turned back. She was there, my mother; she had followed me down the long driveway and now she stood, watching me leave. All the sadness of our final parting showing in the lines of her face. She too understood this was how our story would end.

I was glad I had not asked her for my father's name. I no longer wanted the weight of it, tying me to history. To be an invention was perfect for me. I twirled about and my cloak lifted like the wings of a bird.

My name is Rémi Victoire. I am Rémi Victoire.

I am my mother's child.

I kissed the burn on my wrist and raised it to her in salute.

AUTHOR'S NOTE

The Comédie-Italienne was a theatre in Paris, but this depiction of the place and people is entirely my invention. It began in 1680 as a theatre troupe of Italian professional actors performing commedia dell'arte, but by the late 1700s was presenting plays in French, including plays written by the valiant Olympe de Gouges before the French Revolution. The theatre merged with Opéra-Comique and later Théâtre Feydeau, and by 1802 was located at the present day, Salle Favart, a theatre that has been rebuilt three times in the years since because of destruction by fires. This location was in actual fact a short walk from the home of Jacques Labillardière on Boulevard Montmartre (a real person who also appears in my previous novels). Although the Comédie-Italienne did not exist in the same form and moved locations several times during the early 1800s, my invented Comédie-Italienne became a stable home for Rémi and Pascal.

The travelling St Petersburg Circus is also an invention, although derived from the traditions of travelling performers from the eleventh century in Russia where the *skomorokhs* sang, danced, juggled, used tamed animals, and later performed at fairs in tents along with fortune tellers, contortionists, and even displays of people with deformities. The modern form of circus is attributed to men like Philip Astley or Charles Hughes who built circular amphitheatres to perform horse riding stunts. These circuses were made popular by Catherine the Great in St Petersburg during the 1770s. I thought it was at least possible that a travelling Russian circus as I have described could have been born from these origins.

There are moments of dramatic invention that I could not resist. The Brothers Grimm released their book of tales in December 1812, slightly later than my characters' visit to Marburg. In 1813, the cathedral in Milan was finally completed on Napoleon's instruction, but whether there was an official unveiling is not known to me. Similarly, the movements of the retreating Grand Armée after losses in Russia may not have been in the exact location of my travellers. I hope you will permit these invented scenes as they were intended to show what it was like for people living through the events of history.

The complex political situation, changing allegiances, and geography of nation states are as correct as I could portray them. If I have made mistakes of understanding, I hope they are minor. I found it especially hard to describe events in Germany and Italy before they were the countries we think of today.

Saskia's journey into the battlefields of France was inspired by actual women who disguised themselves as men and went to war. Women like Joanna Żubr from Poland who willingly fought in the Napoleonic wars from 1808 until Napoleon's surrender in

1814 and Eleonore Prochaska who enlisted in the Prussian army fighting against Napoleon in 1813, serving first as a drummer and then as infantry. Most women were ejected from the army after discovery, but Friederike Krüger joined the liberation struggle in Prussia in 1813 and was eventually promoted to sergeant even after her gender was discovered and went on to fight at the Battle of Waterloo.

After Paris was invaded, Napoleon reluctantly surrendered and was allowed to live in exile on Elba. A peace treaty was signed and the borders of France were returned to what they had been in 1792 before Napoleon Bonaparte's French Empire. In this agreement, the Kingdom of Italy was once again turned over to the Austrians to rule. My character Colombina would have been devastated! Inspiration for her character came from the young activists who fought for an independent Italy. At the time, there was a network of secret revolutionary societies forming called the Carboneri. I imagined Colombina's theatre might be one of these. After 1815, literary and artistic nationalism continued to increase and there were several failed revolutions to overturn the Austrians. Unification, the Risorgimento, wasn't achieved until 1871 after the Austro-Prussian wars. Colombina would've been an old woman by that time.

In 1815, while the conquering nations argued over how the remains of his Empire would be assigned, Napoleon escaped from Elba. He returned to France and was restored to power briefly, leading to the Hundred Days War and the Battle of Waterloo where Napoleon was defeated and exiled to the island of St Helena. He remained there until his death.

The fall of Napoleon's Empire in Europe can be attributed to many factors not least of which was the growing spirit of nationalism in the people of the occupied lands who had tired of the suppression of their culture and autonomy. It was their resistance that helped to overturn Napoleon's dominance.

ACKNOWLEDGEMENTS

*T*hank you to all the readers who have come with me on the journey of Marie-Louise Girardin and her son, a story that began in fact and finished in fiction. From the French Revolution to the rise and fall of Napoleon, thank you for taking this tour of French history with me.

I was so fortunate to have my publisher, Annette Barlow, and all the Allen & Unwin team in Australia and New Zealand to bring these three connected books into readers hands (if you are curious, look out for *Into the World* and *Josephine's Garden*). And my agent, Gaby Naher, who found the perfect home for these novels. Thank you all for your skill and support.

Many, many thanks to my fellow writers who braved reading early drafts of *The Freedom of Birds* and offered valuable insights: Robyn Vinten, Greg Johnston and Gaby Naher. I am indebted to the editorial skills of Ali Lavau and Christa Munns who helped me shape this story. Thank you, Ali, for pushing me and asking all the hard questions. I am also grateful for your eagle eye for repetitions and for knowing when to add enthusiastic comments!

Part of this novel was written on an artist residency at Château d'Orquevaux in France, which placed me directly in the region of France where Saskia found herself before the invasion of Paris. Thank you to Château d'Orquevaux for selecting me for this privilege, the Denis Diderot Artist in Residence Grant for assistance, and all the creative people that made the experience of working in a chateau even more amazing.

Thank you, Paul Johnson, for enduring research trips through the fairytale villages of Germany and the majestic cities of Venice and Milan. It's a tough gig. But in all honesty, thank you for your patience and unconditional support, my love.

A special thanks to all the booksellers and librarians I have met on book tour. It has been an absolute delight to be able to meet the dedicated and enthusiastic people who go the extra mile to bring authors in touch with readers. Entering a bookshop is always a pleasure, and thank you to those who have let me sign books and stopped for a chat on my unannounced visits! This novel has a love of story at its heart, so thank you for celebrating and championing stories and literacy.

And a shout out to the book bloggers and reviewers who are doing a wonderful job of sharing the joy of reading through social media. What a fabulous community.

To my loving family and friends who have been encouraging, excited, generous in so many ways and unfailingly supportive from the first. I can't thank you enough, you beauties.